D0324213

THE AUTOBIOGRAPHY OF
JEAN-LUC PICARD

THE STORY OF ONE OF STARFLEET'S MOST INSPIRATIONAL CAPTAINS

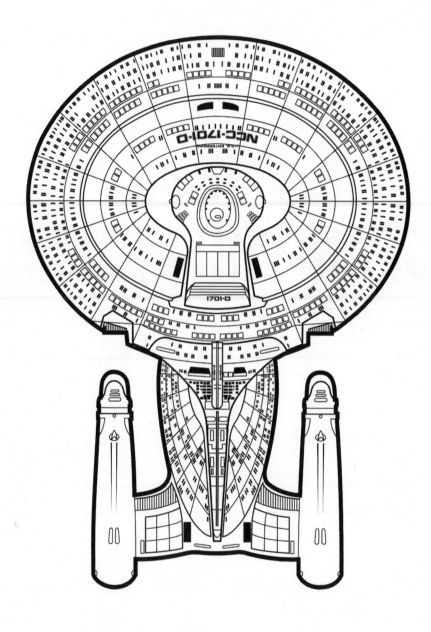

THE AUTOBIOGRAPHY OF
JEAN-LUC PICARD

THE STORY OF ONE OF STARFLEET'S MOST INSPIRATIONAL CAPTAINS

BY
JEAN-LUC PICARD

EDITED BY DAVID A. GOODMAN

TITAN BOOKS

Iosco - Arenac District Library
East Tawas, Michigan

The Autobiography of Jean-Luc Picard
Print Edition ISBN: 9781785654657
E-Book Edition ISBN: 9781785656637

Published by Titan Books
A division of Titan Publishing Group Ltd.
144 Southwark Street, London SE1 0UP

First edition: October 2017
10 9 8 7 6 5 4 3 2 1

TM ® & © 2017 by CBS Studios Inc. © 2017 Paramount Pictures Corporation. STAR TREK
and related marks and logos are trademarks of CBS Studios Inc. All Rights Reserved.

All rights reserved. No part of this publication may be reproduced, stored in a retrieval
system, or transmitted, in any form or by any means, electronic, mechanical, photocopying,
recording, or otherwise, without prior written permission from the publisher.

Illustrations: Russell Walks
Editor: Simon Ward
Interior design: Tim Scrivens

A CIP catalogue record for this title is available from the British Library.

Printed and bound in the U.S.A.

Did you enjoy this book? We love to hear from our readers. Please e-mail us at:
readerfeedback@titanemail.com or write to Reader Feedback at the above address.

To receive advance information, news, competitions, and exclusive offers online,
please sign up for the Titan newsletter on our website: www.titanbooks.com.

CONTENTS

For my father.

FOREWORD

BY BEVERLY CRUSHER PICARD, M.D.,
STARFLEET CAPTAIN

WHEN JEAN-LUC ASKED ME TO WRITE THIS INTRODUCTION, I was overtaken by a flood of emotions. I've been through so much with this man, how could I put into words what he means to me, but more importantly, what he means to the history of the Galaxy? He single-handedly prevented wars, saved civilizations, as well as expanded the boundaries of knowledge—

OH, WHAT DRIVEL! I am the Q. You may have heard of me, I'm somewhat all-powerful and I am rewriting this dull essay by Dr. Beverly. Don't ask how—I have the ability to be in all places and times at once, and I'm improving the introduction as you read it. You know they were in love? We all knew it and it took them years to do something about it. I think Picard talks about that in this book—I assume he does, I haven't read it. Maybe I'll read it right now.

Okay, I just read it.

It's spectacularly mundane, filled with all those dull human tropes of triumphing over adversity and learning from your mistakes. Oh, and the importance of love and friendship. Humans are so predictable. I don't know why I'm even bothering with this, but I am. Maybe it's because next to Picard I am a god, and yet he has been able to get in my way. I could've destroyed him years ago, wiped him from existence. In fact, I still could.

1

I just did.

And I just brought him back. That's how easy it is.

But as much as I hate to say it, Picard gives my life meaning. I've toyed with many of his species throughout the ages; most end up in insane asylums, but not Picard. He is the perfect human: he strives, he achieves, he wrestles with problems until he finds his solutions, and as often as he's right, he's wrong. But, unlike most of you, he admits when he's wrong. You have no idea how rare that is in your species. Maybe that's why you like him. And maybe, pathetic human, you'll like this book. Now back to poor Dr. Beverly.

—it is a testimony to his achievements, but also to the man himself. I hope you enjoy it as much as I did.

PROLOGUE

THE CORRIDOR WAS BOTH OPPRESSIVELY WARM AND HARSHLY COLD. The warmth was the literal temperature; the chill came from a profound lack of emotion. This was the end of my freedom.

"To facilitate our introduction to your societies, it has been decided that a human voice will speak for us in all communications. You have been chosen to be that voice."

I was flanked by two guards, silent man-machine hybrids, in a modern catacomb three kilometers on either side. Starkly white and gray figures, just like the ones standing next to me, stood in rows on stacked floors of a vast metal superstructure. I searched for the source of the voice. There was none, yet it surrounded me. It seemed to come from all the figures, yet their mouths never moved.

This was the Borg. An alien race of cybernetic beings, part-organic and part-machine, linked together into a hive mind. They scooped whole cities off the face of planets, absorbing the people and technology, homogenizing them as part of the collective. And now they wanted me to speak for them to help accelerate the absorption of my people.

This was a fight for civilization. I was in command of the Federation flagship, the *U.S.S. Enterprise*, a *Galaxy*-class starship with a crew of over a thousand. We had been the first to engage the Borg cube, the huge 27-cubic-kilometer starship that had penetrated our sector of space. It had already destroyed the New Providence colony on Jouret IV.

Our first engagement with the Borg cube had not been completely successful. Once I realized we wouldn't be able to stop it, my hope was to at least delay its progress so that Starfleet would have time to gather a superior force to destroy it. This ended up playing into their plans, as the Borg had shown specific interest in me, and when my delay tactics eventually were exhausted, they kidnapped me from the bridge of my own ship.

Now I had discovered why they were interested in me. They said our "archaic civilization" was authority driven and that they needed one voice to talk to it. I wouldn't let myself be used. I was scared, but I remembered that courage is not the absence of fear, but the triumph over it. I had to fight. I had faced many adversaries in my career; my life had been at mortal risk numerous times. I had a wealth of experience to draw from in the coming fight; I was determined to hang on.

I was foolishly naïve.

Without warning, my two guards grabbed me, their grip around my arms like a metal vise. They lifted me off the ground and dropped me on a nearby table. While one held me down by the throat, the other removed my tunic and trousers. I lay naked and helpless.

I looked at the one who held me by the throat. He'd been human once. His right eye was completely covered by a cybernetic implant, tubes and conduit connecting his head to his chest, and his face a ghostly white. He looked at me with the empty gaze of a dead man. Lifting his free hand, three tubules extended from it and pierced my neck. They injected something and everything changed.

I heard voices, softly at first, then like a cresting wave I couldn't escape, they overtook me and I was submerged. Disparate, deafening noise, languages I didn't understand… and then suddenly I understood them all. Hundreds of thousands of minds on this Borg ship alone, connected to billions more, each working individually and together. And it felt like all of them wanted to pry open my mind.

I tried to block them out, but I had no defense; they were already in there. Like a billion hands rooting through a used-clothing bin in an ancient thrift shop, picking and examining what they wanted, tossing aside what they didn't. In my memories they jumped around in time: my first haircut; a laugh shared with a childhood friend; a similar laugh shared with my first officer; my final exam at the academy; my brother pushing me down in the mud; the first woman I was ever intimate with.

Then the search became more discerning and focused on what they were looking for: my casual memory of a starbase commander telling me how his defense shield worked; operating the phaser bank on a *Constellation*-class ship in battle until it was drained; my crew apprising me of their plans for counteracting the Borg weapons.

It didn't stop. The collective now wanted my mind to work: it wasn't just pilfering memories, it wanted my opinion on how to attack my compatriots. I concentrated, trying to present false information, but my deception was ripped away like a paper Halloween mask. My experience and judgment belonged to them. I had an image of myself, it was still there, but I had no control over my mind anymore. It was part of the collective, which used my thoughts and experiences and created a new identity. The morality and ethics and loyalty and affection of Jean-Luc Picard dropped away, a small puddle this new identity stood over.

They called it Locutus. It had access to everything I was. It was me, but it wasn't. I had no strength against it.

And what was left of me watched as Locutus made his plans with the Borg, using what I gave them. I could see it all, how it would all happen. The *Enterprise* would be first; the plan to destroy the Borg cube was laid bare for the enemy now, and the collective had begun work on a defense. And in just a moment, the work would be finished. The *Enterprise* would fail.

I was nothing. A puddle on the floor. I wanted to die. And the collective knew it, heard my plea for death. For a moment, the voices went silent, as if ordered to be quiet. And then came the quiet laughter, malevolent and mirthless.

"Oh, we won't let you die, Jean-Luc," she said. "Not yet."

CHAPTER ONE

THE DOOR TO THE BASEMENT WAS OAK, with five thick vertical slats and two cross-beams, and always locked. The lock had a large, ancient key, which was attached to an oversized metal ring and kept on a hook just inside the hall closet. I had seen my father go through that basement door only a few times. He'd take the key from the closet, turn the lock, enter, and quickly close the door behind him; I could hear the creaky wooden stairs beyond. Eventually, he'd emerge, lock the door, and replace the key.

It is difficult to describe how tantalizing that locked door was to my younger self. Our house was several centuries old, so there were locks on many of the doors, all unused. On 24th-century planet Earth there was no crime, no intruders, no theft or vandalism; there was no need for locks on most of our world, especially in the small, sleepy village of La Barre, France.

Yet *this* door my father locked.

Once, when I was around five, he caught me jiggling the handle to see if it would open. He pulled me back by the shoulder and gave me a stern look.

"You are not allowed in there," he said. His tone was quiet but threatening, and I was so scared I burst into tears and ran to my room.

By the time I reached the age of seven, however, fear of my father's wrath was overtaken, or at least obscured, by the ever-growing curiosity about what lay beyond the wooden barrier. It was the first week of September, the harvest had begun, and I'd been out in the vineyard with my father, mother, and brother sorting grapes. My father had decided the grapes had reached their desired ripeness, and we'd take the bunches from the vines, then separate the fruit from the stems. For a seven-year-old, this was endless, tiring work. There were plenty of machines that could've done the work for us, but my father refused (more on that later). The work held no interest for me, but, like all the work the family did in making our wine, it went without saying that I had to participate. Making matters worse for me, the first harvest's work was always done at night. The heat of the days made the work too straining, and since we were picking grapes, in the daytime the sugar from the fruit attracted all manner of hungry insects.

I had come into the house for one of my frequent trips to the bathroom, many of which were just an attempt to avoid some of the work. On my way back outside, a plan suddenly took shape in my mind. The family was engaged in the harvest; I would have the house to myself for a while before anyone came looking for me. I went to the hall closet and, after a quick look outside, grabbed the ring with the key.

And immediately dropped it.

The loud clatter of the iron against the wooden floor froze me in panic. I slowly moved to the front window (somehow equating that making more noise with my footsteps might be the tipping point in my mission's failure), and saw that no one appeared to be approaching the house. I then went back to the key ring and picked it up. It was much heavier than I imagined.

I went to the basement door and inserted the key. It took both of my small hands to turn the weighty lock. After some struggle, it opened with a satisfying thunk.

I turned the knob, and the door creaked open. The staircase beyond was only partially illuminated by the light from the doorway—after the fifth or sixth step there was complete darkness.

I moved into the unknown. The handrail was very high up for my seven-year-old height, and after two steps I decided to throw caution to the wind and let go of it. When I reached the barrier of blackness on the sixth step, I paused. My eyes adjusted to the darkness beyond, and I could make out the bottom of the stairs. I was sure there had to be a light switch on the wall down there, though I couldn't see one from where I was standing. Excitement overcame nervousness; I proceeded. As I lifted my foot to keep going, however, I was interrupted.

"What are you doing?!"

The voice was behind me. I turned toward it and lost my footing, slipping on the next step. I reached for the handrail in vain and tumbled down the staircase. Though it was perhaps only another six or seven steps, it seemed endless. I landed backwards, slamming my head onto the basement's concrete floor. I howled, then tried to move, but was overwhelmed by an intense pain in my leg. More torture than I'd ever felt, I couldn't catch my breath; it was too much to process. I looked up in panic.

At the top of the stairs my thirteen-year-old brother Robert stood in the doorway, stiff and unsure. He was caught in an unsolvable dilemma: he knew he should come to my aid, but to do so would break our father's strict rule about not going into the basement. At the time I could not appreciate his position, I only saw him staring at me then running off, abandoning me in distress.

Again, I tried to move, gingerly, but the pain was unbelievable. I looked around, overcome with fear, weeping helplessly.

My eyes adjusted to the darkness, and I saw something that momentarily made me forget my agony.

There were faces. They surrounded me, staring. Large ghosts floating in the shadows. I couldn't understand what I was looking at.

"Jean-Luc?!" The voice of my rescuer, my mother, as she ran down the steps. Even in her work boots and overalls, an elegant angel of mercy. She immediately examined my leg.

"Oh, dear, what have you done?" she said. "Maurice, bring the first aid kit…"

"I have the damn kit, calm down," he said as he came down the stairs at his usual unhurried pace, carrying the small black case. Behind him, at the top of the stairs, Robert had returned, and from his expression was clearly now jealous of the attention I was receiving.

My father handed the kit to my mother, who removed a hypo and injected it into my arm. The pain in my leg and head suddenly abated. She replaced the hypo, then took out a small gray device: a bone knitter.

"Maman," I said, whispering, still scared but comforted by her presence. "There are people in the dark…"

"Shhh, I know," she said, as she activated the device and applied it to my leg. "Turn on the lights, Maurice. They're scaring the boy…"

"What doesn't scare the boy?" he said.

"Maurice," my mother said, a snap of condemnation.

Whether the judgment of my mother's tone affected him, his expression didn't reveal, but he went to the wall switch, and the room was illuminated. I could see now the staircase ended in the center of a long hallway dug from the stone beneath the house, three meters high, a hundred meters long. On both sides, the faces became clear; framed paintings and photographs, all portraits, lined the walls. There were dozens. Some of the paintings depicted scenes of ancient Earth, while some of the photographs were more recent. It was a museum of some sort. I turned to my father.

"Who are those people?"

"That," my father said, with grave import, "is the family."

✦

I have to say, the discovery that the secret of the basement was a portrait museum was something of a disappointment. My father had kept the room locked for the mundane reason of keeping the portraiture safe from his often rambunctious sons. However, once my brother and I were in on the "secret," my father began our education of its importance in his life, and, by extension, ours. He wanted us to know the Picards mattered.

This, as it turned out, was not without justification.

The name Picard has a long heritage on Earth that began in ancient Brittany; the line can be traced back all way to the 9th century AD, when Charlemagne, King of the Franks, was uniting Europe. For several centuries, the Picards would hold a family seat in the fiefdom of Vieille Ville in Brittany, where they were elevated to *Vicomtes* (Viscounts), a title of nobility. The name spread throughout France, and by the 14th century there were Picards in Normandy, Lyonnais, and Champagne.

Over time, I would become aware and eventually awed by the important work of my ancestors: Pierre Picard arrived in Quebec in 1629, one of the earliest French settlers in North America; Bernard Picart (an ancestor despite the variant spelling) was a famous French engraver known for his book illustrations of the popular Christian religious text, the Bible, in the 18th century; noted astronomer Jean-Félix Picard, for whom the Picard crater on Earth's moon is named; Joseph-Denis Picard, a divisional general during the French Revolution of the late 18th century; Frank Picard, who won the Nobel

Prize in Chemistry in 2028, and later Louise Picard, who helped found the Martian colony. All of their likenesses were in the basement family shrine, maintained for centuries by their relatives who lived in the vineyard.

The specific history of the Picard vineyard began during the Napoleonic Wars of the 1800s. Henri Picard, a captain in Napoleon's navy, purchased the land in the small village of La Barre, in the eastern French region of Bourgogne-Franche-Comté. The gently rolling hills and sleepy way of life appealed to a man who had spent his life at sea; it was a great tragedy that he never got to enjoy it. The purchase was made shortly before his death in 1805 commanding the French ship *Saturne* at the Battle of Trafalgar.*

His brother, Louis, decided to plant pinot noir grapes on about a half-acre of the 20-acre parcel. The winery took years to produce that first vintage of Chateau Picard, 1815; then it was a very low-yielding vineyard, producing a paltry four hundred bottles. Over time more acreage was planted and the winemaking improved so that by the end of the 20th century each acre of grapes produced six thousand bottles of wine.

In that pre-industrial age of the first vintages, the winemaking methods were determined by the limited technology; grapes were harvested and pressed either by hand or primitive machines. For better or worse, these crude methods became tradition. My family ignored advances in winemaking technology, and, as a result, Chateau Picard has been made the same way for the last five hundred years. This would end up being an unforeseen advantage during the World War in the 22nd century. When John Ericsson, the genetically engineered ruler of Europe, invaded France, he destroyed the country's technological base. So, even during this dark period of the world's history, Chateau Picard survived.**

This first refusal of technology became dismissiveness, and eventually disdain. By the time my father, Maurice, was born in 2270, it had seeped into the bones of our familial culture. Father grew up in a home that reveled in the

---

*EDITOR'S NOTE: There is no official historical record of a Henri Picard or a ship named Saturne at the Battle of Trafalgar. However, it is well known that record keeping of the time was not always accurate; private family histories often contain precise details lost in the more official histories.

**EDITOR'S NOTE: Though Isaac Cody was a well-known and successful developer in the region during the 19th century, there is no record of him selling a farm to Franklin Kirk.

primitive. We worked our vineyard, food was cooked by hand. His leisure time, what there was of it, was spent reading. He developed a love of Shakespeare, which he passed on to his sons, as well as a fondness for Earl Grey tea.[*]

Modern society changed how people consumed and produced wine, the invention of the replicator radically altering the economics of food production. By the 23rd century, anyone manufacturing wine was doing it for the art of it, and my paternal grandparents, François and Genevieve, were experts. They produced some of our most memorable vintages, including the renowned 2247. My father reveled in this reputation, and threw himself into this life, taking over as the winery's cellarmaster at the relatively young age of 29, even though my grandfather was still alive and living at the vineyard.

"He was single-minded," my mother once told me. "Even François [his father] recognized Maurice's passion and determination to make great wine surpassed his own." I suppose if I inherited a character trait from my father it was his single-mindedness, his drive to do something, or create something, great and memorable. In one conversation with my mother she admitted to me that she felt my father lacked some imagination; he not only never physically left La Barre, his mind never did either. He decided to only imagine himself running the family winery. "Of course," she said with a wry smile, "some found this dedication and single-mindedness attractive."

My mother, born Yvette Gessard in 2274, was also from La Barre. She met my father in secondary school, where they began a romance. When she left for university (at the renowned École Polytechnique), he had already proposed marriage, and she had accepted. She was interested in the sciences, but she tailored her education to give her a place on our family vineyard.

"My professors were quite frustrated with my desire to become an enologist," she said. "They felt I was wasting my potential." An enologist is a scientist whose background includes chemistry, microbiology, geology, meteorology, and soil science. Of course, the enologist's only concern with these varied subjects is their intersection with regard to grapes, wine, and especially fermentation. Whether or not my mother agreed with her professors or had any regrets about this decision she never revealed. She always gave the

---

[*]**EDITOR'S NOTE:** A French father passing along a love of the Bard and a very British tea seems to confirm the previous note.

impression of being very content with her life, which consisted of her husband, children, and the work of the family vineyard.

My brother Robert was born in 2299. By the time I was born on July 13, 2305, he was already a dedicated assistant to my parents. Growing up, I became keenly aware of a stifling dynamic; Robert did everything he could to seek my father's approval by imitation. There was no way for me to compete. Robert had six years of wine education and experience ahead of mine. But that wasn't the chief resource he used to dominate me.

"Idiot, you're doing it wrong," he said as I tried to help tie vines, or, "You're as dumb as the moon," as I struggled at using pruning shears to cut stems. It was a cascade of abuse whispered in my ear or shouted aloud at every opportunity, to the point that I grew to disdain our family occupation. It reached a pinnacle one July afternoon. We were standing among the vines as my father gave us one of his many lectures on how to tell when the grapes were ready to be harvested. I asked why we didn't use a computer, which would tell us exactly when they were ready.

"A computer cannot taste a grape," he said, "or tell if the skins are about to burst, or if the heat has eaten the acidity in them." From my little knowledge of computers (I was only eight) I imagined that a computer could probably do all those things. Instead, I decided on a less mature argument.

"Wine is boring," I said.

My father showed no visible reaction, but from the look on my brother's face it appeared as if I'd committed murder.

"Go inside then," my father said. "Robert and I have work to do."

As I turned away, I expected to see pleasure on Robert's face, but instead I saw contempt and judgment. I suppose he was emoting in my father's stead.

I went inside. It may sound like an exaggeration, but this was one of the most important moments of my life. I'd just declared my independence. I wasn't fully conscious of the ramifications, the rift I'd cemented with my father and brother, and the implied decision I'd made about my future—that I wouldn't stay at the vineyard. But the fear and exhilaration made clear to my young self that I was at a crossroads, and that I'd broken free of what felt like a trap. Even at eight, I knew the vineyard and winery would someday be Robert's. He'd guaranteed that path for himself long before I was even born. And the fact was I had no passion for making wine. It seemed so trivial to me. I knew I was on the road to somewhere else, I just didn't know where.

I needed to do *something*. Our computer time was strictly limited to schoolwork. I supposed I could sneak off to my friend Louis's house; his family was not nearly as technology adverse as mine was, and there was an assortment of modern entertainments for children's play. But I sensed from my father that I was being punished, and one rebellion per day seemed enough. Reading was out, I was too restless, so I wandered the house. I eventually found myself in the basement.

This was no longer a forbidden zone. Since my invasion of a year before, my father decided to make use of it. With a natural inclination to take the fun out of everything, he began our rigorous education of the family. We had to learn, by rote, all our ancestors and their achievements. This schooling in our family history had a subtle effect on me. We had a complete family history—a handwritten tome charting every blood relative on the tree and where they lived and what they did—but the forebears in the gallery were all people of great accomplishment: scientists, great writers, explorers. To my young mind it was these people I needed to emulate.

As I strolled through the hall of portraits, I realized I had to do something to distinguish myself, to guarantee my place in this gallery of the skilled and gifted.

I got to the photo of Louise Picard. She was in a spacesuit, standing with several other people on the surface of Mars. They were settlers, jovially holding shovels, as if they would literally be breaking ground on what would be the first human Martian city. Louise was the only photo on the wall of an ancestor who'd gone to space, and though there were others, Louise was the first. As I looked at the picture, I went through in my head my relatives who'd left Earth. There weren't that many… and then a thought occurred to me.

I ran upstairs to our library, and went to the small dais where my father kept the handwritten family history. I scoured the passages of the generations who came of age during space travel, and after a few minutes was able to confirm the hunch I'd had in the basement.

No Picard had ever left the solar system, had ever gone to the stars.

I was eight years old, and I'd found my path.

✦

I began work immediately. However, since I was a child and had limited understanding of what that work should actually be, my goal "to leave the solar system" was as vague as it was grand. I didn't want to ask my parents for guidance for fear of giving away my plan to escape the vineyard. So I devoured whatever books I could find on the technology of space travel and the history of the Galaxy. There were few of these in our home, so most of that reading took place either at school or my friend Louis's house, much to his chagrin (Louis, like most boys our age, wasn't in love with reading). I already had a keen interest in the ancient Age of Sail, when men explored the world in wooden ships, and my study of space travel was a natural extension. I also began building and collecting model spaceships and attempted to become an expert on each one.

My mother indulged this interest, helping me acquire an extensive model collection, and for my ninth birthday we took a trip to the Smithsonian Institution in Washington, North America. I was in awe at the many spaceships on display, including Zefram Cochrane's faster-than-light *Phoenix*, and the first starship *Enterprise*. It was on that day that I acquired a model of that ship, and when we got home I immediately set about its construction. One of the reasons I was interested specifically in the NX-01: my brother Robert had a model of it when I was little, which he never let me play with. He had long since dispensed with such toys, but it had stayed in my memory.

When it was finished, I showed it to my mother, who asked me what I knew about it.

"First ship to go warp 5," I said. "Its helmsman was Travis Mayweather." Like most boys at that age, the most important thing about a ship was how fast it went and who drove it.

"Is that who you want to be?" my mother said. "The helmsman?"

"Yes," I said, "he's the one who flies the ship."

"But he takes orders from the captain, who is the true pilot."

I had never thought about it before. "How do you get to be the captain?"

"You have to go to Starfleet Academy," she said, "and do very well." She left me to a new fantasy. I had of course heard of Starfleet Academy, but this was really the first time I considered that it would be a place that I might go. As I stared at my collection of spaceship models, a different fantasy of the future began to emerge.

That night at dinner, I announced my intention to go to Starfleet Academy. I was met with a derisive laugh from Robert.

"They'll never accept you," he said. "They don't want idiots." He was as predictable as a damp, cold wind in November, yet in my childlike naïveté I still wandered into every interaction with my brother hoping for some wisp of friendship, or at least politeness.

"Robert…" At my mother's warning, Robert withheld his next taunt. Whatever it was, I was certain I would hear it later.

"I'll get in," I said. "I'm not stupid."

"You're not," Mother said. "But it will take a lot of work."

"I'm going to do it," I said.

"Waste of time." This was my father. He was into his second bottle of wine, and had settled into one of his occasional dark moods.

"Well, I think he will," Mother said.

"What do you know about it?" My father snapped this at my mother.

"Obviously," she said, "I couldn't hope to know as much as you. Eat your dinner." Her condescension trumped his, and we sat in silence and finished our meal, though I was just about bursting with plans and determination.

The next day I came home from school. The night before, I'd been dying to research more about the academy, but I had to wait for my free periods in school to gather up all the information I could. There was more than my nine-year-old brain could comprehend, but I was on my way. I had taken copious notes, and was so anxious to go over them that I almost didn't notice the tragedy that was waiting for me.

My new NX-01 model was broken on the floor. At first I thought it had just fallen off the table, but on closer inspection I saw a bit of mud on the broken engine. Someone had stepped on it. Probably a year before I would've burst into tears, but not on this day. I got angry.

I stormed downstairs, the pieces of my new favorite model in my hand, and pushed the front door open. On my way back from school, I'd seen Robert in the vineyard tying off a vine, and made a beeline for him. He didn't see me coming, and just as he turned I got one good shove in. He lost his balance and fell to the ground. He was shocked, but up on his feet and on top of me before I could react.

"You piddly piece of trash," he said. He was enraged that I'd gotten the upper hand on him, even for just a second. He punched me repeatedly, and it was only the sound of my father's voice that put a stop to it.

"What the hell is this?"

My father stood over us, glaring. He pulled Robert off of me.

"He knocked me down," Robert said.

"Because he broke my spaceship!" I said it as I held out the broken pieces as incontrovertible proof of Robert's crime.

"I did no such thing!"

"You're lying!" I lunged at Robert again, but this time my father grabbed me. He took the pieces of the spaceship out of my hand and threw them in the dirt.

"Why did you do that…"

"Get in the house, Jean-Luc! I don't have time for your childish nonsense. There's work to be done."

I had no idea what to say. I had a childhood sense of justice, and I expected my father to enforce it, but he didn't. Tears in my eyes, I gathered up the broken pieces and went back to the house. I was even more determined to escape these bullies who dominated my world.

✦

From that day forward, I took a much more serious attitude to my schoolwork. Acceptance into Starfleet Academy was extremely competitive; less than two percent of applicants were admitted so I was determined to win high marks. I also focused on sports, including track and field, boxing, and fencing. Though I was driven by a desire to both make my mark on the universe and escape the vineyard, the attention I got from my successes was like a drug. My mother was openly delighted by each of my academic achievements. Even my father was impressed, giving me a crisp "very good" for each triumph. Of course, each accomplishment brought a scowl from Robert, which at the time gave me nothing but pleasure. I let myself believe that though he was older and stronger, he wasn't as smart as I was. This was of course not true; he focused his efforts on the winery, and as a result his studies suffered. But feeling the victim of his oppression, I reveled in the pain I was causing him. Looking back, I regret this youthful arrogance, as it cost me a relationship with perhaps the one person who knew me best, and a person I would not fully understand until I was an adult, when it was too late. At the time, however, we were engaged in a battle of wills, and though I gave him no explicit explanation of my escape plans, he seemed to intuit them. From my perspective, he did everything he could to get in the way.

I remember once, I was eleven, in my room, reading a book. It was one of the many biographies of Starfleet Captain James T. Kirk. As I'd begun to study the history of Starfleet, his name kept coming up. He was a swashbuckling hero of a simpler time, and his adventures captured my imagination at that age.

"Father wants you to mix the grapes," Robert said. Lost in the outer space exploits of the book, I hadn't noticed my brother standing in my doorway until he spoke.

I looked up at him. I couldn't be sure that Robert was being truthful. It was quite possible my father had sent him. But the only way to find out would require questioning my father, and I knew that even if he hadn't sent Robert, he'd be annoyed that I would be trying to get out of work, so I'd have to do it anyway.

I put my book away and trudged outside to the barn where we kept our fermentation tanks. This is where the grapes, after they were picked and had their stems removed, would spend about a week fermenting. During this process, the skins separated from the grape, and formed a cap or crust at the top. It was necessary to regularly punch down on that crust, extracting more juice from the skins. To do this, one had to stand above the tank, using a paddle. It was one of many laborious chores that took me away from my new passions.

That day, I climbed up onto the eight-foot-tall tanks, and stood on the gangplank which crossed over it. I grabbed my paddle and began pressing down on the grapes, but my mind was still caught up in the adventure I'd been reading: Captain Kirk, disguised as an enemy Romulan, sneaking aboard their vessel to steal a cloaking device right out from under them… Anxious to get back to my book, I began pressing too hard and fast on the crust, hoping to move my task along quickly. The paddle wouldn't move at the speed I wanted it to, and I slipped.

I fell off the gangplank and landed with a splat and splash into the fermenting wine. The smell, unpleasant enough when standing above it, was truly overpowering. I tried to find my footing, but couldn't touch the bottom; I was around five feet tall, and the fermenting grapes rose to a level higher than that. I stretched for the gangplank, but it was out of reach; I couldn't get high enough to grab it. I tried to move to the side of the tank; the mix of liquid and grape pulp had a consistency closer to quicksand than water. I sank. I took liquid into my mouth; the mixture of juice, alcohol and yeast burned my throat and stung my eyes. I tried to scream, which only made me gulp more of the vile liquid. Every effort I made failed, and panic took over.

"Grab it!"

I looked up. Robert was kneeling on the gangplank. He had retrieved my paddle, and held it out to me. I grabbed onto it, and he pulled. Once I came up out of the muck, he reached down and grabbed my arm. He pulled me up over the gangplank, where I caught my breath and calmed down.

"You're as stupid as the moon," he said. I felt embarrassed, and would soon face punishment for ruining several hundred bottles of wine, along with the added humiliation of having purple skin that lasted several days.

It was only with the gift of hindsight that I realized the only way Robert was there so quickly was that he had to have been watching me. The same was true when I fell down the stairs in the basement, and who knows how many other times. Whatever my brother's feelings for me at the time, he also felt responsible, and for that I owed him my life.

I would eventually leave home and Robert behind; it would take years for me to repent my ingratitude.

✦

"Congratulations," the computer voice said, "your application for entry to the Starfleet Academy Class of 2326 has been approved for final testing. Please report to Starfleet Headquarters, San Francisco, on September 28, 2322 at 0900."

I smiled at the news, and found it in no way surprising. I couldn't wait; my academic achievements led me to expect that I would gain entrance to the academy, and that this was almost a formality. I was 17, and had grown from a quiet, bookish child to a bold, arrogant teen, well past cocky. My life outside in the world was active and social, but things with the family were very different.

I'd become almost a boarder in my own home. Given my size and athletic ability, Robert could no longer effectively bully me physically or mentally, and now that he was in his twenties he had little interest. He was well on his way to becoming the winery's next cellarmaster. He had also gotten what he always wanted—he'd become my father's best friend. They spent most of their time together, talking about their wine, their grapes, their soil, and other people's wines, other people's grapes, and other people's soil. It was an endless wine symposium that they both enjoyed as it fueled my brother's need for approval and my father's need for admiration.

As far as I was concerned, though my father had complimented my academic and athletic achievements, he made no secret that he thought it a waste to use them to gain entrance to the academy. The closer I got to the age of admission, the harsher his disdain for the service and the people in it; it seemed to actually anger him, that somehow my decision was a personal betrayal. This only reinforced my desire to go.

The only person in my family I still had a good relationship with was my mother. I sensed her conflict as a loving parent and a loving wife. And she wanted to encourage my interests but knew that those interests would take me away from her. When I brought her the news of the final step in my application, I could see she was ambivalent.

"That's wonderful, Jean-Luc," she said, "but please keep this to yourself for the moment."

"Why?"

"I want to delay upsetting your father for as long as I can," she said. This was, of course, exactly the opposite of what I wanted to do, but I decided to accede to her request, especially since I needed her help to get to San Francisco.

I would be staying in San Francisco in a dormitory for the three days of testing, so I packed a small bag and we set out early on the morning of the 28th. The day happened to coincide with Robert and my father shipping out a new vintage, so they were properly distracted; we didn't have to say goodbye. We took an air tram from La Barre to Paris, and then my mother surprised me with an energy matter transport to San Francisco. I'd never gone through the process before, and hid my excitement for fear of looking like a child.

The municipal transporter in Paris was outside, a small pad near Notre Dame on the Île de la Cité. The weather was warm and humid, and a technician led us onto the pad. I looked down at it, which was unfortunate, because a moment passed and I was looking down at an almost identical pad. I looked up to see I was now standing in San Francisco near Fisherman's Wharf. The city was covered in fog and a good twenty degrees cooler. I was furious with myself; I'd missed the transposition between cities because I had been looking at my feet.

I'd been to the North American continent several times before, but never to San Francisco. The home of Starfleet Command and Starfleet Academy, this city was the largest spaceport on planet Earth. The crisscrossing of shuttles and trams over the Golden Gate Bridge and ultra-modern skyline was stunning and exciting, and it was impossible to maintain my façade of teenage indifference. Walking the streets was a spectrum of alien life unlike any I'd ever seen. This was the world where I wanted to be, away from what I felt was the primitive, stultifying environment I'd grown up in.

We found our way to Starfleet Headquarters; the testing took place in the Archer Building, one of the older structures, named for Jonathan Archer, captain of the NX-01 *Enterprise*.* After I signed in, my mother gave me a hug as she handed me off to a young female ensign.

"Right this way, Mr. Picard," she said, as she led me to a turbolift.

"Call me Jean-Luc," I said. At this young age, I fancied myself a ladies' man, most days greatly overestimating my appeal.

"No, thank you," she said. She led me to the testing room and gave me a curt goodbye. I entered the room. There were four computer stations arranged in a square each with a chair facing away from the others. Two people were there already, a human male around my age, and a humanoid alien of a species I'd never met in person before, blue-skinned with a ridge running down the center of his face. The human stood and gave me a friendly smile.

"Robert DeSoto," he said as we shook hands.

"Jean-Luc Picard," I said.

"*Parlez-vous francais?*" he responded. I smiled and we had a short conversation in French, which DeSoto seemed to delight in speaking. He told me his mother had been raised in France and taught the language to her children. I broke off our conversation to introduce myself to the other occupant of the room.

"Fras Jeslik," he said.

---

*EDITOR'S NOTE: It is a regrettably common mistake Picard makes here: the Archer Building was in fact named for Jonathan Archer's father, Henry, who designed the warp 5 engine.

"Are you a Bolian?" I said.

"Yes," he said. He seemed surprised. "I have to admit, you're one of the first humans who didn't think I was an Andorian who'd had his antenna chopped off." We began chatting, all of us a little nervous at being there, all immediately recognizing that some of us would not make it through this round of testing. We were soon joined by a young woman, also human. She held out her hand to me.

"Marta Batanides," she said. She was attractive, with brown hair and an appealing smile. I took her hand. In my immature, adolescent mind I decided she must be attracted to me, and depending on how things went over the next few days I thought I might take advantage of it. (It is with embarrassment and a small amount of nausea that I relate my thinking regarding women at this age, but I feel honesty is an essential part of capturing my younger self truthfully.) The four of us engaged in a lively discussion until an officer entered and we immediately fell silent.

"I'm Tac Officer Tichenor," he said. He was tall with curly blond hair that seemed to match his wry, puckish demeanor. "You're here for three days of testing. Right now there are only a few open spots left in next year's class, and there are testing rooms like this all over the Galaxy. If you can't do the math on your chances, you're probably not going to get in." If this was meant to discourage me, it had the opposite effect.

Tichenor showed each of us to a computer console, and we began the tests. Over the course of the three days, the tests covered a variety of subjects ranging from Galactic history, warp physics, and astrobiology. The four of us would finish our testing for the day, go to dinner, then go to sleep. As young and energetic as I was, this was the most stress I'd ever been under, and I was exhausted at the end of each day.

At the end of the third day of testing, Tac Officer Tichenor informed us that we had two tests left, the tactical simulation and the psychological exam. Tichenor told me I was first, and took me out of the room. He led me down a corridor toward an area marked BRIDGE SIMULATOR. I entered and found a detailed recreation of the bridge of an *Excelsior*-class starship. I'd seen pictures of them and had studied the systems with an almost obsessive interest. I was convinced I could operate any of the control panels. I couldn't wait to show off my abilities—I was certain I would impress whoever from the academy was watching us.

Sitting casually in the simulator room were three other students in civilian clothes, all about my age. I assumed they were from another testing group, but before I could introduce myself, Tichenor left, shutting the door behind him. The room was bathed in red light as a klaxon blared.

"Red alert," the computer voice said. I was momentarily startled; this tactical simulation felt very real. I looked at my fellow "crewmen," all of whom seemed genuinely flummoxed. I took this as an opportunity.

"You," I said, pointing to a rotund fellow, "take the science station, activate sensors."

"Where is it?" he said. I realized that my years of studying spaceships probably put me ahead of a lot of my peers. I pointed out the science station just behind the captain's chair, then turned to a young woman.

"Can you get the viewscreen on?"

"I think so," she said, and sat down at the helm station. I turned to the last crewman, a thin reed of a man.

"Man the weapons console," I said, indicating the corner station by the viewscreen. He went over to the console, and tentatively sat down. I then turned to the rotund boy.

"We have anything on sensors?"

"I don't know. I don't know what I'm looking at." He was staring helplessly at the science station control panel. Annoyed, I ran up and activated the sensors. I saw three images of ships closing in on us. Sensors said they had weapons locked on.

"Shields up!" As I yelled, my voice cracked.

"Who are you talking to?" the woman said.

"And what are 'shields'?" Thin Guy said. Unbelievable, I thought. These people think they deserve to be in Starfleet?

Frustrated, I ran to the weapons console and threw the switch to activate the shields. I was too late; the simulator registered a hit and the weapons console shorted out. I looked at the indicators; we now had no weapons. I turned to look at the viewscreen; it was still off.

"Turn on the viewscreen!" I was getting very angry. "We've got to get out of here!"

"I thought I knew how to do it, but I guess I don't..." the woman said. This was insane. Did I have to do everything? I ran down to the helm station.

"Get out of the chair," I said, and the woman got up. I sat down, activated the viewscreen, just in time to see three old Romulan birds-of-prey firing their energy plasma weapons. I keyed the control for warp speed; the simulator recorded another hit. The engineering console shorted out, and the lights dimmed. I looked over and saw that we had no engine power.

"Simulation ended," the computer voice said. Anger overflowed, but I kept my mouth shut. Then someone had to speak and ruin it.

"Sorry," the rotund boy said. The weakness I sensed in his apology set me on edge, and I lost it.

"Sorry?! You're sorry?! Why are you even applying to the academy?!" I'm not sure I'd ever heard myself yell that loudly, but I'd worked so hard to get here, and in my mind these three strangers just ruined it.

"We did the best we could," Thin Guy said.

"Imbecile! Your 'best' would've gotten us killed!" I was making so much noise that I hadn't noticed the sound of the door opening.

"Now, now," Tichenor said, "let's all take a breath." I wheeled to face him; his dry tone made me realize I'd lost control, and I fell into silent embarrassment.

"Picard, I'll take you back," Tichenor said. "The rest wait here."

He led me out of the control room. We walked in silence back to the classroom, where my other three classmates waited. They could immediately see I was upset.

"Hey, Picard, what's wrong?" DeSoto said.

"Tactical simulation went badly," I said.

"It couldn't be as bad as all that," Marta said. I noticed she looked at Tichenor, whose half smile did nothing to confirm or deny Marta's supposition.

"Mr. Picard, you're done for the day," Tichenor said, and then turned to DeSoto. "You're next, come with me." DeSoto followed him out, and I stayed behind and told Marta and Fras what happened.

"I just don't know how that could be considered a tactical simulation," I said.

"Maybe it wasn't," Marta said. "Maybe that was the psych test." That thought hadn't occurred to me, mostly because I couldn't see how it made sense.

"What were they testing?" I said. "How fast I would get annoyed at incompetence?"

"I don't know," Marta said. "Did Tichenor *say* it was the tactical simulation?" I realized that he hadn't said anything; if it was the psych test, I had a sinking feeling I'd failed it spectacularly. And I wasn't even sure what they were testing. Since I was done for the day, I decided to go back to my room and sulk.

The next day, I showed up in the classroom. I hadn't seen my classmates the previous evening, and they all looked somewhat nervous as Tac Officer Tichenor addressed us. He informed us that, of our group, only Robert DeSoto had gained entrance to the academy. DeSoto and I had become friends, but I was also so overcome with jealousy and confusion that it was a struggle to offer him congratulations. He saw through it instantly, reading my expression.

"Yeah, I agree," Robert said. "It should've been you." I was embarrassed at my self-centeredness.

"I'm sorry," I said. "I really am happy for you."

"*Ce n'est pas grave,*" he said. "I'll see you there next year."

Marta and I walked out of the building. I was so lost in thought, it was a moment before I noticed Marta was laughing at me.

"What's so funny?"

"You," she said. "You're so arrogant it's unbelievable."

"Look," I said, "I worked really hard for this…"

"And I didn't?" she said. "In case you hadn't noticed, you weren't the only one whose dreams were postponed." She of course was right, but I couldn't let it go. "Did you even find out whether that was the psych test?"

"No," I said. I had been too humiliated to ask. I didn't want to admit to Tichenor that I didn't know what I was being tested on. This of course was ego, and self-defeating; if I came back next year, I would be no closer to understanding what I needed to do to gain acceptance.

Marta and I said our goodbyes, and made what would turn out to be empty promises to stay in touch. My mother wanted to come pick me up, but I had talked her out of it. This meant I had to take an air tram first to Paris, and then one to La Barre. It was a couple of hours traveling, more time for me to bathe in my own self-pity.

I arrived in La Barre, threw my duffel bag over my shoulder, and walked home from the station. As I passed the familiar trees, I was overcome with a feeling of dread. I knew Robert would take great pleasure in my failure, and I'd been so arrogant in the time leading up to the test, on some level I knew I deserved it. I had no clue as to what my father would do, but I imagined the two of them would share some hearty laughter about it.

I approached the door to our home, which suddenly opened and my mother was there to greet me. She gave me a warm hug.

"It's all right, Jean-Luc," she said softly, and I started to cry. I thought myself such a man, but I was still a child, and my mother's maternal sympathy broke down the false construct of masculinity. She brought me inside and I quickly wiped away my tears.

"Where's Father and Robert?"

"In the barn, still packing wine," she said. "Don't worry, we have a few moments. I want to hear what happened." I told her in some detail, including the mystery of what that last test was.

"It's no mystery," she said. "It was the psych test."

"How can you be sure?"

"You want to leave here and make your mark on the world," she said. "You have for years, and at some point you decided that Starfleet was the way you wanted to do it." My mother could see me so clearly; my youthful arrogance had convinced me that my motivations for self-aggrandizement were well hidden to everyone.

"What does that have to do with it?"

"You were presented with a test that you thought you were quite ready for. Yet there were three incompetent people standing in your way," she said. "Your biggest fear." Realization dawned on me.

"My fear, that I won't have control," I said. And then Marta's comment came back to me. "And that it's all about me." What worried me was that, even with this knowledge, I didn't know what the right way to handle that test was.

"So he's home," Robert said. He and Father had come in from outside. Robert's tone was what I expected, full of derision. They sat down as they removed their dirty boots.

"I'm home," I said.

"And when do you leave again?" Robert said. "Off to the stars, I suppose?" I was confused by this, and looked at my mother, whose expression said that she had not told them.

"I didn't get in," I said. I saw Robert and my father exchange a look, and fully braced myself for an onslaught of ruthless snickering at my expense.

"Oh," Robert said. He didn't laugh. He in fact seemed uncomfortable.

"Well, that's a bit of luck for us," my father said.

"Really? Why is that?"

"We could use your help with the shipment tomorrow," my father said. "If you're available." This last comment had a slight sarcastic bite, but only slight. It has taken me a lifetime to understand that in that moment my father and brother felt bad for me. They took no pleasure in my failure. The next day I helped them pack shipments of wine. It was in some way cathartic for me, helping me move past my failure.

Soon, however, things returned to normal around our house. Robert went back to demeaning me at every opportunity, and I in turn dismissed him with a condescending arrogance. My father continued his loud contempt for my goals, which I pursued with even more fervor. The next year, I succeeded at getting another chance for admission. I went through the testing again, this time with a new group of applicants, still supervised by Tichenor. As with the first time, I did well on the computer monitor testing. On the final day, Tichenor again escorted me to the bridge simulator.

The same three students were there again. Tichenor shut the door and the red alert klaxon sounded.

I was momentarily confused. I had spent the last year going over this situation in my head, preparing what I would do if confronted with a similar test. I had decided that I would take the helm control myself, turn on the viewscreen, and immediately try to pilot the "ship" out of danger, since one man couldn't properly take the three ships on in a battle. But what I hadn't considered was the possibility that the situation would be *exactly* the same, with the same three people. My instinct was to ignore that, take the helm and proceed with the plan, but those other three applicants convinced me that their presence was part of the test.

And then I realized: they weren't applicants. They couldn't be. I decided to ask an obvious question.

"Are the three of you now any more experienced operating this simulator than you were last year?"

"Yes," the rotund boy said. "We've received complete training." I smiled, feeling victorious. I could start giving orders with a fair amount of confidence that they'd be able to carry them out.

Then I hesitated.

The rotund boy's phrase "complete training" stuck in my head. I hadn't received *any* training, I'd just read and studied on my own. I decided on a new strategy.

"If you're all completely trained," I said, "maybe you should take charge."

The thin guy smiled.

"All right," he said, "you take the helm and activate the viewscreen…"

✦

I wish I could say that was the moment I stopped being a cocky bastard, that I learned to show humility and a modest sense of inquisitiveness, but all I did was pat myself on the back for beating the test. I didn't have any real insight into why, and it would cost me dearly.

But right then, all that concerned me was that I passed, and was going to the academy.

A few months later, I left for school. I got up at 4:30am. I had hoped to leave the house without saying goodbye to my family. I knew that, given modern modes of travel, I wouldn't really be that far from home, and convinced myself that I didn't want to deal with my mother's emotionalism. In truth I think I was probably afraid of my own. I gathered my belongings in my duffel and headed downstairs. As I did, I noticed a light in the family room.

"So, you're leaving," my father said. He was sitting in a chair, illuminated by a small table lamp.

"Yes," I said. He didn't have a book or a drink, he was just sitting there. It was impossible for me to believe it at the time, but I think he was waiting for me.

"It is a dangerous path you're on," he said. "Don't do anything stupid." From another man, this might have sounded like a joke, but from my father there was not a hint of humor. At the time, all I read in my father's face was disparagement and rejection, but I see now it was actual concern he didn't know how to express. I regret that at that moment, I turned and left without saying goodbye.

CHAPTER TWO

I WAS ABOUT TWO AND A HALF HOURS INTO THE MARATHON, the last hill just ahead of me. It was almost 30 degrees Celsius, and I hadn't had a drink for almost five miles: the last time people on the route handed out cups of water I didn't take one, I didn't want to risk slowing my pace. My focus was paying off—most of the other runners had fallen behind. There were five of us who'd opened up a lead from the rest of the pack of academy students. The four runners, all ahead of me, were upperclassmen. Cadet Captain Sussman and Cadet Lieutenant Matalas, both fourth-years, were in the lead, followed closely by Cadets Black and Strong. The four were competing against each other; they didn't even realize I was there.

But they would. I decided on my first day at the academy that everybody would.

When I entered in 2323, Starfleet Academy was over 150 years old. Generations of its graduates had helped shaped the events of the last century, and for that reason it was one of the most revered educational institutions in the Galaxy. This fed my own desire for respect and achievement—by being associated with such an admired institution, I assumed I would also be admired. (This belief would lead to one of many rude awakenings.)

The first day at the academy is a trial in and of itself. After being signed in, you are given a large red bag, and sent on an organized scavenger hunt to acquire your needed supplies. In the old days I am told that you would face an angry upperclassman around every corner telling you how worthless you were. This was a leftover tradition from the military academies of old Earth, which had to create soldiers from children, ready to respond to orders on instinct. Over the decades Starfleet was able to chip away at the more barbaric traditions; the individuals of our evolved society respected the chain of command without the need of vicious discipline. Still, that didn't eliminate the difficulties involved in interpersonal relationships.

After I'd gathered my belongings on that first day, I found my way to my room in one of the older dormitories from the original campus, Mayweather House. My roommate lay on his bed, his feet up, the bag of his belongings still packed.

"Jean-Luc Picard," I said. "You must be Cortan."

"I prefer Corey, Corey Zweller," he said. "Pleasure to meet you, Johnny."

We were off to a bad start. No one had ever referred to me by that nickname; I hated it at once, and Corey along with it. I gave him a thin smile, and turned to put my belongings away. As I did, Corey started asking questions about where I was from, to which he received curt responses. Corey himself was from the American continent, the city of St. Louis. He was friendly and outgoing, but I couldn't forgive the nickname.

"So what classes have you registered for? Maybe we've got a few together..." Corey said.

"I haven't registered yet," I said. I had assumed that registration for classes would take place once we got to school, but I could tell from the expression on Corey's face that I was mistaken.

"You better get on it," Corey said. He showed me his computer screen where he had signed in and registered for his classes. I turned to the computer monitor allocated to me; this was a first, I'd never had my own computer. And I was also face to face with how the Luddism of my upbringing disadvantaged me. Unlike every other academy student, who was used to having unlimited access to a computer, I not only hadn't registered for classes ahead of time, I was unaware that I could.

"You never see a computer before, Johnny?" Corey said. He was joking, but I was so embarrassed I could only ignore him by staring intently at my computer as I stumbled through class registration. Corey chuckled to himself, I thought somewhat derisively, then left the room, as I faced the realization that I was already behind.

The education at Starfleet Academy was wide-ranging, with a heavy load of requirements for its cadets in science and engineering, as well as a plethora of courses in the social sciences and humanities, all with a bent to better a cadet's understanding of the Galaxy. There were some courses a student had to take (starship engineering, galactic law, etc.) and some requirements could be filled with one of several courses. I had planned to take a survey course to fulfill my galactic history requirement, but the class was full, and the only history course still open was Xenoarchaeology, a subject I had no interest in because I didn't really know what it was. Nevertheless, I breathed somewhat easier in that at least I'd completed my registration. I was certain that once I started classes things would fall into place.

I was of course completely wrong. The first summer at the academy, before the academic semester begins, cadets face a grueling series of athletic challenges. Starfleet requires students maintain a high level of physical abilities, and the "Plebe Summer" ritual is meant to weed out any cadet who isn't up to the challenge. I had succeeded in school sports, but I grew up on a vineyard; I'd never been through survival training, never carried a hundred-pound pack on a run, never climbed a real mountain. I got through the summer with a barely passing grade.

The feeling of physical superiority I had as a teenager vanished during that summer, and now the surety that I was smarter than everybody else disappeared on the first day of the fall academic semester. Though at the top of my class in my village school, everyone else who was at the academy was also at the top of *their* class. Many of my fellow cadets had been through a much more rigorous education; next to the several Vulcans in my advanced mathematics seminar, I felt like a shambling Neanderthal watching a Cro-Magnon make fire.

After the first day of classes, I sat in my room alone after dinner. Corey had invited me on excursions to find women and drink for the first few weeks, but my standard "no, thank you" eventually led him to stop, even to the point where he dropped his usual "see you later." I sat at my computer console pretending to work, but in fact wondering if I'd made the right choice. I hadn't made any friends, I felt intellectually and physically inferior. I never thought I'd be homesick, but I longed for the soothing voice of my mother, who had made Herculean efforts to stay connected to me, calling and writing at every opportunity. But I kept our conversations short, too proud to reveal to her (and then, by extension, my father and Robert) that the academy might be too much for me. The dreams of going into space and becoming a starship captain seemed very out of reach.

The second day of classes it wasn't much better, especially when I showed up for my first session of Xenoarchaeology. When I arrived, the classroom was empty, and I double-checked to see if I was in the right place. As I did, I was joined by another student, a young man of African-American descent, named Donald Varley.

"Did you get shut out of all the history sections too?" I asked.

"Uh, no," he said, with a smile. "I actually am interested in this. Is it possible there's only two of us?"

"That is my average class size," a man said. We turned to see a man in his seventies, wearing a worn safari vest and carrying a satchel. We assumed correctly that he was Professor Galen. He was a rare breed. Most academy instructors were Starfleet personnel of one form or another; older cadets who'd stayed on after graduation, or officers on leave or retired. Professor Galen however was strictly an academic of the pipe-smoking, tweed-jacket variety.

"Which of you is Varley and which is Picard?" he said as he made his way to the lectern in the front of the room. We identified ourselves, and he motioned us to sit right in front of him.

"The Federation has been in existence for almost two centuries," he said. "It is considered by many of its inhabitants as the greatest civilization in history. The work we will review here will prove the inanity of such a judgment…"

I settled in for what I expected would be a lot of dull photos of potshards and fossils. Instead, Professor Galen took two objects out of his satchel and handed one to each of us. They were small figurines, what appeared to be the torso of some kind of humanoid, perhaps in armor.

"Any idea what you're holding?" Neither of us knew. "That is a figurine from the Kurlan civilization."

This seemed to peak Varley's interest, and he began to examine his very carefully.

"They were created in a workshop by a Kurlan who is now only known as the Master of Tarquin Hill. He used materials and tools several centuries ahead of his time to create those pieces. Any idea of their age?"

"Well," Varley said, "the Kurlan civilization disappeared over ten thousand years ago…"

"Yes," Galen said. "In fact, the objects you hold in your hand are over twelve thousand years old." I now considered the object a lot less casually.

"Because of his artistic eye," Galen said, "and the advanced techniques he used, those objects have survived. Can we make an assumption as to why?"

Varley didn't have an answer, but as I stared at the small object in my hand, I pictured a lonely artist using primitive tools and materials in some ancient workshop. He was focused on his work, and he had only one goal in mind.

"He wanted to be remembered," he said.

"If that's the case," Galen said, "why not inscribe his name on his work?"

"The work is what was important to him," I said. "He left his mark."

"Rather impressively I would say," Galen said. "But, as my old professor said, archaeology is the search for facts, not truth. So we will stick to the facts…" But I wasn't listening. I felt in some way Galen was telepathic; like an archaeologist in my head, he'd uncovered for me my true motivation, which had gotten lost in the insecurity of Plebe Summer and the first day of classes.

I wanted to leave my mark.

It was childish, to be sure. I wasn't interested in accomplishing anything other than my own aggrandizement. I wanted immediate gratification of my desire to make the people here remember me. I saw my answer on my way across campus as I passed a viewscreen with a list of upcoming academy events:

ACADEMY MARATHON REGISTRATION OPENS TODAY.

I'd never run more than ten kilometers at a stretch, and that was during Plebe Summer; I came in almost last, just ahead of a Tellarite cadet, the large, slow-moving porcine species. But the academy marathon was one of the most visible contests the academy sponsored; it was broadcast via subspace, so much of the Federation had a chance to watch it. If I could do well in this, they would have to notice me. I signed up immediately. Now all I needed to do was figure out how to run a marathon.

I did some research, and began my training immediately. I ran five times a week, and quickly got up to a long run once a week, increasing to 20 kilometers in less than two months. Adding this extra challenge further isolated me from my classmates. I suppose in retrospect I was in a kind of hiding; it was easier for me to focus my energies on physical and intellectual activities, rather than face the emotional insecurity I felt. But I rationalized I was happier alone.

One night after a run, I returned to my room to find a surprise. A woman lay on my bed, relaxed with a small bottle in her hand. It took me only a second to recognize her.

"Marta!" I said. I hadn't seen Marta Batanides since our final testing together. I wasn't even aware that she'd gotten into the academy but was very pleased to see her, and that surprised me as well. "How did you find me?"

"Oh my god, Jean-Luc," she said. "Is—is this your room?" She hurried off the bed and stood awkwardly, and I immediately realized she wasn't there to see me.

"Hey, Johnny," Corey said. He came in behind me, having returned, I assume, from the bathroom. "Do you know Marta?"

"Yes," I said.

"We failed our first set of entrance exams together," Marta said. This added to my discomfort—in my constant insecure state, I would never have volunteered to Corey that I'd failed anything. "I'm really sorry. Corey kept saying his roommate's name was 'Johnny,' I didn't know that was your nickname…"

"It's fine," I said, and moved to get my toiletries and towel for a shower.

"Corey and I are going out for a drink," Marta said. "You should come…"

"Don't bother, Marta," Corey said. "Even if Johnny wasn't prepping for the marathon, he wouldn't have a drink."

"You're going to do the marathon?" Marta said. "That's terrific." I gave her a curt smile. Though I had a brief flash of delight upon seeing her, I forcibly suppressed it. In a bit of juvenile pique, I decided I wasn't going to let myself show even friendly interest in someone who'd be friends with Corey. (Looking back I am amazed and ashamed at the extent of my infantile behavior.)

"You're going to win that thing, Johnny," Corey said, as I gave a quick goodbye and headed to the showers. Though Corey's tone seemed sincere, I wouldn't let myself trust it or him. He was taunting me, I was sure of it; no freshman had ever won the academy marathon. When I entered, all I hoped for was a respectable finish, perhaps breaking the standing freshman record. That night, because I was so disappointed that Marta was there to see Corey and not me, I became determined to do the impossible.

The marathon was part of a three-day-long biannual Academy Olympics that took place on Danula II, a planet several light-years from Earth. When it came to the marathon, upperclassmen had a distinct advantage: aside from having more of the academy's physical training under their belt, if they had participated as a freshman or sophomore they had familiarity with the course and could train accordingly. I'd received a superficial description of the terrain when I signed up for the event, but if I was going to win I couldn't let myself be satisfied with such minimal information.

With only a little bit of trouble, I was able to get ahold of the survey Starfleet Academy personnel had done of Danula II in preparation for the athletic events. Their description of the course was a lot more detailed than the one given to the runners, and I saw actual data on the road surface and the incline of the hills. It appeared that the steepest hill was the last one leading to the finish line, and had an incline of 18.1 degrees. I knew I had to design my training runs in San Francisco to imitate it as closely as I could. There was a hill not too far from the academy on Filbert Street, which had an incline of 17.5 degrees, so from then on I always ended my runs there, and practiced holding a little energy in reserve for that final leg.

The day we left for the Olympics was actually a momentous one for me: it was my first trip into space. I was excited to board the shuttle that would take us to a starship in orbit. I crowded in with the other two hundred or so cadets participating in the Olympics; the remaining 12,000 stayed behind and watched the event via subspace. As I strapped myself in, I scanned the small craft looking for a familiar face, but recognized no one, or at least no one I'd had more than a passing contact with. It re-emphasized for me the isolation I'd constructed for myself. I'd been lonely when I arrived at the academy, and all my efforts in my first year only exacerbated that feeling.

"Stand by to launch," the pilot said over a speaker. Shortly we were moving, but I could barely tell. The inertial dampeners on the shuttle kept me from feeling any G-force, and I was seated in the center of the shuttle, meaning my view to the portholes was blocked as other cadets leaned in, as eager as I was to get a look outside. So my first trip into space felt like the equivalent of sitting in a waiting room at a doctor's office, except with a seatbelt.

The shuttle landed in the shuttlebay of the starship that was going to transport us to Danula II. We filed off the craft and were immediately greeted by a yeoman, a man not much older than any of us.

"Tennn hut…" the yeoman said. "Captain on deck."

We stood at attention, as a burly man of about forty, receding hairline, looked us over with a scowl.

"Welcome to the *Enterprise*," he said. "I'm Captain Hanson." We hadn't been told that we were being transported aboard the *U.S.S. Enterprise*, NCC-1701-C, one of the new *Ambassador*-class vessels. Hanson himself was well known to the cadet corps. He'd had a distinguished career already, making captain before he was thirty. I thought for a moment that this said a lot about our status.

"You should all know, I didn't want this assignment," Hanson said, immediately deflating my sense of self-importance. "The *U.S.S. Hood* was supposed to take you children to your reindeer games, but they had to put in for unexpected repairs, so I got stuck with it. This ship is brand new. If any of you do anything to mess it up, I find a scratch on a wall or a crumb on the carpet, I will make sure none of you ever see the inside of a starship again. Is that clear?"

"Yes, sir!" we all said in unison.

"Dismissed." He walked off, giving the impression that we mattered to him not one whit. Later, in my quarters, I tried to discover the meaning of the phrase "reindeer games" but all I could find was an unremarkable movie from the early 21st century.*

The three-day trip to Danula II was almost as unexciting as the shuttle ride. The two hundred of us were confined to our rooms on one deck. We had access to an exercise facility, and a recreation room where we also took our meals. Security men and women kept a strict guard on us; Hanson was serious that we weren't going to interfere with the running of his ship. One of the cadets, a member of the Parrises squares team, tried to sneak past security and get to the bridge. He was quickly caught and confined to the brig for the remainder of the voyage.

When we finally arrived at our destination, I made a concerted effort to get a seat in the shuttle by the window. When we left the shuttle bay, I was

---

*EDITOR'S NOTE: The phrase refers to a lyric in an archaic song, "Rudolph the Red-Nosed Reindeer," written by Johnny Marks. It remains a mystery as to whether Hanson was familiar with the song,

overcome with a strange sense of vertigo: I was sitting upright, but had the overall sensation that I was looking down. Out the porthole was a blue-green Class-M planet, easily mistaken for Earth in my mind. I knew Danula II was a good deal smaller than Earth, and expected that I would be able to tell, but all I saw was a giant world. Then suddenly we were in the cloud layer and heading toward a landing. We flew over a large ocean, heading to the small northern continent.

The planet's sports complex sprawled across my view; the Danulans built it as a gift to the Federation upon its admittance, and Starfleet Command was under some political pressure from the Federation Council to use it for its Olympics, even though it was far from convenient. We were taken to a modern dormitory, spartan but clean.

The marathon was the last event of the Olympics, so I spent most of my time continuing my training. One day, however, I decided to watch the events. The Academy Olympics drew a large in-person audience. As I watched them cheering the cadets, I realized many were family members—excited, proud parents and siblings showing their pride and affection. I hadn't even considered telling my family that I was participating. I found myself jealous of all the goodwill of those friends and families, and I quietly returned to my solitary training.

The day of the marathon was warm, even as early as I got up—I was one of the first to arrive at the starting line. The road we would run on was a wide dirt path, lined with trees that seemed similar to Earth's oak trees but with a purple tint to their trunks and leaves. Eventually my competitors joined me; over a hundred cadets were participating in the marathon, while the others watched. The crowd of onlookers was larger than the events I'd gone to. The marathon was the big event.

The chief judge of the event was the commandant of the academy, Devinoni Grax. He held up a phaser and fired a burst. We were off.

✦

I gave myself an early lead from most of the pack, but the four lead runners quickly passed me, and I let them. Sussman, Matalas, Black, and Strong all ran together, with Sussman out in the lead. They had all run the course before, and the only competitors they were worried about were each other. Over the course of the first thirty kilometers, I slowly closed the distance to them; in the last ten kilometers I knew I wouldn't have the energy to make up a large distance, but also wanted them unaware of me for as long as possible.

Now I saw the final hill coming up. I knew that I was within two kilometers of the finish line. The hill itself was half a kilometer in length, and it looked a lot steeper to me than Filbert Street. I could see Matalas start to kick and pass Sussman as they hit the bottom of the hill. Once he was comfortably out ahead, I saw his pace steady. Now was my time.

I increased my pace, and as I passed Black and Strong first I heard a gasp of frustration. They were not expecting this since they probably didn't even recognize me. My training was paying off; the pain I'd suffered running up Filbert Street was familiar, and I pushed through it. I passed Sussman and closed on Matalas. He was several inches taller than me so his stride was longer. I was less than a meter behind him as I saw the finish line at the top of the hill. (It was often said that whoever designed a marathon course with the finish line at the top of a hill was a unique kind of sadist.) Several dozen officers and academy personnel waited beyond, cheering us on. I pushed up next to Matalas. He turned and looked at me, surprised, annoyed. I'd broken his concentration and that gave me the advantage I needed to get out a centimeter ahead as we crossed the finish line.

I ran only a few feet and collapsed on the other side. There was applause and cheers, and one of the athletic directors came over to help me up. As I stood I saw the ovations came from faculty and staff. Most of the cadets and their families were ignoring me, and congratulating the upperclassmen who'd just crossed the finish line. A few gave me cold stares. I'd just broken a record: I was the first freshman to win the academy marathon. I don't know what I was expecting, but I seemed to have further alienated myself from my colleagues. Or so I thought.

"Johnny!" Startled, I looked up to see Corey and Marta jostle their way through the crowd. "That was amazing!"

"What… how did…" I said. I could barely breathe and I couldn't process the fact that they were there. Neither of them were participating in the Olympics. They grabbed me and took me through the crowd to a table with refreshments.

"Congratulations, Johnny, you're the pride of the class," Corey said.

"It was really amazing," Marta said. She handed me a cup of water, which I gulped down, most of it spilling over me.

"How did the two of you…" I said.

"Commandant Grax, before he left, asked for volunteers to serve as stewards," Marta said. "We've been serving drinks and hors d'oeuvres for the last three days."

"I spilled champagne all over some Vulcan captain," Corey said. "A little on purpose, to see if I could get him mad. But he didn't."

"Why…" I said. I still wouldn't let myself believe they were there to see me.

"Because," Corey said, "what would be the point of winning the marathon if you didn't have any friends to see it?" I'd underestimated him. I wasn't used to this type of person, someone outgoing and personable, someone willing to bend over backwards to be my friend. I had greeted it with suspicion; he hadn't been insulting me by saying I was going to win, he had taken my measure and realized my goal. And I was thrilled. He'd given the race I'd just won a little more meaning.

"Thank you," I said.

"Cadet…" I looked up to see Captain Hanson. We stood at attention. I was shocked; the last time I'd seen him was on his ship.

"Yes, sir," I said.

"At ease," he said, but we didn't. He looked me up and down, and gave a hint of a smile. "Well done." And with that, he turned and left.

"Jean-Luc," Marta said, "looks like you're on the scoreboard."

"Call me… Johnny," I said, and meant it.

✦

"What is ex parte communication?" Rodney Leyton said. He was a recent graduate who'd stayed on as an instructor, and taught my Introduction to Federation Law class. He was a little full of himself but was widely acknowledged to be going places in his career. I wasn't really paying any attention to him anyway, but to the person who answered his question.

"It's an archaic term referring to communication between a judge or juror and a party to a legal proceeding outside of the presence of the opposing party," she said. She was slim, confident, and assertive, and I'd been trying to make eye contact with her for the entire class. Her name was Phillipa Louvois. She was around my age but had already graduated from law school.

"And can you tell me why it's archaic?" said Leyton.

"Though many of the laws guiding the Federation and Starfleet find their origin in ancient British and American jurisprudence," Phillipa said, "some have fallen away."

"For instance?" This was an example where the instructor probably knew less than the cadet; Leyton was using the cadet's knowledge to not only teach the class but himself.

"Well," Phillipa said, "there have been many instances where Federation law has been decided by a Starship captain, without a judge, jury, prosecutor, or defense lawyer."

"And why are those no longer necessary?"

"Trust," I said. They both looked at me, along with the rest of the class, which hadn't really been part of the discussion. At the time it felt like a bold move. It wasn't, but it got her attention.

"What does trust have to do with it?" Phillipa said.

"Something like ex parte communication," I said, "implies that the judge, prosecutor, and defense lawyer cannot be trusted to have communication without all parties present. That implies that either might not follow the law. It appears that our system now trusts that all involved will obey it. It speaks to our evolution as a species."

"Perhaps it does," Phillipa said, "or perhaps it leaves us open to someone waiting to take advantage of it."

"Vigilance, Mr. Picard," Leyton said. "Freedom requires vigilance." He checked the wall chronometer. "That's it for today…"

As the class broke up, I made sure to intercept Phillipa on her way out.

"Do you really think that?" I said.

"What?" She looked at me curiously.

"That someone is waiting to take advantage of us?"

"Why else have lawyers?" She gave me a smile that was at once suggestive and condescending.

"I'd like to talk to you more about the necessity of lawyers," I said, rather awkwardly. But it had its intended effect.

"I take my lunch outside the library every day," she said. "Perhaps I'll see you there sometime…"

This was my second year at the academy, and it was going much more smoothly.

Winning the academy marathon the year before had done a lot for my confidence, and, though the upperclassmen weren't thrilled, my class celebrated me as a hero. I roomed with Corey again, and he and Marta became my closest friends, though the beginning of the year I was still primarily focused on my studies, and begged off on some of their more daring adventures.

But despite my social and athletic successes, the study of archaeology with Professor Galen had taken a dominant role, becoming an unexpected tributary of my ambitions. Growing up, my desire to be a starship captain was unique; it set me apart from my surroundings. Now, at the academy, a large portion of the cadets I met had the same ambition, and I saw that I had come to miss my uniqueness. Galen's mentorship led me to see the potential rewards of being an academic. It appealed to the intellectual side of my personality, and yet was also a form of exploration and achievement. The many discoveries made in the excavations of ancient civilizations on other worlds had led to modern advancements in medicine, agriculture, and terraforming that had changed the face of the Galaxy. Professor Galen had also become something of a surrogate father—a man who understood my inner self in a way my real father never did.

On the last day of the first academic quarter Galen asked me to stay after class. He pulled up an image on the viewscreen at the head of the room.

"You're looking at two paintings; one is Vedalan, the other from Trexia," Professor Galen said. "What do you notice about them?"

There were two ancient paintings side by side. They'd withered with extreme age, but the images were still not difficult to make out. They each represented completely different media and style: the Trexian painting on the right used something similar to oils and was in an almost impressionistic style, with short brush strokes and no sharp edges. The Vedalan painting, on the left, was hyper realistic, almost looked like a photograph. The paintings were from two civilizations that were long dead, and what was interesting was the shared subject.

"They're showing the same scene," I said. The scene showed a scared group of natives, cowering as creatures stepped out of a doorway in the sky. The natives were different; in the Trexian painting they were Trexians, and in the Vedalan painting Vedalans. But the creatures, even though drawn in different styles, on different planets light-years away, were basically the same: lean figures, large-eyed with antenna, and no apparent clothing. And they were both painted gray.

"Yes," Galen said, "should this be of interest to us? We've seen similar myths on different worlds; in fact, Hodgkin's Law of Parallel Planetary Development guarantees that there would be. Are we just looking at two primitive minds expressing their superstitions and fears?" I knew he was testing me, and I enjoyed the challenge. There was another clue in the painting.

"The clothes," I said. "They're different." The natives in the Vedalan painting were cave people; the Trexians depicted were much more advanced, perhaps from a 12ᵗʰ-century Earth equivalent.

"So?" Galen smiled when he said it. I knew I was on to something, but he wasn't going to hand it to me.

"If the paintings were from the same period of time," I said, "they may represent actual events, rather than a depiction of a common myth."

"An archaeologist *did* quantum date the paintings," Galen said, "and they do come from the same period, both created 200,753 years ago."

"That can't be coincidental," I said.

"No," Galen said, "so the archaeologist looked for more clues. For pieces of art to survive the death of these two civilizations meant they themselves must have been considered important. But there were no other clues on either of these planets as to what this scene depicted. So he looked elsewhere." As Galen went to his satchel, I knew that "the archaeologist" he referred to was Galen himself. It was no surprise; I'd come to learn that he was the foremost in his field, having spent the last sixty years of his life uncovering the most famous historical finds of the Galaxy. He had acquired more knowledge in the field than any other living person, and his experience unlocking the mysteries of ancient artifacts was of enormous value to the Federation.

From his satchel, Galen produced a pottery shard.

"This is from a piece of Dinasian pottery from the same time period," Galen said. "And as you can see, a similar depiction of the invader, with the inscription 'the Creature of Air and Darkness.'"

"That's from the legend of Iconia," I said. Up to that point in time, the Iconian civilization was thought to be a myth, conquerors that ruled the Galaxy over a quarter of a million years ago. "You've proved they existed…"

"I haven't proven anything yet," Galen said. "But I have made a proposal to the Federation Archaeology Council to begin a dig on Dinasia; if all goes as planned we will begin next year."

"Wait," I said, "we?"

"I will need help," Galen said.

✦

"That's an amazing opportunity," Phillipa said. "You're not going to turn it down…"

We were outside the academy library. Soon after Phillipa mentioned she regularly had lunch there, I found her and made a point of returning every day with a different culinary delight, which wasn't difficult given the abundance of food replicators on campus. Still, I was making creative choices unfamiliar to her. Today we ate a lamb *vindaloo*. It was the kind of romantic gesture that I've long since abandoned.

"Of course not," I said, and meant it. I was being offered the opportunity to be the protégé of the Federation's greatest archaeologist, putting me in a position to possibly inherit that title myself.

"That's a relief," Phillipa said. "We will be quite a couple." She smiled and I leaned to kiss her. For a while she had playfully discouraged my more assertive romantic overtures, but recently I'd worn her down. Phillipa was ambitious; she saw Starfleet as an opportunity to put her own stamp on galactic law. She took pride in her unusual track of law school and then the academy, and there was something that appealed to her about the road I was on that might lead me to chase archaeology at the expense of an academy career.

That evening, I returned to my room with Phillipa to find Corey and Marta there.

"Pack your bags, Johnny," Corey said.

"What are you talking about?" I said.

"We've got into the flight school on Morikin VII," Marta said. "The three of us." Several weeks previously Corey and Marta had convinced me to apply for training on Morikin VII. It was an elective the academy offered, a ten-week elite flight instruction on a remote world.

"I didn't know you'd applied to Elite Flight," Phillipa said. I had actually forgotten about it, assuming that among the 12,000 cadets in the academy, there was little chance that I would get in. I had a feeling that Corey must have had something to do with our acceptance. It was too much of a coincidence.

"What are you looking at me for?" Corey read the suspicion in my expression. Corey had gotten very good at breaking rules and not getting caught.

"You're not going, are you?" Phillipa said, less as a question than a demand.

I was conflicted. I was half a step from leaving the academy altogether, and I certainly didn't see myself on a path as an elite pilot. And yet, the idea of getting a chance to be stationed on a faraway planet with my two good friends, learning how to fly state-of-the-art ships…

"Have a nice time," Phillipa said, and left the room. I had gotten lost in a bit of a reverie, and hadn't noticed that I'd hurt her feelings. I ran out after her.

"Phillipa, please stop." I caught up to her outside the building and grabbed her arm.

"Let go of me," she said.

"Let's just talk…"

"There's nothing to talk about. I don't want to get in the way of your little jaunt with your drinking buddies."

"It's just ten weeks…"

"Ten weeks with Marta…" Phillipa said, and this was the heart of it. She wasn't comfortable with me having such a close friend who was a woman. The fact was, I thought Marta was very attractive, but I was in love with Phillipa, or at least I thought I was, and I'd told her as much.

"You have to trust me," I said.

"I will," she said. "If you don't go." I don't know what it was about this request, but it rankled me. It showed that Phillipa didn't trust me. I couldn't accede to it.

"I'm sorry," I said. "I want to go." I saw in her reaction a flash of hurt and vulnerability, but only a flash.

"Fine, go," she said. "I'm going to go, too." She turned and walked off. I didn't quite know how it happened, but our relationship was over. I wandered back to my room, a mass of confusion. Corey and Marta were still there. I told them what happened.

"I'm really going to miss her," Corey said.

"Corey," Marta said. Corey, admonished, gave me an apologetic look.

"It's all right," I said. "It probably wasn't meant to be." I was hurt, but also a little angry. It would be a while before I let myself miss her.

"We're going to have the time of our lives," Corey said. I smiled. His enthusiasm was infectious enough that I momentarily forgot my rejection. It was exciting; I was about to go to a new world. And I wouldn't see Phillipa again for over twenty years.

✦

"Probably don't want to unpack your clothes until I fix the moisture problem," the captain said. Marta, Corey, and I were crammed into one of the small shelters on Morikin VII. There were three cots, three dressers, and one closet. And it was raining inside. There was something wrong with the environmental controls and moisture was dripping off the ceiling. "Maybe one of you can give me a hand…"

We had just arrived after a two-week flight on the *U.S.S. Rhode Island*, an antique class J freighter resupplying the flight school. It was my second trip into space and it was only marginally more exciting than my first. My cabin, such as it was, at least had a porthole, and the captain, a jovial man named Griffin who ran the ship with his family, had no problem with giving the three of us the run of his vessel.

It turned out the ship was a lot more pleasant than our destination. Morikin VII was not a very hospitable place. The atmosphere was a combination of carbon dioxide, nitrogen, and sulfuric acid, and the winds often reached hundreds of kilometers an hour. When we arrived we expected to find a state-of-the-art facility; instead we found quite the opposite. We were beamed into a darkened cargo storage warehouse, one of several domed structures connected to each other by underground tunnels. There was a man about sixty, waiting for us alone. As he approached, I was surprised to notice that he was wearing the rank of captain. We stood at attention.

"At ease," the man said with a smile. We relaxed somewhat. "I'm Captain Kirk." Captain Kirk? The same name as the famous starship captain? It was impossible of course; he was much too young, and James T. Kirk had been dead for decades. I decided it must just be a coincidence.

We introduced ourselves, and he led us out of the warehouse on a short tour of the facility, which was only made up of five domes: the warehouse, his quarters, our quarters, a common area for meals and recreation, and a hangar. Corey and I had speculated on the journey what kind of cutting-edge craft we would get to fly. What we saw in the hangar deck surprised us.

"These are class F shuttlecraft," the captain said. We were looking at two dilapidated transports, showing signs of age and wear.

"They're like fifty years old," Corey said.

"More like seventy," Kirk said, with a wry smile. I think we weren't the first disappointed cadets to be under his charge. He then took us to our waterlogged quarters. Marta and I helped him repair the reclamation controls, the source of the problem. He then served us a simple meal of some kind of broiled meat with mashed potato, which he prepared himself. He plated our food, showed us where to clean up when we were done, then went to his quarters and left us alone.

"No replicator?" Corey said. "This has to be some kind of joke."

"I feel that we've done something wrong," I said. Marta looked at us; she seemed to know more than we did.

"You guys know who that is, right?" she said. "That's Peter Kirk, James Kirk's nephew." I'd forgotten that the famous Captain Kirk had a nephew; though he'd entered Starfleet, his career had not been as notable as that of his famous relation.

"That can't be," Corey said. "Did he commit some crime we don't know about? Sleep with the Federation president's daughter or something?"

"No," Marta said. "He started this school. It was his idea."

"His idea," I said, "to create a terrible place for cadets to spend ten weeks?"

"Every cadet who has gone through the program has gotten a prime starship posting upon graduation," Marta said. "He must be teaching something."

The next day he went through a thorough maintenance check of one of the shuttlecraft, then took us for a flight. It was a rough ride leaving the atmosphere; once we got into space it became quite boring. Kirk did not engage us in much conversation beyond familiarizing us with the shuttle controls. He had us take turns flying the ship; it was a leisurely flight to some outlying asteroids. Kirk indicated one of the larger ones.

"There's a Nausicaan mining base there," he said. "Probably want to avoid it." The natives of the planet Nausicaa had been a surly species, historically pirates, only recently reaching an uneasy peace with the Federation. Corey, Marta, and I tried to get a look at the base; it was built into the side of the asteroid. Extending from it were two docking arms with Nausicaan fighters docked.

"They have a base in Federation space?" I said.

"It's been here for over a hundred years," Kirk said. "I think they have a claim." He then turned a ship around to return to Morikin VII, taking back the controls to re-enter the atmosphere. Once back in the hangar, Kirk ordered us to complete another maintenance check on the ship, even though we'd done that before we took off. But as we examined the aged craft, we saw that flying in Morikin VII's atmosphere had caused a lot of damage; the ship needed quite a bit of attention. This ended up being our daily routine: maintenance session, a flight into space, then another maintenance session. Despite all our preparations, we often faced mechanical and electrical failures while flying, and Kirk insisted on letting us fix them ourselves.

Kirk himself seemed something of an enigma. He didn't talk to us much outside of his lessons, and he cooked for us every night, always some kind of food native to his homeland Iowa. We tried to ask him questions about his career, but he didn't seem that interested in talking about it. And though I was filled with curiosity about the man who was his uncle, it seemed impolitic to ask.

Eventually, he began taking us up one at a time, to see how much we could do on our own. On my first solo flight, I successfully piloted the shuttle out of the atmosphere. Once in orbit, however, I noticed an imbalance in one of the engines. In order to check it out, I needed to leave the helm.

"Pretend I'm not here," Kirk said. "What would you do?" I realized he wasn't going to help me, so I put the ship on automatic pilot and headed to the engine compartment in the rear of the ship. Before I reached it, there was a small explosion.

I turned. Kirk was slumped back in his chair, and the control panel was on fire.

I grabbed the fire extinguisher and doused the flame, then went to Kirk. He was unconscious, his face slightly burned. I pressed my finger against his neck and thankfully, there was a pulse.

I would have to tend to him later. I looked at the console; the automatic pilot must have shorted out. The control readouts indicated the main engines were off. The short must have triggered an automatic shutdown. I hit the emergency restart for the engines; the cycle would take two minutes. That's when I noticed our position.

The shuttle was being pulled down to Morikin VII. I would burn up in the atmosphere long before I could restart the engines. The only power I had was in the attitude jets, which were separate from the engines, but they wouldn't give me nearly enough power to escape the pull of the planet. I clicked on the communicator.

"Mayday! Mayday! This is shuttlecraft one. Morikin base, do you read?" It was a futile effort—the communication system was out—and frankly I didn't really believe that Corey or Marta would have any suggestions for me about how to handle this. I looked out the porthole: Morikin VII was filling the view. I would be entering the atmosphere in seconds. I was lost.

"Bounce…" It was Kirk. He was fighting his way to consciousness.

"What, sir?"

"Aim toward the planet…" he said. His voice was weak. "Bounce… off…" He fell back into unconsciousness.

Bounce off what? The planet? That didn't seem likely. Then I remembered something from my studies of ancient spacecraft, about how they used to skip off the atmosphere to slow their descent. It was just a matter of hitting it at the proper angle. I took the controls, and turned the craft directly down into Morikin VII.

The shuttle started to rock, buffeted by atmospheric turbulence. The temperature inside rose as the outer skin began to heat. I pulled the shuttle up hard.

At first the turbulence didn't stop, and I thought I had miscalculated, but then saw the planet begin to fall away out the porthole. The shuttle steadied, and I was in a low orbit.

The engines' restart sequence completed; I had power again. I pushed the throttle forward to move out into a higher orbit, then grabbed the emergency medical kit and tended to Kirk's wounds. He was not seriously injured, and came round after a bit.

"It worked?"

"Yes, sir," I said.

"My uncle taught me that," he said. I took this as permission to say something about his famous relative; I had missed the wistfulness in the way he said it.

"He was one of my heroes growing up," I said.

"Mine too."

"What was he like?"

"You probably know him as well as I did," Kirk said. The heartbreak apparent in his voice spoke volumes, and I decided this would be the last conversation we would have on the subject.

✦

After almost ten weeks on Morikin VII, we felt changed. The mundane routine combined with the poor living conditions and the moments of true terror dealing with old, unreliable equipment had given Corey, Marta, and I a strength and confidence that we'd never had before. It made us all a little cocky (although, in Corey's case, it just made him more so) and led to an incident which would have dire ramifications for me.

Eventually, Kirk let us take the shuttles up by ourselves, and one day I was flying out toward the asteroid field. I wanted to get a closer look at the Nausicaan station. We'd had no contact with the Nausicaans, and I'd never met one face to face, though the images I'd seen made me very curious.

I'd brought my shuttle to within a few hundred kilometers when my communication panel lit up.

"Alien vessel! State your purpose!" The voice was rough and intimidating. I should have just turned the ship around and fled back to Morikin VII, but I was too curious and overconfident.

"Cadet Picard," I said. "I'm stationed on Morikin VII. My vessel is in need of repairs. Request permission to dock." I wanted to get a look inside that base.

"Request denied!"

"Your base is inside Federation space," I said, "and Federation law requires that you help ships in distress." There was a long pause; I didn't know why the Federation let the Nausicaans, who were not part of the Federation, keep a base in our territory, but I made the assumption that they wouldn't want to do anything overt to disrupt that.

"You may dock," the voice said.

I pulled the shuttle up to one of the empty docking arms, and a mooring tube extended to my hatch. I opened it and entered the base. I walked through a cold, dank corridor lined with piping, leading to a catwalk overlooking an ore mining and processing facility. The interior of the asteroid had been carved out; conveyers carrying buckets of ore moved slowly out of a massive cave. Miners, presumably Nausicaans, in environmental suits oversaw the dumping of the ore into a giant fusion furnace, where it was melted. It was both primitive and impressive. Before I could admire it for too long, I was confronted by two Nausicaans.

"Hello," I said.

They were both much taller than me, had ashen skin, large manes of hair, and small tusks surrounding their mouths. They were very intimidating, an obviously predatory species.

"What is wrong with your ship?" the lead Nausicaan said.

"Just a problem with the guidance control," I said. "Shouldn't take too long to fix. I was wondering if I could use your bathroom?"

"Bathroom?" The lead Nausicaan looked like he would kill me without a second thought. "No, you will not use our bathroom."

"Federation law requires that you provide sanitary facilities to ships in distress." I was now lying, there was no such law, but I didn't think these two would know. I tried to walk past them, but the leader grabbed me by the collar.

"Get your ship repaired and get out!"

"Let go of me," I said. I looked him hard in the eye. He laughed, and brought his hand up to strike me.

"Puny human," he said.

I immediately hit him in the center of his chest. The move surprised him, and he was momentarily winded. The other turned to pull out a knife, but I kicked it out of his hand and hit him in the throat.

I turned on the lead Nausicaan, who had gotten his breath back. He swung his large fist at me, but I grabbed it and threw him over my shoulder. He landed on the other Nausicaan, and they both flew back onto the floor of the catwalk. I had clearly overstayed my welcome.

"On second thought, I don't need the bathroom," I said, and ran back through the mooring tunnel to my shuttle, closing the hatch behind me. I started the engines, and disconnected from the docking arm, flying away from the base at full speed. I was initially concerned about being pursued but no craft followed me. The two Nausicaans probably wouldn't make a fuss, I'd just embarrassed them, and as I headed back to Morikin I laughed heartily, exhilarated by my daring.

Soon after, Corey, Marta, and I left Morikin and returned to the academy. I quickly found that I had a new problem. The classroom had very little appeal to me. I'd survived an adventure, and found myself more easily distracted from my studies. I also discovered a new confidence with women, one that is often excused in men as "youthful indiscretion," but was really an insensitive indulgence. I was self-centered, unconcerned with the feelings of the women I pursued. I would pursue them with abandon and cast them aside without a second thought. It was shamefully superficial, and I often find myself mortified by my memories.

"*Vous êtes une femme très attirante.*" I was sitting with a young woman near a large elm tree on the academy grounds. I prefer not to say her name, as I have not seen her since those days and am unsure how she felt about what went on between us.

"What did you say?"

"That you're a very attractive female…"

"Stop it," she said.

"It's the truth. Here, I'll put it in writing," I said. I took out my pocketknife and carved in the tree. When I was done, she looked at it curiously.

" 'A.F.' aren't my initials…" she said.

"It stands for 'Attractive Female,' " I said. She laughed and I was moving in to kiss her when we were interrupted.

"What the hell are you doing?" We looked over to see an elderly man in work boots and overalls, wielding pruning shears rather threateningly. It was the groundskeeper, who I'd occasionally noticed since I'd arrived, but had given no mind to.

"I'm sorry…" I said, stumbling to my feet. My confident masculinity quickly evaporated.

"Don't apologize to me," he said. "Apologize to the tree."

"You… want me to apologize…" I said. I wasn't looking at her, but I could hear my companion quietly giggling at my embarrassment.

"What did that poor elm tree ever do to you?" the groundskeeper said. "Nothing! And you take a knife to it. It's a living thing!" He stood there glaring at me. After a long moment, I turned to the tree.

"I'm sorry…" I said, then turned back to him. "Will that do?"

"It will not. I need help with weeding," the groundskeeper said. "You'll report to me here every morning at six o'clock for the next two months."

"With all due respect, I don't know why…"

"Defacing the academy is grounds for expulsion," he said. He turned and walked off. I sat back down.

"Do you think he'd really get me expelled?"

"I wouldn't mess with Boothby," she said, which is how I learned his name.

For the next two months I met Boothby on the academy grounds every morning and helped him with weeding, pruning, and general maintenance. He didn't talk to me at all except to give me instructions. My childhood on the vineyard made this more natural work for me than it might have been for others, but I didn't enjoy it. And between this and my new romantic adventure with "A.F.," my studies faltered and I actually failed organic chemistry. But that, as it turned out, was the least of my concerns.

One afternoon I received word to report to Professor Galen in his office. It was a cramped room, filled with artifacts from his expeditions. Galen sat at his desk.

"Mr. Picard," Professor Galen said. "The dig on Dinasia has been approved. We leave in two weeks."

"That's wonderful, Professor," I said. I had been dreading this moment since my return from Morikin VII; my recent adventures had muted my desire to be an archaeologist, but I hadn't had the courage to talk to the professor about it.

"You will have to tender your resignation to the academy immediately," he said. I was very conflicted. Professor Galen was very important to me. I decided at that moment that I wouldn't disappoint him.

"Yes, sir," I said.

✦

The next morning I joined Boothby again, this time helping plant a new row of mophead hydrangeas.

"You failed organic chemistry?" Boothby said. This shocked me. It was the first time he'd spoken to me about something personal. I had no idea how he'd found out.

"It doesn't matter," I said. "I'm leaving the academy."

"To spend the rest of your life digging in the dirt," Boothby said. He was showing an almost supernatural clairvoyance.

"How did you know…"

"People talk," he said. "They don't seem to notice I'm listening. Or maybe they don't care."

"Archaeology is important work," I said. "This is an opportunity of a lifetime…"

"Keep saying it," Boothby said. "You may convince yourself." His comments were making me face something I didn't want to face. And I lashed out.

"Look, I don't need career advice from a gardener."

Boothby didn't respond. I should've been thanking this man for understanding me better than I knew myself, but I was too immature, and worked in petulant silence for the rest of the morning. Then, after planting the last of the hydrangeas, he turned to me.

"You're finished," Boothby said. "Your debt to the garden is paid." And he went about the rest of his work. It would be years before I apologized to Boothby, and thanked him for putting me on the right path.

I walked the academy grounds the rest of the day, lost in thought, eventually finding myself at Galen's classroom. He had just finished up a lecture, and there were a few artifacts on his desk. He picked one up and handed it to me.

"Mr. Picard," he said, "can you tell me what this is?" He enjoyed testing me, probably partially because he knew I enjoyed it. I examined the artifact, a stick carved out of stone.

"The images are from Gorlan mythology," I said. "This is a Gorlan prayer stick."

"The ancient Gorlans believed these prayer sticks had the power to grant the owner whatever they desired," Galen said. "I usually would dismiss such superstition, but I acquired this one shortly before my Dinasian dig was approved…"

"I'm not going." I blurted it out. It was tactless and a little cruel.

"What?"

"I've decided to stay at the academy," I said. Galen nodded, then slowly packed up the artifacts into his bag.

"You must decide what's best for you," he said. "If you change your mind, a career in archaeology will always be there." He shook my hand and left the room. I stood there alone, muddled. I had expected him to be angry with me, but he wasn't, or at least didn't seem to be. Looking back, I now know he'd protected my feelings by covering his own. Like a father would.

✦

"And so, Class of 2327, today you are fully-fledged ensigns," announced the president of the Federation. We sat in our dress uniforms, wearing caps for the first time during our enrollment. We were out on the main lawn, a rapt audience for the elderly statesman. The graduating class at the academy didn't always receive an address from the Federation president, except if the current office holder was a Starfleet veteran, as Nyota Uhura was.

"Four short years ago," she said, "you assembled here from all parts of the Galaxy, from all walks of life. Each of you knew what the service meant, or you wouldn't have volunteered. Each of you knew the Federation needs to be cherished and protected, and that sometimes our way of life may require the sacrifice of life itself. From here on, your education must continue in the more demanding school of actual service. Wearing the gold pin of Starfleet, you go out into space to face the great challenges of our final frontier. Your fellow citizens share my confidence that you will serve Starfleet and the Federation with honor and distinction. Good luck."

We stood up and cheered, throwing our caps in the air, continuing a tradition that went back to the early years of the academy when caps were part of the dress uniform. There was backslapping and hugging—we were a joyous crowd. The tumult died down as we broke up to look for loved ones in the crowd.

I found my mother. She gave me a warm embrace.

"It was difficult for your father and brother to get away," she said, responding to a question I didn't ask. I knew that spring was a challenging time of year at home. In the vineyard a time of vigilance for diseases among the grapes, and at the winery removing yeasts and perhaps returning wines to barrels for a second fermentation. But my mother worked just as hard as her husband and son, and she managed to get away.

I'd seen very little of my family and even less of the vineyard since starting at the academy, but my mother wouldn't let me go easily. She made as many trips as she could to San Francisco, and I could tell that the stress of the chasm between me and the other men in my family weighed heavily upon her. But, where my father was concerned, I couldn't consider softening the resolve of my animosity.

"It's all right, Maman," I said. "Let's go get some lunch." As we headed off, an officer intercepted us. I immediately stood at attention.

"At ease, Ensign," Captain Hanson said.

"Captain Hanson, may I introduce my mother," I said. "Yvette Picard."

"A pleasure, madam," he said as he took my mother's hand.

"You are Jean-Luc's new commanding officer," she said. I had told my mother when Captain Hanson had chosen me for a flight controller position on the *U.S.S. New Orleans*. This wasn't just a new ship, it was the first of a new *class* of ship; this would be the third time Hanson would take out the first ship in a new class. I had tried to explain to her why earning a spot with someone considered such an important captain was prestigious, but I could tell she didn't fully understand.

"You should be very proud of your son," Hanson said. "He has already accomplished a great deal." It was a very paternal gesture, though Hanson was only about fifteen years older than I was. He then turned to me. "See you at Starbase Earhart, Ensign." He shook my hand and smiled, then turned to leave.

"He seems very fond of you, Jean-Luc," my mother said. I had always been so nervous around him I don't think I could see that objectively, but it made sense. When I look back on my academy years, the time I spent there was looking for fathers. I hungered for mentors, and found them in both expected and unexpected places. Hanson had been a surprise, showing interest in my career from the moment I won the marathon. Of course, this was all an attempt to fill a hole in my life left by my upbringing.

"Why don't we go home for lunch, Jean-Luc?" my mother said. I had transporter privileges, so we could beam to La Barre. We could be back at the vineyard in less than an hour. I looked at her and smiled.

"I'm sorry," I said. "I'd prefer to eat here."

CHAPTER THREE

"WE GOTTA GET EVEN," Corey said.

Marta, Corey, and I were in my room at Starbase Earhart. It was late, and we'd just come back from an evening at the Bonestell Recreation Center. It had been almost a month since graduation. The three of us, still happily joined at the hip, would all be leaving on our separate missions from this starbase. During our time off, Corey had engaged in games of chance, and I had indulged in some more superficial romantic entanglements that I still regret. In fact, earlier that evening a woman I had successfully pursued the night before discovered that I had a date with her roommate for this evening. My cheek still stung from her slap.

"What did you have in mind?" Marta said. She and I had witnessed Corey losing a game of dom-jot* to a Nausicaan, which had cost him several slips of gold-pressed latinum. This surprised all of us as Corey was well-practiced at the game, and the Nausicaan's victory had been suspiciously quick.

"Well, we can do to him what he did to us," Corey said. "Cheat." Corey had earlier conjectured to us that the Nausicaan had some kind of magnetic device in his belt that allowed him to control the metal ball's path on the table. "Only this time, we rig the table so his device will backfire on him."

---

*EDITOR'S NOTE: Dom-jot is a game with some similarities to both the ancient games of billiards and pinball.

"I know just the thing," I said. My confidence at taking down Nausicaans was still fresh in my mind from my experience back at Morikin. I wasn't really worried about getting caught; in fact, I think I was looking forward to it.

It was a last hurrah for the three of us. We'd spent four years together, and now our respective careers would separate us. We were looking to cause some trouble, and in retrospect it was juvenile, and very dangerous.

But we went ahead.

Late that night, when the recreation center was closed, Corey, Marta, and I snuck in. While Marta dealt with the security systems, Corey and I adjusted the electrical setup that controlled the bumpers on the table to create interference that would block any nearby magnetic device. We got out of there without being detected.

The next evening, we went to the recreation center. I had arranged a date with an older woman who worked as a receptionist in the personnel office. I think she could tell that my mind wasn't on her when I noticed that the Nausicaan had returned with two friends; she soon left me, saying she had to get up early. This was disappointing, but wouldn't be the worst moment of the evening.

"Play dom-jot, human," the Nausicaan said to Corey. "Give you a better chance." Corey happily obliged. Less than thirty seconds into the game, the Nausicaan threw down his cue in frustration; whatever device he'd been using was no longer working.

"Human cheat!"

"I'm cheating?" Corey said. "I don't think so. But if you want to forfeit the game..."

"I do not forfeit to a human," the Nausicaan said. "Humans have no *guramba*." The three of us stood toe-to-toe with the Nausicaans, who towered over us.

"What did you say?" I said, stepping up to the Nausicaan, flanked by Marta and Corey.

"Humans have no *guramba*," he said. I actually had no idea what the Nausicaan had said, since the universal translators wouldn't translate "guramba," but I assumed from context that it was particularly insulting.[*]

---

[*] **EDITOR'S NOTE:** *Guramba* is Nausicaan slang for male genitalia.

"That's what I thought you said." I hit the Nausicaan in the chest, and suddenly the three of us were involved in a melee. I was the only one with experience fighting a Nausicaan, and relied on my previous encounter, which served me well; I had taken out my first opponent with a blow to the chest and neck, and turned to help with the one who was wrestling with Marta. As I did, I felt a sharp pain in my back. It forced me to my knees.

I looked down. A serrated blade, covered with blood, protruded from my chest. I wasn't feeling any pain, and the last thing I remembered was the sound of laughing. My own.

✦

"Ensign?" The voice was distant and unfamiliar. I was in a deep sleep, but was confused. I didn't remember going to bed. I didn't remember anything. I opened my eyes, and it was difficult to focus. There was a doctor, a Vulcan woman, standing over me.

"How are you feeling?" the Vulcan doctor said.

"I'm not sure," I said. Hearing my voice, I realized my mouth was covered by a respirator. "How long…"

"You have been unconscious for three point seven nine weeks," the doctor said, with the usual Vulcan bedside manner. Almost a month?

"The damage to your original organ was too extensive," the Vulcan doctor said. "You were placed in suspended animation until a doctor of sufficient skill and experience could arrive here to perform the necessary surgery." It was clear that the Vulcan was talking about herself. I was so annoyed at her arrogance that I almost missed the meat of what she was saying.

"Original organ? You mean… my heart?"

"Yes," the doctor said. "It has been substituted with an artificial mechanism. It will last many years without having to be replaced." It was too much to take in; I had a mechanical heart?

"When can I get out of here?" I said. I wanted to make a big show that I was ready to leave, but I didn't even have the strength to lift my head off the pillow.

"You will need at least two point four more weeks of observation and physical therapy," the doctor said.

"But my ship…" I said, already knowing the answer.

"You have been temporarily reassigned," the doctor said. "To this hospital bed. You will rest now." She left the room. I lay there thinking about what I had done. That fight had changed everything. No doubt Hanson, leaving on a deep space mission, wasn't waiting months for a relief flight controller to get out of the hospital. What had I done? Had I shattered my whole life trying to cheat a Nausicaan in a game of dom-jot? I felt such a fool. Tears fell from my eyes as I drifted back to sleep.

✦

Within a few days, I had mostly recovered, and was able to review several messages that were left for me. The first was from Corey.

"The doctors assure me you're going to be fine, Johnny. I hope so," Corey said. He was bruised and bandaged, having recorded the message shortly after the bar fight. "I'm sorry I can't stay around; the *Ajax* is leaving. Right after you got stabbed, the security boys showed up and stunned the Nausicaans. They got arrested, and were extradited back to their homeworld. Starfleet security had some questions for me and Marta, but they didn't dig too deep about what exactly happened, which I guess is good." That was something of a relief, since I don't think Starfleet would've looked kindly on three officers riggings a dom-jot table to cheat someone, even if it was a Nausicaan. I looked at Corey on my viewscreen: his usual bravado was gone. I could see he was very remorseful. "I'll check in as often as I can to see how you're doing, but the *Ajax* is headed out to the Romulan Neutral Zone, and Captain Narth is pretty strict about using subspace for personal communications. Sorry I… sorry I got you into all this. Take care of yourself." Corey signed off.

Marta's message was much more emotional. She had obviously been crying before she made it.

"The *Kyushu* is leaving today, and I don't want to go," Marta said. "It's very difficult leaving while you're unconscious. The doctors say you'll be all right… I just wish I could stay." She broke down again. "I should've stopped you guys," she said. "It was so stupid…" She wiped her eyes, and composed herself. "I love you, Jean-Luc. Please be well…" She signed off. Jean-Luc. She hadn't called me that in years. I watched it again, and regretted that Marta and I never took the time to explore how we felt about each other. Perhaps one day.

I also got a short written message from Captain Hanson, wishing me a speedy recovery. I couldn't help but interpret it as disappointment in my rash actions. I promised myself I would never be so foolhardy again.

During my convalescence I devoted a lot of time to looking for a new posting. I was anxious to make up for lost time, so I rearranged my priorities. My hope to be a flight controller on a ship whose assignment was deep space exploration would have to wait, as there were no postings available. So instead, I looked at the openings on ships assigned to Starbase Earhart's sector; a vessel close by would at least get me on active duty sooner. I found one on the *Reliant*, an opening for a junior science officer. The ship was a small one, assigned to routine patrol in this sector of space. It wasn't really what I wanted, but I was qualified—though I'd failed organic chemistry, I had high marks in astrosciences and archaeology. I submitted my application, and received a call via subspace from the ship's commander.

"Ensign," Captain Quinn said, "I don't like troublemakers." Gregory Quinn was a large man, with a soft, intimidating voice.

"I understand, Captain," I said. I tried to think of what I could say to convince him that I was no longer a firebrand, and decided instead to stay mum. Despite my recent indiscretion, my transcripts had been adequate enough for him to seriously consider me.

"I don't know Captain Hanson, or why he wanted you," Quinn said. "But this isn't that job. Are you sure being a junior science officer is going to be exciting enough for you?"

"I'm not looking for excitement, sir," I said. "I'm looking to serve." On the viewscreen, I could see that Quinn was studying me, trying to tell if I was being sincere. I honestly didn't know if I was, I just knew that was the only appropriate answer to give. It seemed to be enough for him.

"I need to fill this opening, so you've got the job. I'm not sure if I'm happy about it, but it's the situation we're in. *Reliant* will be docked at Earhart by 0800. Report to Lieutenant Nakamura then," he said, and signed off.

✦

"Welcome aboard," Nakamura said as I stepped off the transporter, my duffel in tow. "Captain wants you to have a stem-to-stern tour." Nakamura was the senior science officer, friendly if a little officious. He had me drop my belongings in my quarters and then led me through the small, clean ship. There were only thirty-four crewmembers, and by the end of the first few hours on board I'd met a good number of them. The only part of the ship I didn't get to see was the bridge.

"You only go there if you're reporting for your shift, or if you're called," Nakamura said. "Captain Quinn doesn't like extra people up there." After our tour, Nakamura took me to a room about the size of a large closet, just large enough for a computer console, table and chair.

"Welcome to the science lab," Nakamura said, with a smile.

"This is it?"

"This is it." Nakamura showed me what I would be doing as a junior science officer. There was no real research on a ship this small; most of what the science officers did was take in data. The ship ran on four six-hour shifts; I would be serving on two: 1900 to 0100 in the science lab, and 0100 to 0700 on the bridge. While on the bridge, the science officer, aside from providing information to his commanding officers, coordinated whatever scientific information was coming into the ship, whether significant or trivial: sensor data, reports from planetary surveys, communications from Starfleet or Federation planets. The officer serving in the lab, when not assigned to an away team, was to make sure the information routed from the bridge was properly categorized and catalogued, and reported to Starfleet Command. This was one of the pillars of our civilization: ships all over the quadrant were taking in information and sending it to Starfleet Command, where it became part of the collective knowledge of the Federation.

It was also very tedious work. My first shift in the lab was spent sorting data and preparing reports to be approved later by Nakamura before being sent off. Whatever fantasy I had of serving aboard a starship, six hours sitting alone in a room staring at a computer screen wasn't part of it. But what got me through the tedium and disappointment of that first day was my anticipation of reporting to the bridge. At the end of my shift in the lab, I closed it up and went there.

Like most starships, the *Reliant* duplicated Earth conditions of day and night, so I was reporting on what would be considered 1am; the lighting in the corridors was low, as it was on the bridge. It was the familiar layout, though smaller than what I expected. I was a few minutes early for my shift change, and reported to the commanding officer in the captain's chair, a woman in her thirties: Commander Shanthi, the ship's first officer.

"Ensign Picard, reporting for duty," I said. She turned and looked at me.

"You are early, Ensign," she said. She had a thick East Indian accent, and a formality that I found a little intimidating. "Report to your station." I went to the science station, and met the other junior science officer, a man about my age. He stood up; I was surprised how much taller he was.

"Walker Keel," he said. He smiled and held out his hand. I shook it. He looked familiar.

"Jean-Luc Picard," I said. "Have we met?"

"Yeah," he said. "You and your friends almost started a fight with me and mine at a bar on Tau Ceti III." I remembered the incident: Corey, Marta, and I were on our way home from Morikin, and had had a little too much to drink.

"Sorry about that," I said.

"No apology necessary," Walker said. "We were all a little full of ourselves." I was relieved there were no hard feelings, as it turned out he was my roommate; we hadn't seen each other yet due to the staggered shifts.

"I relieve you, sir," I said, indulging with full seriousness the ceremony of my first duty shift on the bridge. Walker chuckled.

"I stand relieved," he said, amused at my obvious pleasure. I took the science station, as the other crewmen were relieved by their graveyard shift replacements. This shift was a young one. The ship's second officer, Lieutenant Commander Altman, who was only a few years older than me, relieved Commander Shanthi. I looked out the large viewscreen. The beautiful blue-green planet that was home to Starbase Earhart filled the bottom quarter of the screen. The rest was stars.

It wasn't exactly what I wanted, but it was close enough.

✦

"Sir, I want to make a proposal," I said. It was during one of my duty shifts in the science lab. Lieutenant Nakamura had stopped by to review a few reports I'd completed for approval.

"Proposal?" he said. I could tell he just wanted to get through his work and sign out for the day, but I had to make my pitch now or it would be too late.

"Yes," I said. "Since we'll be in orbit of Milika III for one more day, there's an archaeological site that we should investigate." We'd come to Milika III delivering the new Federation ambassador and his staff to the planet. It was an arid planet, home to an advanced species of humanoids. The Milikans until quite recently had been a culture ripped apart by religious differences, but in the last few decades had united under one government and quickly gone into space. There were still pockets of religious dogmatists on the world, but the Federation had determined that the planet fit enough of the guidelines for admission to the Federation, and the government began the process of opening diplomatic relations. *Reliant* had been assigned to set up a Federation embassy on this planet. It had been a stressful time for Quinn and the crew, as the ambassador, an elderly man named William Smithie, had been exacting in his demands. I, on the other hand, had very little to do so I'd been reading everything I could about the planet and stumbled upon a native archeologist's research paper on a recently discovered site.

"What is so important about this site?" he asked. I could see Nakamura was getting a little annoyed, but I had to push on.

"It contains Vulcan artifacts," I said. "A local archeologist discovered them last month, and the Federation has not confirmed the find yet. If they are authentic, it might mean the ancient Vulcans had an unknown colony on this world."

"I don't know if we have anyone on board qualified in the procedures to authenticate a site like this," he said.

"Actually, I'm qualified, sir," I said. My years of study with Professor Galen had left me prepared for this opportunity. I could tell, however, that Nakamura's annoyance had now grown to frustration. "If I authenticate the find, it would save the Federation Archaeology Council from having to task another ship."

"Give me the proposal," Nakamura said, "and I'll take it to the captain." I was ready for this and handed him a PADD with my proposal on it. He wasn't happy. No one on this ship would care about Vulcan artifacts, especially the captain. But I'd presented him with an opportunity that he had to take up the chain of command. The Federation Archaeology Council would certainly ask for the site to be authenticated before sending a team to explore it further. The efficiency of my proposal was compelling, even if it was also a little annoying. Because Nakamura knew that the main reason for my suggesting it had nothing to do with science.

I wanted to go on an away mission.

My eighteen months on the *Reliant* had been pleasant. I'd begun to make friends among the crew, and the work was rarely demanding. It was also rarely interesting. I wasn't going to let that affect my performance, and I completed all my duties quickly and effectively. I didn't see much of the captain: he came on bridge duty just as I was signing out. My vague impression was that my work ethic had done a lot to ease his initial concerns about offering me the posting.

But I hadn't left the confines of the ship. If there was an away mission that required a science officer, Nakamura usually went, and if he didn't go, he sent Walker. I was getting the shipboard equivalent of "cabin fever" and was looking for some way to justify walking on solid ground. The obscure archaeology journal I'd found in the database from Milika III gave me my opportunity.

As the day went on, and I hadn't heard anything, my hope began to dim. We were due to leave orbit the next morning at 0900, and by the time I reported for my duty shift on the bridge, I assumed that my proposal had either been turned down or ignored. When Nakamura relieved me at 0700, he said the captain wanted to talk to me. I stepped down into the well of the bridge near the captain's chair. Quinn, having just taken over from Altman, was reading his shift report. He didn't look up.

"Archaeology, huh? Was never that interested in it myself," he said.

"Yes, sir," I said.

"How long would you need?"

"Once at the site, the scans would take less than thirty minutes," I said. It would actually take a lot less than that, but I didn't want whoever was leading the away mission to rush me. Turns out that wouldn't be a problem.

"You will be leading the away mission," Quinn said. "Pick an assistant and a security officer, report back to the ship in one hour. Dismissed." Quinn never looked up from his report, but I'm sure he could tell I was dumbfounded. *Leading?* I was leading an away mission? I'd never even been *on* one. Quinn finally looked at me.

"I gave you an order," he said.

"Yes, sir!" I stumbled out of the bridge, eager and queasy.

✦

"Thanks a lot," Walker said. We had just beamed down to Milika III with a security officer. It was like being shoved into an oven: it was over 43 degrees Celsius, an intense dry heat. We were a few kilometers outside the capital city, near a small congregation of ruins many thousands of years old. I'd assigned Walker to come, for the simple reason that, though I was in charge of the mission, every officer on the ship outranked me. Although he wasn't pleased that I'd conscripted him during his off-duty shift, I was at least assured he wouldn't be challenging my already shaky authority.

The security officer, Ensign Cheva (her full Thai name was Chevapra-vatdumrong, but she used the shortened version), examined her tricorder.

"Vehicle approaching," she said. We turned to see a floating vehicle, an air raft, open with four seats but only one occupant. It slowed as it got near, and settled softly to the ground. Its driver, a squat, brown-faced figure with ridges above his eyebrows, climbed out. He ran up to us, his flowing tan robes fluttering behind him, and excitedly held up his hands in the traditional Milika greeting. As was customary, I placed my palms against his, briefly.

"You must be Picard," the Milika said. "I am Mantz. I'm so delighted you read my paper."

"It was my pleasure," I said. I introduced the rest of the away team. Mantz started talking about how he had been working this dig site for over a decade, and went into what would be a lengthy lecture about its history. After several moments, Walker gave me a look, and I took the hint.

"You should probably show us the artifacts," I said. "We are somewhat pressed for time." Mantz apologized much too profusely, and led us down into the dig site to an excavated room. He took us to a sealed case which he opened; it contained catalogued artifacts. He indicated a broken sculpture inside. I kneeled down and scanned the pieces with my tricorder.

"Pottery?" Walker said. "We're baking in this heat for some pottery?"

"It's not just pottery," I said. I picked up part of the sculpture; it was a head with pointed ears, and the base had a symbol on it. "This is a *katric* ark."

"Is it authentic?" Mantz was very excited. I completed my scan.

"It was made out of native materials, but the design and age would indicate that it is," I said.

"What's a *katric* ark?" It was Cheva who asked the question, but it was also apparent from Walker's expression that he didn't know either.

"Upon death," I said, "a Vulcan's 'living spirit' is transferred to a *katric* ark."

"Transferred?" Walker said.

"Telepathically," I said. "Supposedly, the spirit exists there indefinitely."

"Come on," Walker said.

"I'm being serious. Captain Jonathan Archer supposedly had the *katra* of Surak in his head…"

"This confirms my theory," Mantz said. "There was a Vulcan colony on this planet."

"We would need more evidence to reach that conclusion," I said. "But this artifact is at least authentic. The Federation Archeology Council will certainly send a team." We were interrupted by a call from the ship. I opened my communicator.

"*Reliant* to Picard," Nakamura said. "We're beaming you up immediately."

"Yes, sir." I could hear the red alert klaxon over the speaker. I turned to Mantz. "We'll have to come back later."

"But what's the matter? I have more to show you…" Mantz looked apoplectic.

"I know, I apologize, but we must go," I said. Walker, Cheva, and I stepped away from him. "Picard to *Reliant*, we're ready to beam up."

"Stand by," Nakamura said. "Belay that, transporter not functioning." I turned to Cheva, who had her tricorder out.

"There's a particle-scattering field," she said. "It wasn't there before."

"Someone doesn't want us to beam up," Walker said.

"Picard to *Reliant*, we're detecting a particle scattering field. Do you read that as well?"

"Affirmative, stand by," Nakamura said. His tone was unusually taut.

"What is going on?" Mantz said.

"Please, sir, I need you to be quiet," I said. "You're safe with us." That of course was a lie. If we were the object of the scattering field, then he was completely unsafe with us, but I needed information.

"Picard, this is the captain," Quinn said. "The Federation ambassador has been kidnapped. The scattering field was set up so we can't beam him up, or beam anyone down."

"Who kidnapped him?"

"Religious extremists," Quinn said. "They've demanded the removal of the embassy, and want the Federation off their planet by tomorrow, or they'll kill the ambassador." I noticed Mantz listening to this, registering understanding. "Stay out of sight until we resolve this. They're hiding somewhere in the old section of the capital city. It's unlikely the extremists even know you're there. *Reliant* out." I turned to Mantz.

"You know who these extremists are?" I said. Mantz nodded.

"They call themselves the Xaalas. They continue to adhere to the old beliefs. You must understand they represent only a small minority of our people." He seemed embarrassed and worried by the act of his fellow natives. I decided to use that to our advantage.

"Mantz, can you take us into the city?" I said.

"Captain told us to lay low," Walker said.

"Because they don't know we're here," I replied. "Which is exactly the reason we should try to ascertain the situation." Walker smiled, and nodded.

✦

We waited until nightfall, and then flew to the city in Mantz's air raft. Mantz picked up clothing at his home for us, and in a short time Walker, Cheva, and I were covered in the flowing robes the natives wore. We then headed for the old section; unlike the modern glass and steel constructions of the capital, the buildings in the old section were made of brick and mortar. The streets narrowed to alleys, and the air raft became too conspicuous, so Mantz parked it, and the four of us moved through on foot. Cheva was on her tricorder, tracking the ambassador's life signs.

She stopped us two streets away from the ambassador's location. She indicated down an alley to a three-story building. We could see several Milikans with weapons patrolling the streets around it. I gave Cheva permission to leave us to perform a closer scout. Walker and I were a bit taller than the average Milika, but Cheva was an appropriate height, and could move among them unnoticed, especially at night. After she left, I turned to Mantz.

"Mantz, you should go," I said. "Thank you for your help."

"I am not leaving," he said.

"I don't want to put your life in danger..."

"*They* are the ones putting us in danger," Mantz said, referring to the guards. "I want to help." I was surprised and impressed by how personally

Mantz was taking the actions of his fellow Milikans. This was a man who was standing up for progress.

"All right," I said. I handed him a communicator and showed him how it worked. "Go back to your air raft. I may need you to come in a hurry." Mantz nodded and left, just as Cheva returned.

"They're on the third floor," she said, showing us the scans she'd taken with her tricorder. "In a central room with no windows. Two guards on the street, one on the roof, one at that third-floor window, and one in the room with the ambassador."

"Too many for us to make a frontal assault," Walker said. "Or even one by stealth." Walker was saying what I was thinking. Any attack might give the extremists enough time to kill the ambassador.

"We might be able to get him if they had to move him," I said. I looked around and saw, two blocks away from our target, a ruined structure, destroyed in some kind of fire or attack. It had been a three-story building like the ones surrounding it, but less than half of it was left. "Cheva, scan that building. Any life signs?"

"No, sir," she said.

"Get on the other side of it and wait for my signal," I said. "When I tell you, blow it up." Cheva nodded and disappeared into the dark. Walker and I then headed to a spot in an alley opposite the entrance to the building the extremists were in, and crouched behind a refuse receptacle. We had a view of the only door to the building; Smithie was too old to climb out a window, if they were going to escape with him it would be from here. I took Walker's communicator. "Picard to Mantz…"

"I hear you," Mantz said.

"In a few moments, you will hear an explosion. When you do, take the air raft and head to the alley directly south of the building where they're holding the ambassador."

"Directly south, I understand," Mantz said. I then switched frequencies on the communicator.

"Picard to Cheva, report," I said.

"In position," came her voice.

"Wait for my signal," I said, then switched the frequency once more. "Picard to *Reliant*."

"This is *Reliant*." It was Quinn.

"Captain, I've found the ambassador," I said. "And I have a plan to rescue him, but I won't carry it out without your order." There was an excruciatingly long pause.

"All right, let's hear it."

I laid out the situation and what I had in mind.

"What if they decide to just kill the ambassador?" Quinn said.

"It seems unlikely, unless they feel they have no way out," I replied. "They will try to escape." I don't know why I was so sure of myself, but it appeared Quinn agreed with me.

"Make it so," Quinn said. This was the first time I'd heard Quinn use this expression, and it wasn't until he added, "Good luck," that I realized he'd given me permission. I turned to Walker.

"Set phaser for stun, widest possible beam," I said. Walker nodded. I opened my communicator. "Picard to Cheva: go, repeat, go."

After a short moment, the ruined building down the alley exploded. The vibration shook the nearby structures; the guards on the street turned and immediately started shouting. We heard responses from the guard up in the window, who ran inside. The guards on the street took up positions near the door. We watched as two more Milikans came out of the door, dragging the ambassador.

"Fire," I ordered. Walker and I shot at the group. They were all clustered together; the Milikans and the ambassador were bathed in a red glow, and then fell to the ground unconscious. We moved out of the alley and headed for them.

"Wait," I said. "There's one missing…" We both looked up to see the Milikan on the roof, aiming his weapon at us. He was hit with a red beam, and fell backward. We turned to see the source of the shot was Cheva, running to join us, phaser in hand.

"We gotta move," Cheva said. "They could have friends in the neighborhood…"

We grabbed the still unconscious ambassador, and carried him, just as Mantz's air raft landed at the end of the alley south of the building. We got on board and flew off.

In the air raft, Cheva took position in the rear to watch for pursuit. Walker patted me on the back.

"Good job, Jean-Luc," he said. I smiled. I noticed that Ambassador Smithie was slowly regaining consciousness. He looked up at us, frightened and confused.

"It's all right, Ambassador," I said. "You're safe."

✦

"Come in, Picard," Quinn said. He was sitting at his desk in his quarters, which I had never seen. They were simple and efficient, like the man himself. I entered; he indicated a chair across his desk, so I sat.

"Good work down there," Quinn said. Thanks to my actions, the extremists had been rounded up, the Milikan government had apologized, and the embassy had been established.

"Thank you, sir."

"You know, it's rare that I have to apologize to one of my officers," he said.

"Sir?"

"When I was unable to beam you up, my first order to you should've been to reconnoiter and get me more information. That's what the book says, but..." Quinn paused. "But I didn't have enough faith in you. So you did my job for me, and now I will get credit for saving the ambassador."

"Sir," I said, "you don't owe me any..."

"You showed better command judgment than I did," he said. "You saved a man's life, at great risk to your own. And there was no loss of life on the other side, which helped repair a delicate diplomatic situation." He took out a small wooden box, and set it on the desk.

"You're wasted as a science officer," he said. "You need to be on a command track. Flight controller, right? That's what you originally wanted?"

"Yes, sir," I said.

"Unfortunately, there's no room for you on this ship in that position," he said. "My flight controllers are good at their job, and I don't have any reason to transfer them. Same goes for all my command track positions, at least for the time being." He slid the small wooden box over to me. "Open it."

I did. Inside were lieutenant bars.

"You're promoted," he said. "A 23-year-old lieutenant is going to get noticed, and you deserve it."

"But, sir," I said. "I'd like to stay…" I was truly stunned. I had felt a bit of victory saving the ambassador, but it was all in an effort to solidify my place on this ship. I had no intention of leaving.

"You need to be on a bridge, and not at the science station," he said. "And even if it was this ship, puttering around a safe sector like this one, it's going to take you too long to do the work you were born to do. Get out to the edge. Dismissed."

I left Quinn's quarters in a bit of a daze, and wandered back to my quarters. Walker was there, and saw my new rank.

"You just lapped me," Walker said, as he pinned the lieutenant bars on my uniform. "How did that happen?"

"He wants me to transfer," I said.

"You bastard, you're ruining my day." Walker and I spent the next hour looking at the available postings. There were a few on bigger ships, more prestigious names, but there was only one opening that appealed to me.

"You ever hear of the *Stargazer*?" I said.

"No," Walker said.

"*Constellation*-class ship," I said. "It's got an opening for a relief flight controller." We both looked at the record; the ship had just returned from a five-year exploration of the unexplored mass of the Galaxy, and it was about to be sent out again.

"Do you know Captain Humphrey Laughton?" Walker said. I didn't. We did a quick search: he had a very impressive record of exploration.

"Wow," Walker said. "That's a lot of new worlds. Are you going to apply?"

"I just did."

✦

"Starbase 74, this is *Reliant*," Altman said. "Request permission to assume standard orbit."

We arrived at Starbase 74 during the gamma shift, my shift on the bridge. Though I now outranked Walker, I didn't see a need to take his shift, since I was leaving the ship so soon. Altman was in command, and on the viewscreen the massive space station hung in orbit around another blue-green world.

"*Reliant*, this is Starbase 74," a female voice said. "You are cleared for orbit."

"Thank you, Starbase 74." Altman said, "We have one passenger for transfer."

Altman gave the order to put the ship in standard orbit near the station. Normally, a ship would enter the massive doors and berth inside the cavernous interior dock, which could hold several large starships. However, *Reliant* was only there to drop me off.

I had submitted my application to the *Stargazer* and got an almost immediate reply offering me the post. The *Stargazer* had a maintenance overhaul scheduled at Starbase 74, which was not too far off the *Reliant*'s course. Captain Quinn agreed to drop me off here, and I would only have to wait a little over a week for the arrival of my new ship.

But now that I was here, I faced a problem: I hadn't said goodbye to anyone. There were over thirty people on the ship; I had come to know some of them very well, but not nearly all. Do I go to every department and say goodbye? Since this was the gamma shift, a lot of them were still asleep. Do I wake them up? That seemed presumptuous. On the other hand, if I didn't make that effort, would they think me arrogant? The way Starfleet operated I could easily find myself serving with some of them again, and I didn't want to leave anyone with a bad impression. And yet still, the idea of walking through the entire ship looking to say goodbye to people… it seemed an unsolvable dilemma.

I finally decided that I would send a group message to the crew saying what an honor it was to serve with them. I wrote that first: "It was an honor serving with you all," and looked at it on the screen. It seemed a little perfunctory, but I couldn't figure out what else to say. It was then that I noticed Lieutenant Nakamura was standing next to me, quite a bit early for his shift. He looked at me, smiling.

"Attention on deck," he said, quite loudly. I had been so focused on how I was going to say goodbye, I hadn't noticed that a good portion of the crew had squeezed onto the bridge, including Walker, first officer Shanthi, and the captain. They were all standing at attention. I hurriedly stood up, stunned by the courtesy.

"Thank you," I said. "It's… been an honor serving with you all." Somehow saying it out loud seemed to convey a little more weight than writing it. Or at least I hoped so. Captain Quinn stepped forward and shook my hand.

"Good luck, Lieutenant," Quinn said.

"Thank you, sir," I said. I stood there awkwardly for a moment.

"Crew dismissed," Quinn said. "Back to work." I had the distinct impression he sensed my discomfort. He turned to Walker. "Ensign, get this man off my ship."

"Right away, sir," Walker said, and we got on the turbolift and took it to the transporter room. My packed duffel was already there. Walker shook my hand.

"Maybe with you gone, I can finally get a promotion around here," Walker said. I laughed. I got up on the pad, and Walker operated the controls. The hum of the transporter beam coincided with Walker and the *Reliant* fading from view.

✦

I had guest quarters on Starbase 74, and it ended up being a relatively quiet first few days as I waited for the *Stargazer* to arrive. The station was well equipped and pleasant, and I spent the time reviewing what I could about the *Stargazer*'s systems, as well as practicing navigation in one of the station's simulators. I was getting used to the relaxed schedule when early one morning I was awakened by a voice on the intercom.

"Lieutenant Picard," the voice said. It was one I didn't recognize.

"Yes," I said. My voice was more of a croak, as I was fast asleep when the voice came through.

"Report to Shuttle Bay One in fifteen minutes," the voice said. "In your dress uniform." I sputtered a response but whoever it was had ceased communications. It sounded like an order. Could the *Stargazer* be early? It seemed unlikely. And why wear a dress uniform? I didn't have any time to figure it out, so I cleaned up, got dressed, and reported to the shuttle bay. When I got there, I found about a dozen officers, all in their dress uniforms, and a waiting shuttlecraft. None of them had any more information pertaining as to why we'd been called. We didn't have a long wait to find out.

An elderly man, also in a Starfleet dress uniform, approached us. I silently guessed he was about 100 years old. As he got closer I noticed three more things: he was an admiral, he wore the insignia of the medical branch of the service, and he seemed annoyed at all of us.

"What are you all waiting for? Get in the damn shuttle."

"Excuse me, sir," I said. "May I ask where we're going?"

"Nobody told you?" He seemed even more annoyed. "We're going to down to the planet for Spock's wedding. You're going to be the honor guard. He doesn't want an honor guard—too bad, he's getting one. Now get a move on, we're going to be late. That's a blasted order."

We all quickly filed onto the shuttle, and as soon as we were settled on board, it launched. Starbase 74 was in orbit around Tarsas III; the planet itself was the site of an old Earth colony that had terraformed the planet.

But to a man and woman on the shuttle, no one was interested in the *where*, but the *why*. We all knew who Spock was, probably one of the most well-known veterans of Starfleet, as well as a distinguished ambassador to the Federation. And he was getting married, and this doctor, whoever he was, had decided to provide an honor guard made up of any officer he could find.

Doctor. I stared at him as he pulled a small flask from his jacket pocket and took a healthy swig. I felt like such an idiot. This was *McCoy*. For the short ride, I tried my best to get a look at him without letting him know. I was not successful.

"Something I can do for you, Lieutenant?" he said, after catching me.

"No, sir," I said. "But it's an honor to meet you…"

"Stow it," he said, sat back in his chair, and closed his eyes. After a few minutes he was snoring peacefully. The rest of us exchanged amused excitement.

"Who is the senior officer here," I said, "besides the admiral?" A woman, a lieutenant commander, realized she was, and immediately understood why I asked.

"Let's all figure out what we're going to do once we get there," she said. "I imagine we're all a little rusty at marching drills…"

✦

We landed on Tarsas III, at the spaceport a few kilometers outside the main city. Since its inception, Tarsas III had undergone a stark transformation thanks to modern terraforming techniques, and where once natural growth was confined to a small area around the city, it was now over the entire continent. We were taken by hovercraft to the city. It was made up of twelve boulevards that radiated out from a town square. When we got to the square, we saw that preparations were made for a sizable event. There were chairs set up around an altar. It surprised me as the whole thing had a very human flavor. This was not, from what I understood, how Vulcans got married. Our hovercraft stopped, and McCoy turned to us.

"Don't embarrass me," he said, and got off first. There were fourteen officers, so, with the lieutenant commander leading, we formed two lines of seven, and marched out of the hovercraft. We stayed in formation until we reached the altar, then split so there was seven on each side. We stood there at attention as the guests trickled in.

And what a guest list it was. The president of the Federation, the commander-in-chief of Starfleet, members of the Federation Council and dignitaries from dozens of worlds. There was nothing "Vulcan" about this event. Which probably meant the bride was not a Vulcan.

"Lieutenant," a man said, "I have a query." I was at the end of the line on the left side of the altar, and kept my movement to a minimum so as not to break formation. I glanced sideways at the person talking to me.

It was Sarek. Sarek of Vulcan. One of the greatest figures in history, a man who helped shape the modern Federation. I hadn't forgotten he was Spock's father, but the whole human flavor of the event made me forget he would probably be here.

"Um..." was all I could get out in response.

"I am unfamiliar with human wedding traditions. Is there a specific section for the blood relations of the groom?"

I just stood there, grinning like an idiot. The lieutenant standing next to me leaned in to answer, telling Sarek that it would be first row, whatever side the groom was on. Sarek nodded in acknowledgment, looked at me briefly, and sat down.

The ceremony began shortly thereafter. The president of the Federation stood under the altar to officiate, and Dr. McCoy walked in with Spock. Spock did not seem nearly as old as McCoy, and had the quiet power that came from the inner peace his species enjoyed. They stood only a few inches from me, and I heard a quiet conversation.

"I distinctly requested no honor guard, Doctor," Spock said.

"It's not for you," McCoy said. "It's for her. Now shut up, you're getting married." A string quartet began to play Vivaldi's "The Four Seasons," and the bride walked down the aisle. She was human, but wore a veil; it was impossible to get a good look at her. When she approached the altar, Spock lifted the veil. From where I was standing, I couldn't turn to look and see who she was.

"Dearly beloved," President Uhura began, "we are gathered here today to join in the bonds of matrimony, Spock and…" At the moment President Uhura said the bride's name, an elderly guest in the front row coughed loudly, so I missed it. The wedding continued in a very human tradition, ending with President Uhura giving Spock permission to kiss the bride. He did so, and when he did I happened to have a direct line of sight to Sarek, in the front row. He wore an expression that I could only describe as disgust. At the intermarriage? No, that couldn't be, Sarek himself had married an Earth woman. Maybe the display of affection? It was impossible to know.

The wedding ended, and I and the rest of the honor guard returned to Starbase 74. The whole trip back I was in a daze at the company I'd just been in. Once I returned to my quarters, I looked for information on the wedding on the Federation news services, but I couldn't find anything. Some of the biggest names in the Federation had just come to a private affair that had no publicity. And I had been there too.

✦

I sat in the lounge of Starbase 74, with a book on the history of the Federation, reading about the people that a few days ago I'd actually been around. I'd chosen this spot to settle in and wait for my new ship, scheduled to arrive sometime that day. Through the bay windows in front of me was the cavernous interior docking compartment of the station. There were several starships berthed inside, undergoing various degrees of repair and maintenance. I was interrupted from my reading by an announcement over the public address system.

"U.S.S. *Stargazer* arriving Bay 3." I looked up; after a brief moment, the *Stargazer* slowly came into view directly in front of the windows. In the pictures I'd seen it had seemed much smaller than it actually was. That was probably due to its squatness. It was much less sleek than the modern starship design. I remembered the ancient American naval officers used to refer to their ships as "tin cans," and somehow that moniker fit this vessel.

I loved it.

I practically ran back to my quarters, picked up my packed belongings and made my way to Bay 3. I'd spent weeks brushing up on my navigation skills and couldn't wait to sit at my new station on the bridge. I had very poetic thoughts that I was "plotting the course to my future." I found myself standing at the doorway to the airlock to Bay 3, pausing dramatically at the control pad that would open the hatch. As I keyed the panel, I said quietly to myself…

"On the other side, destiny awaits…"

The door opened and something hit me. It went splat across my chest, and dropped to the floor. An egg. Somebody had just hit me with an egg. As the slime of the white and yolk slid down my tunic, there were squeals of delighted laughter. I saw two boys—one around twelve, the other a little younger. They seemed to have been waiting for someone to open the airlock door. I stood there stunned. They stuck their tongues out at me and ran off, just as an officer came up from inside the ship.

"Anthony! David! Get back here," the officer said, but the boys were gone. The officer turned to me. He was in his thirties and had commander bars.

"Lieutenant Jean-Luc Picard," I said, a little lost. "Reporting for duty."

"Glad to meet you, Lieutenant, I'm Commander Frank Mazzara," he said. "I'm the exec. Let's get you cleaned up, and then I'll take you to the captain." He led me into the ship, and I was too confused as to what had just happened to even be aware of my surroundings.

"Who…" I said, "who were those boys?"

"Oh, those are my sons," he said. "Great kids."

"They're on the ship?" I'd never heard of children being allowed on board a starship.

"Yeah," he said, with genuine enthusiasm. "You will love them once you get to know them."

About that, he would end up being wrong.

Commander Mazzara took me to my quarters, where I quickly changed into a clean tunic, and then he took me to the captain. Along the way I was able to refocus on where I was. The ship was bigger than *Reliant*; just on the walk from the airlock to my quarters and then up to the captain's quarters I saw more crewmen than I served with on my old ship. Mazzara was affable, and filled me in on how the ship ran and what would be expected of me. There were three shifts instead of four, and I would serve on the bridge as second shift flight controller—a great improvement over the graveyard shift on *Reliant*. I began to relax and regain my enthusiasm for my new position. We reached the captain's quarters, buzzed the door chime and were ordered in.

The captain's quarters were larger than Quinn's on *Reliant*, but seemed much tighter. Wall space was completely filled with art. There were shelves groaning with books and knick-knacks, as well as stacks of PADDs and piles of papers. Paper had never been used for record keeping in Starfleet, so I couldn't imagine what it all was. It seemed less a captain's quarters and more a family attic.

In the center was Captain Laughton, naked except for a towel around his waist, sitting in the chair at his desk, which was piled high with much of the same debris that was spread throughout the room. Laughton was a large man, very overweight by Starfleet standards. Directly in front of him a small space had been cleared for a plate of food: a half-eaten meal of curried chicken with rice, which I identified by the pungent odor. I stood at attention.

"Lieutenant Jean-Luc Picard, reporting for duty, sir."

"Our new junior flight controller," Laughton said. "You can stand at ease, Lieutenant, we don't go in for all that." That clearly went without saying. "So, the hero of Milika III. Made quite a name for yourself already." His air was subtly taunting.

"Thank you, sir," I said, doing my best to ignore his tone.

"We could use a few more heroes around here, right, Mazzara?"

"Yes, sir," Mazzara said.

"Well, just so you know," Laughton said, "I like people to pitch in even if it isn't in their job description. I hope you don't have a problem with that."

"No, sir," I said, having no idea what he meant.

"Good, welcome aboard." He took a healthy forkful of chicken curry, and as he chewed said: "Mazzara, put him to work." Laughton fully engaged with his meal as Mazzara led me out.

"The captain's something else, isn't he?" Mazzara said, once we were in the corridor. I might have said the same thing, except not with Mazzara's admiring tone.

Mazzara had to return to duty on the bridge, so he took me with him. As we walked through the corridors, maintenance workers from the station had already begun to stream on board the ship. We would be in spacedock for at least a week for repairs and upgrades.

"Truth be told, the old lady could probably use a month," Mazzara said. We arrived on the bridge, where the second shift was on duty, and the person sitting in the captain's chair was a bit troubling.

"Anthony, get out of the chair," Mazzara said to the older of the two boys who had egged me. "Where's your brother?"

"Don't know. Said he was going to play in the warp core," Anthony said, still sitting in the captain's chair.

"I want you to apologize to Lieutenant Picard," Mazzara said.

"For what? We didn't do anything. It was David who threw it…"

"Anthony," Mazzara said

"It's fine, no need," I said. The other bridge officers were watching this, their first impression of me, and I just wanted it to end.

"All right," Mazzara said. Anthony continued to sit in the captain's chair, as Mazzara took me around to meet the other officers on the bridge. I wasn't a parent, but I knew terrible parenting when I saw it.

The next week I threw myself into helping with the ship's repairs and upgrades, and it quickly became apparent to me the *Stargazer* was in terrible shape. Some of the systems were very outdated, and regular maintenance had not been performed on everything from the engines to the hull to the coffee cups, so everything felt worn and dilapidated. This went for the crew as well. Lieutenant Christoph Black, who'd been one of the cadets I'd passed in the academy marathon, was a communications officer. One day I joined him for lunch in the ship's wardroom and asked him tactful questions about Mazzara and his children.

"He's a single dad," Black said, "and Laughton wanted him, so this was a condition of him coming on board." Black was also being politic; neither one of us was going to reveal how we felt about the two boys. He then asked me how I ended up on the *Stargazer*. I told him I applied for the open position, and the derisiveness of his laugh cut me like a razor.

"Probably should've done a little more due diligence," Black said. I didn't need to ask him why he thought that.

Finally, it was time to leave spacedock. The ship was scheduled to depart in the middle of my shift. I was at the flight controller station and Mazzara sat in the captain's chair, in command for this shift. I was nervous; I was about to fly a starship for the first time. Every free minute I'd had I'd practiced in the simulator, but I still wasn't sure I was ready to handle a ship this large with an engine this powerful. Black turned to Mazzara.

"Dock command signaling clear," he said.

"Inform the captain we're ready to depart," Mazzara said.

"Captain acknowledges and is coming to the bridge," Black said. Mazzara moved from the captain's chair.

"Conn," he said to me,* "Captain might want to take a look at the final maintenance report. Have it ready." I nodded and went to the science station to get a PADD, then downloaded the report onto it to give the captain. When I finished, I headed back to my chair, only to find someone was in it.

"I'm going to fly the ship," David said, the younger of the two Mazzara children.

"That's my job," I said. I looked for Mazzara, who was nowhere to be found. I assumed he must be in the washroom behind the viewscreen.

"No, it's my job," David said. This was a true no-win scenario. I had to get this child out of my chair before the captain arrived, which would be any second. I looked around helplessly, but every bridge officer was avoiding my silent plea. All of them had been veterans of the *Stargazer*, some if not all had probably been victims of the tyranny of these imps.

"Well," I said, "how about I let you have a turn when I'm done?"

"It's my ship, I'll do what I want." He spun back and forth in my chair. He knew he had power. Absolute power corrupting absolutely. I was hoping Mazzara would return before Laughton arrived, but I couldn't risk it. I wanted to tell the spoiled rodent that I would wring his neck if he didn't get up, but threatening my superior officer's child seemed ill-advised. I wracked my brain for another plan, and then realized I was over-thinking it. I looked over David's shoulder to the empty captain's chair.

"Were you sitting in the captain's chair?"

"No."

"Oh," I said, and walked over to the chair. "I guess finders keepers…" I pretended to reach for something in the chair, and David immediately got up from the conn station and ran over.

"My dad was sitting there, whatever it is it's mine…"

---

*EDITOR'S NOTE: Conn is shipboard parlance for the officer manning the flight controller station.

With a quick step I was back in the conn chair, just as the turbolift doors opened and Laughton strode onto the bridge. David, realizing he'd been fooled, ran back to me.

"Hey, I was sitting there…"

By then, Mazzara was out of the washroom.

"David," Mazzara said. "Go to our quarters."

"But I was sitting…"

"Go now," Mazzara said. He gave a slightly worried glance to Laughton, who didn't seem interested. David looked me in the eye—I'd made an enemy today. He then shuffled off the bridge.

"All right, Mr. Picard," Laughton said. "Take us out. And try not to side-swipe the door jamb." After what I'd just been through, getting to handle the ship seemed a relief. I also decided when I became a captain, children wouldn't be allowed anywhere near my ship, let alone the bridge.

CHAPTER FOUR

"SET COURSE FOR THE NORTH STAR COLONY," Mazzara said. "Maximum warp." The order, like many I'd carried out, made little sense, but after four years on this ship I'd learned to accept such things.

"Course set," I said. "Engaging at warp factor 7." The ship shook a little as we went into warp; the inertial dampeners were old and always in need of adjustment. We'd just been examining the Kobliad system, a binary star system with one sparsely populated planet. We were about to make contact with its inhabitants when the captain gave the order to change course and go to the North Star colony. This almost certainly didn't come from Starfleet Command. I knew this because we hadn't heard from Starfleet in weeks.

Laughton had crafted his image at Starfleet as a great explorer. In the first part of his career on the *Stargazer* he'd catalogued a record number of new worlds for a shipmaster. He was now living off that reputation, and had been for some time. He was still making new discoveries, charting new systems, meeting new species, but not nearly as rapidly. However, the *Stargazer*'s age and condition meant it had little use anywhere else, so even if the reports of new systems were down to a trickle, the Admiralty still felt it was getting its "money's worth" from the old bucket.

But because they gave him such a long leash, Laughton took ridiculous privileges. The current situation was a perfect example: one more day and we could've finished the survey of the Kobliad system, but instead, we were heading off at high warp for some unknown reason that was almost certainly frivolous. Whatever it was, we would have to turn around and come right back to finish the survey. It was inefficient, indulgent, and an infuriating waste of time and resources. And it would invariably involve me doing something I didn't want to do. As he mentioned on my first day, Laughton liked officers to "pitch in" outside their job description.

When we reached colony a few days later, I got a call from the captain to come to his quarters.

"I need you to take a shuttle to the surface," Laughton said. He was in a bathrobe, which was better than the towel. "You're to pick up a piece of equipment from a man in the main city; I'll give you his contact information. You'll pay for the equipment with one of our power converters."

"Yes, sir," I said. "What kind of equipment am I picking up?"

"You'll find out when you get there," he said. "Oh, also, have someone come in here and take out this desk."

So he bought a new desk.

This was his modus operandi; he was a collector and spent all his free time scouring subspace marketplaces for things that struck his fancy. It wasn't just his quarters that were filled with his acquisitions: storage spaces all over the ship were stocked with objets d'art, books, furniture, and rare documents. Now he found a desk he wanted and had taken his ship and crew away from its duties to pick it up. He could just have it beamed into the cargo bay, but in his mind that would be too conspicuous. Somehow, by tasking me with this, he thought only I would know about it, not taking into account all the people I would have to deal with on the way. But I'd learned there was no point in trying to explain this to him.

I took the information from him and went to engineering. The chief engineer, Lieutenant Commander Scully, a large, usually affable man, looked annoyed when I asked him for a power converter.

"They don't grow on trees, son," he said.

"The captain..."

"All right, all right..." he said and walked off to retrieve one. He handed it over, and I then went to the shuttle bay and informed the bridge that I was taking a shuttle to the surface on orders from the captain. Nobody questioned anything, no one asked for any more detail. They all knew what was going on.

I took the shuttle down to the surface. The North Star colony (not to be confused with Polaris, the "North Star" in the Earth's nighttime sky) was a pleasant throwback. Some time in the 19th century on Earth a wagon train had been abducted by aliens called the Skagaran, who used the humans for slaves on this planet. Eventually the humans rose up and took over the planet, and when they were rediscovered in the 22nd century by the first starship *Enterprise*, they'd built an entire town that looked like it was from the 19th-century North American West, complete with horses and buggies and gunslingers. It still exists to this day, but now with many modern conveniences.

I landed at the starport and then made my way to the address the captain had given me. It was a small adobe-like home. I knocked on the door. A hunched, wizened old man named MacReady answered.

"I'm here from the *Stargazer*," I said. I gave him the power converter. The old man nodded and led me into his home.

He was a woodworker, and the whole house was set up as a workshop. The old man gestured toward a wooden desk. It was quite stunning, polished dark wood, and very large. Troublingly large. Larger than any desk I'd ever seen on a starship.

I took out my tricorder and did a quick scan of its measurements; it wouldn't even fit through a turbolift's doors. Again, there would be no point in trying to explain this to the captain, so I just decided to get it back to the ship and deal with it there.

"Do you have an anti-grav unit?" I said. The old man shook his head, then handed me four pieces of wood attached as a square, with wheels on the bottom. It appeared to be a primitive device called a "dolly," used to move heavy objects. With some difficulty, I got the desk up on the dolly, and slowly pushed it out the door and down the street, back to the starport. It was a difficult trek, as the desk was much larger than the dolly, and it took some effort to keep it balanced as I pushed. I used my time on this excursion to ponder, as I often did, how I might extricate myself from this ship, but every attempt I made to get transferred was denied by the captain. He seemed to understand that he was getting in my way, which is why the previous year he had promoted me to lieutenant commander. The new rank did nothing to help me haul this giant piece of wood.

I finally reached the shuttle, and realized I had another problem: there was no hatch on the shuttle big enough for the desk. The only solution seemed to be to beam it up, but I wasn't going to do that. A few weeks earlier, the captain had me on a similar errand to pick up a statue of Kahless, the ancient Klingon leader. The most efficient way to get it back on the ship was to transport it, but when he found out that's what I did he was furious and threatened to demote me. Black had quietly explained to me that transporter logs were very detailed, and Laughton didn't want an official record of all the cargo he was bringing up. I didn't want to risk his ire again, so I had to come up with another plan.

There was a life-support belt in the shuttle; it projected a low-level force field around the user, providing oxygen in case of emergency. I adjusted the field so that it would surround the desk, and attached it. Then I secured several magnetic clasps to the surface.

I got in the shuttle and lifted off, hovering a few feet off the ground, and then maneuvered the shuttle over the desk. I slowly lowered the shuttle until I heard a thunk as the magnetic clasps attached themselves to the belly of the craft, and then I began a slow ascent into space. I hadn't had a lot of time to calculate how much acceleration those clasps could take, but as long as we took it slow I figured I should be all right.

That was when the captain called.

"Laughton to Picard," he said. "What the hell is taking so long?"

"Uh, sir, there was some difficulty..." I said.

"We've just received a distress call, get back to the ship immediately," he said. This was a problem. I was pulling out of the atmosphere but still inside the planet's gravity well. If I increased my acceleration, I wasn't sure the clasps would hold against even the limited air resistance.

"Picard, acknowledge!" Laughton was a little panicked, for good reason. If the *Stargazer* failed to acknowledge a distress call because we were busy getting him a new desk, he could lose his command.

"Acknowledged, sir," I said, and pushed the throttle forward. It seemed to be all right for a moment, and then there was a slight jolt. I checked my scanner; the desk was tumbling back toward the planet. I switched on the communicator.

"Picard to Transporter Room," I said. "Emergency."

"Transporter Room, this is Chief Mazzara," the voice said. Wonderful. Anthony Mazzara, now 16, had been made a transporter chief petty officer. He had not matured in the least since throwing an egg at me four years ago.

"There's an object falling away from my shuttle," I said. "You need to lock onto it and beam it aboard."

"What is it? Is it dangerous…"

"I'm giving you a direct order!"

"Okay, okay. Calm down…" I was fast approaching the shuttle bay of the *Stargazer* and had to deal with my approach and landing, so I couldn't monitor what was happening with my cargo. As I settled onto the landing pad, I heard from the transporter room.

"It's a desk. What am I supposed to do with it?" It was a very good question.

I informed Chief Mazzara to just get it off the transporter pad and wait for instructions. I then raced to the bridge, where his father was at ops and Captain Laughton was in command. I took over the conn and hoped that I would have time later to properly explain to the captain why I had to use the transporter to retrieve his "equipment."

The ship had gone to maximum impulse power soon after I'd landed and we were headed to the inner part of the system. The planet closest to the sun had a large mining operation. One of the miner's ships had lost engine power and was now being pulled into the star. By the time I assumed my post, the magnificent orb was growing in the center of the viewscreen. The mining ship wasn't even visible against the orange conflagration.

"Are we in transporter range?" Laughton said.

"Not yet, sir," Mazzara said. I silently hoped his son had gotten the desk off of the transporter pad.

"Try to raise them," Laughton said. Black, who was at communications, said there was no response. It didn't mean they were dead—there were still three life signs on the mining ship, and this close to a star's magnetic field older communications systems had a tendency not to work well. Or at all.

"How long until we're in transporter range?" Laughton said. I checked my board.

"Eleven seconds," I said. Though Laughton was often a strange man with deplorable priorities, he also knew how to be a captain when necessary. He sounded cool and confident, which, with a sun growing on the viewscreen, went a long way in keeping the rest of us calm.

"Transporter Room," Laughton said. "Stand by to lock onto the crew of that ship." I had a moment of fear over what the response would be.

"Acknowledged," Anthony said. "Standing by." Good, he must have moved the desk out of the way. I again looked down at my panel. We were a few seconds from transporter range when an alarm flashed.

"Sir," I said. "We've got an ion surge in helm control..."

Before I could finish my sentence, my panel erupted. The force of the blast sent me tumbling backwards out of my chair. I looked up, and saw that my console was on fire. The ship's fire control system immediately doused it. The sound of the blast caused me to momentarily lose my hearing; there was silent chaos around me. I tried to get to my feet, and saw Frank Mazzara standing by the captain's chair.

Laughton was slumped back, and his eyes were open; a piece of debris from my panel was lodged in his head. He was dead. Mazzara looked stunned, then turned to the bridge crew. My hearing was returning, and I took over Mazzara's post at the ops panel—the conn was a charred mess.

"Status," he said. Even with my impaired hearing, Mazzara sounded shaky.

"We're in transporter range," I said. "We've got no helm control up here." Mazzara turned to Black.

"Inform the transporter room to beam the miners on board," he said. "Bridge to Engineering—"

"All impulse and warp control circuits completely burned out," Scully said. "We must have had a build-up of ions on the hull, and it induced transients..."

"It doesn't matter what happened," Mazzara said. "We need to get control of the ship back."

"I don't know what to tell you," Scully said. "The engines have shut down, but we're still traveling at close to the speed of light. All I've got is maneuvering thrusters, they won't slow us down. I need some time to rig something up..."

"Transporter Room reports the miners are on board," Black said. But Mazzara wasn't listening. He was staring at the viewscreen, where the sun was growing in size.

"Distance from the star," Mazzara said.

"One point five million kilometers," I said. Our shields were still protecting us, but with no engines to escape the sun's gravity, they wouldn't help us if we ended up inside. There was one possibility as long as we did it before we got too close. I started a quick calculation, when I was interrupted by Mazzara's order.

"All hands abandon ship," Mazzara said. He'd also been doing a calculation: at this distance, shuttles and escape pods would still escape the sun's gravity.

"Sir, I think we can—" I said, but Mazzara cut me off.

"Get to your assigned evacuation stations," Mazzara said. I could see his mind was somewhere else—his family, his children. He was playing it safe for them. Then he did something truly startling.

He left the bridge.

This act left the bridge crew momentarily stunned. I wanted to explain my plan to everyone who remained, hoping to convince them we had a chance, but I was out of time. The other members of the bridge immediately began shutting down their stations, preparing to evacuate. There was no time to explain. I had to act.

"Belay that order," I said. The remaining crewmen turned and looked at me. By abandoning the bridge, Mazzara had left me in command even though he hadn't stated it explicitly. I could see doubt in the faces of most everyone, especially Black, who until a short time ago had outranked me. But they obeyed and didn't leave their posts. Mazzara hadn't just abandoned the bridge, he had abandoned *them*, and, with their captain lying there dead, they wanted some hope. Black signaled a cancellation of the abandon ship signal. I leaned into the intercom.

"Bridge to Engineering, Scully, fire all port thrusters," I said.

"Aye, sir," Scully said. "They won't last long…"

"They won't have to," I said.

"Mazzara to Bridge, what the hell's going on up there? Who countermanded my order?"

"One moment, sir," I said. I checked our position; as long as we started the maneuver before we reached the distance from the star equal to its diameter, we still had a chance. The star was eight hundred and seventy-five thousand miles across—I'd fired the port thrusters at over a million kilometers out. It would work.

"Mazzara to Bridge, answer me!" On the viewscreen, the sun started to slowly move to the left.

"Sir, this is Picard—the thrusters, our momentum, and the sun's gravity are moving us into a high orbit around the star. This should buy Engineer Scully enough time to make repairs." There was a long pause.

"Shield status?"

"Sixty-five percent," I said, which would give us plenty of protection for the time being. Though I'd saved the ship, I took no pleasure in the fact that Mazzara was humiliated. I needed to change the subject. "Your orders, sir?"

"Have damage control teams make reports. I'll be right up," he said. "Inform sickbay to make arrangements for the captain."

"Aye, sir," I said. I looked at Laughton. He'd done so much to define life on the *Stargazer*, it was hard to imagine what this ship would be like without him. I stood over him and closed his eyes.

✦

"Laughton had an ex-wife," Captain Mazzara said. "She lives on the New Paris colony, and he left instructions to bring his belongings to her in the event of his death. Once there, I want you to handle it personally, Number One." Since I'd become his first officer, Mazzara had referred to me as "Number One," an ancient Earth term for the first officer on naval vessels. I assumed it was something he learned on a previous posting, because Laughton never used it. But I didn't mind it.

"Yes, sir," I said. Mazzara was behind his desk in his quarters, which he shared with one of his sons, David, who was now 14. Anthony, now a crewman, was quartered with another engineer. Though he'd been promoted, Mazzara had not moved into the captain's quarters because of the sheer amount of Laughton's possessions. (With the giant desk in there, it was now almost impossible to get inside.)

"Don't bring an away team," Mazzara said. "Go see her yourself first. She's not human, and I don't know anything about her species. I would go, but…"

"Yes, sir," I said. "Better for you to stay on board." A first officer's duty was to protect the life of his captain, even if he didn't have any respect for him. Mazzara didn't like leaving his sons. As a father it was admirable, as an officer, disgraceful.

"That'll be all," Mazzara said.

"You heard him—get lost," David said. David had been sitting in the back of the room, playing a game on a PADD and looking at us intermittently. Mazzara snapped an admonishment at his son for his rudeness but as usual it did little good. From the first day I came aboard this ship, David had decided to be my personal nuisance. I'd long since learned to take pride in the fact that he couldn't faze me, which only provoked him more. My new position undoubtedly made things worse. I smiled at the captain and left.

In the wake of Laughton's death a month before, Mazzara had promoted me to First Officer. Mazzara never mentioned my countermanding his order. I'd committed a court martial offense, but in order for him to press charges he would have had to mention to Starfleet Command that he'd left the bridge in a moment of crisis. His first act as interim captain, preceding the rest of the bridge crew in an evacuation, did not violate any regulation, but went in the face of thousands of years of heroic tradition: the last man off a sinking ship is always its captain. Starfleet Command would've frowned on his behavior, and it might have kept Mazzara from getting the captaincy.

So though he had the rank, Mazzara had completely undermined his authority. Crewmen snickered about his cowardice. I was in the rec room having dinner with Black, Chief Engineer Scully, and two other officers one evening when I discovered just how bad things had gotten. Black was relaying a story about showing up late for his shift.

"…I'm pulling on my clothes as I run to the bridge, get on the turbolift with my shirt over my head, and when I pull it down, there's Captain Quitter who must've gotten on before me…" The other officers laughed at the story, but I had a different reaction. The nonchalance that greeted the moniker troubled me.

" 'Captain Quitter'?" I said. "Where did that come from?"

"Oh," Black said, realizing that as first officer I might not have been privy to it. "Yeah, someone nicknamed him that, I don't know who…"

"It was me," Scully said. Scully was so vital to his job that he knew it wouldn't cost him anything to admit responsibility. He was also old enough that he didn't care if it did.

"I don't want to hear it again," I said. "Next person who says it in front of me goes on report." I got up from the table and took my tray to the recycler.

"What's the big deal?" Black said.

"The big deal is he's the captain," I said, "and even if he wasn't, he has two sons on board." I then walked out, and considered that it might seem puzzling that two boys who were such irritants to me could arouse this level of compassion. I suppose, looking back, I might have been jealous that they had a father who was so devoted to them he had essentially destroyed his own career to prioritize their safety.

✦

New Paris was one of Earth's oldest and largest colonies, dating back before the founding of the Federation. It had a population of over three million, and the planet had a wide variety of populated ecosystems. When we arrived, Mazzara provided me with exact coordinates of the home where Laughton's ex-wife lived.

"Shouldn't we try to call first?" I said. "It seems strange to go in unannounced."

"Laughton's instructions were to do just that," Mazzara said. "She doesn't have a communicator. Wants her privacy." Me showing up with no warning seemed to fly in the face of that desire, but I decided to follow orders.

I went to the transporter room. Anthony Mazzara was on duty. I gave him the coordinates.

"Kind of hard picturing fat Captain Laughton finding a wife," he said.

"Belay that," I said, and got on the transporter pad. There was no bottom to the depths the Mazzara boys would dive.

I beamed down to find myself in a lush thicket of trees and vines. I could hear a soft rain high above, but the canopy of leaves kept much of it from reaching me. It was a serene and beautiful environment.

I took out my tricorder and detected a structure not far away. There were no life-form readings, however. I moved through the thicket and in a few moments found a house, one story high, set in amongst the forest, made of indigenous wood and stone. It had a natural camouflage making it impossible to see until I was almost upon it. But my scanning for life-forms was still unsuccessful.

"Hands in the air," a woman's voice said, behind me. I did as she told me. The woman circled around me. She wore a long gown and a wide-brimmed hat, and held a large, formidable-looking rifle, aimed right at me.

"How did you find me? I know it wasn't that tricorder, I can fool those stupid things."

"Um… I'm from the *Stargazer*. Captain Humphrey Laughton…"

"Figured that loser would come bothering me," she said. "What does he want?"

"I'm very sorry to inform you…"

"Wait a minute…" she said, breaking out into an infectious smile. "You're Jean-Luc Picard… Oh my, it's been such a long time, and I didn't recognize you with all that hair." This caught me off guard. I'd never seen this woman before. But she obviously knew me. She lowered her rifle, so I dropped my hands.

"I'm sorry, you have me at a disadvantage," I said. "You know me?" Her demeanor suddenly changed. She seemed slightly awkward with the situation, but also amused.

"Oh… no… sorry, I thought you were someone else."

"Someone else named Jean-Luc Picard?"

"Yes, strange coincidence, he's a bald guy, lot older," she said. "I'm Guinan, nice to meet you. Sorry about the 'hands up' thing." She shook my hand, her grin filled with Cheshire cat irony. "So you're in Humphrey's crew?"

"Well, yes, in a way. On behalf of Starfleet and the Federation, I want to express my condolences on his death."

"Oh, that's very nice, but Humphrey was three husbands ago," she said. "It's been thirty years since I've even seen him." Thirty years? She already seemed quite a bit younger than the captain, but that was in human terms. The mysteries were multiplying. "Now, I'm going to need you to get me out of here. They've known I was on the planet for some time, and they were probably keeping track of your ship because they knew Humphrey was one of my husbands."

"Wait…"

"I don't have time to wait; if they detected your transporter beam…"

"Who are we talking about?"

We were interrupted by a blast from a pulse weapon, which knocked the bark off a tree right next to me.

"Them," she said, taking my hand and leading me off in a run. More blasts, each just missing us. We reached a large stone, and she had us hide behind it. I tried to get a look at our assailant. He had taken up a position about twenty meters away.

"Who's shooting at us?"

"Some mercenary or bounty hunter," she said "And he's not shooting at me, he's shooting at *you*—he wants me alive." Every answer she gave led to more questions, but I had had enough. I took out my communicator.

"Picard to *Stargazer*, two to beam up..." There was no answer.

"He's probably jamming you," Guinan said. "I'm worth a lot." She held up her rifle. "If you make a run for that big tree over there, it'll draw him out and I can get a clean shot." I looked to where she was indicating; it was a distance.

"Don't take too long to aim..."

"Don't worry," she said. Her confidence was reassuring.

"Ready?" I said. She nodded. I took off. After about three steps I heard a blast that didn't sound like our assailant's.

"You can stop running," Guinan said. I turned and saw a prone figure on the ground. I went over to him. It was a species I didn't recognize in camouflage clothing, with a ridge bisecting his forehead. I took his weapon, found a device on his belt that was jamming communicator transmissions, and shut it off.

"I'll take him back to the ship and turn him over to the New Paris authorities," I said.

"You're taking me too," she said. "I can't stay here anymore."

"But..."

"No buts; I had a perfectly good hiding place till you showed up. Where are you guys going?"

"Well, our command base is Starbase 32..."

"That sounds fine," she said. She smiled. "Besides, aren't you interested in getting to know me?"

In truth, I was.

✦

Captain Mazzara wasn't happy about our new passenger, but was at least relieved that she let us store Laughton's cargo in her home on New Paris. After

I had enlisted several crewmembers to transfer our former captain's extensive collection of artifacts and memorabilia, we left for Starbase 32.

During the week-long trip, I spent a fair amount of my free time talking to Guinan. I did not learn much about her, however. She was an El-Aurian, a species I knew nothing about, and she gave me almost no details other than there were very few of them left in the Galaxy, and that they lived extremely long lives. This led to rumors about their blood being a source of immortality, which made them the victims of unscrupulous bounty hunters.

Though I couldn't draw much more information out of her, I unexpectedly found myself quite comfortable sharing my personal details. She was a compelling listener, and with very few questions I opened up about my history and feelings quite easily. I disclosed thoughts and ambitions that I had never mentioned to anyone. I quickly formed a connection with this woman, but there was nothing romantic about it. She just wanted to be my friend. I didn't know why, but it was comforting nevertheless.

It was, however, difficult for me to imagine her married to Captain Laughton, and she laughed when I mentioned that.

"You should've seen Humphrey at 28," she said. "Full of drive and ambition. He was going to explore the universe and make it his own." I didn't know whether it was a coincidence that the age she picked to mention just happened to be mine.

"He had quite a career," I said.

"In the beginning," Guinan said. "He started out as an explorer, but over time he decided the self-aggrandizement was more important to him, and he lost sight of his goals. His life became empty. And so did he. So he started collecting."

"I think it's easy to lose sight of your goals," I said. "It happens to me all the time."

"You have responsibilities, they can distract you."

"Yes, they can," I said. I was verbalizing something that had been in the back of my mind since Laughton's death. Out of a sense of loyalty, I had not broached the subject of a transfer to Captain Mazzara. I thought he would be more open to it than Laughton was, but I also knew that to ask too soon after Laughton's death was inappropriate. Now, however, a month had gone by and the ship was running as smooth as it ever had.

"You look like a man with a mission," Guinan said. I had become preoccupied by my own thoughts. I smiled and excused myself, and called the captain on the intercom. He was in his quarters, and I requested to see him.

On my way there, I let myself enjoy the possibility of finally leaving this ship. I was so energized and preoccupied that I walked into the captain's quarters without buzzing. He was playing a game of three-dimensional chess with David.

"What, you don't knock anymore?" David said.

"Sorry, sir," I said.

"It's all right, Number One," the captain said.

"You should call him Number Two," David said. I knew that this was some kind of insult, since David said it all the time, but I never learned what it meant.

"David, please," Mazzara said. "Give us a minute." David begrudgingly got up and left.

"What can I do for you, Jean-Luc," Mazzara said. "You want a drink?" Mazzara went and got a bottle of green liquid that I later discovered was Aldebaran whiskey. I didn't feel like drinking, but I also didn't feel like saying no, so I took a glass. Mazzara indicated a seat in front of him. He seemed to have forgotten that I was the one who asked to see him; there was a lot on his mind.

"I've been thinking a lot about the captain," he said.

"Yes, sir," I said. "A tragedy."

"I know he wasn't popular," Mazzara said. "And now, I feel a lot of sympathy for him. You can't understand command till you've had it. It's the loneliest, most oppressive job in the whole universe. It's a nightmare."

"Sir," I said, "you've been quite good at it…"

"Yeah, as soon as I got it I ran right off the bridge," he said. "I'm sure the crew has come up with plenty of nicknames for me by now…" I had not considered until then what must be going on in Mazzara's mind. Of course, a moment of bad judgment would haunt him, as it would any of us.

"Sir, I think everyone has forgotten about it," I said.

"I doubt that," he said. "In any case, I haven't. I'll remember it till the day I die. Everyone's life turns on a few crucial moments, and mine turned that day on the bridge." He took a long pull on his drink and placed the glass down on the desk. "I'll be resigning my commission."

"Sir, you should reconsider." This was, in my mind, tragic. Mazzara was letting one mistake define the rest of his life. "You're a good officer…"

"That's very kind, but I've already informed Starfleet Command. When we arrive at Starbase 32, this ship will have a new captain." Oh, wonderful, I thought. What broken-down failure had they found to take this ship? I couldn't risk staying around to find out. I had to get Mazzara to approve my transfer immediately.

"Sir, with all due respect to your situation, I came to talk to you about something. I would like a transfer…"

"Jean-Luc, I think you'll be needed here…"

"I understand, but I have my own career to think about, and I just don't think my future is on the *Stargazer*."

"Really? Even as its captain?"

"Yes… wait… what?" The word "yes" was already on the way out of my mouth when I processed what he had said. "Me?"

"You," Mazzara said. "It was my suggestion, and frankly I don't think command had any captains they wanted to spare. Or no one wanted it. *Stargazer*'s class is too large to be commanded by a commander, so you'll skip a rank and be promoted to full captain. Or I can approve your transfer."

"No, sir," I said. "I mean, yes, sir. I'll happily accept. Thank you, sir."

"Congratulations," Mazzara said. He picked up the bottle and poured himself another drink. "Dismissed."

I'd arrived at his cabin determined and excited to leave the *Stargazer*, and now I left having inherited it.

I had no idea what to do. Do I tell everybody? There was no one I really wanted to tell, so I wandered the ship for hours and I found myself alone in the observation lounge. It was at the top of the primary hull and faced the stern of the ship. I stood there for a long time, watching the stars streak away at warp speed.

"Good news?" It was Guinan. I hadn't heard her come in.

"What? Oh, yes… wait, how did you know?"

"You were smiling," she said. "Can you tell me?"

"I'm… I'm the new captain." Saying it out loud, I had to laugh. I felt joy over this news. I was 28 years old and was a captain. I'd only graduated from the academy six years ago.

"That's wonderful," Guinan said. "Some childhood dreams do come true." She already knew me well enough to know this, as well as a lot of other things. "What's going to be your first act as shipmaster?"

"I'm going to make a sign," I said. " 'No children allowed.' "

CHAPTER FIVE

"TO CAPTAIN FRANK MAZZARA, COMMANDING OFFICER, *U.S.S. Stargazer*, stardate 13209.2, you are hereby requested and required to relinquish command to Captain Jean-Luc Picard as of this date…"

I stood on the deck of the main shuttlebay next to Captain Mazzara as he read the order off the PADD, in front of a good portion of the four hundred people who made up the crew. Mazzara turned to look at me. I played my part.

"I relieve you, sir," I said.

"I stand relieved," Mazzara said, then looked up and addressed the ship's computer. "Computer, transfer all command codes to Captain Jean-Luc Picard, authorization Mazzara Beta Alpha 2." The computer immediately responded.

"*U.S.S. Stargazer* now in command of Jean-Luc Picard…" It was an amazing thing to hear. A computer voice had just made it official. I looked around at all the faces of the crew. I had fantasized my whole life about what this would feel like, and my imagination had never gotten it right. Because, as I stood and looked at all those expectant faces waiting for my first command, I realized in a flash that I was responsible for all of them.

"If you don't mind, I'd like to leave right away." It was Mazzara, in a hurry to get off the ship. I hadn't been fully aware of his embarrassment until he relayed it to me in his quarters, but since then it was all I could see. He didn't make eye contact with the rest of the crew, and he certainly wasn't staying around to say goodbye.

"Of course," I said. I turned to the crew. Here it was, my first order as captain. It was going to be nothing special. "All standing orders to remain in force until further notice. Prepare shuttlebay for launch. Dismissed." I then escorted Mazzara to the shuttle, where his two sons awaited him.

"It was a pleasure serving with you, sir," I said. I held out my hand and Mazzara shook it perfunctorily. I then turned to Anthony and David. "Good luck to you both."

David ignored me and followed Mazzara onto the shuttle. It probably wasn't David's best day that I, the officer whom he seemed the most disdainful of, now had his father's job. Anthony, however, hesitated a moment. His father, before I assumed command, had had his son transferred off the ship. It was only then that I realized that perhaps Anthony didn't want to go.

"Um… sorry about the egg," he said. "I hope I can serve with you again." I smiled, nodded, and he boarded the shuttle. As the hatch shut, I thought to myself: *Over my dead body.*

✦

We were circling Starbase 32, a planetary facility on Tagan III. There were limited dry dock services in orbit, but I planned to make use of them as much as I could. I had one goal in mind: get as many repairs and upgrades done as possible to the *Stargazer* before my replacement crew arrived. I needed a new conn officer (to replace me) as well as a new ops officer, security chief, and doctor. And one of those positions would also be my first officer.

I headed back to my cabin and passed a lot of crewmen in the corridors, exchanging friendly nods. I had enough relationships on the *Stargazer* that I felt there was plenty of goodwill at my promotion. Still, there were some officers who I knew did not take the news well. One of them intercepted me outside my cabin.

"May I speak with you a moment… sir?" It was Lieutenant Commander Black, the communications officer. I noticed that the "sir" took an extra moment; he wasn't comfortable with the change in our relative status. I ushered him inside.

"I would like to make a request," Black said. Undoubtedly, he wanted a transfer, which I would grant. Though he would actually be a big loss to the ship—it was doubtful I could find anyone with his experience—I didn't want to stand in the way of anyone who didn't want to be here.

"Go ahead."

"I'd like to throw my hat in the ring for first officer."

"Oh." This I did not expect. I was all set to offer to give him a recommendation to another ship. "I've already offered the position to someone else. I'm sorry." I'd only just assumed command, but had made arrangements for a new first officer a few days before.

"I see," he said. "That's disappointing. You're not... you're not replacing me are you?"

"No."

"Good, thanks," he said. "I'm really looking forward to serving under your command." With that, he left. This came as a considerable surprise to me. Somehow, despite Black's obvious jealousy of my promotions over him, I'd earned his respect. Just that bit of amity made me think if I hadn't already had someone else ready to take that post, I might have considered him.

A few minutes later, I had put on my new rank pin, and headed "upstairs." I wanted to sit in my new chair.

"Captain on the bridge," Black said, as I entered. This was a leftover protocol from the days of the Earth navies; when a captain entered the bridge, it was carefully noted in a written log so that if there was a grounding or collision, the captain's presence was a matter of formal record. On a starship, the sensor logs placed me and every other member of the ship at all hours. Black indulging in it was a show of respect, one he'd never shown to Laughton or Mazzara.

I looked around the room: the overall impression was of anarchy. Half the control panels in the room were open; maintenance crews were either scanning underneath them with tricorders or ripping out and replacing the innards with new parts. I went toward the captain's chair and stopped. An engineer stood on a small anti-grav platform and rewired optical cabling in the ceiling. The small floating disk was almost directly over the captain's chair. I would have to ask him to move to sit down. I decided against it, and instead walked past the captain's chair to the ops station, where Engineer Scully worked underneath the control panel. He noticed me as I approached.

"Hey there, sir," he said. He managed to walk the line between informality and respect, and I had to accept him as he was. Forty years older than me, and having served on the ship since before I was born, it was a lot more his than mine.

"How go the upgrades?"

"The ship's systems weren't really designed to handle a lot of this new stuff, but we're doing the best we can," he said. The technology of the *Stargazer* was years out of date, and the best I could hope for, barring a complete refit, was patchwork repairs. The ship would never be top of the line again, but as I stood there on that mess of a bridge, it didn't matter. The old lady was mine, and I loved it.

"Sir, Starbase 32 signals crew replacements standing by to beam aboard," Black said. This was sooner than I expected. I just had to hope there might be a delay in getting my orders so that most of the work I'd had started could be completed. I left the bridge and headed down to the transporter room.

As soon as I found out I was getting command, I knew I wanted a friend as my first officer. I thought of Corey and Marta, but knew they were both already up the chain of command on much better ships than the *Stargazer*: Corey was chief of security on the *Ajax*, and Marta was already the first officer of the *Kyushu*. Maybe I didn't want to put them in an awkward position, or maybe I didn't want to face rejection, but I didn't ask either of them. The only person I asked gave me an immediate yes, because for him it was a big step up.

"Request permission to come aboard, sir," Walker Keel said, as he stepped off the transporter. I warmly shook his hand. We hadn't been in touch that much since I left *Reliant*, but I knew he was ready to move on. With him on the pad were my new security chief, conn officer, and doctor. Three humans and one Edosian.

"Lieutenant Cheva reporting for duty, sir," Cheva said. I'd gotten her a promotion and was happy to have her as my chief of security. I hadn't forgotten the vital role she'd played on Milika, and how that had changed my career. Behind her, the new medical officer stepped forward.

"Commander Ailat," I said. "Welcome aboard." I'd never seen an Edosian in person before. Her orange skin, three arms and three legs fascinated me. Walking seemed impossible—as each leg took a step forward, her lower half rotated; three steps was a full circle.

"Thank you, Captain," Ailat said. Her voice was high-pitched, with a staccato speech pattern.

"And let me introduce your new conn officer," Walker said. I'd been so riveted by Ailat I'd ignored the young man standing toward the back. Walker had recommended him; he knew his family and had helped him get into the academy, which he'd just graduated from a couple of years before. Despite his slightly awkward bearing, he had an affable smile.

"Ensign Jack Crusher, reporting for duty, sir," he said.

✦

"You have all your crew replacements," Admiral Sulu said, "so I'm hoping you're ready to leave." I was in my quarters, and she was on my desk viewscreen, speaking from her office on Starbase 32. Though she was the commanding officer for this entire sector, she was sociable and engaging, and seemed very young for someone in her sixties. I never wanted to disappoint a superior officer, and Demora Sulu's casual authority heightened that need.

"Yes, ma'am, we're ready," I said. That was pretty far from the truth; I'd begun too many repairs and upgrades, gambling they'd be finished before *Stargazer* might be sent into action.

"Good," she said. "We've lost contact with a scientific research facility in system L-374. We'd like you to check it out."

"Can you tell me what the nature of their research is?"

"It's all in the briefing packet I'm sending now," Admiral Sulu said. "It's an old research facility that's been studying an ancient derelict spaceship. You're to depart as soon as possible."

"Right away, Admiral," I said, again not really sure if I could leave.

"Sulu out," the admiral said, and the picture went off. I then called Scully on the intercom.

"Scully here," he said.

"How much longer to complete all the repairs and upgrades?" I said.

"We're done with some stuff, but there's still more I'd like to do. How much time do I have?"

"About ten minutes," I said. "Sorry."

"All right," he said, with a heavy sigh. "I can do some of it on the fly after we go, but before we leave I'm going to have to reconnect the conn and op controls. And I won't be able to do anything about the engine circuit upgrades, so don't make me go too fast. Scully out." It was clear that this was a large inconvenience, but Scully never complained. I was about to read the briefing packet when the door chimed. I opened it to find Guinan.

"Guinan, I'm a little busy…"

"I won't take too much of your time," she said. "I just wanted to say goodbye." This shouldn't have come as a surprise; she wasn't a member of the crew, and all she had asked of me was to take her to the starbase. Still, I was very disappointed.

"Are you sure? You are welcome to stay aboard."

"Thanks, but I don't really have a job here," she said. "And there isn't one I really want."

"What would you like to do?"

"I don't know, tend bar?" I smiled at the joke.

"Well," I said, "in that case, I have something for you." I pulled out a bottle of Aldebaran whiskey. "For the bar you eventually tend."

"Where'd you get this?"

"Mazzara gave it to me," I said. "But it was from a case that I think he stole from Laughton, so it belongs to you anyway."

"Thanks."

"Where will you go?"

"Oh, I'll be here and there. Don't worry, you and I will run into each other again." She smiled, and, just like on that first day I met her, it seemed like she was engaging in some private joke. She gave me a hug. "Thanks again for saving my life."

"You're welcome," I said, and she left. I sat back down.

She was probably one of the most unique personalities I'd ever met. Her presence had a strange calming effect on me, and I was sorry that there wasn't a place for her in my crew. I was sorry we didn't have a bar on the ship.

I looked back at the briefing packet on my viewscreen to familiarize myself with the mission ahead, as I tapped the button for the intercom.

"Picard to Bridge," I said, "stand by to leave orbit."

✦

"Dock command signaling clear, sir," Black said.

I was in my chair, but that was about the only thing considerably different from the previous day. A lot of control panels were still open, and a lot of crewmen had their heads inside them. But we had to leave. Jack Crusher was at the conn, Walker at ops, and Engineer Scully was lying on the floor between them, working underneath their stations.

"Set course for system L-374, Mr. Crusher," I said.

"Uh, sir, I don't have any helm or navigation control..."

"Just one more second, sir," Scully said. "Okay, try it now..." Crusher operated his controls.

"Still nothing, sir," Crusher said. My first moments on the bridge as captain were off to a terrible start.

"Oh, okay, got it now," Scully said. "You're good to go..." Crusher tried the controls again.

"Course plotted, sir," Crusher said.

"Engage," I said. On the viewscreen, Tagan III fell away, and we leapt to warp. The stars streamed by. And then the inertial dampeners strained, and we all were pulled forward as the ship came to a sudden stop.

"Report!" I said.

"We're no longer at warp," Crusher said.

"That much is clear," I said.

"That was me, that was me," Scully said. "Sorry, okay, here we go..." The screen changed again as we went back to warp. I held my breath, waiting for another breakdown, but it didn't come.

"On course for system L-374," Crusher said. "ETA 47.9 hours."

"Communications," I said. "Put the image I sent to you up on the main screen."

"Aye, sir," Black said. On the main viewscreen the image of a kilometers-long structure hung in space, a dark tube with an immense mouth on one end, tapering to a point on the other. Its immense size was apparent by how it dwarfed the three starship tugs hanging near it. I got out of my chair and walked near the screen.

"What is that?" Walker said. I was about to answer when someone did it for me.

"That's the planet-killer, isn't it?" It was Jack Crusher. I was impressed that he recognized it.

"Yes," I said. "About eighty years ago that machine entered Federation space and destroyed four solar systems."

"How?" Walker said. I turned to Crusher.

"Ensign?"

"It used an anti-proton beam to destroy planets and ingest the debris from those planets for fuel. It was very difficult to destroy because its hull is solid neutronium." Once Crusher said that, there were sounds of recognition from the rest of the bridge crew. This object, made out of the ultra-dense matter that exists in the center of a neutron star, was part of academy legends.

"Okay, this is coming back to me," Walker said. "Kirk stopped it, right?" I nodded. The planet-killer had all but destroyed the starship *Constellation*, though it had left its impulse engines functional. Kirk himself had driven the wrecked ship inside the deadly machine and beamed off just before blowing up the *Constellation*'s impulse engines. It was one of the many swashbuckling stories of Starfleet's most famous captain that had inspired generations of cadets.

"The object was immobilized," I said. "And for the last eighty years Federation scientists had been studying it in system L-374, trying to unlock the secrets of its construction. Yesterday, Starfleet lost contact with the science team, and now there's heavy subspace interference in the area."

"The neutronium itself is the cause of the interference," Crusher said. "The science team used signal boosters to counter it. They must be malfunctioning."

"Or destroyed," Scully said. I'd forgotten about him, still lying on the deck with his head under the conn and ops consoles. But he had hit Starfleet's concern—that someone had decided to steal the planet-killer. Still, there was no proof of that.

"The *Stargazer* is the closest ship available," I said. "We're going to see what's going on, so let's not jump to conclusions. However, Number One, schedule some battle drills."

"Who's 'Number One'?" Walker said. He was serious and I realized I'd unconsciously adopted Mazzara's penchant for that nickname. It was an interesting lesson to me; you could cherry-pick aspects of someone's command style even if you disdained them as a whole. I enjoyed that Mazzara had called me "Number One," a charming relic of the days of sail.

"That's you," I said.

It would take two days to reach our destination, so I tried to give Scully as much help to complete the repairs and upgrades as possible without compromising other ship's functions. However, it would turn out we wouldn't have the full two days; about ten hours from our destination, sensors picked up the planet-killer, moving at warp speed.

"How is that possible?" I said.

"I don't know," Walker said. "I thought Kirk destroyed its engines."

"It's on a course away from us," Crusher said.

"Heading?"

"It's a precise heading for the planet Romulus." That gave me pause. The Romulans? The Federation had not heard from them in decades. Had they snuck into Federation space to steal this artifact? It seemed unlikely. But I had a more pressing problem.

"We need to intercept it before it enters the Neutral Zone,'" I said.

"Its speed is warp 5.9," Crusher said. "To catch it before it reaches the Neutral Zone, we'll have to go to warp 8.3." Engineer Scully would not be pleased, but I didn't see that I had a choice. I couldn't risk pursuing it into Romulan space, even if they were the ones stealing it.

We changed course, and after a few hours we closed in on the behemoth. When we were in visual range, we were able to determine how it was able to travel at warp: it had a large girdle built around it, with two warp engines attached.

"That's Starfleet equipment," Walker said. "The Federation science team must have had the Corps of Engineers build it so they could move the thing." I noticed an engineering compartment at the base of the engines.

"Scan for life signs," I said.

"One human, very faint," Walker said.

"All right," I said. "We'll have to beam aboard and try to ascertain what is going on."

---

*EDITOR'S NOTE: Picard's concern about entering the Neutral Zone dates back to the treaty negotiated at the end of the Romulan War in 2160. The Neutral Zone was a border area between the Federation and Romulan Empire. The treaty states that entry into it by either Federation or Romulan ships constituted an act of war.

"If the Romulans are responsible," Walker said, "it's possible there's a cloaked ship nearby that we can't detect." The Romulans, the last time Starfleet had seen them, had perfected their ability to "cloak" their ships from Starfleet detection devices. No doubt in the intervening years their technology had continued to improve.

"I'm still not sure why the Romulans would risk this," I said.

"Even with no power," Crusher said, "it is a formidable weapon. Send it into a system at warp speed and it might be difficult to stop before it crashes into an adversary's planet. The destruction from such an impact would be catastrophic." I wasn't that impressed with Crusher's theory, because it neglected the obvious.

"Stealing it and taking it back to their homeworld?" I said. "We would know they had stolen it. What do they gain from such a bold move?" I needed more answers.

"Scully to Bridge," Scully said on the intercom. I knew what this was about.

"Yes, Engineer," I said, anticipating his demand, "I know we've got to slow down…"

"And soon," he said, "or we're all going to be a big pile of scrap metal."

"I understand, Picard out." I checked our distance from the Neutral Zone; we had maybe twenty minutes. I turned to Walker. "We need to regain control of that ship. Mr. Crusher, you're with me." It was a difficult thing, after acquiring a ship of my own, to then leave it in someone else's hands. But I felt like I had to solve this problem myself.

"You have the bridge, Number One," I said.

With Security Chief Cheva and Dr. Ailat, Mr. Crusher and I beamed into the engineering compartment. It was clean and efficient, a series of control panels surrounding a warp reactor. Dr. Ailat took out her tricorder.

"The life sign is over here," Ailat said. Cheva and Ailat led the way and we found a human in a Starfleet engineer's uniform. He was unconscious, lying in a pool of his own blood.

"He's been stabbed repeatedly," Ailat said. She immediately got to work, using her three hands to treat and close the wounds.

"Stabbed?" I said. "With what?" Cheva had her phaser out. Crusher meanwhile was checking the control panels. Ailat's hands glided from her patient to her medical bag and back; she spoke to me without looking up.

"Difficult to determine at this stage," Ailat said. "I will have to do more study at a later time." I went over to Crusher.

"Sir, the controls are locked out," he said. "I can't shut down the engines or adjust the course or speed."

"*Stargazer* to Picard," came Walker's voice over my communicator.

"Go ahead," I said.

"Engineer Scully apologizes, but he reports we have about ten seconds before he has to take us out of warp, or the engines will overload." This was not very convenient. If the *Stargazer* dropped out of warp, the planet-killer would leave it behind, and it would be almost impossible for it to catch up. I quickly went through my options, and decided I had to stay on board.

"Beam back the rest of the away team and Dr. Ailat's patient."

"Request permission to stay on board," Cheva and Crusher said in unison.

"Denied," I said.

"Sir, I think I can stop this thing," Crusher said. He had a very earnest look, and since the only idea I had was firing my phaser into the warp core and possibly blowing myself up, I decided he was worth the gamble.

"All right," I said. "*Stargazer*, beam back Cheva, Ailat, and her patient." After a moment, the three of them disappeared.

"Picard to *Stargazer*, do you have them?" There was no answer. I assumed, hoped, they had made it before my ship had to drop out of warp. In any event, Crusher and I were by ourselves.

"Enlighten me, Ensign. What is your plan?"

"I've done some calculations," he said, "and I think the reason this thing is going warp 5.9 is that the structural integrity of the girdle pushing such a large mass won't handle a higher speed."

"You said we couldn't adjust the course or speed."

"Not with these controls, but we could use our phasers to open up the plasma injectors to increase our speed. I estimate at warp 6.2 the girdle will crack and we'll drop out of warp drive." What he was proposing was very dangerous.

"Did you do all these calculations in your head?"

"Yes," he said. Now I was starting to be impressed.

After a brief conversation about our procedure, we took our phasers, and each went into a Jefferies tube leading to each of the two engines. I found the plasma injectors, and programmed my phaser to fire automatically for one nanosecond on an extremely tight beam. I had to fire several pinprick shots to put extra holes in the injector so that more plasma could flow out of it, but if my phaser stayed on a millisecond too long, the beam would hit the plasma and ignite it, and I'd be consumed in a radioactive fire. I took careful aim, and fired the shots. The phaser went on and off automatically; there were now three almost microscopic openings in the injector. More plasma started to flow out of it, and after a brief moment the Jefferies tube began to vibrate. I climbed out and rejoined Crusher in the engineering compartment, who was already at the controls.

"It's working," he said. "Our speed's increased to warp 6.1... 6.2..." We heard the creaking and groaning of straining metal. Crusher checked his board. "Structural integrity at forty-three percent... twenty-eight..."

"Hang on..."

There was a loud crack that reverberated through the room. The room went dark and we were thrown forward over the console to the deck. I hit my head on something, and in my mind I saw myself on the floor of my family's basement all those years before...

✦

"Captain... Captain..." My vision cleared and I was looking up at Ailat. Emergency lighting was on, and her orange skin was bathed in red, making a color I couldn't quite recognize.

"Crusher?" I said.

"I'm fine, sir," he said. I looked to see he was standing with Cheva and Walker.

"You did it, sir," Walker said. "The planet-killer dropped out of warp just short of the Neutral Zone."

"Crusher's idea," I said, and pulled myself up. I looked hard at Walker.

"You all right, sir?"

"Yes, I'm just wondering who the hell is in command of my ship?"

Later, back on the *Stargazer*, the crewman we rescued, an engineer by the name of Lounsbery, had recovered. Walker and I interviewed him in sickbay, but unfortunately he had little information to offer.

"I didn't see whoever it was," Lounsbery said from his sickbed. "I was alone on the graveyard shift. I'd received word from our base that our long-range communication array had been sabotaged. Then someone stabbed me and the next thing I knew I was here." I told him to get some rest then went to talk to Ailat in her small office attached to the exam room.

"Any more indication of what the weapon was?"

"It was an efficient blade designed to cause a great deal of damage," Ailat said.

"Could it be a *d'k tahg*?" I said.

"The wounds are consistent with such a weapon," Ailat said.

"A Klingon weapon?" Walker seemed dubious. "They stole the planet-killer for the Romulans? Why would they bother?"

"They weren't stealing it," I said. "They were doing what Ensign Crusher proposed it might be used for, sending it at high warp on a collision course to Romulus." I could see that Walker was putting it together.

"And making it look like we did it," he said.

"Even if the Romulans had been able to stop it," I said, "they would've responded with an attack on the Federation."

"And even though *we* stopped it," Walker said, "we don't have any evidence that the Klingons are responsible."

"Lounsbery's stab wounds. Hardly conclusive." I would make a report to Starfleet, but there was little to be done. The Federation had been engaged in peace talks with the Klingons for sixty years. The alliance was never a solid one, always on the verge of falling into conflict. And it was becoming clear that the Klingons weren't really interested in peace. It appeared that they were looking to ignite a deadly Galactic war. They would even resort to subterfuge to gain an early advantage—putting the Federation in conflict with the Romulans would do that quite nicely.

"At least one good thing that came out of this," Walker said.

"What's that?"

"You gotta like that Crusher kid," he said.

He was right, I did.

✦

Out of the blocks on that first mission, I learned some very important lessons. 1) Lean on your officers. If I hadn't had Crusher with me, I'm not sure I would have come up with a solution that left me alive. And 2) Don't lie to your admiral about the condition of your ship. I was fortunate that our next assignment was a general star-mapping mission of an unexplored region so we had breathing room for Scully to finish a good portion of the upgrades and repairs. I settled into a routine and soon found myself exploring what kind of commanding officer I wanted to be.

There are many different types of captains. Some find it most effective to govern their ships with a god-like detachment. But given my age and relative inexperience, I found myself approaching my role less a master and more a servant. The needs of the crew were foremost on my mind, and the best way to learn about those needs was through conversation. I enjoyed walking my ship from stem to stern for at least an hour, if not longer, every day. During these walking tours I'd talk to fifty or so crewmembers, giving me an up-to-date snapshot of what was occurring below decks. Unfortunately, my daily walkabouts led to an increasing pile of administrative work left undone, which I eventually left in the hands of my first officer. Walker complained sarcastically, though I rationalized he was getting his own education on the requirements of being a captain.

As time went on, I learned whose opinions I could rely on and constructed a web of crewmen throughout the *Stargazer* who gave me a good gauge of where problems might arise. Along with Walker, Scully, Crusher, and Cheva, I relied on a junior officer working in the torpedo bay named Ensign Vigo, who seemed to trade in the most intimate levels of gossip and helped me avoid management difficulties with his extensive knowledge of the state of the crew. Ironically, the ship's designated personnel officer, Lieutenant Felson, was too formal with me and seemed uncomfortable sharing what she considered unseemly personal details. The walkabouts also let me know where there were technological challenges, which we had in abundance.

I became increasingly comfortable as captain of the ship, which in turn, made my crew more comfortable. With Laughton and Mazzara gone, the vessel was alive with a new atmosphere—I could see it as the crew went about their duties. I soon allowed myself the luxury of friendships. A trio of sorts formed: Walker Keel, myself, and, surprisingly, Jack Crusher. I began to identify with him; he was like a different version of me, as if the bookish intellectual I'd been in my youth had been encouraged, and I'd avoided becoming the ego-driven teenager whose arrogance almost got him killed.

Stargazer moved into an unexplored region of the Alpha Quadrant. Much of our time was spent exploring systems with no sign of advanced technology, and over the next year or two we catalogued dozens of planets and countless forms of life. The ship, unlike the *Reliant*, had better scientific facilities, which Walker oversaw as part of his operations duties. I became quite proud of the work I was doing, and it went to my head. I fell into the trap early on that some starship captains had: I began to see myself as infallible.

"The asteroid is 3.2 kilometers in diameter," Crusher said. "It will strike the planet in less than a day." We were in an uncharted system, formerly designated HD 150248, and discovered an asteroid on course to impact the fifth planet in orbit, Class M. I ordered a scan of the planet.

✦

"That asteroid…" I didn't have to finish the question. Everyone knew what I was asking.

"It will exterminate all life on the planet," Crusher said.

"The poor inhabitants won't even know what hit them," Walker said.

"Can we divert it?"

"It's too late," Walker said. "Too close to the planet."

"Any signs of civilization?" I said.

"Yes, primitive, fifth-century Earth equivalent, agrarian. Spread across the northern continent," Walker said.

"I want to take a look." I could see that some of the bridge crew were uneasy at this suggestion. Walker stepped over to me.

"Jean-Luc, it's too dangerous," he whispered.

"We should have some record of this," I said. "Some memory of who these people are." Walker wasn't happy, but he wasn't going to disobey an order.

✦

I had the transporter put me and the away team down on a hill overlooking a village and some surrounding farms. It was me, Cheva, and Jack Crusher. We hid at the edge of a vast forest, over 4,000 kilometers square, out of sight of the natives. Cheva scanned for possible approaches by native life, while Crusher and I used our recording binoculars to film some evidence of this civilization that was about to die.

"They're bipeds," Crusher said. "The village seems to be some kind of fortress."

"No doubt," I said, "providing temporary shelter in case of approaching enemy hordes."

"I think I found a farmer," Crusher said. I looked where he was pointing and could see a stocky creature tilling the soil with some sort of plow.

"Captain," Cheva said, "picking up life signs approaching. We should go."

"Hey," Crusher said, "he's got an assistant." I watched as the stocky creature was joined by another that looked very similar, only a good deal smaller.

"Not an assistant," I said. "A son."

"Assuming they're male," Cheva said. Her point was well taken, but I was lost in a memory. I was a child, following my father out in the vineyard, helping him plant the grapes. A few brief minutes, just my father and me—no Robert. I had forgotten there were such moments…

"Sir," Cheva said, "they're closing in…" She indicated to the left of us a group of four of the local inhabitants, about 100 meters away. They carried spears, and moved cautiously toward us.

"All right, let's go," I said. We stepped into the forest, and as Cheva had us beamed up, I watched through our recording binoculars as the farmer placed his child up on his shoulders.

"We've got to do something," I said. I could see from his expression that Walker had now decided I was certifiable.

"Jean-Luc, it's about to enter the atmosphere…"

"We have a responsibility to try," I said.

"Sir," Crusher said. "The Prime Directive specifically states we can't interfere with the natural evolution of a society…"

"It's a captain's prerogative to interpret the Prime Directive," I said. "I don't think it applies here. This society should have a chance to survive to evolve naturally."

"Mass extinctions play a large role in evolution," Crusher said.

"We're not going to discuss this further," I said. "I want to try to cut the asteroid into smaller pieces."

"If we'd gotten here a week ago, we might've had a shot. But now…"

"Walker," I said, "that's an order." I ordered an analysis of the asteroid and its possible weak spots and found myself growing optimistic that we would succeed. Crusher and Cheva targeted phasers and photon torpedoes.

"Weapons locked," Cheva said.

"Fire," I said. We watched on screen as *Stargazer*'s weapons tore into the large rock, breaking it up. Cheva aimed the weapons, slicing pieces into smaller and smaller chunks. Dust from the debris filled our view.

"The debris is interfering with our targeting sensors," Cheva said. "I can't maintain a lock anymore…"

We hadn't done nearly enough to reduce the size of the asteroid. There were still too many large pieces that would cause catastrophic damage. If they hit land they would bring up enormous amounts of ash and dust, blocking out radiation from the sun and causing an "impact winter." The global temperature would drop, causing a mass extinction. I stepped over to the weapons console.

"Let me take over," I said. Cheva quickly got up, and I sat at the console. I switched the targeting sensor off, brought up a real-time view of the debris, then opened the switch to fire the phasers and held it open. It was an excessive use of phaser power; I used it like a knife, slicing back and forth through the remaining pieces. Eventually, the *Stargazer*'s phasers powered down; I'd completely drained them.

"You've done it, sir," Crusher said. I went back to the captain's chair and watched as the hundreds of pieces of asteroid began their descent through the atmosphere. There were some larger pieces, but nothing that would cause the catastrophic damage that the original would have. I was feeling quite proud of myself. I could see that Walker, however, wasn't sharing my optimism.

"The forest…" he said. I didn't initially understand what he was implying. Walker then changed the viewscreen to feature this grand stretch of trees, and it dawned on me.

From even a high orbit I could see flaming debris striking across the length and breadth of the 4,000 square kilometer woodland. Within minutes, a wall of flame stretched across and kept growing. I realized that it would have the same effect as if the asteroid had impacted whole: soot and ash from a fire that was impossible to extinguish would fill the atmosphere and block out the sun. The mass extinction would happen anyway.

A species would die that I'd felt I had gotten to know through one moment of joy between a father and son.

✦

"Sensors are picking up a ship," Walker said.

"Let's see it," I said. On the viewer, a small, scout-sized craft. Its engines were forward of the ship, and the general shape of it reminded me of a hammerhead shark. It was drifting, plasma leaking from one of its engines.

"Two life signs," Walker said. "Unknown species, but if they're oxygen breathers they're in trouble. I'm reading minimal life support."

"Hail them," I said.

"No response, sir," Black said. I did not have a lot of experience dealing with adversarial situations, but I was on guard. Despite the apparent helplessness of the vessel, its design appeared predatory.

"Shields up, Mr. Crusher," I said. "Then move us in closer." The *Stargazer* moved within a few hundred meters. There was no change in the other ship. I told Black to put me on a hailing frequency.

"Unidentified ship, this is Captain Jean-Luc Picard of the *U.S.S. Stargazer*, we stand ready to assist." I waited, still no answer.

"Sir, it's possible they don't understand us," said Crusher. "Our universal translator works by comparing frequencies of brainwave patterns, or by processing language that it's hearing. If the aliens are unconscious, it's possible the universal translator doesn't have enough information to translate your hail."

"And if they haven't developed the universal translator yet," I said, continuing his thought, "they're hearing gibberish." There was, however, no way to prove this was what was happening. The ship could still be laying some sort of trap.

"I advise caution, sir," Cheva said. "The damage and radiation signatures seem consistent with the ship being in proximity to an exploding impulse engine. I'd say they've seen some action." Though she echoed my concern, I was still left with no choice.

"Bridge to Dr. Ailat, report to the transporter room." I couldn't bring the survivors on board without knowing who they were, but I also couldn't ignore people possibly in distress. "Cheva, Crusher, you're with me. Number One, drop shields long enough to beam us over."

"Sir, may I remind the captain…"

"I know, I'm not supposed to go on away missions," I said. "But I'm going."
Walker had given up fighting me on this. The captain was supposed to stay on
the bridge, and the first officer was supposed to lead the away missions. But I
had only served as a first officer for a little over a month, so I still enjoyed the
hands-on experience.

Dr. Ailat, Cheva, Crusher, and I beamed over to the small scout vessel. We
found the two crewmen, both unconscious, with lacerations and burns. They
had pronounced ridges on their heads and neck, giving them an almost
reptilian look. They wore matching armor; they were definitely part of a
military. Ailat scanned them.

"They are alive, though their internal systems are unfamiliar," she said.

"Can you help them?"

"I believe so," Ailat said. "Their unconsciousness seems to have been
caused by severe concussions."

"That would be consistent with the damage to the craft," Cheva said.

"Very well," I said. I had Dr. Ailat beamed back with the two survivors,
while Crusher, Cheva, and I continued to examine the ship. It was very small;
there was only one crew quarter, presumably for the commander—it had
framed medals on the wall. There was a bridge and an engineering
compartment. Every other available bit of space was used for storage.

We then set out to understand the workings of their machinery. The
language of the control panels was unfamiliar, but our scans of the systems told
us they were consistent with a level of technology close to our own. This is
where my background in archaeology was helpful; I'd been taught by Professor
Galen how to translate ancient languages of lost civilizations by finding a key.
If said civilization had a developed understanding of mathematics and science,
all you needed was to find some written example of a constant, like pi or the
speed of light, or even better the periodic table of elements, and with the help
of a computer the whole language could be deciphered. This was much simpler
on a spaceship with advanced equipment scanning the heavens around it.

"Sir, I think I found something." Crusher was looking at a display. "This
is measuring radiation… see, there's the *Stargazer*'s engines, and that graph
there must be background radiation." He was right, and we were able to use
this as a basis for our language key. Once we could translate the displays, we

would be able to make a determination of damage to the ship. Cheva, meanwhile, was taking stock of the armaments and defensive capabilities, as well as examining their handguns. Their energy weapons were less technologically advanced but quite durable and probably very deadly (there didn't seem to be a stun setting).

We then returned to the *Stargazer*. Walker met us at the transporter room, and the two of us then went to sickbay to see to our guests, who were awake. Two security guards stood by the door.

"I am Glinn Hovat," one of them said. The universal translator had had enough time to translate their spoken language. The posture and bearing of this being told me he was in command; what helped to confirm it was that his companion did not attempt to speak. What I'd seen on the other ship—their weapons and medals indicating a martial philosophy—made me suitably wary of them.

"I'm Captain Jean-Luc Picard," I said. "You're aboard the Federation ship *Stargazer*."

"I demand you release us immediately," Glinn Hovat said, "or you will face serious consequences."

"You are not our prisoners," I said.

"Oh?" Glinn Hovat said. "The presence of the guards would indicate otherwise." I smiled; this was a shrewd man. I could tell from the aggressiveness of his remarks that he was testing me and my resolve.

"Glinn Hovat, forgive me," I said, "but I am forced to take precautions. That includes not letting strangers have free run of my ship."

"What is the status of my vessel?"

"Life support is still operational," I said. "But our unfamiliarity with your systems and language make it difficult to tell the extent of the damage." I was lying to him, in an effort to gain some advantage. But it was clear I was failing; this man didn't believe a word I was saying. "Can you tell me what happened to it?"

"Captain... Picard was it? You are strangers to us, and you understand I am forced to take precautions. That includes not telling you events that may be classified." He was throwing my cautious attitude back at me, and I would now get nowhere with him. I had begun badly, and now there was no way back.

"Well, yes, but..." I fumbled, trying to find some way to keep him talking, but he wasn't interested.

"Thank you for rescuing us, but if you will allow us to leave, we must return to our ship." I turned to Ailat, hoping the plea in my expression would tell her I wanted them to stay longer, but she either didn't read it or didn't care.

"I would recommend rest," Ailat said, "but they appear to have recovered from their wounds."

"Very well," I said. "Are you sure there isn't anything else I can do for you?"

"Yes," he said, after a brief pause, "I'd like a glass of water."

"A… glass of…?"

"Your doctor was kind enough to give me one earlier, and I'd like another." I don't know why this seemed like a very strange request, but it was. There was no reason to refuse. Dr. Ailat didn't wait for my permission; she went to the wall replicator, made the request, and a glass of water appeared. I noticed Hovat watching intently as Ailat brought it back to him. He took a healthy sip, and then asked to be taken back to his ship.

A few hours later on the bridge, we watched on the viewscreen as the small ship's engines came back online.

"Those guys must have been working nonstop," Walker said. "The damage report you brought back was pretty extensive."

"The place was packed with spare parts," Cheva said.

"Why would they carry so many spare parts?" Walker said. "If they had replicators, much of what they'd need…"

"Wait," I said. "Did you notice a replicator?"

"Oh," Cheva said. "No, you're right, I didn't." We'd missed an important piece of information in taking stock of that ship. Then I looked at Walker.

"You remember the glass of water?" Walker realized what I was getting at.

"He wasn't thirsty, he wanted to see the replicator in action again." We turned and looked at the screen. The ship moved away and leapt to warp.

"If that's the case," Crusher said, "then they're very dangerous."

"What do you mean, Mr. Crusher?"

"Replicator technology eliminated need on planet Earth," Crusher said. "A lot of exploration previous to the invention of the replicator was about the hunt for resources. That invention more than any other helped make us a peaceful society."

"And without one," I said, "a society might be more aggressive."

"They'd have to be," Crusher said. "Without replicators, space travel is very expensive. And resources are never freely given by anyone." The message was clear to everyone in the room. We may just have discovered a new adversary. I was constantly impressed with Jack Crusher's view of the Galaxy. It challenged me to be more thoughtful. I was lucky to have him in my crew.

"Did they ever tell us the name of their species?" Walker said. We never asked them because Crusher had discovered it while searching the ship.

"Those medals framed on a wall in the quarters," Crusher said. "I translated the inscriptions. They all read: 'For the glory of Cardassia.' They're Cardassians."

✦

"Go and talk to her," I said to Jack Crusher. He, Walker, and I sat at a bar on Sigma Iotia II. Across the room was a young woman around Crusher's age, sipping an elaborate cocktail and occasionally looking our way. The bar was called The Feds, and the woman, as well as everyone else in the place, was in a 23rd-century Starfleet uniform, or a close approximation of one. In fact, just about everyone on the planet was dressed that way. And none of them were actually in Starfleet.

"I think Jean-Luc is right," Walker said. "She looks interested."

"They're always interested in the real ones," Crusher said. He was a little insecure when it came to women, although in this case, he was right: actual Starfleet officers were considered something of celebrities on this world, which was one reason why it was such a popular shore leave destination.

"How did this place get like this?" Crusher said.

"Oh, no," Walker said. "Why are you going to bring that up? Now we're going to have to listen to another Starfleet legend..."

"It's an amazing tale," I said. "A starship discovers the planet, which, a century earlier, had been contaminated by its exposure to the history of 20th-century Earth. Everyone on the planet acting like Al Capone..."

"Who's Al Capone?" Crusher said.

"This is going to take forever..." Walker said.

"It's not," I said, though I'd had a few drinks and was having a little trouble staying succinct. This was true alcohol, and though I'd been raised on it, I hadn't had much since I'd left home. "Now, where was I... oh, yes, so, the starship shows up and tries to fix the contamination, but all that happened was that he *altered* the contamination… but he saved these people by doing that…"

"So instead of pretending they're El Cabone…"

"Al Capone."

"Al Cabone, instead everyone pretends they're in Starfleet," Crusher said. "That's better?"

"It is," I said. "Much better. They used to kill each other every day; now their focus is on education, diversity, and a brighter future. That's what a captain's supposed to do, fix things…" I'd had too much to drink, but I was enjoying myself. During my lecture however, I'd failed to notice the woman making her way over until she was already talking to Jack.

"I was wondering if we could have a drink," she said, looking him in the eye. He smiled.

"I'm here with my friends," he said. "Sorry." She shrugged and walked off. Walker slapped his palm into his forehead.

"What the hell, Jack?"

"Guys," Crusher said, "I'm not going to meet the woman I want to spend the rest of my life with in a fake Starfleet bar on some nutty planet." Through my liquored haze, I admired this grounded but also romantic view of the world. He did not need womanizing conquests to buttress his self-esteem. It made me think that perhaps I was the insecure one. The thought faded, and I decided to resume my good time.

"Another round!" I shouted to the bartender.

✦

"The government of Tzenketh is accusing us of spying on them," Admiral Sulu said. "They say they've captured a Federation insertion team, and that they're going to execute them."

"*Are* we spying on them?" It was an obvious question, though it seemed to catch Admiral Sulu off guard. She was tightly framed on the viewscreen in my quarters, and I noticed that she glanced away; there must be someone else in her office. She quickly looked back at me.

"Whoever they have captured are not Federation spies," she said. She hadn't quite answered the question, but there was no need for me to pursue it.

"We need you to go there immediately, Jean-Luc. They've specifically asked for *Stargazer* to parlay for their release."

"Really? Do we know why?"

"*Stargazer* made first contact ten years ago, that might have something to do with it. Check your former captain's logs. But above all, you need to get those hostages out safely."

"I understand, Admiral."

"I'm not sure you do," she said. "You've got to get them out *with* the permission of the Tzenkethi government. No rescues—we need to keep the peace."

"Yes, Admiral," I said, and then we signed off. I called the bridge and ordered Walker to set a course for Tzenketh, while I stayed in my quarters and did some research.

Captain Laughton's logs contained some information on the Tzenkethi, all of which was now part of the Federation database. They had an unusual appearance for bipeds: they had four arms—two for strength and two smaller ones for more meticulous work. Their skin resembled a rhinoceros hide and their heads were similar to that of a hadrosaur, with a large duckbill sweeping back behind them. They were fierce creatures who had managed to venture out into space and achieved warp drive shortly before *Stargazer*'s encounter with them. But on the subject of the events of the actual first contact, Laughton's logs were disappointingly sparse. There were no clues as to why the Tzenkethi would ask for the *Stargazer*.

I went to the bridge and informed the command crew of our mission. We were still an hour away from the Tzenkethi system when Crusher picked up three of their ships closing in on our position.

"Their speed is warp 6," he said. I turned to Walker.

"When *Stargazer* discovered them ten years ago, they were only capable of warp 2," I said. I'd just read that in Laughton's log.

"Maybe we *should* be spying," Walker said.

"Captain," Cheva said, "they're locking weapons. Looks like they've got disruptor cannons…"

"Shields up," I said.

"Their ships had projectile weapons back then, too," Walker said.

"Curiouser and curiouser," I said. I got a strange look from Crusher. "It's from *Alice in Wonderland*." His expression told me he'd never heard of it.

"Receiving a message, sir," Black said. "Audio only. They're ordering us to follow them to orbit."

"Acknowledge the message," I said. "Crusher, follow them in. Lieutenant Cheva, conduct a discreet scan of those ships. I want as much information as you can get."

We followed the ships into a standard orbit, and I was almost immediately talking to the leader of their world, called the Autarch, named Sulick. His large head nearly filled the viewscreen. He wore a gold helmet that fit over the duckbill on top of his skull. The image was both frightening and comical.

"We have your spies, Federation," Sulick said.

"I can assure you, Autarch Sulick, they are not spies."

"They were digging a secret base to carry out attacks on us. They thought by choosing a forgotten part of our land we wouldn't detect them." Digging a base? This didn't provide me any clues as to who the prisoners might be.

"What did they say they were doing when you caught them?"

"Their lies matter not," Sulick said. I had to cut to the meat of things.

"Sulick, what can I do to secure their release?"

"We will trade the spies for Laughton," Sulick said. I exchanged a look with Walker. That's why they asked for *Stargazer*, and they didn't know that Laughton was dead.

"Why do you want Laughton?"

"I was commander of the ship that met Laughton when he was here. He will know why I want him," Sulick said. "Once he is here, you may have your hostages."

"And if Laughton cannot come to you?"

"Then they are dead."

"I will get back to you shortly." I gave Black the cut sign, and Sulick disappeared from the screen.

"You can't lie to them," Walker said.

"I know," I said. "But if I tell the truth, that Laughton's dead, there's a good chance they'll think I'm lying and kill whoever it is they have down there." I needed more information about what happened when the *Stargazer* visited the first time. It was then I remembered that there was one crewmember on board who might be able to fill in some of the blanks. I ordered Scully to come to the bridge.

"Stupid, mean creatures," Scully said. "How they ever got into space is beyond me. Their ship was two hundred years behind ours, but they came at us guns blazing."

"What did the captain do?" I said.

"Laughed at 'em," Scully said. "He let them fire off all their projectile weapons, and once they bounced off our shields, he figured they'd be more willing to talk."

"Were they?" I said. Scully laughed.

"Nope," Scully said. "So the captain decided to have a little fun with them. He locked onto the ship with a tractor beam and took it for a ride. See, their ships were maybe capable of warp 2—that day they broke the warp 5 barrier." It was unlikely that a primitive warp ship could internally handle that speed; the crew was undoubtedly bounced around, if not worse. I'd come to accept that Laughton lived by a different set of rules than most starship captains yet was also always surprised how far he'd taken things.

"Fun with them?" Walker said. "He completely humiliated them."

"And unlucky for us, the captain of that ship is now in charge," I said. There was a lot going on here: hostages being accused as spies, a considerable technological leap by a hostile species, and a mess left by my predecessor. It seemed an unwinnable situation. And then a thought occurred to me.

"Cheva, what's their sensor capability?"

"Not as advanced as ours," she said. "They can detect life signs and species. Roughly equivalent to our 22nd-century technology." That was what I needed to hear.

"Poker faces everyone," I said. "Black, open a hailing frequency." Sulick was back on the screen.

"Well, human, what is your decision?"

"Captain Laughton has agreed to turn himself over to you," I said. "In exchange for the hostages." Despite my order that everyone put on their poker faces, Walker glanced at me with some surprise. Fortunately, I don't think the Tzenkethi had the ability to read human expressions.

"Very well," Sulick said. "Have him use your transporter to beam down, then we will give you coordinates—"

"I'm afraid we need a little more of a guarantee," I said. "So Captain Laughton will board one of our shuttlecraft and leave the *Stargazer*. Once he does, you must give us the coordinates for the hostages, or he will return to the ship." I saw Sulick consider this proposal.

"Agreed," Sulick said. I had Black cut off the transmission, and briefed everyone on my plan.

Thirty minutes later, we watched a shuttlecraft leave the hangar deck and hold station a few hundred meters from *Stargazer*.

"*Shuttlecraft Tyson* to *Stargazer*, I've cleared the hangar deck." It was Laughton's voice on the intercom; it was a simple program Crusher had put into the shuttle's main computer. It duplicated Laughton's voice and gave programmed responses. There was also a transmitter on board that was fooling the Tzenkethi sensor into believing they detected a human male at the helm. Cheva reported that the Tzenkethi were scanning the shuttlecraft.

"Acknowledged," I said. "Tzenkethi vessel, transmit the hostage coordinates." There was a pause, and then Black nodded that he'd received the transmission. I had him send the coordinates to the transporter room. A short time later, Scully called from there to report the hostages were aboard.

"*Stargazer* to shuttlecraft *Tyson*," I said. "The hostages have been recovered."

"Acknowledged," Laughton's voice said.

The shuttle started to move toward the lead Tzenkethi ship, and then suddenly took a sharp turn away.

"*Shuttlecraft Tyson*," I said, "return to your course immediately, acknowledge." Then for a little more drama, "Acknowledge, damn you!" I watched as the Tzenkethi craft moved in pursuit of the shuttle, and had Black turn off the speaker.

"Make it look good, Mr. Crusher," I said. Crusher nodded. He had control of the shuttle from his console, and put the shuttle through a series of evasive maneuvers, eventually taking it out of orbit. I signaled Black to put me back on hailing frequency.

"Laughton, you'll never make it!" After Black cut me off again, I turned to Walker. "Too much?"

"We're about to see…" he said. We watched the screen as the Tzenkethi ship fired on the shuttle. It was destroyed in a single blast. After what I determined to be a pause that would convey confusion on my ship, I had Black connect us. Sulick came back on the screen.

"Sulick, I must protest this attack," I said.

"We have what we wanted, Picard," he said. "And you have what you wanted. Now withdraw." He disappeared from the screen. I smiled at my crew. "Well done, everyone. Mr. Crusher, set a course for Starbase 32."

I left the bridge to find out who the hostages were. I was very proud of myself. I'd pulled off a clever ruse that had saved innocent lives and done it with a bit of flare, like my heroes had done before me. I was becoming the kind of captain I wanted to be.

I found the hostages in sickbay, getting a physical from Ailat, and was in for another surprise.

"Mr. Picard," Professor Galen said. He was sitting on a diagnostic bed as Ailat scanned him with a medical tricorder. Three other people were there, one Vulcan female and two human men, all much younger than him.

"Professor Galen," I said. "It's a pleasure to see you." I offered a warm handshake; his response was cold and perfunctory.

"I suppose we have you to thank for our lives," he said. There was no gratitude in his voice.

"Yes," I said. I was about to tell him how we'd done it, but could see he wasn't interested, so I decided instead to satisfy my own curiosity. "What were you doing on Tzenketh?"

"During my Dinasian dig, I discovered an ancient text with a star map that, once I compensated for stellar drift, led to Tzenketh. There was an Iconian base on this planet. My team and I would have found it before we were captured by the natives."

"Did you ask for permission…?"

"Permission? For what? I wasn't coming to steal anything; I would've shared everything I discovered. I'm not Starfleet, barging in with phasers blasting." That last remark was directed at me. I realized that when I had turned down his offer all those years ago, though he hadn't shown any resentment over my decision, it was clear it had been there.

"Well," I said, "I'm glad you're all right. We'll do our best to make you comfortable while you're here."

"Thank you, Mr. Picard." I wanted to tell him it was Captain Picard but decided against it. I nodded and walked out, leaving him, and that piece of my past, behind.

CHAPTER SIX

"MOTHER IS VERY ILL," ROBERT SAID. "She may die soon."

He stared at me from the viewscreen, locked up with grief. I was in shock. She was only 68.

"What's happened?" I stared at Robert. Hard physical labor in the sunlight had caused him to age quite a bit in the fifteen years since I'd left Earth.

"Something called Irumodic Syndrome," he said. "She hasn't been herself for some time. You wouldn't know that, of course." Though his physical appearance was different, his bitterness toward me had not diminished. I also felt a pang of guilt; I had been diligent in staying in contact with Mother, but the last few months had been busy and I hadn't spoken to her.

"Fortunately, we are on our way back," I said. "I should be there in a few days."

"Very convenient for you," he said.

"How is Father?"

"How do you think? His wife is dying." I saw now that Robert had no interest in talking to me, but that familial obligation required that he call to tell me of our mother's condition. I decided to put him out of his misery.

"I will let you know when I achieve orbit," I said. "Please update me if her condition worsens." Robert nodded and the transmission ended. I then called Dr. Ailat, and asked her what she knew about Irumodic Syndrome.

"It is a neurological disorder," Ailat said. "It can have varying symptoms as it deteriorates the synaptic pathways."

"Is it always fatal?"

"Yes, though there are many cases where humans survive for many years with it. Do you know someone who has it?"

"Yes," I said, but decided not to reveal my personal reasons for asking, and signed off. I went to the bridge.

"Status?"

"On course, Captain," Walker said, "Holding at warp 6, ETA to the Sol system in 97.1 hours."

"Increase speed to warp 8," I said. Walker stared at me briefly, then gave the order. Nine years as my first officer, he knew me well enough not to ask why Robert had called, and why we were increasing speed.

Almost a decade of exploration, and we were finally heading back to Earth. The *Stargazer* under my command had been a success, and we'd been ordered home, though I wasn't exactly sure why. The ship would be in dry dock for several weeks to finally receive upgrades that had been put off since the day I took over. My hope was that I would be moving on to a new ship. I loved the *Stargazer*—it held a special place as my first command—but I was also looking forward to piloting something that wasn't always on the verge of breaking down.

A day and a half later, as we passed Saturn's familiar rings, I was reminded how much I missed Earth. I'd seen many wonders out on the Galactic rim, but the familiar planets of our home solar system offered a strange kind of comfort.

"Passing Luna," Crusher said. We passed the moon, and Earth filled our view. There was an audible sigh from the bridge crew. Home.

Spacedock gave us clearance, and we entered the huge bay. Inside, I saw something that made me gape with envy.

"Will you look at that," Black said.

"That's the *Horatio*," I said. "*Ambassador*-class vessel, fresh off the assembly line." The clean blue lines, grand saucer, and sleek engines made the *Stargazer* look like the jalopy it was. I secretly hoped that I'd be offered command of that ship.

We docked at the bay, and I knew that everyone who had relatives on Earth were anxious to disembark—given Earth's centrality in the Federation, this went for many of the non-human crew as well. Once all the ship's systems were shut down, I granted everyone but a skeleton crew shore leave.

Before he left, Walker asked to see me in private.

"I'm leaving the *Stargazer*," he said. "I've been offered a ship." He was sitting across from me in my quarters, and I was thrilled. I hadn't actually told him my plans, since I didn't know what they were, but there was no doubt in my mind that Walker deserved his own command.

"Wonderful," I said. "What ship?"

"The *Horatio*," he said. The shock must've registered on my face, and he reacted to it. "You don't think I deserve it?"

"No," I said. "Of course you do. I'll be honest, I'm envious." I was having trouble processing this; if the newest ship off the assembly line was going to my first officer, what ship would I get?

"When are you due to leave?"

"I haven't even begun to put the crew together, so I'll be here for a while," Walker said. "I won't poach anyone from *Stargazer* without checking with you first."

"Thanks," I said. "If I have to come back to this bucket, I'm going to need all the help I can get."

"I wouldn't worry. They must have big plans for you," Walker said. I supposed he was right, but given that he'd just gotten what I wanted, I couldn't imagine what those plans could be. "Now, how about joining me and Jack for a drink? There's a woman I'm going to introduce him to."

"No, thanks," I said. "I'd better get home."

I had just enough time to get to the vineyard and see my mother; the next morning I had an appointment with Admiral Hanson, who'd been promoted the year before and put in charge of Starfleet Operations. I assumed he would be giving me a new assignment.

Beaming into the La Barre station was not the sentimental experience I thought it might be. It was night in France, and as I approached the vineyard I was overcome with dread. Somehow my fifteen years out in space, all those experiences, adventures, and the maturing that came with them—or that I thought came with them—were wiped away. I was a child again.

By the time I reached the house it was one o' clock; all the lights were off except one downstairs. I entered as quietly as I could.

"You look tense, Jean-Luc," my mother said. I turned and saw her in the living room. She was fully dressed, in a bright purple and silver blouse, wearing silver earrings, her ghostly white hair perfectly coiffed up.

"Maman," I said. It was a strange tableau: one lamp on, her sitting at a table with a silver tea set.

"Come and have a cup of tea. I'll make it good and strong the way you like it. We can have a nice, long talk." She started to pour some tea into a cup. I walked over and gave her a kiss.

"Maman," I said, "how are you feeling?"

"Oh, I'm fine," she said. "Now, tell me about school."

"School?"

"Yes, school is very important to your future…" I'd read about the confusion this disease caused, but I didn't expect it. I was at a loss as to what to say.

"He's not in school," my father said. He was in his dressing gown, standing in the hallway. He looked exhausted, but I don't think he'd been asleep. "Yvette, what are you doing up?"

"I wanted to have some tea with Jean-Luc when he came home from school."

"I just said, he's not in school anymore." Father was very aggravated, impatient with what must have been a tragic situation for him. "He's a grown man."

"I know, you don't have to tell me," mother said, but her voice wavered. Then it looked like she'd started to remember. "You were in space."

"Yes, Maman," I said.

"You're the pilot… you always wanted to be the pilot…"

"Come to bed," Father said.

"I'm having tea with Jean-Luc…"

"I said come to bed!"

"We'll have tea in the morning, Maman," I said. I helped her to her feet, and my father took her hand and walked her out of the room. I sat alone in the room.

Nothing I'd seen in my years of command prepared me for this.

✦

I slept in my childhood room that night, unchanged since my departure for the academy. When I woke the next morning, I looked over my spaceship collection, and the carefully repaired NX-01, still there among the rest. I picked up a *Constellation*-class ship I'd built when I was nine, identical to the vessel

I'd been commanding for almost a decade. I had been living the dreams of my childhood, dreams that I had used to escape the unhappiness of my years in my father's house. And now I'd come home to an even harsher reality: the one person who I knew loved me was fading away.

I dressed in my uniform and went out into the kitchen to find my father and brother eating breakfast in silence.

"So, you're home," Robert said.

"Yes," I said. "Where's Mother?"

"Asleep," my father said. There was a baguette and a few wedges of cheese on a cutting board in front of them. I sat down and helped myself.

"That service of yours requires you wear a uniform to breakfast?" Robert said.

"I have to go to headquarters," I said. We continued to eat in silence. It was a strange experience. I hadn't seen either of them in 15 years. Even if there hadn't been a pall hanging over our home, they still would have had no interest in the life I had been leading. I certainly wasn't in a mood to share it.

"I'm going to request a leave of absence," I said. "I will be around more." Robert looked unaffected by this.

"Your mother will be pleased," my father said. I could forgive that he said this without the least bit of indication that it would please him as well.

"What do the doctors say about the progression of the illness?"

"It has progressed very quickly," Robert said. "They have not been optimistic." We ate in silence for a few more minutes, and then I got up.

"I will be home by dinner." Neither one said anything, and I left.

The problem with instantaneous travel by transporter on a planet is the time difference, so I arrived in San Francisco the night before, and had time to kill before my morning meeting with the Admiral. I wandered the city for a few hours, then headed to Starfleet Headquarters. Entering the Archer Building in my uniform, surrounded by members of my service, I was more at home than I had been at breakfast at home. I found my way to the top floor of the building, occupied by the offices of the Admiralty, where a yeoman escorted me to Admiral Hanson's office. When he saw me he practically bounded from the other side of his desk.

"Jean-Luc, get yourself in here," he said, shaking my hand. "How 'bout some coffee?" I said yes, and the yeoman brought in a tray with coffee and sandwiches. The admiral dismissed the yeoman and poured the coffee himself. I was a little taken aback by the attentiveness. It had all the warmth that had been missing from my own father.

"I've been keeping tabs on you," Hanson said, as he handed me a cup. "I'm just sorry you weren't able to serve under my command so I could take more credit for all your accomplishments."

"Thank you, sir," I said. "And congratulations on your promotion."

"Well, I enjoyed being in the center seat," Hanson said, "but they need me here. I probably don't have to tell you we're facing a potentially devastating conflict..."

"The Klingons?"

Hanson nodded.

"They've increased ship production two hundred and fifty percent, and we'd had some hope of negotiating a new, more far reaching Khitomer Accord*, but they're more interested in trying to surround us with enemies. Your work has given us valuable information. Aside from that incident with the planet-killer, we have a fair amount of circumstantial evidence that they're the ones arming the Tzenkethi. And they've reaffirmed their alliance with the Romulans. The Federation could be facing a war on three fronts."

"The Romulans don't know about the incident with the planet-killer?"

"Oh, they do," Hanson said. "The Klingons told them, said rogue elements in the Federation were responsible. We were never able to find more conclusive proof of Klingon involvement, so we couldn't counter their misinformation."

This was a troublesome turn of events. I had studied war my whole life but had not experienced it. War on a galactic scale could cost billions of lives. Even Earth itself might be threatened in such a conflict.

"How does Starfleet plan to deal with this situation?"

"You're going to find all that out soon enough," Hanson said. "You have a big role in this." I had come to the office with the purpose of asking for a leave of

---

*EDITOR'S NOTE: The First Khitomer Accords, signed in 2293, established peace between the Klingon Empire and the Federation. The Second Khitomer Accords established a permanent alliance between the two governments. As of 2342 (the year Picard is writing about) negotiations had not begun.

absence to spend some more time with my mother in what might be her final year, yet the obligations of service were pulling me in another direction.

"Yes, sir," I said. "Whatever you need." How could I ask the admiral to put my own priorities above those of the Federation? The answer was, I couldn't.

"Good," he said. "I want you to be my chief of staff."

"What?"

"You'll be stationed here, and help me whip the fleet into shape. We've got a lot of work to do, and I think your experience out there will be of immeasurable help. What do you say?" My head was a mass of confusion. Hanson was offering me a compelling opportunity, the chance to help prepare Starfleet and protect the entire Federation. This work could end up shaping the quadrant for the next two decades. It also meant that I could be home for my mother.

"Of course, sir," I said. "I'd be honored."

"Great," he said. "I'd like you to start as soon as possible."

"Yes, sir," I said. I knew that this was the moment I should let him know about my personal situation, but I could not bring myself to say the words. "I still have a few things to wrap up on the *Stargazer*."

"Yes, of course," he said. "Also, I understand your mother is facing some difficult challenges. Please send her my regards. I remember meeting her at your graduation. Lovely woman."

He really had been keeping tabs on me.

We said our goodbyes, and Hanson then had the yeoman show me my new office. It had a window with a stunning view of San Francisco. I could see the academy and the Golden Gate Bridge. I'd just spent fifteen years crammed into an outdated ship, and now I was literally on top of the world. Yet something at the edges of my mind gnawed at me. I didn't want to be a deskbound officer, I wanted a captaincy. But I consciously pushed these thoughts away. This is where it was decided I was needed. It implied respect and esteem, not just by Hanson but by Starfleet itself. Whatever my personal desires were, I tried to let this cascade of approval overwrite them.

I left the office, and had myself beamed up to *Stargazer*. There was, as typical when the old lady was in spacedock, a lot of maintenance work underway. On the bridge, I found Jack Crusher supervising all of it. As he took me through the repair and upgrade schedule, I realized I probably wouldn't be serving with him much longer. I would however make sure that Starfleet was aware that *Stargazer* had a good replacement for Walker as XO. When we finished, I decided to indulge my curiosity.

"I heard Walker fixed you up last night," I said. Crusher brightened.

"She's nova," Crusher said. "Medical student, really smart… beautiful." His expression revealed a lot more than his words.

"Not someone you'd meet in a bar," I said.

"Well, maybe," he said, "but not someone who'd go home with me if I was drunk." I laughed. It appeared Walker had hit the mark.

I took a short tour of the ship, and, satisfied that Crusher had things well in hand, told him to call me if there were any difficulties.

When I returned home, I had another surprise waiting for me. There was a woman in the kitchen I'd never seen before, cooking. She met me with a smile. She was fair-haired with blue eyes, a stunner in a plain dress and apron.

"You must be Jean-Luc," she said. Her hands were deeply involved in kneading dough, but she quickly wiped them off to shake mine. "I'm Jenice."

"I'm sorry," I said. "Do you work here?"

"Your father didn't tell you?" she said. I shook my head. "Oh, well, since your father and brother have to spend their days in the vineyard, they requested an aid from the Federation Health Service, who sent me. I've been helping take care of your mother."

"I see," I said. "Thank you."

"Have you had a chance to see her?"

"Yes, last night." She read my expression very well.

"She has good days and bad," Jenice said. "It's a very difficult time. She's sitting out back. I'm sure she'd love to see you." Jenice indicated the window in front of her, and I could see my mother in one of the wooden chairs that overlooked the vineyard in the back of the house. I thanked Jenice again and went outside.

Mother sat staring at the vineyard. She was in a heavy bathrobe, and her hair was ill kept. It was a stark contrast to the well-presented image she'd had the previous night. As I approached, she looked up at me.

"Hello, Maman," I said. She smiled at me.

"Hello," she said. I could see she was confused, but trying to hide it. Her "hello" had no recognition in it.

"I'm Jean-Luc," I said. She nodded, still smiling. I didn't know whether she didn't recognize me, or just didn't have the words. "I'm just going to sit here awhile, if that's all right?" She nodded, and looked back out at the vineyard. I sat in the chair next to her. She held her hand up, indicating the long stretch of vines.

"Look how pretty," she said.

"Yes," I said.

✦

She passed away two weeks later. There had been flashes of lucidity, but the disease progressed very rapidly, and in her last days she was lost in a private world none of us could see. We buried her in the local cemetery, in a plot surrounded by Picard ancestors. The service was small: my brother and father, Jenice, as well as Walker and Jack, whom I hadn't told about my mother's sickness but had managed to find out anyway. There were also a few people from the town who knew her, including my childhood friend Louis. My father said a few words: about how my mother would not have wanted us to fuss about her death, about what a strong person she was, and how much her sons meant to her.

Afterward, I thanked my friends for coming, said goodbye to them and Jenice, and went home with my father and Robert. When we arrived, my father went to his room. My brother and I exchanged few words, and then I suggested we open a bottle of wine. I thought we might find a way to speak about our loss, but the dialogue never came. We drank in silence.

A short time later, my father appeared. He'd changed into his work clothes.

"Come," he said to Robert, "we have things to do." Even Robert was surprised by this, but, after only a brief pause he stood up and went to change. My anger, however, boiled over.

"Do you really think it's appropriate," I said, "on the day of our mother's burial…"

"I don't expect you to do anything," he said. "Stay here and wallow in wine and self-pity…"

"I don't have to listen to this."

"No, you don't," he said. "Fly away on your toy spaceship, the men have work to do." He walked outside. Furious, I threw my wine glass and it shattered against the wall, the red juice dripping down to the floor.

I went to my room, packed my bag, and left without saying goodbye. I don't remember the walk to the transporter station, I was so engulfed in white-hot rage. There was a short line of people waiting to use the transporter pad, and I got in line to wait my turn.

"Jean-Luc," Jenice said. "What are you doing here?" She was standing right in front of me, but I'd been so lost in my fury I hadn't noticed her.

"I'm going back to San Francisco," I said.

"I see." She seemed to understand, which shouldn't have surprised me, since she'd spent time with my family. Her presence made me suddenly ashamed of my display of anger. I tried to hide what I was feeling in a forced gentility.

"Where are you headed?" I said.

"Home to Paris." I nodded. She stared at me, gave me an empathetic smile.

"Thank you… for everything you did," I said. The line of people in front of us had disappeared; it was now just the two of us waiting for the pad.

"I wish I'd known your mother longer," she said. "She was a lovely person." She placed her hand on my arm. The fugue of rage I was in dissipated, overcome by a wave of sorrow.

"Yes." I wanted to run past Jenice and get on the pad, escape before it overcame me.

"She loved you very much. You made her very proud," Jenice said. The ire I felt toward my father was spent, and all I could think about was my mother, and that she was gone. Tears welled; I wanted to say something else to try to fight it off, but I had no words. I soon found myself in Jenice's embrace, crying softly.

✦

I was in deep mourning, and I wouldn't leave it for several months. I tried to distract myself with work, and this would have a temporary effect, but being on Earth brought my mother to mind often. Eventually, the pain of her death became dulled, though there are still days where it comes back at me full force. She taught me more about compassion, love, and learning than any one person in my life, and I owe so much of who I am to her.

But as she went on in her life, I went on in mine. Though still grieving, I returned to San Francisco and forced myself to focus on my role as Hanson's chief of staff. He put me to work organizing fleet construction, trying to remove

Top: Jean-Luc at 7 with his brother Robert, age 10.
A rare pleasant shot of Robert, who was enjoying the new gift of a toy spaceship.
Bottom: Picard with Jack Crusher, shortly after Crusher was promoted to First Officer of the *Stargazer*.

FEDERATION ARCHIVE: FILE/PICARD, JL
REF/01445.28

Picard upon graduating from Starfleet Academy.

Top: The *U.S.S. Stargazer*, Picard's ship for over 20 years.
Bottom: The command crew of the *U.S.S. Enterprise*, *1701-D*.
Clockwise from upper left: Worf, Geordi LaForge, William Riker, Picard, Deanna Troi, Beverley Crusher, Data.

FEDERATION ARCHIVE: FILE/PICARD, JL
RET/81255.8B

This picture was found in 1962 among the personal letters of Samuel Clemens bequeathed to the University of California/Berkley. Picard would remain unidentified by historians for over 400 years. The inscription from Picard reads: "A great man once said 'Truth is stranger than fiction, but it is because fiction is obliged to stick to possibilities. Truth isn't.' Thanks for the possibilities! J.L.P." In quoting Clemens himself, Picard created a conundrum: He met Clemens in 1893, four years before Clemens would publish that quote.

SHADOWS OF KATAAN

An Evening of Music and Discourse with Captain Jean-Luc Picard

TEN FORWARD
47451.2
1930

All Shipboard Personnel Welcome

FEDERATION ARCHIVE: FILE/PICARD, JL
RET/00102.4L

An unused poster created by Commander Data for Picard's lectures on his experiences on Kataan. Data suggested hanging them in the corridors, but Picard denied him permission.

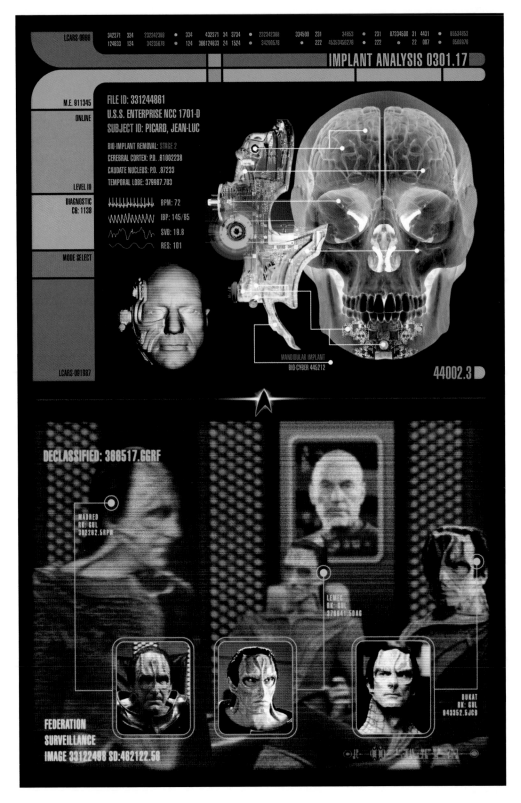

Top: A scan Beverly Crusher took of Picard's skull when he was assimilated by the Borg.
Bottom: Part of a transmission obtained by Starfleet Intelligence of three Cardassians: Gul Madred, Gul Lemec and Gul Dukat, discussing Picard, shortly before his capture and torture at the hands of Madred.

Captain Beverly Crusher, M.D.
Starfleet

and

Captain Jean-Luc Picard
Starfleet (Retired)

Request the pleasure & honor
of your company at their wedding

Saturday, October 8, 2383
Picard Family Vineyard
LaBarre, France

Seven o'clock in the evening
Reception to follow

The betrothed respectfully request no gifts

Picard and Beverly Crusher's wedding invitation.

A recent photo of Picard in front of his portrait in the gallery beneath his home.

FEDERATION ARCHIVE: FILE/PICARD, JL
REF/110705.2B

logjams that had slowed down new ships coming off the assembly line, and making sure that ships already in service were properly equipped for potential conflict. Hanson also tasked me with personnel recommendations for captain and first officer postings, with an eye to shoring up command teams with at least one command-level officer who had combat experience. Ironically, my first assignment in this area was finding my replacement for the *Stargazer*.

Despite the intensity of the work, I started to lead a very different life. The work days could be long, but it was nothing like being on *Stargazer*. When you're serving on a ship, you are always occupied; the life never allows you to truly relax. You lose some of your personal identity to your responsibility to the people you serve with. This is especially true when you're captain. The lives of the people under your command depend on you being fully attuned at all hours of the day and night.

So however busy life as Hanson's chief of staff was, I still found myself with time to relax. After a long day of work, I would often meet Jack Crusher and Walker Keel for drinks. I also began a relationship with Jenice, beaming over to Paris for dinner or a weekend. (Serving on ships, weekends are irrelevant.) The emotional vulnerability that I'd revealed to her opened me up to an intimacy I'd never had before. She and I became very close, very quickly. We spent many days and evenings together. It was unlike any connection I'd ever had with a woman. She was intelligent and lovely, and though our bond was still very new, the pull I felt toward her was compelling. I could easily lose myself to her.

I was having a good, happy life. And it was beginning to drive me mad.

It wasn't happening consciously, there were just snippets of annoyance over trivial things that I couldn't explain: restless sleep, slight indigestion, having to wait a moment too long for a transporter. The moment I became aware something was wrong was in a meeting with Admiral Hanson. The maintenance on *Stargazer* was almost complete, and I was going over my recommendation for my replacement.

"Edward Jellico has been first officer of the *Cairo* for five years," I said. "Relatively young for a captain, but an exemplary record. He would make a fine captain of the *Stargazer*."

"Milano won't like losing him," Hanson said, referring to Dan Milano, the captain of the *Cairo*.

"Captain Milano has forty years experience in command, and will undoubtedly be adept at training a replacement."

"You recommended Crusher for XO of the *Stargazer*," he said. "A good mix with Jellico?"

"I've never served with Jellico, but Crusher knows *Stargazer* almost as well as I do, and Jellico will need that expertise. I've also left him an experienced command crew."

"Okay, done. I'll recommend that Jellico gets *Stargazer* at the Admiralty meeting tomorrow," Hanson said. There was something about the finality of this that left me uneasy. Hanson read my expression, and smiled.

"Hard to give up your first girl to another guy," Hanson said. "Even if she isn't the prettiest one on the block."

"Yes, sir," I said. I smiled, but in truth his anachronistic, and rather offensive, metaphor did not make me feel better. I felt a great sense of loss, and it stayed with me the rest of the day.

That evening, as I routinely did, I met Jack and Walker for a drink in the 602 Club.* I told them about the new captain of the *Stargazer*. We all were a bit wistful.

"Hard to imagine the ship going on without you," Walker said.

"Jack'll have to carry the flag for the three of us," I said. I had another piece of news for Crusher. "And assuming the Admiralty approves Jellico, *Stargazer* could ship out as early as tomorrow."

"Is the *Cairo* here?" Crusher said.

"No, it's at Starbase 11," I said. "So, you have to take *Stargazer* and rendezvous with him there." I thought Jack would be thrilled at this news; though I'd left him in charge of the bridge from time to time, he'd never been in command for that length of voyage. His reaction, however, wasn't what I expected: he looked forlorn.

"I thought you'd be more excited," I said.

---

*EDITOR'S NOTE: The 602 Club was a famous watering hole frequented by Starfleet officers since the 22nd century. It was unfortunately destroyed in 2375 during the Dominion war when the Breen attacked Earth.

"No, I am," Jack said. "And I really appreciate what you've done, Jean-Luc... but I've got to go." He hurriedly finished his drink and left. Walker laughed.

"Our boy's in love," Walker said. "He didn't expect he'd have to say goodbye to Beverly so soon." I hadn't met Jack's girlfriend yet but he was clearly enraptured.

"Another drink?" I said, but Walker shook his head.

"I should probably get going, too. Still have some work to do tonight if *Horatio* is going to ship out on time." He left and I found myself alone in the bar, ignoring the other patrons. I was supposed to see Jenice the next afternoon in Paris and had the thought I could call her tonight. But instead, I just stared at the walls.

I wasn't staring at nothing. The walls of the 602 Club were adorned with pictures and souvenirs of past Starfleet heroism. Directly in front of me was a photo of A.G. Robinson, the first man to break the warp 2 barrier. To the left of that was the famous Captain Garth of Izar. On the right, two young captains, Matt Decker and Jose Mendez, who'd brought a superior Klingon force to a stalemate in the Battle of Donatu V. Looking at the past, I felt my future was slipping away.

"Can I get you something else?" The voice was familiar. I looked over and was surprised to see a new bartender on duty.

"Guinan," I said. "What... what are you..."

"I wanted to tend bar," she said. "They had an opening." I hadn't seen her in nine years, and she didn't look a day older.

"Finally started losing your hair," she said. My hair had been thinning lately, and this, again, seemed to be some kind of private joke between her and me, except I didn't know what it meant.

She had been living on Earth for over a year but was rather mysterious about how she'd come here or what she'd been doing in the intervening years. As she had done in the past, her listening skills effortlessly shifted the focus to me. I filled her in on what I'd been doing since coming to Earth. She looked at me with a slightly sardonic expression.

"What?" I said.

"Nothing," she said. "You sound very happy. Working in an office, helping out an admiral."

"It's a little more important than that," I said.

"Of course it is," she said. As she poured me another drink, she referenced a picture on the wall of a middle-aged Starfleet officer receiving a medal. "You know this guy?"

"Yes, of course," I said.

"To work here, you're supposed to memorize every picture. You know what he got the medal for?"

"Was it for bringing the humpback whale forward in time to save the Earth?"

"No," Guinan said, "I don't think he got a medal for that. I think this was when he saved the president's life at Camp Khitomer... or maybe it was after stopping the V'Ger probe..."

"Can't be," I said, "the uniforms were different then."

"You're right," she said. "Who knows, the guy did so much."

"I feel like you're trying to make a point," I said.

"I am? What point would that be?" I didn't answer her question, because it was obvious. I finished my drink and left the bar. Emboldened by alcohol, I decided to visit Admiral Hanson at home.

This was not a short trip; Admiral Hanson had his own personal transporter, so he could live anywhere in the world. He chose to live in a small home on Cape Kidnappers, on the east coast of New Zealand's North Island. It was daytime when I arrived there. A yeoman took me to the admiral, who was seated outside, overlooking the rocky coast and a beautiful blue ocean. When he saw me, he looked concerned.

"Jean-Luc? What's the matter?"

"Sorry to disturb you, Admiral," I said. "I was wondering if I could have a word." He looked at me curiously, then offered me the empty chair next to him, and dismissed the yeoman.

"What can I do for you?" Hanson said.

"I appreciate all you've done for me," I said, "but I'd like to return as captain of the *Stargazer*."

"Why?" He was clearly disappointed, but I couldn't say he looked surprised.

"I feel I can do more good out there."

"You're doing a lot of good down here," Hanson said. "You've already made yourself invaluable to me, and as Starfleet officers we unfortunately don't always get to choose our postings."

"I know, sir," I said. "I can only make the request; if you decide not to grant it, I understand."

"If you wait just a little longer," Hanson said, "the *Melbourne* or the *Yamaguchi* will be off the assembly line, I'll make sure you get one of those. That way I'd get a few more months out of you." As attractive as a brand-new ship might be, they didn't interest me. I felt a need to *get out*.

"Yes, sir," I said, "but if it's important to have experienced captains out there now, the right choice is to put me back on *Stargazer*. The old lady is temperamental, and anyone else in that chair may not have time to get used to her before we need to put her in action."

Hanson considered me for a long while, then sighed. I knew he was worried about the situation with the Klingons, and my appeal went to the heart of those concerns. He wanted people he could rely on in positions of command. He looked out at the ocean. A flock of gannets flew over.

"Beautiful, isn't it?"

"Yes, sir," I said. "It's paradise."

"What we're trying to protect," he said.

I could see I'd made my point. Though I was making his job easier on Earth, he wouldn't let his own privileges get in the way of his commitment to the service.

"All right," Hanson said. "You ship out tomorrow."

"Thank you, sir," I said.

I left his home, momentarily pleased. This was what I wanted, to be out on the edge, in charge, and participating in the making of history. I still had this overwhelming desire to make my mark, and being the captain of a ship, even an old tin can like the *Stargazer*, fulfilled that desire.

The only remaining problem, of course, was Jenice. My desire to get back on a ship right away was fueled in part by my fear that saying goodbye to her would only become more difficult, if not impossible. Right then, I thought I could walk away; a few more weeks, I wasn't sure. We were set to meet at the Café des Artistes in Paris the very next day. I would tell her then. It would be a difficult parting, but I knew it was best for me. If I didn't say goodbye then, I might never.

✦

"Captain on the bridge," Commander Black said, as I walked on.

It was the next morning, and Black had received my transfer of command order, so by the time I beamed up the whole crew knew. I'd gotten warm greetings and handshakes all the way from the transporter room to the bridge.

Crusher was there at the conn, Cheva was at ops. Vigo, who'd been down in the torpedo room, was now the bridge weapons and security officer, and Scully was at the engineering console. And though I'd skipped over Black again to be first officer, I'd gotten him a grade promotion, and he seemed happy to stay.

As I stepped off the turbolift, they all applauded, and I couldn't help but laugh. I looked around; the maintenance the ship had undergone had breathed new life into it. Or maybe I was seeing it with new eyes, I didn't know.

"Status report, Number One," I said.

"Dock command has signaled we're clear for departure," Crusher said. "All stations report ready." This caught me a little by surprise. I was supposed to meet Jenice at noon in Paris; it was ten o'clock Paris time then. I could have delayed our departure three hours. No one would know why or even question it.

I was going to order a delay, and stopped myself. I pictured seeing her, saying goodbye. She would understand, she'd let me go. I had to go see her, but if I did…

"Orders, sir?" Crusher said.

I was at war with myself. I felt a pull, a need, to delay our departure so I could go see Jenice. And, in that moment, I was overcome with a new perspective: I thought I wanted to be back here, on this bridge, but Jenice's smile, her eyes, her presence in my mind diminished the desire for this ship to a shadow. We'd only just started our romance, but Jenice embodied love, affection, and desire. This machine, the "old lady," couldn't compete. If I went to see her, Jenice might let me go, but I was suddenly unsure, face to face, that I could leave her.

"Stand by to depart," I said. I couldn't say goodbye. I wanted my career.

I was a coward.

✦

"The raiders came in the middle of the night," Governor Harriman said. "They were in a small scout ship. They wore armor…"

"Take your time," I said. He was lying on a cot in the infirmary on Hakton VII.

About 80 years old, he'd been the governor since its founding a decade before. Dr. Ailat tended to a gash on his forehead, as other members of the *Stargazer's* medical team worked with colony doctors administering care to the rest of the patients, victims of a recent attack by persons unknown.

"They were very aggressive," Harriman said.

"They weren't Klingons," I said.

Harriman shook his head. "They were more civilized in one way, but there was an arrogance about them," he said. "They landed, we went to greet them, and they came out firing. I immediately surrendered; they were better armed than we were. They rounded up most of us, picking just a few to load equipment into their ship. And then they left."

"You acted properly," I said. "You probably saved a lot of lives by cooperating."

"I hope so, because it just felt like cowardice."

I tried to look reassuring, then excused myself and went outside. The infirmary was in the center of the colony. The colony itself was an orderly collection of single-story buildings made of stone in a unified architectural style, designed to coexist with the natural surroundings.

We'd received the distress call less than an hour before. Fortunately, we were already on our way to Hakton VII, delivering supplies from Starbase 32. But we hadn't made it in time to stop the raid. I was immediately met by Cheva and Vigo, returning from their scout of the area.

"I examined the blast marks from their weapons," Vigo said. "Some kind of disruptor."

"What did they steal?"

"That's the strange thing," Cheva said. "They didn't take any of the colony's weapons, they were only interested in replicators." The jigsaw was slowly coming together in my head when Crusher called from the ship.

"*Stargazer* to Picard," he said. "I've picked up an ionization trail. We can track that ship."

"Beam everyone up but the medical team," I said. "Go to red alert."

We were lucky: the small scout vessel was slower than *Stargazer*, and it didn't take long before we were closing in on them. The unmarked ship's hammerhead design was very similar to one I'd seen before. I had Black open a hailing frequency.

"This is Captain Jean-Luc Picard, of the Federation ship *Stargazer*. We are investigating an attack on the Federation colony on Hakton VII. Please secure from warp drive…"

I was cut off as the ship rocked, the result of an impact by a torpedo on our shields.

"Vigo, report on their weapons," I said.

"Standard photon torpedo," Vigo said. "We can take 'em, sir."

"Lock phasers," I said. "Target their engines and weapons." Vigo complied and the *Stargazer* fired on the unknown ship.

"Sensors report we've knocked out their torpedo launcher," Cheva said. "But they haven't slowed down."

"Reading an overload building in their warp reactor," Crusher said. "We damaged them, but they're trying to ignore it." I checked the scan of the ship; its reactor was reaching critical mass.

"Transporter Room, lock onto that ship, and beam—"

I was cut off again, this time by the ship exploding. Whatever their mission was, they didn't want to get caught. I had Crusher extrapolate their destination based on the course they were on, and ordered him to stay on that course. I thought that perhaps by finding their destination, we might gather some clue as to their purpose.

We soon found ourselves entering an uncharted system with fourteen planets. The raider's course led us to the largest one, the eleventh planet—a Class-M world. Sensors showed an extensive and ancient humanoid civilization. A formidable-looking space station was in orbit. It was a strange design, dark, almost skeletal, like a giant incomplete gyroscope. Arms curved up and down from the hub of the station, where spaceships were docked.

"That station is heavily armed," Vigo said. "Photon torpedoes, disruptor cannons, some other weapons I can't identify. And their shields just went up."

"I'm also detecting a lot of active machinery," Cheva said. "Some kind of ore refinery operating there."

"We're being hailed," Black said.

"On screen," I said. A member of a species I'd met only once before appeared on the viewscreen. He gave me a smile that I can only describe as malevolent.

"Unidentified ship," he said. "I am Gul Dukat, commander of the station Terok Nor, and Cardassian prefect of Bajor. Please state the nature of your business."

"Captain Jean-Luc Picard, Federation ship *Stargazer*. We were pursuing raiders who attacked one of our colonies. They were heading to this system."

"Really? How terrible," Dukat said, with oily sincerity. "And what happened to the raiders?"

"Their ship was destroyed," I said. I decided to be as vague as possible regarding my role in the ship's destruction. Dukat, however, could see through my deception.

"Well, whoever they were," he said, "I'm sure they won't be missed."

"So you can't provide us with any information about them?"

"I'm afraid not. As governor of this system, I have much more important things to concern myself with."

"Forgive my ignorance," I said. "We've never visited this system before. You said it was called... Bajor?"

"Yes," Dukat said. "It is a protectorate of the Cardassian empire. We defend the peaceful Bajorans from a hostile universe, and in exchange we only ask for a modest payment from their abundant planetary resources. It is an equitable exchange." Though he wasn't being explicit, I felt Dukat's meaning was clear: they had enslaved the Bajorans, and they didn't plan to stop there.

"We are explorers," I said. "We would enjoy the opportunity to perhaps learn more about the Cardassian–Bajoran relationship."

"As I mentioned," Dukat said, "I'm quite busy. Perhaps another time. But if you do return, I will happily demonstrate how we protect Bajor from unwanted intruders."

Cheva reacted to something on her board, and she leaned in to me. "Sir," she said, "they've locked weapons on us." I knew *Stargazer* would not last long in a battle with that station, and Dukat knew it too.

"Well," I said, "thank you for your time." Dukat smiled that terrible smile, and his face disappeared from the viewscreen. I had Crusher set a course out of the system, back to Hakton VII, to pick up our medical personnel.

"He was lying," Crusher said, very matter-of-factly. "He probably ordered the raid."

"Yes, but why?" Cheva said.

I asked Cheva to give me the inventory of what had been stolen from the colony. "They want a replicator," I said. I referenced the list of stolen items. "They ripped three replicators out of the walls of several structures, leaving potentially more valuable technology alone."

"This is a dangerous situation," Crusher said. "They want that technology and are willing to sacrifice the lives of their own soldiers to steal it."

"Why don't they just ask us to trade for it?" Vigo said.

"A sign of weakness," I said. "They wouldn't want to reveal their position to a potential adversary."

"And I bet they think they could get more by just taking it," Crusher said.

As we went on our way, I realized Starfleet had a lot more to worry about than the Klingons.

✦

It was in 2346, two years into returning as captain of the *Stargazer*, and I began to understand why "you can't go home again" is an enduring cliché. I was happy to be back but it wasn't nearly the same. Many of my officers remained, but they had all grown over time. I also came to the captain's chair with more experience and a little less wonder and enthusiasm. And of course, Walker Keel was gone. I still had my friendship with Jack Crusher, but he had also changed. He'd taken to the responsibilities of first officer very naturally and his boyish eagerness was gone. In fact, he was often quiet, and sometimes even despondent. I had been blind to the cause, so I asked him about it.

"Oh, sorry, Captain," he said, one day at lunch. "I'm just a lovesick fool." His relationship had gotten very serious, and since we'd left Earth almost two years before, he'd only seen her by subspace communication. She was a student in the Starfleet medical program. Because of the separation caused by their respective careers, they had been having discussions about the reality of the future of their relationship. It would be years before they could be together, and that was only if they were posted to the same ship.

"How many years at the academy does she have left?"

"Two," Crusher said, "and then another four of medical school." Starfleet Medical Training had become that much more complicated as more and more species fell into the Federation's sphere of influence. A Starfleet doctor had to have working knowledge of the physiologies of hundreds of species, and an even larger number of medical ailments. I couldn't do anything about the medical training, but the academy education was another matter.

"What if Beverly completed her academy years aboard the *Stargazer*?"

"Really? Could we get approval for that?"

"I would think so," I said. "As first officer, it would be your job to make sure she completed the curriculum. And if she worked in sickbay I would imagine she might be able to gain medical credit as well."

"Jean-Luc… are you sure?"

"Absolutely," I said. "Though I have to insist on separate cabins until you're married."

Crusher laughed. "Thank you."

"Don't thank me yet," I said. "We're not due to go back to Earth for some time; you'll have to figure out some way to get her out to us."

"That," Crusher said, "I can handle."

He was a man determined. We shortly received orders to rendezvous with a squadron near the Federation–Klingon Neutral Zone, and Crusher found out that one ship assigned to the squadron, the *Hood*, was coming from Earth. He was able to not only get approval for Beverly to complete her academy degree aboard the *Stargazer*, he also got her passage aboard the *Hood* within three hours of the ship's departure from Earth. Watching Jack receive the news that Beverly was winging her way to him, I saw some of his youthful zeal return.

When we reached the rendezvous, ten ships had gathered, and I had to face some of my own decisions. Among the ships were the *Melbourne* and the *Yamaguchi*, still relatively new, both of which had been offered to me by Hanson. The *Stargazer*, twelve years after I'd taken command of her, was worse off than ever, and, as I looked at the clean lines and powerful grace of those new ships, I had to wonder what it would've been like if I'd had a little more patience.

The lead ship, the *U.S.S. Ambassador*, signaled for me and my first officer to beam over immediately. Crusher and I headed to the transporter room, and when we arrived, Transporter Chief Youlin informed me that someone was beaming over from the *Hood*. A woman materialized on the transporter pad, and it appeared that Crusher was embracing her before the process was even complete. She had red hair; the rest of her face was momentarily obscured as they were locked in a passionate kiss. I exchanged an awkward glance with Youlin, who stifled a laugh. I finally cleared my throat, and Crusher broke from his embrace.

"Captain Jean-Luc Picard," Crusher said, still quite flushed, "may I introduce Cadet Beverly Howard." She smiled and gently pulled her hand from Crusher's, who hadn't realized he was holding it.

"An honor to meet you, Captain," Beverly said.

"Welcome aboard, Cadet," I said. "Unfortunately, Mr. Crusher and I are late for a meeting." She quickly stepped off the transporter platform, and as Crusher and I beamed off the ship, she blew him a kiss.

✦

The captains of the squadron and their execs gathered in the enviably spacious conference room of the *Ambassador*, which easily held us all. Out of the large view ports we could see all the ships lined up aft of the lead ship. *Stargazer* was the runt of the litter. I knew most of the men and women in the room, if not personally, then from my work as Hanson's chief of staff. Only two were more than an acquaintance: Robert DeSoto, the friend I'd made on my first academy testing day, now captain of the *Hood*. He greeted me with a hearty "Bonjour, mon ami!"

The other friend was a lovely surprise: Marta Batanides. She had been promoted to captain of the *Kyushu*. We got to say a brief hello before the meeting. She gave me a hug, which made me a little self-conscious in such august company.

"It's been too long," she said. I studied her face: the youthful woman was still there, behind a touch of gray. She then leaned in closer to me. "I heard about your mother; I'm so sorry." I thanked her. I'd forgotten what a close friend she had been, and I wanted to talk to her more, but then we noticed our leader was at the table, and we all took our seats.

We didn't need to be told to come to order, because no one in the room was as impressive as the person at the head of it: Andrea Brand, shipmaster of the *Ambassador*, the Federation flagship. Even without saying a word, she was a formidable presence.

"The Klingons are planning a surprise attack," Brand said. "We can't stop them, but we can track their ships." This statement was counter-intuitive: the Klingons still had cloaking devices, so their ships could gather in secret, within striking distance of their target, and we wouldn't be any the wiser until they launched their attack. But, as I looked at Captain Brand, I knew she must have the answer to such an obvious question.

She stood up and activated the viewscreen on the wall behind her. A star map appeared, and, at every star, groups of red markings.

"These symbols on the map represent every Klingon ship in existence," she said. "Starfleet Intelligence has kept close watch on Klingon ship movements and construction, and thanks to their diligence, we now have a complete inventory of their entire fleet, as well as each ship's current whereabouts."

There was a murmured response of disbelief.

"Captain Brand, how do we know they don't already have a mass of ships under cloak?" This came from Owen Paris, a few years ahead of me at the academy, and the captain of the *Al-Batani*.

"For the simple reason," Brand said, "that this project started over sixty years ago. After the first Khitomer Accords allowed Klingons access to Federation space, Starfleet Intelligence began a clandestine cataloguing initiative, monitoring individual ship movements as well as construction projects." It was so simple, and yet brilliant: even if the Klingons knew we were monitoring them, a Klingon ship couldn't stay under cloak that long. Eventually it would appear and be tracked.

Brand continued, pointing out an area along the Klingon–Federation border.

"As you can see, they've concentrated the bulk of their ships in this area, in easy striking distance to Starbase 24 and Starbase 343." It would be the right move to attack those bases, since they were the closest Federation outposts to Klingon space. If they were destroyed, it would limit Starfleet's ability to repair and resupply ships in an extended conflict.

Brand then adjusted the controls under the viewscreen. Blue markings appeared on the map.

"Our plan is simple," Brand said. "Each of your ships will proceed to a preassigned route. Using long-range sensors, and without crossing the border, you will surreptitiously monitor the Klingon ships on your patrol station. If you lose contact with any of them, we will assume they've cloaked, and you will report to the command ship immediately. Where they launch their ships from should give us some information as to what the Klingons plans are."

It was very clever. I must have been smiling.

"Something amusing, Captain Picard?" It was Brand; because I'd been lost in thought, I didn't notice her looking at me. I decided to be honest.

"Not at all, Captain," I said. "It's brilliant. It reminds me of a blockade from the age of sail, when a frigate would be assigned to keep enemy ships bottled up in harbor."

Now it was Brand's turn to smile.

"Can you tell me," Brand said, "the one problem with that comparison?"

"Sometimes the enemy ships slipped through," I said.

✦

The ten ships left the rendezvous and moved to their assigned routes. I regretted that I didn't have more time to spend with my friends, but duty called. Our patrol station was near the Federation outpost on Ajilon. We pretended we were on leisurely patrols, training all our sensors on the Klingon outposts on the other side of the border. *Stargazer* was responsible for monitoring twenty-five ships of various sizes. It was apparent to me that I'd been given what was considered a low-risk patrol sector; we were the furthest away of any of the ships from Starbase 24 or Starbase 343. If the Klingons were going to attack those two bases, they would certainly launch from a closer location. But we kept a careful watch nevertheless.

During the two weeks we were on patrol, I was beginning to get to know the love of Jack's life. She was young and soft-spoken, but I soon learned her manner hid a passionate intellect. Crusher himself was also different around her, a little more brash as well as occasionally, well... silly. He seemed to enjoy making her laugh.

"...and he was sitting in your chair?" Beverly said. The three of us were in the rec room having dinner. Crusher had prompted me to tell her why I didn't approve of children on my ship.

"That's nothing," Crusher said. "Tell her about the egg." I suppose some captains might think such informality would undermine their authority, but I'd learned I could trust Jack with these confidences, and now that trust seemed to naturally extend to the woman he loved.

"You can tell her," I said. "I want to check in with the bridge."

"They'll call if they detect anything," Crusher said. "What are you worried about? I don't think the Klingons are going to attack here, do you?"

"What we think doesn't matter," I said. "We have our duty."

"Excuse me for asking, but aren't we near Archanis?" Beverly said. "That might be a prime target for them."

"It's not the most strategically valuable," Crusher said.

"No," Beverly said. "But the loss of Archanis in 2272 was a humiliation for them. Warfare for the Klingons is as much about honor as it is about strategy." Crusher and I exchanged a look. She had insight into the current situation because academy lessons were fresh in her mind. And as if to confirm it, Cheva called from the bridge.

"Red alert," she said. "Captain Picard to the bridge." I clicked the intercom. "Bridge, this is Picard, report..."

"All the Klingon ships, sir," she said. "They're gone."

✦

A few hours later, we were at Archanis. I'd contacted Brand, and she agreed with my analysis (really Beverly's), that the Klingons were headed there. Brand would be coming with the rest of her squadron to buttress Archanis's defenses. There were three Class-M planets in the system, several orbital facilities, but currently no starships. Until help arrived, *Stargazer* would be alone.

The situation of our patrol had gone from dull to dire. It seemed unlikely we would survive the day.

But all we could do was wait. I paced the bridge, occasionally staring at the starfield. I remember reading that the original Klingon cloaks caused a slight distortion of the stars, and so I searched, vainly hoping for some forewarning before those ships appeared. I looked around at the faces of the bridge crew: they wore expressions of determination, but fear was just below the surface.

"There's a spike in neutrino emissions," Cheva said. "Could be cloaked ships."

"Bearing, Mr. Crusher?"

"Directly ahead of our position," Crusher said. I looked back at the viewscreen. The stars began to shimmer…

"Shields up," I said. "Stand by all weapons."

Twenty-five Klingon ships solidified into reality, filling my screen, blotting out the stars. Their forward torpedo launchers were all trained on us, all glowing red.

"They've all locked onto us," Cheva said. We would not survive that onslaught.

"Phasers, lock onto the lead ship," I said. "Fire…"

And then suddenly, the ships shimmered again, dissolved, and disappeared. All of them.

"Sensors, report!"

"They're gone, sir," Cheva said. "I've got nothing."

"Stay sharp," I said. We remained at the ready. I glanced at the chronometer; thirty seconds passed. I checked our boards: no neutrino emissions, no sensor contacts, nothing. I looked back at the chronometer. Now a minute had passed.

"They had us," Crusher said. "What happened?"

"Sir, message coming in from Captain Brand," Black said.

"On screen," I said, and turned to see Brand on the spacious bridge of the *Ambassador*.

"Captain," I said, "the Klingons were here, but they… left."

"I don't think they're coming back," Brand said. "They're needed elsewhere. There's been an attack on two Klingon colonies." This seemed unbelievable; the Federation had never initiated a war. She immediately read the confusion in my expression. "The Romulans have attacked Narendra III and Khitomer. The Klingons have another war to worry about."

It turned out that the Romulans had not believed the Klingons regarding the event with the planet-killer, and had been planning their own military action in retaliation. They were both warlike societies, and I suppose the

Federation was lucky that they turned their hostility to one another. However, the war between Romulus and Qo'noS* was not without casualties for Starfleet. When the Romulans attacked Narendra III, the inhabitants sent a distress call. The only ship to answer it was the *U.S.S. Enterprise*-C, the first ship that had taken me into space. The vessel, under the command of a woman named Rachel Garrett, engaged four Romulan warships in an attempt to stop the attack. The efforts of Captain Garrett and her crew of 700 were unsuccessful. The ship was lost with all hands, and the Klingon outpost destroyed. I was discussing the tragedy the next evening at dinner with Jack and Beverly—meals with them were quickly becoming a regular event. Crusher was going over the crew list of the *Enterprise*-C. He found the name of someone he knew, the ship's helmsman.

"I knew Richard Castillo at the academy," Crusher said. "Good guy, very earnest. Sad that he had to die for nothing."

"Maybe not for nothing," Beverly said.

"What do you mean?" I said.

"There's been an intense focus on Klingon culture in my classes at the academy," Beverly said. "I think the commandant knew war was coming. In any event, one Klingon warrior sacrificing himself to protect other Klingons is a very meaningful act of honor, even if he or she fails. It guarantees them a place in the warrior's afterlife."

"I don't understand what you're getting at," Crusher said.

"Well, seven hundred Federation 'warriors' on the *Enterprise*-C sacrificed themselves to save Narendra III..." Beverly said. "If they are true to their own customs, there may just be the possibility of real peace between our two societies."

Beverly would turn out to be right, and as the days went on I became more impressed at this person who'd come into my friend Jack Crusher's life. And as we sat down to eat, and I watched how she looked at my best friend, I found myself envious that she hadn't come into mine.

---

*EDITOR'S NOTE: Qo'noS (pronounced "KRO-nus") is the homeworld of the Klingon Empire.

CHAPTER SEVEN

"AND SO, IT IS MY HONOR TO UNITE YOU, Jack Crusher, and you, Beverly Howard, in the bonds of matrimony…"

It was a sunny, humid spring day in the small village of Cornwall, in the state the ancient Americans called "Connecticut." Jack said that his family went back several centuries in this town: his maternal grandmother, Clara Sedgwick, who officiated the wedding, had regaled the visitors the night before about her ancestor who served in the United States Civil War.*

The village had remained almost as rural as when it was founded. The wedding took place at Jack's family home, set amongst a stretch of woods. It was the second wedding I would attend in my dress uniform, this one however as best man. I stood next to Jack, who faced Beverly. Though still a cadet, she eschewed a uniform and instead wore a white dress and veil in the ancient Earth tradition. She wore it with grace and splendor, and stared soulfully into my best friend's eyes, never noticing my rapt gaze.

Clara had them say their vows and exchange rings. Jack lifted Beverly's veil and they kissed. The audience of about a hundred people broke out into

---

*EDITOR'S NOTE: The ancestor was John Sedgwick, born in Cornwall Hollow, Connecticut, who served as a general in the Union Army, and was killed at the Battle of Spotsylvania Court House in 1864. Upon viewing the placement of Confederate sharpshooters, his famous last words were "They couldn't hit an elephant at this dist—."

spontaneous applause, and I joined in. The joy I felt for my friends was tempered by the feelings I'd developed for Beverly over the past two years.

After the service, Jack was thanking his grandmother, when Beverly stepped over to me.

"I hope you don't mind, Captain," she said. She leaned in and gave me a soft kiss on the cheek. "It means so much to us that you're here."

"I wouldn't have missed it," I said, returning her smile. I felt my face flush. Uncomfortable with our closeness, I stepped back. "You're both very special to me." Jack came back over and shook my hand warmly.

"Thank you, Captain," he said.

"None of that 'Captain' business today," I said. We joined the other guests, including several members of the crew. I noticed Scully already with a drink in his hand. I did my best to engage with the merriment. When I felt I'd given an appropriate amount of time to the party, I made my excuses and said my goodbyes. My last image was of Jack and Beverly absorbed in a lively dance, sharing their joy, surrounded by loved ones. I withdrew, headed to the center of town, alone.

My thoughts went to my own family. I reached the Cornwall transporter station, very reminiscent of the one in my hometown. I'd been avoiding going back to the vineyard, but there was unfinished business waiting for me there. I stepped forward to the technician at the control panel.

"Destination?" he said.

"La Barre, France," I said.

An hour or so later I was standing in the barn that held the wine tanks.

"So, you're home," Robert said—his standard greeting. He stood on the gangplank over one of the wine tanks, pressing down the skins with the large paddle.

"I can't stay long," I said.

"I didn't expect you would," he said. Robert was infuriating. He continued on, pressing the paddle into the sloshing purple mess. He wasn't going to make this easy for me.

"How was the funeral?"

"Very simple," Robert said. "Just me and some people from town. Smaller than Mother's."

"I am sorry I wasn't here," I said. "I was several hundred light-years away when I found out." This was the truth; I was out at the Cardassian border when

I'd received word of my father's death. It would've taken me weeks to get back home. And the truth was, upon hearing of my father's passing, the memory of his coldness toward me when Mother died was still fresh in my mind. It left no room for sorrow.

"He wouldn't have wanted a fuss," Robert said. He stopped what he was doing; I felt like I'd passed some test by bringing up the awkward subject of my father's death. Robert took the paddle and laid it across the gangplank, then made his way to the ladder on the side and climbed down.

"Come with me."

He led me into the house and into the kitchen. There was a small lockbox on the table.

"Father left you that," Robert said. This was a surprise; I hadn't expected him to leave me anything. And I was correct not to; I opened the box, and took a quick glance inside. There was a PADD, and on it was a letter from Starfleet Academy. It began "Dear Mr. Picard: we are sorry to inform you..." It was my rejection letter from when I first applied.

"What is this about?"

"I don't know," Robert said. "It was the only thing he left in his will to you."

I didn't understand it. It seemed to be an insult from the grave, but the purpose of which I couldn't comprehend. A reminder of a failure? I looked at Robert. I could see he wasn't interested in this. He had another agenda, and I immediately knew what it was.

"This was all he left me," I said. "That's what you want me to know."

Robert stood still, unable to meet my gaze. I had no expectation that my father would leave me anything, but Robert's concern was the vineyard. It was his now, and he wanted me to know it. I looked at him. He was almost 50, and though he would probably live a lot longer, he'd devoted his whole life to the family business. It was his entire past, and the only possibility of a future. I didn't know what Robert's plans were, though I assumed he would want a family to pass the vineyard onto as my father had to him. Yet, I was stung by Robert's lack of generosity. He didn't want to risk sharing any of it with me. We'd lost both our parents, and though that might have brought some brothers closer together, in our case, it only cemented our distance. We were both victims in a sense; my father hadn't dealt with this situation with respect for either of us.

"Good luck," I said. I shook his hand. He wouldn't look me in the eye. When I left, I expected this would be the last time I would see him. I walked back to the transport station in La Barre, and beamed back to the *Stargazer*.

✦

"Beverly's pregnant," Crusher said.

"Congratulations," I said, giving him a warm handshake. He had just returned from his honeymoon and found me in engineering, where Scully and I were reviewing the completed maintenance we'd done while in Earth orbit.

"That was fast," Scully said. "Wedding was only two weeks ago." Crusher and I exchanged a glance and laughed.

"Yeah," Crusher said. "I guess you didn't notice the shotgun her father was holding." This was of course a joke. Jack told me that his and Beverly's families had known that Beverly was pregnant before the wedding. It was a fait accompli that they were going to marry, and humans were beyond such narrow-mindedness that said they *had to* because the woman had got pregnant.

Crusher and I left Scully and headed up to the bridge. I asked him where his new bride was.

"Actually, that's something I wanted to mention to you," Crusher said. "She's decided to finish her studies on Earth. With your approval, of course."

"Why?" This news caught me off guard. I'd been steeling myself for her return, and now I was sincerely disappointed not to be seeing her again. "I certainly hope she didn't think I would have trouble with a pregnant crewman."

"She wasn't worried about the pregnancy," Crusher said. "She was worried about what would happen afterward."

"I don't understand."

"Come on, you're not exactly a fan of having children aboard your ship," Crusher said. "And since we weren't sure where *Stargazer* would be seven months from now, she decided she wanted to avoid the potential awkwardness of that situation."

"That was very thoughtful," I said. But this revelation had left me embarrassed and a little somber. That my stories of difficult children on board the *Stargazer* had been the deciding factor in Beverly not returning upset me. I somehow felt I'd hurt her, which I knew was ridiculous.

"Well," I said, "when she's through with the academy, I hope she'll consider a posting on this ship."

"I hope we're not still here." As we got on the turbolift to the bridge, I could see beneath his good cheer was a sadness.

"Was it difficult to leave her?" I said.

"Leave *them*," he said. "I have a family now."

"I'll get you back to them," I said. He smiled, and we exited to the bridge.

✦

"The Cardassians have destroyed the colony on Setlik III," Captain Ross said. He was on the viewscreen, calling from the bridge of his ship the *Crazy Horse*. Over the past few years, incidents of Cardassian raids on ships and colonies had escalated, so Starfleet sent a task force commanded by Ross to the border with Cardassian space. This was supposed to prevent a conflict, but it had in fact seemed to ignite one, as now the Cardassians had wiped out a Federation colony.

"Code One?" I said. Ross nodded.

Code One. We were at war.

"I have new orders for you, Captain," Ross said. "The *Stargazer* has been detailed to my task force, while we await further reinforcements."

"Yes, Captain," I said. I looked at Ross. A beefy man with a hangdog expression, he was still several years younger than me. I'd often been in the position of giving orders to older people, and now I would find myself on the opposite end of that awkward relationship.

"You are to proceed to Starbase 32 and pick up a shipment of supplies that will arrive there tomorrow from Earth," Ross said. "I'm sending the manifest now. We're about to find ourselves in a shooting war, and we're going to need those supplies as soon as possible."

"Acknowledged," I said. "We won't let you down." I signed off and Ross left the screen. "Mr. Crusher, set course for Starbase 32, warp 6, engage." As we entered warp, I noticed the crew looked uneasy. We'd engaged in the occasional skirmish and had faced down a fleet of Klingon ships, but none of the crew had ever fought in an actual war. That, unfortunately, was also true for their captain. Still, I had to find some words of comfort and encouragement.

"War is something to be avoided at all costs," I said. "But when circumstances don't allow you to, then all you can do is your best. This ship has survived a long time and accomplished a great deal, because its crew understood where its duty lay. This war will be no different. We will do our duty, and we will succeed."

As it turned out, I was right, but not quite in the way that I thought.

I assumed that once we picked up the supplies at Starbase 32, *Stargazer* would join Ross's task force. But Ross had a string of newer, faster, better-armed ships than mine, and the "milk run" became our chief duty. We transported supplies and personnel back and forth between Starbase 32, other starships and the ships on the front line. During the first two years of the war, the *Stargazer* participated in no battles. It gave one the ambivalent feeling that you were both safe and somehow not doing enough.

A few months into our third year of war, however, one person aboard got something out of the situation. We were in the recreation room one evening playing poker (I had started a regular game with Jack Crusher, Dr. Ailat, Scully, and Cheva). We had just delivered dilithium and photon torpedoes to Ross's task force. The game helped relieve the monotony on these long trips back and forth. I was dealing five-card stud when Jack told us the news.

"Beverly and Wesley are on Starbase 32," Jack said. I was overcome with a wave of anticipation. I had not seen Beverly since she'd left the ship, and she had faded from my mind. I'd seen photos of her and their young son, but having her far away made me forget the feelings I'd had for her. Now that I might be seeing her again, they came flooding back. I focused intently on the game, and let the others ask the questions that were on my mind.

"That's wonderful," Cheva said. "Just visiting?"

"No," Jack said. "She's finished with the academy, and is going to complete her medical training at the starbase hospital."

"It is an exceptional teaching facility," Ailat said.

"You're going to get to see a lot of them," Cheva said, and Jack smiled. He hadn't met his son face-to-face yet, only over subspace communications. It had been weighing on him, and he told me he'd even been toying with the idea of resigning his commission. I had encouraged him to find another solution, and it seemed he had.

"Could we focus on the game, please?" Scully said. "Looks like the captain's dealt himself a straight draw." Scully read my hand well: I had a two, four, five showing, and my hold card was a three.

I dealt everyone's last card. I got a six of spades, completing my straight, a very difficult hand to get in this game. The betting started. Jack had two kings, a nine and ten up: his best possible hand was three of a kind, which wouldn't beat me. He bet heavily and Cheva, Ailat and Scully folded. The betting got to me and I raised; I knew I had a better hand than Jack. Jack, however, didn't seem to care, or thought I was bluffing. He raised me.

I looked at my hole card, then his hand, playing coy because I knew I had him beat.

"Well, Jean-Luc," Crusher said. "Raise, call, or fold." If I raised, he would probably raise as well, and I would take all his chips. But I looked at this man, my friend. I thought of his anticipation of the warm embrace of family, one that I'd never really experienced. I don't know why I did what I did next.

"Fold," I said, flipping the cards over, and pushing them into the center with the other folded hands, so no one could see what I had.

"Funny," Jack said. "I thought you had me beat."

"No," I said. "You had the better hand."

✦

"This is Captain Picard," Jack said. He held his toddler son, Wesley, who hid his face in his father's neck when I tried to say hello. Beverly gave me a hug. She looked lovely. We had arrived at Starbase 32 and were standing at the airlock hatch. I'd come to greet Jack's family, which in some ways I regarded as my own.

"Please come have dinner with us, Captain," Beverly said.

"Thank you," I said. "But I have some work to finish up." Seeing the three of them together, I felt the connection that I wasn't a part of, and certainly didn't want to be in the way. I watched them leave and headed back to the bridge.

After over two years of coming to this base, the shore facilities held little interest for me, so after completing my shift on the bridge, I retired to my cabin for dinner.

I sat down at my desk for a meal of soup and bread. I intended to read some dispatches, but I couldn't focus. My mind wandered to Jack holding his young son, and I tried to recall being held by my own father. He must have picked me up at some point, I just didn't remember.

I hadn't thought about my father since I had returned home, but now I was distracted with the one unsolved mystery of his death: the PADD he had left for me with my rejection letter from the academy. I hadn't looked at it since Robert had given it to me.

I dug out the PADD from the storage container that I'd tossed it in. Why would my father leave this for me? I started to read it, which I realized I hadn't really done when I first got it from Robert, and immediately noticed something. The date was wrong.

March 13, 2287. My first application to the academy was in 2321. I kept reading. It was the same letter. Except for the "Dear Mr. Picard" it was a form letter. And then I saw and understood—I wasn't the "Mr. Picard" it was addressed to.

It was addressed to Maurice Picard.

My father.

I couldn't believe what I was reading. My father, at 17, had applied to the academy and been rejected. He'd kept this a secret, maybe even from my mother, and decided before he died to let me know.

There was so much to process. For my entire adult life he had denigrated my ambitions; in my hand was the key to understanding why. He resented not just that I was living my dream, I was living *his* dream, which had been denied to him. What had looked to me like disapproval had actually been jealousy. It brought back so many memories, placing them all in a different context, and it raised as many questions as it answered. When I was rejected the first time, he couldn't express any empathy in a situation *that he himself had experienced*. It was hard for me even as an adult to see how small a man my father was.

And the broken ship model, the NX-01, which I blamed on Robert, who claimed innocence. I remembered how angry my father got when I accused my brother. I was suddenly sure that Robert *was* innocent; the boot that had stepped on it had in fact belonged to my father.

The anger dissipated, replaced by loss and regret for a connection that could have been—if he'd been a different man, a man who could communicate with his son, share his dreams, who didn't let his envy and frustration get in his way. And then I felt envy, envy of that young boy I'd just met who had a father to hold him.

✦

"We have read your report," Admiral Blackwell said. "I'm sorry to say we weren't convinced." I was in a large conference room on Starbase 32. At the table were two admirals, senior members of the Admiralty, and a third watching from a viewscreen. I knew none of them personally. This was a large gamble, one I had to take, not just for the war effort, but for everyone close to me.

The duty *Stargazer* drew was taking its toll on the ship and crew. Everyone understood the importance of keeping our ships supplied with those valuable assets that our replicators couldn't make, but as news of Starfleet's losses reached us, my ship's crew (and its captain) desired a more important role. I contacted Admiral Hanson, and made my pitch. Hanson arranged the meeting for me, though he couldn't be there; he was still on Earth. His task of keeping fleet production on its vigorous pace was even more vital.

The day-to-day operations of the war effort were in the hands of a few admirals, two of which were in this room and the third was sitting in a darkened room from an undisclosed location somewhere in the Galaxy. He was the important one, the one that I was counting on. The eldest of the three, at least 100 years old, didn't introduce himself, and seemed to be willing to leave me to the other two. But I was hoping when the moment came he would speak. Only he might have the information that would sell my plan. He in fact was the one admiral I'd asked Hanson to get in the meeting.

"I understand, Admiral Blackwell," I said. "But I have new information to add. I will keep it brief." I directed most of my presentation to Margaret Blackwell, a reserved woman in her fifties, as she at least offered some courtesy or the pretense of it.

I went to the viewscreen on the wall and brought up my chart.

"As I pointed out in my report," I said. "All the raids on Federation shipping and colonies before the Setlik III massacre were focused on specific technology. Technology related to our replicators."

"Yes, yes," Admiral Janeway said. "We told you we read your report already." This was Edward Janeway, clearly a man who wanted to be anywhere else. And I really couldn't blame him. Starfleet crews were losing their lives daily, and he was responsible for them.

"Captain Picard," Admiral Blackwell said, "your theory that the Cardassians became interested in Federation technology after having observed the replicator aboard your ship is interesting. But to suggest they went to war over it…"

"That's not what I'm suggesting," I said. "The raids were about the technology. The war is about us settling on Setlik III and establishing Starbase 211." Starbase 211 was the newest Federation outpost, built only a few light-years from the Cardassian border.

"Those were completely separate events," Janeway said. "The Starbase began construction long before the raids started, and the Federation colony on Setlik was not a Starfleet operation."

"There is no way the Cardassians could be sure of either of those facts," I said. "It is easier for them to believe that we knew of their lower technological level, and assume that we planned on taking advantage of it by invading from two new outposts."

"That is not the Federation way," Janeway said.

"No, but it is the Cardassian way," I said. "They projected their own motivations upon us." I could see that I wasn't making any progress. This was all in my original report; I was repeating a case I'd already argued unsuccessfully. But I had to keep going. "There is a way to end this conflict. We offer them the technology they were trying to steal before the war started."

"If, as you say," Admiral Blackwell said, "the raids are about replicator technology, then surely by now they've got it."

"Exactly," Janeway said. "We've lost several ships and bases. They must have salvaged something by now."

This was the moment I was waiting for, the reason I had stuck my neck out to make my case. I knew that Starfleet had intelligence operations behind the lines, operations that I didn't have clearance for. But one person in this meeting did. Now I looked over at him.

He was old, and gray. He had been a Starfleet officer since he was 22 and was now in charge of Starfleet Intelligence. I would love to have spent a day with him and learned about his incredible career, serving on two ships named *Enterprise*. But right now I just needed him to answer Blackwell's query.

He looked up and cracked a smile. The other two turned, sensing that their older companion was about to speak.

"The Cardassians haven't got it," he said, his voice thick with a Slavic accent. "Or they haven't figured out how to make it work. Their people are starving, and the military continues to promise that victory will feed their children."

This was what I needed. Blackwell and Janeway exchanged a look. "Wouldn't giving them replicator technology," Blackwell said, "violate the Prime Directive?"

"Do you think if it ended the war," Admiral Chekov said, "anybody would care?"

"The ends do not justify the means," Janeway said.

"Do what you want," Chekov said. "The kid's idea deserves a shot." He disappeared from the viewscreen. It took me a moment to realize that, at the age of 48, I was the "kid." Blackwell and Janeway exchanged a silent glance. Janeway sighed, resigned, and was the first to speak.

"Walk us through your plan once more."

✦

It took us five days to reach the Cardassian border. I'd chosen an area that was known to be well patrolled; it was important that I get their attention, but not be so close to their homeworld as to appear a threat.

"Approaching Sector 21503," Crusher said, from the conn.

"Hold station," I said, then turned to Black, and had him open a hailing frequency. I sent a general message to any Cardassian ship in the area that I was there to parlay for a truce.

It wasn't long before I received a response.

"Ship closing," Cheva said. "*Galor* class." This was the newest type of Cardassian vessel, and I'd suggested this area specifically because several of these newer class of ships had been encountered here. The *Stargazer* was no match for it, and that was the point. I wanted the Cardassians to believe my intentions were sincere. To get them to agree to a parlay, I would be offering a replicator. I was certain that it would show our good faith, and the relative weakness of my ship would show I was no threat.

The vessel hung in front of us.

"Sensors detect they've locked weapons," Vigo said. "Should I do the same?"

"Negative," I said. "We will take no provocative action." I had Black open another hailing frequency.

"Cardassian vessel, please respond," I said. "I bring greetings from the United Federation of Planets, who wishes to negotiate a ceasefire."

Still no response. I could tell them what I had to offer, but with them not responding I was doubtful they would believe me. They were aggressive and suspicious, and I expected they would think I was setting some kind of trap. I needed something to change the game.

"As a gesture of goodwill," I said. "I will lower my shields." Crusher turned and looked at me.

"Captain," he said, "I think we should give it a few more minutes." I thought about his suggestion; I suppose it had some merit. But I had already told the Cardassians what I was going to do, and so I was committed.

"Carry out my order," I said. Crusher turned back to his console, and Cheva lowered the shields. "Cardassian vessel, as you can see—"

I was thrown off my feet as a Cardassian disrupter ripped into the saucer section of the ship. Consoles exploded on the bridge.

"Direct hit," Cheva said. "Weapons systems damaged..."

"Shields up," I said, pulling myself off the deck.

"Shields non-responsive," Vigo said.

"Get us out of here..."

The Cardassian ship fired. I watched as the engineering console caught fire.

"Impulse engines off-line," Crusher said. I leaned over him. There was a course plotted away from the Cardassian ship, and I saw the warp engines were still online. I threw the switch to engage them, and we jumped to warp speed.

"Report!"

"We're at warp 2...warp 3..." Crusher said.

"Cardassian ship pursuing... they're at warp 4... warp 5..." Cheva said.

"Engineering," I said, talking into the intercom, "Scully, we need more speed..."

"I can give you warp 6," Scully said, "but we won't be able to hold it for long... it's a mess down here. Why did we lower the shields?"

"Just give me what you can," I said, ignoring his question. I was slammed forward—the Cardassian had hit us again with a torpedo. It looked like there was no salvaging this peace mission.

"Weapons status," I said.

"Forward and aft torpedo bays damaged, phasers inoperative," Cheva said.

The only reason we were still alive is the Cardassians had focused on taking out our weapons first. They'd been certain I was laying a trap.

"Black, send out a distress call," I said.

"They're jamming transmission," Black said. I checked the status of the Cardassian ship; it was overtaking us. This was bad and getting worse.

"Ship coming in," Cheva said. "It's the *U.S.S. Crazy Horse.*" The "cavalry" had arrived, ironically named after a Native American. The *Crazy Horse* raced past us, and opened fire on the Cardassian ship, who turned and ran.

"Subspace interference is fading," Black said. "Captain Ross calling." Captain Ross appeared on the viewscreen, smiling at me from the bridge of the *Crazy Horse.*

"Nice try, Jean-Luc," Ross said. "We'll get this guy off your back." I thanked him and headed for the barn. My "big swing" was a complete failure. We would stay on supply duty for the foreseeable future.

A few months later, the *U.S.S. Cairo,* under the command of the newly promoted Edward Jellico, took three ships, surrounded a *Galor*-class vessel and demanded a parlay. They respected the strength he showed and agreed to a temporary ceasefire… in exchange for a replicator and the instructions on how to build one. Jellico and Starfleet Command had seen the truth in my proposal, but I got no credit for it because my method almost lost me my ship. I wasn't sure my situation could get much worse.

How wrong I was.

✦

"They're called the Chalnoth," Ailat said. "My people have avoided them."

We had entered the Chalna system, which had one habitable world. The system was uncharted, but we'd entered an area of space not far from the Edosian homeworld, so I had called Dr. Ailat to the bridge to see if she could provide us with any information that wasn't in our computer memory.

"Do they have warp capability?" I asked.

"They did," Ailat said. "Their society fell victim to narcissistic leaders, and has since devolved into anarchy. Such unrest makes maintaining a space-going infrastructure impossible. Which, I would say, is fortunate for its neighboring systems."

"Put us in a standard orbit," I said. I watched on the viewscreen as we approached the brown and yellow planet.

"I'm detecting orbital structures and ships," Cheva said. On the screen, a large space station floated toward us. "No power signatures or life signs."

As we got closer, it was very clear that the station had been abandoned for a long time. There were signs of battle damage, breaches to its hull caused by energy weapons and projectiles. A number of ships of various sizes were drifting nearby, all dead. The scene was foreboding.

"Scan the planet," I said.

"Heavily populated, signs of some advanced technology," Cheva said.

"Have they scanned us?"

"No, sir," Vigo said. "No sign of scanners or advanced ground-to-space weapons systems."

"There's a lot of dilithium down there," Cheva said. I looked over at her scanner. There was a highlighted section on the planet, a rich vein over a hundred kilometers square. It was very tantalizing. Starfleet had no source of the valuable substance—responsible for powering starships—in this section of the Galaxy. Having a mining treaty in this sector that could supply Starfleet with dilithium would be a vital resource given the current political situation. We had a ceasefire with the Cardassians that could break down at any moment, and though the Klingons were no longer threatening the Federation, they had armed the Tzenkethi, who were making aggressive moves. The possibility of war was never far off.

"What does the Prime Directive say about a planet like this?" Cheva said.

"They had warp drive once," Crusher said. "And those ships aren't that old. They're aware of other worlds and other cultures."

I looked over at Ailat, who nodded.

"The Chalnoth have been in space in my lifetime," Ailat said. "It is unlikely they've forgotten that other worlds exist." The Prime Directive specifically stated that any contact with a primitive society with no knowledge of the other star-faring species meant that could not be revealed to them. However, if they were already aware, the Federation could trade with them.

"And we've got to have something they want," Crusher said. I smiled, knowing what was behind Jack pushing this mission. He'd recently gotten other offers to be first officer on better ships than this one, and turned them all down. He maintained he was only going to leave for a ship of his own. But I knew he was staying out of loyalty to me, and I also knew it would only be a matter of time before someone gave him a captain's chair. Until that happened, he'd taken it upon himself to get me out of my career purgatory. A treaty to mine dilithium on Chalna might do the trick.

"Still," I said, "it seems dangerous to beam down without knowing more."

"We can't beam down near the dilithium vein anyway," Cheva said. "There's too much interference."

"All right," I said. "Cheva, you, Vigo, and Dr. Ailat take a shuttle, scout the area and report back." I stared at the derelict spaceships hanging in front of me. They felt like a warning. One I didn't heed.

✦

"*Shuttlecraft Erickson*, do you read?" Black said. There was no response.

We'd lost contact with the shuttle just as it cleared the cloud layer. They were flying low over the area when Cheva reported they'd been hit by an energy weapon and lost engine control.

"I've got them," Crusher said. "They've crashed."

"Life signs?"

"Faint," he said. "Difficult to read with all the interference."

"Transporter Room," I said, into the intercom, "can we lock onto them and beam them up?"

"Negative," Transporter Chief Youlin said. "All that interference from the dilithium is disrupting their patterns."

"What about the emergency transporter in the shuttle?" Crusher said.

"It's not powerful enough to reach the ship at this distance," Youlin said.

"It doesn't have to be," Crusher said. "We can operate it remotely to act as a pattern enhancer so we can beam down to *them*." Transporter-to-transporter beaming was always much safer; Crusher's idea was brilliant. Once there, the shuttle's transporter could be used to enhance our lock on the survivors.

"If it's still operational," Youlin said, "that should work, but we can only send one person at a time. More than that is too risky."

"All right," I said. I had decided it was my responsibility to rescue Cheva and the landing party. I had ignored the danger signs, and now they might die because of it. "Mr. Crusher, you have the bridge…"

As I reached the turbolift, Crusher moved to intercept me.

"Request permission…" he said.

"Denied," I said.

"With all due respect, sir," Crusher said, "we have no knowledge of who shot the shuttle down, no knowledge of the damage it has sustained. It is reckless for you to beam in there with so little information." I looked at him; he felt responsible too. And, as much as I hated to admit it, he was right. As cowardly as I felt staying behind, it was irresponsible of me to beam myself into an obviously dangerous situation with absolutely no knowledge of the conditions awaiting me.

"Very well, Mr. Crusher," I said. "Proceed." I watched him leave the bridge, wishing I'd had another choice.

A few minutes later, Crusher had beamed into the shuttle, and immediately managed to activate the onboard communicator. We had a visual image of the interior of the damaged craft. Cheva, Ailat, and Vigo were all unconscious, bleeding from head wounds.

Crusher scanned them with a medical tricorder.

"They've got concussions," Crusher said. "Looks like it was a pretty rough ride."

"Is the shuttle operational?" I said.

"Negative," he said. "But we should be able to beam everybody up, one at a time." He picked up Cheva and brought her to lay under the shuttle's emergency transporter.

"Youlin, one to beam up."

"Picking up life signs closing in on the shuttle," Black said, sitting at ops. I looked at the readout: five life-forms were closing on the shuttle from all directions.

"Did you hear that, Jack?"

"Affirmative," Crusher said. We watched as Cheva energized and disappeared. Crusher then picked up Ailat and put her in the same spot. The shuttle was suddenly rocked. Someone or something was trying to get in from outside. Crusher braced himself as the craft slid back and forth. "Youlin, you've got another one, energize!"

"Can we fire weapons from here? Stun those intruders?"

"We won't have an exact lock," Black said. "And if we hit the shuttle, even on the stun setting, it might negatively affect the transport." We watched Ailat disappear. Crusher was already hauling Vigo out of his seat and bringing him to the transporter.

A gash suddenly appeared on the shuttle wall, which looked to be caused, incredibly, by a *knife*. It must have been made of a fantastically hard metal. And whoever was wielding it tore through the bulkhead like it was tin.

And then another knife sliced another part of the hull. And another.

"Looks like I've got company," Crusher said, as he dragged Vigo, a head taller than him, achingly slowly. I wanted to get down there and help him, but there would be no use, it would just slow down his escape. So all I could do was watch.

He finally laid Vigo into place. "Youlin, go!" Crusher said, as he stepped away and drew his phaser. The first intruder had now opened a hole in the shuttle revealing his face: a mane of red hair and small tusks around the mouth reminiscent of a Nausicaan but with a wild-eyed fierceness. It cut away an entrance big enough to move through.

Jack fired his phaser, and the creature fell back, only to be replaced by another. Vigo finally energized, and disappeared. Crusher went to the transport area.

"Beam him up!" I said. I watched as two more Chalnoth forced their way into the shuttle. Jack fired again. One went down as the other moved across the craft, slashing his formidable blade across Jack's neck, just before he disappeared in the transporter beam.

I ran down to the transporter room. A medical team was wheeling out Vigo as I raced inside. Two medics were standing over Jack, who lay on the pad. Blood flowed freely from a laceration that went across his neck and up to the top of his head. The medics worked on closing the gaping wound as I kneeled down beside him.

"Jack," I said. "We got you…"

He looked up at me, in pleading disbelief. A gurgling sound came from his neck. The medics closed the wound, placed him on a waiting gurney, and hurried out with him. I stayed where I was, kneeling in a wide pool of my friend's blood.

✦

"It's good of you to come," Beverly said. It was overly formal; she was struggling to hold back her emotions.

"It's the least I could do," I said. We walked slowly through the corridor of Starbase 32 heading to the morgue. I had arrived with the *Stargazer* to bring Jack back to his family. We were withdrawn, both mourning the loss of the most important person in our lives. Jack had died because he was protecting me. He was my friend, my family. I felt a loss that was immeasurable. And yet I knew it was nothing next to the loss Beverly was experiencing.

We entered the morgue and approached the table where Jack's body lay, covered with a sheet. I knew what was under the sheet. I'd watched as Dr. Ailat, still recovering from her own injuries, worked with her medical team to try and save Jack's life. The image of my dead friend was branded in my memory. I turned to Beverly.

"You shouldn't remember him like this." She looked down at the sheet, stoic.

"It's important to me," she said. "I have to face the fact that he's gone."

I nodded and reached for the sheet. It seemed to take all my strength to lift it up. Jack lay there, white and still. Beverly took a moment, leaned in, and kissed his forehead. Her tears began. I covered Jack and held her a moment. She forced herself to recover.

"I've got to go find Wesley," she said.

"He doesn't know?" I said. She shook her head.

I went with her back out into the corridor, and we made our way to one of the station's schoolrooms. Wesley, now five years old, sat at a table, playing with geometric toys. The teacher in the room had obviously been informed; she ushered the other children to another part of the room as we knelt down next to him.

"Wesley," Beverly said. "You remember Captain Picard." He looked at me, unsure. We'd only met a couple of times, and I'd kept my visits short. He held up the geometric toys.

"I'm building a model of the atomic structure of dikironium," he said. I looked at the toys and realized that he had indeed made them to resemble an atomic diagram. "It's an element that can only be created in a laboratory."

"That's very clever," I said.

"Wesley," Beverly said, "I have something to tell you. Dad… is… he's been hurt. I'm sorry… he died."

"Did he go to the doctor?"

"He did, but the doctor couldn't help him." Beverly was holding back her tears, her arm gently around the little boy's shoulder.

"Oh," he said. "Can I finish my model now?"

Beverly smiled and nodded. "Sure," she said, kissed his forehead.

"Can we stay and watch you?" I said. Wesley nodded, and I sat down with Beverly and watched as he worked on his remarkably complex model.

Later, I said goodbye to Beverly, and told her that if there was anything she needed I hoped she would contact me. But I knew that she wouldn't; I was an unpleasant reminder of how the man she loved was taken away from her. I had given the orders that led to his death. I expected I would never see her again.

The love I felt for her could never be returned.

I returned to the *Stargazer*, lost and empty, about to embark on what would be my last mission as its captain.

✦

"Phasers coming to full charge, sir," Black said. "Torpedoes armed."

Smoke was filling the bridge. I stared at the strange wedge-shaped ship on the viewscreen, circling away from us.

"Who are they?" I said to Black, but he had no answer. I couldn't expect my new first officer to know any more than I did. We had been charting the Maxia Zeta star system, and were near a moon near the seventh planet. We'd passed over a large crater, and then suddenly we were hit. Our adversary must have been lying in wait for us deep inside, shielded from our sensors by the moon's mineral deposits. Our shields were down, and the first attack took out our impulse drive and shield generator. The second attack destroyed our life-support systems, including fire suppression. Fires broke out on the bridge.

"They're turning for another pass, sir," Black said.

"We can't take another hit, Captain," Vigo said. It was clear their intention was to destroy us. Sensors indicated they had a weapons lock. I had to fool that lock…

"Set course 7-7, mark 20," I said. This course would move us to within a few hundred meters of the enemy. It was a risky maneuver, one that would not work against a more experienced captain.

"Ready phasers and lock," I said. "Stand by on warp 9." My conn officer, Lieutenant Lee, still relatively new to the job, keyed in the course, despite his obvious confusion about what I was doing. By jumping to warp, we would appear to this enemy ship to be in two places at once; for a brief moment, their weapons lock would be on our former position. I would only have a second…

I watched as the adversary turned full on to face us.

"Engage!" The enemy ship zoomed in; the underside of its hull filled our viewscreen. "Fire!"

Torpedoes and phasers overwhelmed the enemy's shields and cut through the hull. There was a cascade of explosions, and then it was gone. I considered myself lucky; it was entirely possible that his shields might have held against that attack, and then we'd be finished. As it was, my ship was in deep trouble.

"Engineering to Bridge," Cheva said. After the first attack, we'd lost contact with engineering and I'd sent Cheva down to take stock of the situation. "I can't get the system back online, and the fire control teams have more than they can handle. It's spreading out of control."

"What about the life-support system?"

"Completely fused, sir, can't be repaired," she said. With fires throughout the ship, and a failed life-support system, the air would be gone in a matter of minutes.

"Where's Scully?" I said.

"Chief Engineer Scully… is dead, sir," Cheva said. "Killed in the first attack." I was stunned. Scully had survived so long, *Stargazer* was more his than mine. And now he was dead, and our ship along with it. A brutal and merciless enemy had just attacked us.

There might be more of them. I had to try to get the crew to safety.

"All hands, abandon ship," I said, then turned to the bridge crew. "Get to your evacuation stations."

✦

I was crammed inside a shuttle with about twenty crewmen. Cheva was at the piloting controls. I took the seat next to her, and watched out the view port as the rest of the shuttles left the bay.

"We're the last, sir," Cheva said. "Ready to depart."

"Make it so," I said. I'd never used that phrase before; it had belonged to Captain Quinn, my first commander. It took me only a little while to understand why.

We flew out of the ship, and joined a string of shuttlecraft and escape pods, all moving in formation away from *Stargazer*; a flotilla, limping away from our dead home. I had sent a distress signal to Starfleet before we evacuated, laying out the course our ships would be taking. The crew was under strict orders to maintain radio silence on their shuttles and escape pods. I knew it was a futile gesture—if an enemy ship was nearby and looking for us, they would find us long before help from Starfleet arrived.

Ailat and her medical team were on three medical shuttles tending to the injured. We'd had twenty-three deaths in the attack—I made sure Black kept a record. If we were to survive I had to inform their families. Was it my fault they were dead? I couldn't let myself think about that, I had to make sure I concentrated on the survival of the rest of the crew. I focused on protocol: I had to mark the time and date that I'd left the ship. A captain abandoning his vessel was an act Starfleet would scrutinize.

I looked back at the old lady, wrecked and lifeless. A fount of so many memories: Laughton, Mazzara and his children... becoming a captain, Walker and Jack coming on board... Beverly...

I couldn't let myself get lost in sentiment. I had work to do. I opened the log. That's when I noticed the date.

I remembered the first time I heard Captain Quinn say, "Make it so": he was giving me the order to save the ambassador on Milika III. That had imprinted on me as the defining moment of my career. Unconsciously, I must have known abandoning my own ship was one, too. I looked at the date again.

July 13, 2355.

My 50th birthday. And I'd just lost everything.

CHAPTER EIGHT

"THIS COURT-MARTIAL IS NOW IN SESSION," Admiral Milano said. Six other officers, captains and admirals, joined him on the court-martial board. I sat opposite their table in courtroom #3 of the Bormenus Building, headquarters of the JAG* at Starfleet Command. The clerk, on a nod from Milano, activated the computer, and the familiar female voice read the charges against me.

"Charge: Culpable Negligence and Dereliction of Duty. Specifications: In that on stardate 33994.5, by such negligence and dereliction of duty, Captain Picard, Jean-Luc, did cause both loss of life and destruction of *U.S.S. Stargazer*, NCC-2893..."

I sat with my defense counsel in a bit of a daze. Across from us was the prosecutor. The whole event was surreal. Only two months ago I was still in space, limping along with shuttles and escape pods with the remainder of my *Stargazer* crew. We had been traveling for weeks when we were rescued by the hospital ship *U.S.S. Caine*. They saw to our needs; Dr. Ailat had done a superb job keeping the wounded alive, but many of them needed further treatment. The rest of us were suffering from fatigue and post-traumatic stress.

---

*EDITOR'S NOTE: The Starfleet Judge Advocate General's Corps (JAG) is the branch concerned with Starfleet law and justice. The building was named after Bormenus, an Andorian, who, before serving as president of the Federation in the 23rd century, was one of the first Starfleet Judge Advocate Generals.

We arrived back at Earth, the *Caine* moored in the orbital dockyard. I received word to report to Starfleet Headquarters to give a debriefing. As I was leaving the ship, I found many of the survivors of the *Stargazer* crowded in the corridor by the airlock. At the front of the pack were Cheva, Ailat, Vigo and Black.

"Everything all right?" I said.

"Yes, sir," Black said. "The crew and I just wanted to say goodbye."

I realized, as they must have, that, given the vicissitudes of the service, it was quite possible I might never see them again.

"I hope we can serve together again," Cheva said.

"I hope so, too," I said. I then turned to the crowd.

"We owe you our lives," Vigo said.

"Oh, no," I said. "We all owe our lives to that ship who protected us longer than anyone ever expected her to, and the crew who sacrificed their lives so that we could survive. And now, it's up to us to keep the memory of our fellow crewmen, and the old lady herself, alive by continuing to serve as you all have done, and as they did, with integrity and distinction."

"Hear, hear!" Black shouted, and the rest joined in, cheering and applauding. I smiled at them all, and waved goodbye, wondering when I'd see them again. It turned out for some, it was sooner than I could imagine.

✦

I had been told to report to Admiral Quinn's office. I was looking forward to seeing him. He was now in charge of Starfleet's Operational Support Services. When I arrived in his office, he wasn't alone.

"Jean-Luc, good to see you," Quinn said. "Glad you made it back in one piece." He then turned to introduce me to his guest. I was too stunned upon seeing her to tell him we'd already met. "This is Commander Phillipa Louvois of the Judge Advocate General."

I hadn't seen her in over 25 years. Her hair was short, but other than that she looked much the same as she did at the academy. I was filled with a nostalgic affection for that more innocent time. I walked over to greet her and was met with a metaphoric wall of ice.

"Captain Picard and I know each other from the Academy," she said. She couldn't have been clearer if she'd been a telepath: Quinn wasn't to know about our former relationship. I held back; I could certainly respect her position.

"Nice to see you again, Commander," I said. If Quinn picked up on anything between us, he didn't let on. He made a gesture for me to sit down. I took the chair next to Phillipa as Quinn went back behind his desk.

"Captain," he said, "the commander has informed me that the Judge Advocate General is convening a court-martial regarding your loss of the *Stargazer*."

"On what charge?" I said.

"There is no charge as of yet," Phillipa said. "It's routine. A court-martial is standard procedure when a ship is lost. My preliminary findings don't indicate any other charges. As of yet."

"*Your* preliminary findings?"

"I am prosecuting this case, yes," she said. "Someone in my office will be contacting you to serve as your defense counsel. Now, I hope you'll excuse me, I have another appointment." Phillipa got up and left the room.

"Jean-Luc," Quinn said, "I've read your report. I don't think you have anything to worry about. She's just doing her job."

I thought about telling him about our past, and that I thought she was pursuing an old grudge, but that seemed silly, and I couldn't tell him without it looking like I was unfairly trying to impugn her motives. So I let it lie.

Admiral Quinn invited me to join him for dinner, but I declined. I was assigned quarters in San Francisco and went back there that evening to think about my situation. A court martial? I hadn't even considered that was a possibility. I'd been mourning the crew that had died and the ship I'd lost. And now I found myself concerned about Phillipa. We'd had a brief romance, I wondered if that would affect her prosecution of my case. Would it lead her to be vindictive? I couldn't imagine that it would.

My brooding was interrupted by the doorbell. I went to answer it and found a Starfleet lieutenant commander in his thirties. He was overweight, balding, and somehow familiar. He carried a briefcase.

"Hello, Captain Picard," he said.

"Hello," I said. I felt I knew him, but I couldn't figure out from where. He saw my confusion.

"My apologies, sir," he said. "I'm Lieutenant Commander Anthony Mazzara. I look a lot different than when we last met."

A strange surprise. I hadn't seen him since he left the *Stargazer* when he was 17. Between seeing Phillipa in Quinn's office and now Anthony showing up at my door, it felt like an aphorism about chickens returning to roost was appropriate. I had a fair amount of questions about what he was doing there, but I had too many things on my mind at that moment to indulge my curiosity.

"Anthony," I said, "it's nice to see you, but you're really catching me at a bad time…"

"I'm sorry again, sir," he said. "This isn't a social visit. I've been assigned as your defense counsel by the JAG office."

"You've been assigned…"

"Yes, I'm sorry no one informed you," he said. "May I come in?"

In a bit of a daze, I gestured for him to come inside. This felt like a terrible practical joke, but there was no one alive who would know to play it. With little choice, I joined him at the table.

"You're a lawyer?"

"Yes, sir, I've been in the JAG corps for seven years. I'll do my best to help you."

I knew Phillipa, and I knew him; I thought she would eat him alive.

"Seems like quite a coincidence, you getting assigned to me."

"Truth be told," he said, "when I heard you were being court-martialed, I asked to be made defense counsel."

"Really? Why?"

"I felt like I still need to make up for the egg."

I couldn't help but laugh. I had no choice but to embrace the absurdity of the situation.

"All right, Mr. Mazzara," I said. "What do we do?"

✦

He spent the next two weeks asking me questions about my service aboard the *Stargazer*, as well as the specific events leading up to the exodus from it. Though I might have been initially reticent about being defended by Anthony Mazzara, those concerns quickly vanished. He had grown up on the *Stargazer*, and he knew much about the specific challenges of serving on and commanding that ship. There was so much I didn't have to explain to him; we saved a great deal of time. And I felt I had a sympathetic ear.

But, as the trial date approached, I became more concerned about Phillipa. Anthony knew her, and said that the staff in the JAG office had never seen her so driven on a case. My worries were confirmed the day before the trial when Mazzara came to my quarters, looking grave.

"She's charging you with culpable negligence and dereliction of duty," he said.

"On what grounds?"

"That I don't know," he said. "She has the same evidence I have. I don't think she has a case."

The next morning, Anthony met me at the courtroom, and as we headed inside, I saw Phillipa approaching. I asked Anthony to let me talk to her alone.

"As your counsel, I have to strongly advise against that."

"I'll be all right," I said.

"Watch what you say." Anthony went inside. I intercepted Phillipa before she reached the courtroom.

"May I have a moment?"

"I don't think that's a good idea," she said.

"Phillipa, why are you doing this?"

"What I'm doing is my job," she said. "I don't know who you told about us…"

"I haven't told anyone…"

"Whether you have or not, I can't afford to let people think I'd make it easy on an old boyfriend. Now, if you'll excuse me." She walked past me into the courtroom, and I realized she still cared about me. But she was going to prove that her feelings wouldn't get in the way of her work. I thought, as I walked into the courtroom, this made her a lot more dangerous.

✦

After the reading of the charges, Phillipa called her first witness.

"Please state your name and rank for the record," Phillipa said.

"My full name is Tcheri Chevapravatdumrong, Lieutenant Commander," Cheva said. "I use the last name 'Cheva' for short." I could see that Cheva was nervous on the stand. She was concerned that something she might say would get me in trouble. Phillipa began asking general questions about how long she served with me, and then got into the specifics about the events leading to my order to abandon ship.

"We'd suffered catastrophic damage. The impulse drive was inoperative, the shield generator destroyed, the life-support system was fused and the fire suppression system was offline, among other things."

"That seems like an awful lot of damage," Phillipa said.

"They hit us with our shields down."

"As operations officer, making sure *Stargazer* is up to date on its scheduled maintenance is part of your duties?"

"Yes," Cheva said.

"And was it?"

"I'm sorry?"

"Did *Stargazer* adhere to the Starfleet schedule of maintenance?"

"No…" Cheva said. The trial board looked surprised by this response, but I knew what she was going to say. "*Stargazer* was over sixty years old. Starfleet's maintenance schedule wasn't strict enough, so the captain had the chief engineer devise a more rigorous one."

"Thank you, Commander," Phillipa said. "No further questions." Unlike the board, Phillipa wasn't surprised by Cheva's answer. It appeared that this was the answer she expected, even wanted. It was Anthony's turn to ask questions.

"Lieutenant Commander Cheva," Anthony said, "in your opinion, as an officer experienced in space combat, was there any action Captain Picard took that you would characterize as being directly responsible for the disabling of the *Stargazer*?"

"Absolutely not, sir," Cheva said. "In fact, Captain Picard's actions saved the lives of the surviving crew."

"Thank you, Commander," Anthony said. "No further questions."

Over the next two days, Phillipa interviewed other crewmembers. They all confirmed Cheva's version of events. But Phillipa always continued questioning with some aspect of their work that indicated the difficulty of working on a ship as old as the *Stargazer*. She'd done her research: she had Black recount my first day taking the *Stargazer* out, with Scully repairing the helm as we did; Vigo relayed our disastrous encounter with the Cardassian ship; Dr. Ailat spoke of the difficult stress the crew was constantly under because the ship was often on the verge of breaking down. Anthony always cross-examined them, emphasizing the ship's achievements. Toward the end of the second day, Phillipa called one last witness.

"Prosecution calls Captain Jean-Luc Picard to the stand."

Anthony reacted immediately.

"Objection, Your Honor," he said. "Starfleet and Federation law plainly state that Captain Picard is not required to testify as a witness for his own prosecution."

"Prosecution concedes this," Phillipa said. "Captain Picard is free to decline."

"I need a moment to confer with my client," Anthony said. He leaned into me and spoke very softly. "You don't have to do this. If you don't take the stand I think I can get a dismissal. She hasn't come close to making a case for culpable negligence or dereliction of duty."

"She's hoping I make the case for her," I said. Anthony nodded. I looked over at Phillipa, back at her table, giving me a challenging stare. I then scanned the faces of the trial board. The men and women were impassive, difficult to read. I knew that if I didn't take the stand, there might be some of those captains and admirals who'd assume I had something to hide. Phillipa knew how much my reputation meant to me, and she assumed that it would compel me to put myself in a vulnerable position. And, of course, she was right, I had no choice. I stood up, and walked over to the witness stand. I saw Phillipa smile.

✦

"…we moved into position, and fired everything we had," I said. Phillipa had made me go through the battle, and my account bore little difference from the other witnesses.

"Very clever," Phillipa said. "Please tell the court, were you surprised at the amount of damage your adversary caused the ship?"

"No," I said, "the fact that the shields were down, combined with the *Stargazer*'s age…"

"So you think that the ship's age played a role in it being so easily disabled?"

"I don't know for certain…"

"Do you know what the average life of a ship is in Starfleet, Captain?"

"I do not," I said.

She immediately walked over with a PADD in hand. "I would like to offer into evidence Starfleet Exhibit 2, the Starfleet Ship Inventory," she said. She handed me the PADD. On the screen was a spreadsheet of all the types of ships currently in active duty in Starfleet, along with their ages.

"Please read me the average ship age of all the ships in the fleet, Captain." At the bottom of the sheet, the average ship age had been calculated.

"16.2 years," I said.

"And, as has been previously testified, *Stargazer* was over 60 years old. Is that correct?"

"Yes," I said. "63.7 years in fact."

"Thank you. Did you ever consider that *Stargazer* was too old to be in service?"

"That was not my decision to make," I said. But I began to understand where Phillipa was headed.

"Did you ever consider recommending to the Admiralty that they take *Stargazer* out of service?"

"No," I said.

"Why not? If, as has been testified, the ship's age caused it to be plagued with difficulties, required a much stricter than average maintenance schedule, caused undue stress on its crew, and made it more vulnerable to catastrophic failure after an attack, wasn't it your duty to inform Starfleet that the ship was unsafe?"

I glanced at the faces of the court-martial board. They looked annoyed. One of them, Admiral Dougherty, shook his head slightly in frustration. It appeared that Phillipa's line of attack was working. I looked back at her waiting for my answer; she knew my weakness. If I'd informed Starfleet that *Stargazer* was unfit for service, I'd have been potentially giving up my command, with no guarantee of another. And perhaps that pride and ambition had kept me from seeing the danger I was putting the crew in.

"Court will direct the witness to answer the question," Phillipa said.

"It may have been my duty," I said.

"No more questions," she said, and sat down.

Admiral Milano, the court-martial board chair, turned to Anthony. Anthony, however, wasn't paying attention; he was furiously typing into another PADD.

"Defense counsel," Milano said, a little annoyed. "Any questions for the witness?"

"No questions," Anthony said without looking up from the work he was doing. I could see this surprised Phillipa.

"Defendant may step down," Milano said. I went and rejoined Anthony at the table. "Does the prosecution wish to call any more witnesses?"

"No, sir," Phillipa said. "Prosecution rests."

"If defense has no objection," Milano said, "the court suggests we adjourn till tomorrow, and defense can begin its case."

"Actually, Your Honor," Anthony said, looking up from his PADD, "defense moves all the charges and specifications in this matter be dismissed. The prosecution has failed to make her case for culpable negligence or dereliction of duty."

"Objection, Your Honor," Phillipa said. "I have shown that Captain Picard ignored the condition of his craft and unnecessarily put his crew's life at risk."

"In fact, Your Honor," Anthony said, "she has not. Captain Picard did not ignore the condition of his craft. He worked to make sure that it was in proper working order. And, for twenty years, he succeeded, until it was brutally and mercilessly attacked. The prosecution, having never served as part of a crew, does not understand if a vessel is space-worthy; the requirements of the service necessitate the captain 'make do,' which Captain Picard did. Historical precedent is on the side of the defense."

"What historical precedent?" Phillipa said.

"I just did a record search," he said, holding up his PADD. "No captain in the history of Starfleet has ever suggested to the admiralty they decommission their own ship. I submit this as Defense Exhibit 1." Anthony brought the PADD over to Milano, and then he stood in front of the board.

"Captain Picard never hid the condition of his ship from the admiralty. His maintenance and repair reports were quite thorough in their description of the *Stargazer*'s deficiencies. He did his job. It was up to the admiralty to decide whether the ship should be decommissioned, not its captain."

"The board will consider defense's motion," Milano said. "Court stands adjourned until tomorrow."

Phillipa, annoyed, left the courtroom. I turned to Anthony.

"I'm not sure this will work," I said. "She made a very convincing case."

"Not to them," Anthony said, referring to the board as it filed out of the room. "Did you see their faces?"

"Yes," I said, "they looked angry."

"At *her*, not you. Almost all those officers have been in command of a ship, and I bet they've all had to live with substandard equipment at one time or another. None of them would want to have been held to the standard Louvois is trying to hold you to."

I considered Anthony's point. The fact was Phillipa's argument had landed with me. But I appreciated this man's passion in my defense.

"How about some dinner?" he said.

"Sure," I said. "I'm in the mood for eggs."

Anthony looked at me and laughed.

✦

"Congratulations, Jean-Luc," Quinn said. I was back in his office three days later. Two days before, the trial board had ruled in favor of Anthony's motion and dismissed the charges, clearing me of any wrongdoing. I had tried to talk to Phillipa, but as soon as the court was adjourned, she was gone. It turns out my exoneration had ramifications for her as well.

"You'll be happy to know your prosecutor resigned," Quinn said.

"What? Why?"

"Judge Advocate General thought her prosecution was unnecessarily aggressive from the start, but against his advice she went full steam ahead anyway. The fact that the trial board ruled against her only confirmed her superior's opinion, so she drew a reprimand. I heard she quit on the spot."

That was unfortunate. I was never sure what was behind Phillipa's uncompromising prosecution of my court martial. The romantic egotist in me wanted to believe that it was an attempt at retribution for a broken heart, but I think it was simply that she liked to win. I was sorry to hear that it had ended her career.

"So, now that you're a free man," Quinn said, "what are your plans?"

"Well," I said, "I'm hoping for a new command."

"I'm going to be straight with you, my friend," Quinn said. "That's not going to be possible for a while."

"Why not?"

"Phillipa did land a few punches, mostly on the admiralty. She made us look bad by implying we left *Stargazer* in service too long. A complete re-evaluation of the fleet is underway. We're going to be pulling a lot of ships off the line and getting new ones going. I need to put you on a desk for a while."

This was far from what I wanted to hear, and I also knew he was leaving out the most important fact: I had lost a ship. There were some ways Starfleet was still quite traditional, and, no matter the circumstance, losing a ship was not something that was going to be rewarded. Which also meant I wouldn't be seeing a promotion anytime soon.

"All right," I said. "What did you have in mind?"

"If you come work for me," he said, "I promise to get you back on a bridge, and it'll be the right ship, I assure you."

"It would be my honor to serve with you, Admiral," I said. He shook my hand and had a yeoman show me to an office. It was much like the one I'd had when I was Hanson's chief of staff, but unlike that job, I would see little of this room.

Though Quinn had described this as a "desk job," he and the admiralty had an agenda that required I be dispatched to starbases and shipyards to deal with a variety of issues regarding construction, upgrades and personnel. But before I left, I made sure to see to a couple of important loose ends.

I used my influence with Quinn to try to find the crewmen and women of the *Stargazer* prominent positions throughout the fleet. Cheva, after twenty years serving with me, deserved her own command, and Quinn approved her posting to command of the *U.S.S. Roosevelt*. Ironically, it was much easier to get her a ship than to get one for myself. Black also deserved his own vessel, and with some prodding Quinn was able to get him posted as captain of the science vessel *Bonestell*. Dr. Ailat took a leave of absence from Starfleet, but I secured her promise to return if I ever had a command again. I found positions for many others as well, and felt good that, despite my difficulties, my crew wouldn't be tarred with the same brush as me.

Soon after, Quinn briefed me on my specific agenda. Our department was working with Starfleet Tactical to move ships and personnel so that there would be a strike force ready at a moment's notice near Sector 003. Quinn couldn't fully brief me on why; that would have to wait until I arrived at Starbase 3, the last stop on my journey. I accepted the secrecy without question. Nothing I knew about the major civilizations in that sector—Tellar, the Vega Colony and Denobula Triaxa—made me think that any of them would provide a threat.

The first leg of my trip was a short one: the Utopia Planitia shipyards in orbit of Mars. I requisitioned a shuttle and flew there myself. The trip took less than an hour, but it was still pleasant being back at the helm of a ship. When I entered orbit of Mars, I took a leisurely tour of the web-like dry docks arranged above the red planet. A diverse assortment of ships were in various stages of completion. I had a specific ship to visit and headed for its coordinates. The vessel was the first of a new class of starship Starfleet was developing and was still under construction. I was there to prod the captain and chief engineer along, in the hopes that the ship might be of use in the upcoming mission. But as I approached, I knew this was an impossibility: much of the saucer section of the ship was still just a skeleton. Still, I'd been sent by Quinn to try to move things along, so that's what I would do. I received permission to berth the shuttle at the dry dock's center of operations and disembarked.

The center of operations was a buzz of activity, monitoring all the teams of crewmen in spaceships working on the hull through the large windows of the operations center. Two people greeted me: a gray-haired captain and a young woman.

"Welcome aboard, Captain Picard," the captain said. "I'm Tom Halloway, this is Chief Engineer Sarah MacDougal." Halloway was in command of the ship under construction. "Can we show you around?"

"That would be splendid," I said.

"He doesn't want a tour, Tom," MacDougal said. "He wants to know why we're so far behind."

I have to say that despite her rather rude manner, I appreciated her cutting to the point.

"Well, Admiral Quinn did want me to get an update on your current schedule," I said.

"It's the damned holodecks," MacDougal said. "It's impossible to get one of them working properly, let alone *seven*."

"Holodecks?" I said. "What's a holodeck?"

"Oh crap, are you cleared for this?" MacDougal said.

"My god, Sarah, what have you done?" Halloway said, in mock dismay. He clearly enjoyed teasing her.

"I have level 10 security clearance," I said. "Now, what's a holodeck?"

"We'll show you," Halloway said, then turned to MacDougal. "It's on the tour."

They led me out of the operations center down to a docking tunnel to a docked support vessel. We walked through a corridor over to a control panel near a large hatch.

"This holovessel was designed specifically to test the holodeck in space," MacDougal said.

"I still don't know…"

"You from Paris, Jean-Luc?" Halloway said.

"Actually, a small village named La Barre," I said. Seemed a strange question to ask at that moment.

"Well, I don't know if that's in the memory banks, but let's see," Halloway said. He leaned into the computer panel, "Computer, location, La Barre, France, Earth, Picard home, nice autumn afternoon." I couldn't imagine what he was doing.

"Program complete," the computer said, and Halloway led me to the hatch; it opened automatically.

I almost fainted.

I was standing in front of my childhood home, with the large wooden wine barrels next to the front door. I felt the slight breeze, the smell of fermented grapes. It was impossible. I was seeing my whole vineyard—the area took up an area larger than the ship itself. I bent down and grabbed a handful of the gravel beneath my feet. I stood back up and let it roll around in my hand. It was real. I was back at home. I half expected Robert to walk by.

And then he did.

Robert exited the barn, wearing an apron covered in wine stains, wiping his hand with a dirty cloth. I knew it was a computer simulation, but he still conjured an adverse reaction. Until he gave me a big smile.

"Good morning," he said. "Welcome to my humble home."

I reached out and gently touched his shoulder. He was *there*; it wasn't a hologram.

"Are you quite all right?" he said.

"Computer, freeze program," Halloway said. Robert froze in position with that ridiculous and unnatural smile. "Pretty good, huh?" I looked back and saw Halloway and MacDougal standing in an archway by the door leading to the ship's corridors, which bluntly interrupted the view down our path to the village.

"It's unbelievable," I said. "How does it…?"

"It combines transporter and replicator technology for the simpler forms like plants, trees, buildings," Halloway said, "and holograms and force fields to create the people and animals." Almost before I could finish, the scene disappeared. As it did, the walls seemed to move in; the winery and the horizon along with it were an illusion. Now I was standing in a large black box, segmented by a grid of yellow lines on the walls, floor, and ceiling. MacDougal went to the archway control panel.

"It shorted out again," MacDougal said. "This is why we're behind; this holodeck is actually hooked up through the dry dock to *Enterprise*'s power grid, but it keeps overloading it."

"We'll solve it," Halloway said, "but you've got to tell Quinn it's going to take time."

"Understood," I said. I was still processing the experience, and what it meant for starship travel. Such a convenience would be an amazing advantage: it would reduce the need for shore leave, as well as providing a multitude of training and technical simulations.

"Was it nice going home?" Halloway said.

"Oh, it was wonderful," I said. I decided quite rightly that, in this case, the truth was completely unnecessary. I would never be using a holodeck to go home again. Still, the *Enterprise* was going to be quite impressive when they were done.

✦

I left Utopia Planitia as a passenger on the *U.S.S. Saratoga*, which was under the command of a Vulcan captain named Storil. It was a small ship, similar to the *Reliant*. *Saratoga* was going to take me to Starbase 2, and then I would get other transportation to Starbase 3.

I was surprised to discover that there were children aboard the ship. A few officers and crew had their families with them. One night, Captain Storil invited me to join him for dinner in his cabin. We were enjoying a vegetarian meal, though mostly in silence, when I decided to ask him about it.

"It is Starfleet policy that having families aboard is a captain's discretion," Storil said. "It is logical that if Starfleet personnel have made the decision to have families, they will perform their duties more efficiently if they are not separated from them."

"Still," I said, "aren't children a disruption?"

"If rules are properly enforced," Storil said, "children follow them." I couldn't really mount an argument to this, but I also couldn't imagine inconveniencing myself to this level.

I thought I would enjoy being back on a ship, but the week I spent on the *Saratoga* ended up being far from relaxing. My first few nights I was restless and unable to sleep. I took to getting up and wandering the corridors, hoping some exercise would relax me. This ended up being useless, and by the third day I was a physical wreck. I didn't understand what the problem was; I'd spent my adult life on starships and I'd never had any trouble sleeping. But every time I lay down in bed, I had a strange and unsettling impression of danger lurking nearby. I'd get out of bed and stare out a porthole for hours, trying to see if I could make out if some enemy ship or undiscovered anomaly was threatening the vessel. All I saw were the stars. I came to know that my feeling, whatever it was, was unfounded, but I couldn't shake it.

On the fourth night, having reached my limit, I went to sickbay in the hope of receiving some medical help to get to sleep. When I got there, it was empty except for one young cadet, a woman who couldn't have been much older than 20. I had trouble believing that this woman in a cadet uniform was also a doctor, but I'd learned never to presume anything.

"May I help you, Captain?"

"Yes," I said. "I'm having trouble sleeping and was hoping you could give me something."

"I'm not allowed to prescribe medicine," the cadet said. "The *Saratoga* medical staff is short-handed, so they have me serving the graveyard shift, but I'm to wake one of the doctors if they're needed."

"No," I said, "it's not necessary…"

"You seem very anxious," she said. This bit of insight surprised me. And then I noticed her deep black eyes.

"Are you Betazoid?" I said. The Betazoids were natural telepaths; it was possible this woman was reading my mind.

"I'm half-Betazoid, on my mother's side," she said, then held out her hand. "Deanna Troi."

"Jean-Luc Picard," I said, shaking her hand. "Serving part of your academy time on the *Saratoga*?"

"Yes, I'm training in Starfleet's new ship counselor program."

I was vaguely aware of it: Starfleet had decided that on larger starships it was preferable to have a trained psychologist who was separate from the ship's doctor.

"Well, good luck," I said. I suddenly felt a strong desire to leave. I certainly didn't feel like I needed to have my head examined. I moved toward the door.

"I do think your insomnia is related to your anxiety," she said.

"I do not need to be psychoanalyzed by a cadet," I said. My tone was unnecessarily sharp, and I immediately regretted it.

"Forgive me, Captain," she said. "I didn't mean to pry."

"No, no," I said. "My fault." I stood there. I wanted to leave, but there was something comforting about this young woman that kept me there.

"Would you like to sit down for a moment?" she said. She sat at a small table near one of the bio beds. I paused, and, not quite understanding why, I joined her. We sat in silence for a moment.

"How did you know I was anxious? Did you read my mind?"

"I'm not a true telepath," she said. "My father was human. But I can read strong emotions. Do you know what it is you're anxious about?"

"No."

"I see." She considered me for a moment. "Is this your first time on a starship?"

"Hardly," I said. "I just finished twenty years as captain of the *Stargazer*."

"Oh," she said. "What made you decide to leave?"

"I didn't decide to leave," I said. "The ship was disabled in an attack, we had to abandon it."

"I'm sorry," she said. She appeared genuinely saddened. "Did you lose any of your crew?"

"Yes." The images of the people who'd died on that ship that I left behind came forward in my mind. What kept me from sleeping suddenly made sense. I'd made some association with being on this ship and their deaths on *Stargazer*; my mind had tried to push them away. But they had lurked there, an "impending danger."

"That's terrible," she said. "I can feel they meant a lot to you." I was resentful that this woman was prying into my emotions. I wanted to escape, but I couldn't. Somehow, by sitting down with her in the first place, I had consented to her meddling. Her questions made me uncomfortable, but I wanted them.

She waited a few moments; it might have just been seconds, but it felt a lot longer.

"Do you think being on the *Saratoga* is reminding you of their deaths?"

I didn't answer her. I couldn't. But she properly read that as affirmation.

"It's not uncommon," Deanna said, "for someone to feel they've done something wrong surviving a traumatic event that others did not."

"I was the captain," I said. "It was my responsibility to protect them."

"You were the captain. You are also just a man. Some situations are out of your control." We again sat there in silence for a few moments. The feeling that had held me there initially eased. I knew I could get up. But now I wasn't sure I wanted to.

"What do I do?" I said.

"There's a voice inside of you telling you to avoid the memory," she said. "But there's also a part of you that wants to remember them. They meant a lot to you. I think you should try to listen to that part of yourself."

I nodded, and got up.

"Thank you, Cadet," I said. She smiled, and I left the room.

I went back to my quarters and lay down on the bed. I thought of my late friend Scully, underneath the bridge helm controls of the *Stargazer* trying to reconnect them so the ship could leave spacedock. I smiled a sad smile and drifted off to sleep.

✦

A few weeks later, I'd finished the final leg of my journey and reached Starbase 3. One of the oldest of the Starfleet outposts, it was a planetary facility built on the smaller of two M-Class worlds circling Barnard's Star. The architectural style of the starbase reflected the fact that Starfleet, in its original inception, was an Earth-based service and the facilities were built to resemble something that felt familiar to humans. Space travel took much longer back then, and the designers of the early Starbase program wanted personnel posted there to feel like it could be home. It was effective; when I beamed down to the main administration building, I felt like I'd arrived in the Earth city of Denver, despite the orange sky.

A yeoman ran out of the building to greet me and escorted me to the administrator's office. The man behind the desk was about my age with gray in his beard and stood up to greet me.

"Good to see you, Jean-Luc," Admiral Leyton said. "Been a long time."

"Introduction to Federation Law class," I said. "Right?" Leyton laughed. I had seen him at the academy after that class, but not since graduating. He'd recently received the promotion to vice admiral and this posting. Though he was more than deserving of the rank, when renewing acquaintances with old colleagues I was often left with the feeling that my career was standing still.

The yeoman left us alone, and I made my report to Leyton regarding the readiness of ships to be moved to this sector. I could see that the news I'd brought wasn't what he wanted to hear.

"Fifteen ships ready now," Leyton said. "That's all?"

"Another twenty will be available in three weeks," I said, but this didn't seem to make him feel better. "Perhaps if I knew what this was about…"

"I'm sorry you had to be kept in the dark, Jean-Luc," Leyton said. He then tapped the communicator on his chest. "Leyton to Lieutenant Data, please report to my office."

"Acknowledged," the voice said. A moment later, a Starfleet lieutenant from a race I'd never seen entered the room. He seemed human except for his golden-white skin and yellow eyes. His demeanor was simultaneously pleasant and distant.

"Lieutenant Data," he said.

"Captain Jean-Luc Picard." I extended my hand. He looked at it curiously for a strange beat, then shook it. There was something inorganic and forced about his touch, like an expert imitation of a human handshake. It was then that I realized who this was.

"You're the android," I said. The words came out of my mouth involuntarily.

"Yes," Data said. It was a matter of some note that an android, created by noted cyberneticist Dr. Noonian Soong, had graduated from Starfleet Academy, but I was in no way prepared to meet it and quickly realized I'd been rude.

"Forgive me for calling you 'the android.' "

"There is no offense," Data said. "As I am the only android in Starfleet, referring to me as 'the android' is an accurate description."

"Lieutenant," Leyton said, "please brief Captain Picard on the situation related to his mission."

"Yes, Admiral," Data said, walking to the large computer interface on the wall. He brought up an image of a planet. "This is an image of the planet Denobula taken with long-range sensors."

"As you know," Leyton said, "Denobula withdrew from Galactic affairs after the Romulan War when the enemy fleet killed three million of their people…"

"Three million, seven hundred sixty-three thousand, two hundred seventy-one," Data said.

"Just show him what you found," Leyton said.

I could see that the android lieutenant had not picked up on Leyton's annoyance at the pointless correction. Data adjusted the image, which magnified to reveal another globe in orbit of the planet.

"Is that a small moon?" I said.

"Negative," Data said. "It is an artificial construct, perhaps a space station."

"It's larger than any space station I've ever seen," I said. "Are we able to determine its purpose?"

"That's the difficulty," Leyton said. "It's projecting an enormous amount of subspace interference that disrupts our long-range scans. Starfleet Tactical is concerned it's a weapon of some kind."

"The Denobulans were allies," I said.

"Who we haven't heard from in two hundred years," Leyton said.

"The Denobulans do have a long history of war in their culture," Data said.

I was fascinated by this creation. His delivery of information somehow immediately engendered trust in me.

"There is also the message," Leyton said.

"Message?"

"Starfleet Intelligence intercepted a coded message sent throughout the Alpha and Beta Quadrants," Data said.

"A message," Leyton said, "which only Data was able to decode."

"The code was based on a Denobulan lullaby," Data said, "which was commonly known in Denobulan culture, but virtually unknown anywhere else. This led me to hypothesize that the message was meant only for Denobulans, perhaps some who might still be residing on other planets."

"What did the message say?"

"Two words: 'Come home.' Along with a date." Data indicated a date on the screen.

"That's about two weeks from now," I said. "Is that a deadline?"

"It would appear so," Leyton said. "Starfleet Tactical is concerned that that globe is a first strike weapon, and that's the date they plan to use it. We have to destroy it."

"We're going to attack? The Federation has never committed a first strike..."

"There is no better alternative," Leyton said. "The Denobulans won't respond to our attempts to communicate."

"Have you told them you plan to attack?"

"How can we do that, Jean-Luc?" Leyton said. "If it really is a weapon, we'd be giving them another advantage. We have no choice. I need you to find me more ships. Lieutenant Data will help you."

I had my orders, but I didn't like them. This situation was very troubling. The idea that Starfleet might make a first strike was a terrible precedent and undermined the philosophy of peace that the Federation had lived under for centuries.

But the one positive in this mission was Data. As I spent the next two days with this artificial man, I went from fascinated to awed. He had an amazing ability to process a wide variety of information from multiple sources, as well as having a veritable encyclopedia of knowledge in his own brain. And though he claimed to have no emotions, he had a cheerful desire for learning and acceptance. I soon looked to him as an indispensable resource.

One day while we were going over the repair schedules of ships in the sector, I hit on an idea.

"Data," I said, "what do Denobulans look like?"

"There are twenty-three thousand, one hundred seven images in the Federation database," Data said.

"Choose one," I said. Data pulled a picture up on the viewscreen in his small office. I was only vaguely familiar with the species I was looking at: it had a prominent forehead, outlined with ridges that extended down to its cheekbones. Though I'd learned about Denobulans in history, I don't think I'd ever seen one in person.

"Now, cross-reference this photo with facial recognition software and see if any resident of a Starfleet or Federation facility has similar features." I thought that if there were still Denobulans living in the Federation, they might be living incognito.

"I have found one," Data said. He brought the picture up. It was a similar being to the one we'd just looked at, although a great deal older. "His name is Sim; he is a resident of Starbase 12 where he has run a facility since the year 2314." There was something familiar about Sim, but I couldn't put my finger on it.

"Facility? What kind of facility?"

"A bar. It is named 'Feezal's.' "

"Check and see if he's still there."

"He has left. He filed a flight plan yesterday… for Denobula." Data looked up at me; he seemed impressed that I'd been able to track down a Denobulan in the Federation. "Intriguing. This person may be a source of valuable information."

"He almost certainly knows why he's going home," I said. "His course will take him fairly close to Starbase 3, correct?"

"Yes, sir," Data said. "In six point seven days. But it would seem unlikely that he would voluntarily provide us with the information we seek."

"He won't have to," I said. A plan was forming in my mind. One that I hoped would avoid a military incursion that would stain Starfleet for generations.

"Let's go see Admiral Leyton," I said.

✦

One week later, Data and I were in a small, somewhat ancient Tellarite scout vessel, floating in space without engine power. Our warp reactor had been sabotaged. By us.

Also, we were disguised as Denobulans.

The prosthetics we wore were quite convincing, and small devices that Lieutenant Data had created made us read to any scanner as being Denobulan. I hoped our deception would succeed. Leyton had recognized that this was a good intelligence-gathering opportunity, but had given me a strict time limit: if he didn't hear from me in four days he was going to proceed with his attack.

"I'm detecting the transport," Data said.

"Send the distress signal," I said. I needed to wait until the last possible moment. I couldn't risk another ship answering our faux plea for help, but it had to be general enough to avoid looking suspicious.

"The transport is responding," Data said.

"On screen," I said.

On the small viewscreen, an elderly Denobulan appeared. It was Sim. This was a particularly long-lived species, so the fact that Sim appeared elderly meant he must be of a considerably advanced age.

"What have we here?" the old Denobulan said. Despite his age, he had a youthful bearing.

"I am Phlogen," Data said. "This is Mettus." Data and I had agreed ahead of time that I would let him do most of the talking. He had in his head more information about the Denobulans than anyone, which was how I was able to sell Admiral Leyton on this spy mission.

"How interesting," he said. "I named one of my children Mettus. I am Sim. What seems to be the trouble?"

"Our engines have failed," Data said. "We do not possess the necessary tools or expertise to fix them." I realized that there was a downside to letting Data speak: he was overly formal. I hoped that our friend wouldn't notice.

"I don't know that I can help you, I don't really have much mechanical expertise," he said. "Were you heading home?"

I nodded.

"Well, if you're willing to abandon your ship, I can, as the humans say, 'give you a lift.' "

"That would be greatly appreciated," Data said.

Sim docked with us, and we boarded his ship. It was a small craft, crammed with cages holding all manner of creatures and plants.

"Forgive my menagerie," he said. "And I suggest you keep your hands free of the cages." He led us to two seats behind his at the control panel. He took the helm, disconnected from our derelict craft, and headed off to Denobula.

A bat in a cage near me tittered noisily.

"What kind of bat is that?" I said.

"Pyrithian," he said. "Careful, she enjoys the taste of fingers."

"You have quite a collection."

"I was a doctor in a previous life, back when practicing space medicine relied on live animals and plants for cures, so I would collect flora and fauna from whatever planet I visited. Medical technology has long since made this kind of thing obsolete, so I stopped practicing medicine, but I haven't been able to cure myself of the habit of collecting."

"How long have you been away from Denobula?" I said.

"Oh, I haven't lived there in over two hundred years," he said. "But I've been back to visit. What about you? What took you away from home?"

I glanced at Data. I wanted him to answer this question.

"We are geologists," Data said, "exploring other planets looking for solutions to the seismic problems on Denobula."

"A worthy effort," Sim said.

I was relieved but not surprised. I'd spent enough time with Data to know that he could tap into the historical database in his head to reference Denobulans who'd left their homeworld and use the information to craft a believable answer. What interested me about Data as a creation was that, if instructed, he had the ability to lie. And he did it very convincingly.

We had to travel several hours to Denobula, and Sim chatted with us the entire time. Data did an incredible job maintaining our cover, while I waited for an opportunity to find out what Sim knew. I had to be careful and wait for the subject to come up naturally. Eventually it did.

"I have to say," Sim said, "I was surprised they were able to complete the project so quickly."

"Yes," I said, "it's quite an accomplishment."

"Hmmm," Sim said.

"You seem conflicted," I said. "Do you think we're making the wrong decision?"

"No," he said. "But I have made a lot of friends in the Federation. I will miss them."

I glanced at Data—this had an ominous ring to it. I was afraid that Leyton might be right. But, as I had been spending time with Sim, memories started to nag at me. His face was still familiar. I decided to try to figure out why. I got him talking about his bar on Starbase 12.

"Why did you decide to settle there?"

"I don't talk about it very often," he said. "I served in Starfleet. I still enjoy the company of their officers."

"When did you serve in Starfleet?" Some lost piece of memory was fighting its way forward to the front of my brain...

"Oh, before they founded their Federation. I was part of something called the Interspecies Medical Exchange, and served on one of their starships."

I remembered, and a split second before I could stop him, Data did too.

"The name of that Denobulan," Data said, "was Phlox."

"Yes, I changed my name a while back," Sim said. "I knew that I had gained some notoriety in the Federation, and was looking to live out a quieter life. You've heard of me?"

Heard of him! When I realized who he was, I had to stifle a gasp of recognition. Phlox was the doctor on the NX-01, the original *U.S.S. Enterprise*. But I'd momentarily forgotten that I was disguised as a Denobulan, and that a Denobulan might not be so well versed in the personnel on humanity's first starship.

"Yes," I said, "you're well known among scientists like us. You blazed a lot of trails."

"Oh, I think you exaggerate," Phlox said. "But it's nice to know I'm remembered back home."

I had so many questions I wanted to ask but held back—Data and I had almost blown our cover. Still, our companion's identity only made the situation harder to accept. Everything I knew about Phlox, his compassion and scientific integrity, made it impossible for me to believe he would accept his people launching some kind of attack against the Federation. Yet if he did accept it, I couldn't take the risk to reveal ourselves. I had to see the plan through.

We arrived at the Denobulan system, and this was where my plan to be picked up by Phlox paid its greatest dividend: Phlox had a clearance code for his ship, and they let us enter the system with no difficulty. We approached the planet, passing the large artificial globe that hung in a wide orbit. It was a monstrosity. Its dark metal skin and vibrant internal energy seemed to confirm a malevolent purpose.

Phlox took his ship to a landing pad on the planet. The entire Denobulan population was on one continent, and when we landed the population density was startling, even at the spaceport. The Denobulans themselves seemed very comfortable with close physical proximity. It seemed many were returning home, receiving enthusiastic greetings from friends and family.

"It was a pleasure meeting you," Phlox said. "I'm sure I'll see you again."

"I hope so," I said.

"We greatly appreciate you 'giving us a lift,'" Data said. His inflection was stiff and unnatural, but Phlox laughed—he seemed to take it as a bit of humor. We went our separate ways.

Data and I journeyed into the main city off the starport. In the sky above the city, even in daylight, the giant artificial globe was visible. It was incongruous to the sight of the city itself. The homes and buildings were close together, and Denobulans seemed in the midst of an extended celebration, singing, drinking, and enjoying each other's company.

"Is this what a warlike species looks like?" Data said.

"Hardly, Mr. Data," I said. "We have to get more information about what that device is. How much time do we have?"

"The date the Denobulans originally gave is now three point seven three five days away."

Leyton would stick to the timeline he'd given me—he wasn't going to wait past the deadline. It was imperative for him to destroy that device rather than risk it being used on the Federation. So Data and I had two days to get into our roles as Denobulans and hopefully find out something useful, and then get off the planet to intercept Leyton and his fleet.

I was immediately overwhelmed by the general hospitality and openness of this species. The Denobulan culture was focused on family; they gave freely of shelter and food, and celebrated familial relations in a way I hadn't seen on any other world. Men and women had multiple wives and husbands, and there were many children from those connections. It felt like a vibrant, advanced society where individuals were firmly connected to one another. My companion agreed with me.

"It would seem," Data said, "that Starfleet's concern that the Denobulans have returned to their historic warlike period is unfounded." We had just left a large meal with a Denobulan family, who had invited us in off the street.

"Then why build a giant weapon?" I said. "And if it's not a weapon, why hide its purpose with subspace interference?"

"There is one possibility we have not considered," Data said. "Perhaps the subspace interference is not intended to hide its function, but is just a necessary aspect *of* its function."

"A giant subspace transmitter? What would it be used for?"

"You don't know what it is?" The voice surprised both of us, and we turned to find ourselves facing a young Denobulan, probably ten years old. He had been at the dinner that we'd just enjoyed, and must have followed us out. Not sure what to do, I paused. Data did not.

"No, we do not. Can you tell us?"

"It's a subspace engine," he said. "Everybody knows that." With that, the child scampered off.

"A subspace engine?" I said. "Have you ever heard of such a thing?"

"They are theoretical," Data said. "It has often been postulated that since we use subspace to send faster than light communication, it might also be used to transfer objects."

"We need more information," I said, "and I'm afraid we're going to have to take a bigger risk."

We set out, with the help of a directory, to find our way to Phlox's home. When he answered the door, he looked genuinely pleased to see us. His home was filled with children and adults, and Phlox seemed intent on introducing us to all of them, including his son named Mettus. Eventually, I found a moment to take Phlox aside.

"We need to talk to you alone about a matter of some urgency," I said. He could see I was concerned and took us to a more private room.

"What is the problem, Mettus?"

I looked at Data, and I knew he had no idea what I was planning to do. Nor would he know how to give me any support for it even if he did.

"I'm not Denobulan. I'm human. Captain Jean-Luc Picard from Starfleet."

"Really?" He started looking over my disguise. "Quite convincing..."

"We came here to find out why your people have built a subspace engine," I said. "Starfleet is greatly concerned."

"They have no need to worry," Phlox said. "It was built to take Denobula and its sun away."

" 'Away'?"

"Yes," he said. "In a few days, it will generate a subspace field that will remove this entire system from our Galaxy, and transfer it into subspace."

It sounded incredible. I looked at Data, who nodded.

"That is theoretically possible," he said.

I turned back to Phlox. "Why are you doing this?"

"My people never recovered from the deaths caused by the great attack," he said. He was referring to the attack on the planet that had occurred two hundred years before. "Three million Denobulans were killed; those deaths touched every family on the planet. We've seen the hostilities Starfleet has recently engaged in, with the Cardassians and the Tzenkethi, there was almost a war with the Klingons, and the Romulans still loom large. It is only a matter of time before our world is pulled into conflict again."

I couldn't tell him how correct he was: Starfleet itself was planning an attack as we spoke.

"So we are pulling ourselves from the Galaxy. Replicators give us everything we need. The effective radius of the engine will include our sun and the other bodies in the system. The invention has been tested; our scientists assure us our star system will survive in subspace. And we will survive in peace. But you, my friends, must leave, unless you wish to spend the rest of your lives here."

"That would be most intriguing," Data said.

"But not preferable," I said. "Can you help us?"

✦

"I don't know that I can afford to trust this, Jean-Luc," Leyton said. It was a day later, and I was on the bridge of the *U.S.S. Excalibur*, the lead ship in the fleet

Leyton had assembled. We were a few light-years out from the Denobulan system, and Data and I were still in our disguises. Phlox had been able to get us to a spaceship, and we'd intercepted the fleet.

"You have to trust this, Admiral," I said.

"It is not a weapon, sir," Data said. Leyton looked at him; it was hard to argue with Data. "They have no harmful intent."

"Sir," the ops officer said, "I'm reading a massive build-up in subspace interference."

Leyton looked at us, annoyed. We'd delayed him, and, in his mind, perhaps doomed him.

"Shields up, red alert," Leyton said. "All ships, stand by to—"

Before he could finish, the ship was hit with a shockwave that knocked us all off our feet. Leyton and his conn officer crawled back to right the ship. Data helped me up. When we looked on the screen, I knew it was all over.

"Message to all ships," Leyton said. "Engage course to Denobula."

"Sir," the conn officer said. "I can't. It's gone."

"What?"

"The star, the planet, they're not there."

I looked at Data and smiled. The Denobulans had got what they wanted, a universe without war. And as I watched Leyton, simmering with frustration that events hadn't played out the way he'd expected, I knew such a universe would escape the rest of us—at least for a while.

✦

Over the next few years, I found satisfaction in my job as a troubleshooter for Quinn. The work I was doing was active and engaging, and the desire to command a ship began to fade. Quinn seemed to have forgotten his promise to put me back in command, and in any event I felt I had made a transition to another career, maybe one I would find as satisfying as being a starship captain. I also took delight in being free from the confines of one ship; I'd been on the *Stargazer* for so long, I felt like I was discovering a whole new generation of people who'd come out of the academy and begun to make their mark on

Starfleet and the Federation. And I found satisfaction in sharing my experience with them, acting as a kind of elder statesman.

One such person I met while I was serving as interim commanding officer of Starbase 23. The old commander had unexpectedly passed away, and a new commander was en route, and since I was the most senior officer in the area, Quinn had me take over running the facility. Starbase 23 was a space station in a system with no Class-M planets, but one that did have an abundance of asteroids, on which the Starfleet Corps of Engineers had built mining facilities. Part of my duties were regular inspections of those asteroid facilities. One day, leaving for a round of these inspections, I had the shuttlebay officer of the deck assign me a pilot.

When I showed up in the shuttle bay, the young officer greeted me. He wore an unusual device over his eyes, a gold visor made of a light metal. I introduced myself, and we shook hands.

"Lieutenant Geordi La Forge," he said.

We were on a tight schedule, so I refrained from indulging my curiosity about his eyewear and we got on board. La Forge took the controls, and went down a complete checklist of all the shuttle's systems. (I would've usually dispensed with this protocol, but this was a young officer trying to make an impression, so I let him go through with it.)

On our short trip out to the asteroid, I found out a little bit about him. He was from Earth, had served on the *Victory* and was between assignments, so he volunteered for shuttle pilot duty. I decided to ask about his accessory.

"It detects electromagnetic signals and transmits them to my brain," Geordi said.

"That sounds like a useful device," I said.

"Especially when you're blind," he said.

"Excuse me?"

"Oh, I'm sorry, sir, I assumed you knew. I was born blind. The visor lets me 'see,' kind of."

The man piloting my shuttle was blind. It was at times like this I marveled at the age in which I lived that such a thing was in no way worrisome.

We returned from the inspection of the first asteroid mining facility and parted company for the evening. I returned to the shuttlebay the next morning for my tour of the next asteroid facility. La Forge was already there, working on the shuttle. He looked very tired, and I asked him what he'd been doing.

"I refitted the fusion initiators, sir," he said. "Just finished."

"That must have taken all night," I said.

"Yes, well, I thought I should do something about it when you commented on the engine efficiency…"

This was strange; I had no recollection of saying anything about the engine efficiency.

"I think you must be mistaken…" I said.

"When I went down the launch checklist and reported the shuttle's engine efficiency was 87 percent, you said: 'Probably not what it should be.' They should be up over 95 percent now."

If he'd done it to impress me, he'd succeeded, but I could tell that it wasn't his motivation. He sincerely just wanted to make a piece of equipment work better. A short time after, La Forge received a posting on the *Hood*, but I knew this was someone I was going to remember.

✦

"*U.S.S. Constellation* arriving Bay 2," the announcer said.

I was packing up my office at the starbase, which looked out on the internal bay. As I looked up and saw the ship pulling in, I had a moment of déjà vu. The *U.S.S. Constellation* was the same class as the *Stargazer* and looked virtually identical. When I had first seen that old ship of mine, it was pulling into the bay of a starbase; now it felt like I was reliving that moment 25 years later. My temporary assignment was over, and I would be leaving on the *Constellation*. In command, if only for a little while.

Cliff Kennelly, shipmaster of the *Constellation*, had just been promoted to vice admiral and would be taking command of Starbase 23. Since Kennelly was taking much of his command crew with him to the starbase, and much of the rest of the crew was being reassigned, someone had to get the *Constellation* back to the Sol system, where it would be decommissioned and its parts recycled. I was ambivalent about the mission, but Quinn needed me back on Earth, and this was a very efficient way to get me there.

Kennelly reported to my office, and I released the starbase command codes to him. Though I'd read his reports on the condition of his ship, he gave me a quick briefing on its handling. He was an ambitious man, at least ten years my junior. Just a few years earlier I would've been jealous of his success, but I had found some peace in the intervening years of not being in command, or I thought I had.

Later, after I'd gathered my belongings, I went to the *Constellation*. The ship was as old as the *Stargazer*, and on the inside looked much the same. I walked along the corridors with a little sense of nostalgia, mournful for the friends who'd died, accepting of the loss. My interaction with Deanna Troi years earlier had helped me to fully process that terrible tragedy.

When I got to the bridge, an unusual sight greeted me.

There was only one officer there, an ensign. Who was a Klingon.

"Captain on the bridge," the Klingon said. The fact that he was announcing it to no one made the situation that much more strange.

"You must be Ensign Worf," I said. I had read the records of the crew of the *Constellation*, and had learned a little about this unique officer.

"An honor to meet you, Captain Picard," he said. Like many of his species, he was large and intimidating, with an almost animal growl under every word out of his mouth. I'd met a few Klingons over the years, but had never found common ground with any of them. This one, however, had an amazing story: he was one of the last survivors of the Romulan attack on Khitomer. He spent much of his childhood on the farming colony on Gault, raised by human foster parents of Russian origin, and was the first Klingon to graduate from Starfleet Academy.

"Glad to be aboard, Ensign," I said.

"I studied your battle at Maxia when I was a cadet at the academy," Worf said. "Your victory was worthy of a Klingon warrior."

I hadn't heard anyone put the event quite that way. I looked at this young officer. No matter where he was from, I decided it was my responsibility to contribute to his education.

"Did you also study the Duke of Wellington?" I said. Worf looked at me confused.

"Duke of…?"

"I'd like you to tell me why I might not see it as a victory, and use the Duke of Wellington as your guide."

"Yes, sir," Worf said. "Now, sir?"

"On your first free shift," I said. "Now I'd like you to make preparations to get underway." He turned and recalled the bridge crew to duty. While he did, I took the command chair.

We left orbit a few hours later. About half the crew had disembarked at Starbase 23 for other assignments. The ship's maximum speed was warp 6, but I kept it at warp 4—Kennelly had warned me it wasn't up to specs. For the entire trip back, there were only four of us on the bridge: Ensign Worf at the ops station, Ensign Tania Lotia at the helm, and doing double duty of engineering and communications was Lieutenant Lexi Turner.

It was going very smoothly. We were only a few days from Sol and it felt as if it would be a very dull trip. During my one shift off, I spent the time alone in my quarters. Off of Worf's remark that he'd studied "The Battle of Maxia" at the academy, I decided to investigate what exactly it was that was being taught. I found in the database the academy text "Strategies and Tactics of Starship Combat" and was startled to discover something called the "Picard Maneuver." My last-ditch tactic on the *Stargazer* of jumping to warp against my unknown enemy had made it into a text.

I watched a computer simulation of the event linked to the text: the ships moved in a dance that looked choreographed. It was horrifying to me. The text had taken out all the desperation and risk. This wasn't a game—people had died. I turned off the screen.

I began writing a formal complaint to the academy commandant. This seemed like a terrible way to teach students. Halfway through, I took a pause. Yes, my experience had been fraught and difficult, but because of what I'd had to go through, perhaps some future captain in a similar position might benefit from my experience. I deleted my letter. My reverie was interrupted by the door chime.

"Come," I said.

The door opened revealing Worf.

"May I come in, sir?"

"Certainly, Ensign." I offered him a chair, which he declined.

"I've completed my assignment," Worf said, handing me a PADD. "I have studied the career of Arthur Wellesley, the First Duke of Wellington. Perhaps one of Earth's greatest warriors."

"Is that why I had you study him?"

Worf took a long pause.

"No," Worf said, "I believe it was because of a quote he was well known for. In an ancient correspondence he was reflecting on the loss of comrades, and wrote: 'Nothing except a battle lost can be half as melancholy as a battle won.' You take no joy in your victory; it is only slightly less sad for you than defeat. You do not celebrate your victory at Maxia for this reason."

"Yes," I said. This young officer had passed the test with flying colors. "Do you agree with me and the Duke of Wellington on this?"

"The honor is to serve," Worf said. "If they died well, in service, there is no reason for… melancholy."

"And yet you understood what I wanted you to glean from it."

"If you'll forgive me, sir," Worf said, "I have lived with humans my whole life. I understand their proclivities." This was an interesting man; straddling two worlds and doing it quite well.

My little seminar on war was interrupted by a call from the bridge.

"Receiving a distress call from the Federation colony on Carnellia IV, " Turner said. "Several of the colonists have accidentally crossed into an old minefield. There are severe injuries. The *U.S.S. Roosevelt* has also responded."

"Set course, maximum warp," I said. "Inform the *Roosevelt* we will stand by to assist." Worf and I left for the bridge in a hurry. Without a full crew compliment or dedicated medical staff, I wasn't sure we would be that much help, but, as Worf said, the honor was to serve.

When we arrived at Carnellia IV, the *Roosevelt* was already in orbit. The colony was very new; about one hundred people had settled on the planet after it was charted. Soon after they arrived, the colonists found evidence the original inhabitants of the planet had died out long ago. I beamed down with Worf and every crewmember who had any sort of medical training.

A field hospital had been set up near the minefield; it was a nightmare of injured people, some missing limbs. The *Roosevelt*'s doctors were already hard at work treating the victims. I instructed our medics to lend a hand, while Worf and I headed to the scene of the accident.

We followed the sound of a man howling in pain, and found the ship's captain at the edge of the minefield. There was evidence that several mines had exploded—blood and body parts were scattered around. It was horrific, but that wasn't what I was focused on.

In the middle of the carnage, a Starfleet ensign was looking intently at the ground as she slowly but steadily walked through it. A few feet in front of her, the source of the unnerving screams was a middle-aged man, his left leg blown off at the knee.

I approached the captain, who didn't take her eyes off her officer.

"Captain Cheva," I said. She turned and glanced at me.

"Captain Picard," she said, "I wish we were meeting under better circumstances." Her focus was on her officer, a young woman who was no more than 25. I watched as she slowly picked up her foot, and gently placed it forward. Another step.

"Can't we just beam the man up?" Worf said.

"We don't know anything about these mines," Cheva said. "The energy from the transporter, or even a scanner, might set them off."

"Your ensign is very brave," I said.

Cheva nodded. "Natasha Yar," she said.

"How is she determining where to walk?" I said.

"She's making judgments based on her own experience planting mines," Cheva said. "Inexact to be sure. Tasha's from the Turkana colony." That was a violent, unforgiving place, and if this woman had survived it and made it through the academy she was special indeed.

We watched as Tasha took another careful step. She was now inches from the injured man, whose howling was unnerving us all. Tasha carefully knelt down, and injected the man with a hypo. He fell into unconsciousness. She then lifted him up over her shoulder and slowly stood up. Blood from his wounds soaked her uniform as she slowly retraced each of her steps out of the minefield.

"Warrior," said Worf, quietly. I couldn't have agreed more.

✦

It quickly became clear that *Constellation*'s presence on Carnellia was superfluous. Cheva and her crew of the *Roosevelt* were quite able to take care of the injured, as well as determining how to deactivate the minefield. So with Cheva's permission, I left. It was quite a thing to see my former officer now in command, and I felt in some sense the torch had been passed. It was the next generation's turn to take over.

I returned the *Constellation* to Utopia Planitia, and on my way, I reflected on the terrible effect of war: the close brush with Denobula, the carnage on Carnellia IV. I'd had my fill of it. It wasn't enough to just be a Starfleet officer, one had to commit oneself to peace. I decided as I ended what I thought would be my last command that I had new purpose.

We reached Utopia Planitia, and the crew disembarked without fanfare. I turned all the necessary paperwork over to the yard commander, then requisitioned a shuttle to take me to Earth. But before I got very far away from Mars, I received a call from Tom Halloway, who asked me to come meet him back on Utopia Planitia. I turned the shuttle around, and headed to the dry dock where the *Enterprise* was still being built, now almost complete.

As I closed in on the all but complete ship, I took it in. It cut a grand profile, the largest Starfleet vessel in history. I docked, and Halloway met me in the operations center.

"A beauty, isn't she?" he said. We were looking again at the *Enterprise*, this time through the bay windows of the operations center. "They've designated her the Federation flagship." This was quite an honor; in the absence of an admiral, the flagship's captain would have implicit seniority over other captains and ships in the fleet.

"You've done an amazing job," I said. "Almost ready to launch?"

"Yeah, taking her on a three-week shakedown cruise on Monday," Halloway said. "Then after that, to Earth where she'll be someone else's problem."

"You're not going to stay her captain?"

"I'm a 'first captain,'" Halloway said. He was making reference to the old naval tradition of the United States Navy where the first captain of a ship was only responsible for building it; it was the second captain who took her out.

"Well, someone is very lucky then," I said.

"That's actually what I wanted to talk to you about," someone said. I turned to see that Admiral Quinn had just walked in.

"Admiral," I said. "What are you doing here?"

"I wanted to hear who you thought should be captain of our new ship," Quinn said. "Halloway, can I borrow your office?"

Quinn and I went to a small office off the operations center.

"So," Quinn said. "Who do you recommend?"

"Well, Andrea Brand..."

"She's only a couple of years away from being promoted to Admiral," Quinn said. "I want someone who is going to stay a while."

"There's Jellico, DeSoto, Bill Ross..." Quinn dismissed all of them with a wave of his hand. I was finding this little game, whatever it was, quite annoying.

"We had someone else in mind," Quinn said.

"Who?"

"You," Quinn said. "Unless you just want to stay in your current job."

This took me by surprise for a lot of reasons. In that moment, I realized how much I had been protecting myself from disappointment. I'd wanted a captain's chair again, but had rationalized that that part of my career was over because I didn't think it was possible.

"You've done excellent work the last few years," Quinn said. "Your mission to Denobula alone was enough to rehabilitate you in the eyes of the Admiralty. I could've put you on a ship before this, but it felt like the *Enterprise* was the right one, so I held you back. I hope that's all right." He'd made me captain of the Federation flagship, the highest honor a captain could achieve.

"Thank you, Admiral."

"Don't let anyone ever say I don't keep my promises," Quinn said.

CHAPTER NINE

"**CAPTAIN'S LOG: STARDATE 41153.7.** Our destination is the planet Deneb IV, beyond which lies the great unexplored mass of the Galaxy. My orders are to examine Farpoint, a starbase built there by the inhabitants of Deneb IV. Meanwhile, I'm becoming better acquainted with my new command, this *Galaxy*-class *U.S.S. Enterprise*. I'm still somewhat in awe of its size and complexity…"

I was in my new quarters, grand, plush, and comfortable, staring at the stars distorted by warp speed. I'd put a lot of thought into what I was going to say in that first log entry. I was recording a moment for posterity, and my words were carefully crafted to disguise the mass of chaotic feelings that threatened to overwhelm me. I had a new ship, a new crew, a new life. And I was surrounded by strangers, there were children all over my ship, and I was on my way to see the one woman in my life I'd ever truly loved.

Several weeks previous, while Halloway was still "shaking down" the *Enterprise*, I was in my rooms at Starfleet Headquarters going over personnel choices. There were over a thousand crewmen tasked to this ship, almost a complete city in space, and I wouldn't choose them all; I picked department heads and they in turn staffed their sections, though I could certainly make strong "suggestions" if there was a junior officer I liked. Because the *Enterprise* was the Federation flagship, Quinn had made it clear that I had my choice of any officer I wanted. Though this was a boon for me, it had a downside as I would be taking talented people away from captains I knew, many of whom were my friends.

THE AUTOBIOGRAPHY OF JEAN-LUC PICARD

I had spent hours reviewing the service records of all the candidates I was considering for first officer. It was becoming impossible to tell them apart. They were all very much the same: accomplished young men and women from countless species, all with glowing letters of recommendation and spotless records. It was telling that the one that caught my eye was the one whose record had a "spot."

William Thomas Riker, first officer for my friend Robert DeSoto on the *Hood*. He'd disobeyed a direct order from his captain and refused to let DeSoto beam down to Altair III, because Riker deemed it unsafe. He risked a general court-martial to, in his mind, protect the captain and the ship. I decided to look into this one.

"Bonjour, mon ami," DeSoto said, from the monitor in my quarters; I'd contacted him via subspace. "You going to steal my first officer?"

"It is a possibility," I said. "I'm assuming your letter of recommendation was honest?"

"Not entirely," DeSoto said. "He's got a sense of humor; I left that out because some captains don't like that."

"Good to know," I said. "Was he joking when he wouldn't let you beam down to Altair III?"

DeSoto smiled. He knew what I was getting at.

"Anybody who's had this job, Jean-Luc," he said, "knows you're alone in a thousand decisions, and a bad one can cost lives. Do I need to tell you that you need people who will stand up to you when they think you're making a bad call?"

"No, you don't," I said. This was the heart of it. I knew how hard it must have been for this young officer to stand up to his captain, because I had been in that position myself. I had disobeyed Mazzara's order to abandon ship, risked my own court-martial because I thought the captain was wrong. It was a lonely, scary moment, and an important one.

"Anything else?" DeSoto said.

"Yes," I said. "If I were you, I'd start looking for a new first officer."

After picking my XO, there were other key positions I already had people in mind for. I contacted Cheva and asked her if she'd mind giving up Natasha Yar, whom I wanted for my chief of security. Cheva chuckled at the idea that she would turn down a request from the man who'd gotten her a command.

The *Enterprise* was also one of the first vessels to have a ship's counselor, and Deanna Troi, the young woman I'd met several years before on the *Saratoga*, was my only choice.

I also had to get Data away from Leyton. I offered Data a promotion to lieutenant commander, but Leyton didn't want to let him go—he knew how lucky he was to have him. I had Quinn put in a call and it was done. I hired my blind pilot Geordi La Forge as my conn officer, and gave Ensign Worf a promotion to lieutenant, and suggested him to Yar as a security officer.

When it came time to choose a chief medical officer, I thought my decision had been made. Dr. Ailat had been on Earth at Starfleet Medical Headquarters since her time on the *Stargazer*. I'd told her years ago that if I got another command, I would be asking her back. I didn't question this course of action until I came across a resume I didn't expect.

Beverly Crusher. She had put in for duty in the *Galaxy*-class program because it made room for families; she had never remarried and had raised Wesley on her own. When Quinn had given me the news that the *Enterprise* would have families aboard, I was aghast—children on my ship. I was in no position to argue, I wasn't going to give up the post, but it rankled me. Until, that is, the moment I realized it might mean I'd see Beverly again.

It occurred to me that she might not know I was captain, and if I offered her the position she might turn it down. And then there was the problem that Ailat might be expecting the position. It seemed irresponsible to alter my decision for such personal reasons. Beverly, though competent and skilled, wasn't nearly as experienced as Ailat was. I decided to call Ailat; perhaps she wasn't expecting me to make the offer. She was in her office at Starfleet Medical; I spoke to her via my computer monitor.

"You've heard I've been made captain of the *Enterprise*," I said.

"Yes," Ailat said. "Congratulations. You will need a chief medical officer."

"Yes," I said. "I would love for you to accept the post." I realized that I had to, in good conscience, offer her the job. She was the most qualified, and I'd had a long, comfortable working relationship with her. But my heart ached at what I was giving up.

"I am honored," Ailat said. "But are you aware that Beverly Crusher is also available?"

"Wh-what?" I sputtered, confused, embarrassed. "No... I mean, yes, her service record came my way... but..." Why was she bringing up Beverly? Were Edosians telepathic?

"Captain," Ailat said, "I served with you a long time." Her tone was as flat as it always was. She looked at me with those strange Edosian eyes set apart in that giant orange skull. Edosians didn't smile the way humans did, and certainly didn't seem warm or friendly. But Ailat was taking care of me.

"I owe you, Ailat," I said. I disconnected from her and immediately sent a request for Beverly Crusher to be posted to the *Enterprise* as chief medical officer. I stared at my computer console waiting for a response. There was still a lot of service records to look over, other posts to fill, but I couldn't concentrate.

Finally, a message. A simple moment of joy.

"Position: Chief Medical Officer. Candidate: Beverly Crusher. Candidate accepted."

✦

"Here are your orders, Captain," Quinn said, handing me a PADD. I was in the Admiralty Meeting Room with him and Admiral Norah Satie. Satie was one of Starfleet's most senior admirals. Her presence was a testimony to the prestige of the command I was being given. I was set to take command later that afternoon; Halloway had finished his shakedown cruise, and brought the *Enterprise* to McKinley Station for final adjustments.

"Anything I should be aware of?" I said. Admiral Satie sat silently for a moment; her stare was penetrating, and it unsettled me.

"After you've solved the mystery of Farpoint Station, your mission is chiefly exploration," Satie said. "You are headed into an area of space that we still have very little information about. And of course, there are security concerns."

0"And, Captain Picard," Satie said, "command of the Federation flagship is a vital responsibility. We're giving it to you because we trust you to protect us from our enemies without and within."

" 'Within'?" I said. "I'm sorry, Admiral, I'm not sure what that means."

"It means, Captain, be vigilant." There was definitely more to this than what she was saying, but she wasn't going to elucidate any further. I took my leave and headed to the main San Francisco starport. I was surprised to see Tasha Yar waiting for me by a shuttle.

"Security Chief Natasha Yar, reporting for duty. It's a pleasure to meet you." I found her formality unusual; she seemed to think she needed to introduce herself.

"Yes, Lieutenant, we met on Carnellia IV," I said.

"I wasn't sure you'd remember me," she said. I was incredulous.

"I watched you walk through a minefield. I chose you to be my chief of security because of it."

"Sorry, sir," she said. Her unique strength seemed to hide a bit of insecurity, at least around me.

"No apologies necessary," I said. "Shall we go?"

We boarded the shuttle, and flew over San Francisco as I'd done many times before. Tasha however appeared amazed at the views.

"It's so beautiful," she said.

"You went to the academy, surely you've seen it before."

"Yes," she said. "I've never gotten used to it. And I don't want to." I remembered then that Tasha came from Turkana IV, a truly violent world, a place where civilization had fallen apart.

"I understand," I said. "I guess I take paradise for granted."

"You've earned it, sir," she said. "The example you've set in your career has raised the bar for the rest of us."

I wasn't used to hero worship, and my instinct was to put a stop to it. But her feeling seemed so genuine, I think I would've regretted discouraging it.

Tasha piloted us toward the *Enterprise*. McKinley Station looked like a giant metal crab that was gripping the ship from above. We went into one of the smaller shuttle bays, and Tasha led me out.

There was a relatively small group of crewmembers in the bay. As there was still plenty of work to be done so we could launch, both Captain Halloway and I had agreed to dispense with a grand "transfer of command" ceremony.

"Commanding Officer *Enterprise*, arriving," Tasha said. The group stood at attention. I went to a small lectern that had been set up in the bay and read my orders aloud.

"To Captain Jean-Luc Picard, stardate 41148.0, you are hereby requested and required to take command as of this date. Signed Rear Admiral Norah Satie, Starfleet Command." I nodded to Tasha.

"Crew dismissed," Tasha said.

I walked over to Deanna Troi and Lieutenant Worf. "Welcome aboard, Captain," she said.

"It's an honor once again to serve with you, sir," Worf said.

"Thank you," I said. I noticed that not only Worf but the rest of the crew present looked at me with a kind of reverence I hadn't before experienced. It was both satisfying and unnerving. "Resume your posts, stand by to get underway." I left the shuttle bay and headed to my quarters.

As I walked the corridors, I was struck by the ship's beauty. Even with the activity the ship had an inherent tranquility. It felt like the pinnacle of civilization. For a moment at least…

"Ow!"

I'd come around the corner, and something had hit me in the shins. It took all my willpower to regain my composure. I looked down to see what had collided with me: a boy.

A child. On my ship.

Merde.

"Harry!" A man in a science uniform ran over to us and helped the boy up. He then saw who his son had run into and looked genuinely horrified. "I'm so sorry, Captain…"

"It's quite all right," I said, lying.

"I'm Dr. Bernard, sir," the man said. "This is Harry. Harry, apologize to the captain."

"No," Harry said.

"It's quite all right," I said, again lying. I left them quickly and headed to the turbolift. Once on it, I thought of my first day on the *Stargazer*, the frustration I felt at having to deal with Mazzara's children. And now there were about seventy-five on this ship. I tapped the communicator on my chest.

"Picard to Lieutenant Yar," I said.

"Yar here, sir," she said.

"From this point forward, no children allowed above Deck Two," I said. This, at least, was something I could do to limit my exposure.

"Aye aye, sir," she said. I could hear a little confusion in her voice, but I didn't mind.

I'd just posted a sign: NO CHILDREN ON THE BRIDGE.

✦

"Captain on the bridge," Data said as I stepped off the turbolift.

My first view of the bridge was quite startling. It was large and comfortable. I initially felt ill at ease walking in such a large room; bridges in my mind were compact and efficient. This almost felt like a living room.

Data was at the ops station, Lieutenant Torres at the conn, serving there temporarily. Tasha was on the upper level at the security and communication station. Worf stood behind her, operating the defensive systems. I stopped by Data at ops.

"Good to see you, Mr. Data," I said.

"It is… good to see you too, sir," he said, as if unsure he was understanding what he was saying.

"For the future, you won't need to announce my presence on the bridge," I said.

"Aye, sir," Data said. I felt the formality didn't go with the setting. This place was to be our home. I then sat down next to Counselor Troi. She looked at me and smiled. There was something behind it.

"Something wrong, Counselor?"

"Nothing at all, sir." She leaned in closer. "Your enthusiasm is infectious."

I smiled, a little awkwardly; it would take a little getting used to being around an officer who could read my emotions so clearly.

"McKinley Station reports we're clear to depart," Yar said.

"Take us out," I said.

McKinley Station's crab-like claws lifted away, and the ship moved out of orbit. As I gave the orders for us to set a course for Deneb IV, I took in the room; we had the most up-to-date technology and an accomplished and gifted crew. I felt a great deal of anticipation for what awaited us. I was confident I was ready. My first encounter on Deneb IV brought home that my youth was long behind me.

Shortly after arriving in orbit, I stood on the deck of the hangar as a small shuttle came through the forcefield and landed. I stepped forward to greet its esteemed passenger, Starfleet's most senior physician who was going to inspect our medical layout. I hadn't seen him in a very long time, and was looking forward to our reunion.

"Admiral McCoy," I said, "Nice to see you again."

"Have we met?" He was much older, over 130 years old, white haired and stooped, but had lost none of his irascibility.

"Yes, I was in the honor guard, in Ambassador Spock's wedding."

McCoy grunted. I felt foolish; of course he wouldn't remember me.

"I was quite a bit younger," I said.

"Did you have hair?"

"I did," I said. We stood for a moment in self-conscious silence. I realized he had no interest in talking to me.

"Someone going to take me around? I'm not getting any younger."

"Of course sir." I decided to assign Lieutenant Data to the task, and returned to my duties. A few years earlier I would've felt obliged to take such an esteemed man around myself, and suffer through an awkward interaction out of a feeling of obligation. Now, however, I spared myself the indignity.

Thinking back, some of my strongest memories of that first mission center around what the circumstance revealed about members of my new crew.

Commander Riker came on board, and immediately and enthusiastically fell into his role as my first officer. He was a man of action, reminding me of my younger self, and we quickly fell into a rhythm that was efficient and complementary. I also gave him the unenviable task of trying to make me look genial with children. Geordi La Forge took his place at the conn, and my bridge crew was complete.

My first encounter with Beverly, however, was a little less satisfying. Within days of assuming command, I was on the bridge when I noticed the turbolift doors open. A teenager was standing there.

"What the hell?" I said. "Children are not allowed on the bridge."

Then Beverly stepped out of the turbolift. My breath left me. I remembered this feeling before. It was as if I was always surprised at how beautiful she was, that I couldn't hold her true beauty in my memory.

"Permission to report to the captain," she said. She was strained—this was difficult for her, too.

"Dr. Crusher," I said. I suddenly felt I'd made a terrible mistake. As her captain, any hopes for a relationship with Beverly would be impossible. I had created a new purgatory for myself.

"Captain," she said. "Sir, my son is not on the bridge, he just accompanied me on the turbolift."

"Your son?" I said. I felt a fool. I knew Wesley had aged, yet locked in my mind was the image of him as a toddler.

"His name is Wesley," she said. Of course I knew his name. How could she think I'd forget his name? Then I realized she didn't know I'd been thinking about her since the day we parted. I felt the urge to apologize for my initial coldness, so I broke my own brand-new rule, and invited Wesley on the bridge.

As he left the turbolift, I had a moment of intense déjà vu. I remembered his father, stepping off the transporter back on the *Stargazer*. This boy had the same awkwardness. The more I looked at him, the more I saw my friend.

Jack was back from the dead. I hoped I wouldn't have to see a lot of him.

✦

"Thou art directed," Q said, "to return to thine own solar system immediately."

He strutted around my ship dressed as Christopher Columbus. His primitive costume belied his virtually limitless power; he'd stopped my ship with an energy force field that stretch to every horizon of space. He changed his appearance in a flash of light and was suddenly a marine from the ancient United States, expounding about the need for "a few good men." A flash, and then he was a soldier from World War III, in battle armor sniffing amphetamines before he went into combat. All very dramatic, meant to intimidate us. Q had the power to do to us whatever he wanted. But he didn't want to destroy us, he wanted to sit in judgment.

Any student of Starfleet history knows of the extraordinarily advanced beings in the Galaxy. The Organians, the Excalbians, the Metrons—all very much like Q, judging "lesser" beings, sometimes for what they considered the greater good, sometimes just for their own amusement.

On that first mission, Q promised that if we failed in discovering the truth about Farpoint Station, we would all be sent back to our home planets, confined for eternity. I had a lot of questions as to whether he could and would have carried out his threat if we hadn't solved that mystery;* as I look back, I'm convinced he would've regretted it. He's enjoyed toying with me and my crew too much.

✦

"Captain," Riker said, "I'd like to talk to you about Wesley Crusher." I had a regular morning meeting with Riker in my ready room. Though we would go over a wide variety of issues involved in running such a huge ship, I never expected Wesley to make the agenda.

"What about him?"

"He's shown remarkable aptitude at understanding the ship's systems, with very little training," Riker said. "I tested him on the flight simulator, and he's as good a pilot as I am."

"Please don't exaggerate," I said. Riker's record as a pilot was exemplary—he literally had the best ratings of the entire crew.

"I'm not," Riker said. "His score on the flight simulator was higher than mine." I could tell that Riker was serious. "I think we should take him under our wing. He'd be an incredible resource."

"Why is it necessary? We have a full crew compliment." I was resisting the idea, although at that moment I didn't understand why.

"Well, sir, one of the arguments for having families on board was the opportunity for Starship captains to identify potential academy candidates among the relatives of the crew. This appears to be one of those opportunities." I envied Riker, his ability to get along so easily with everyone, while also not losing his authority. And I knew he'd formed a bond with Wesley. I was pleased

---

*EDITOR'S NOTE: Farpoint Station was in fact not a building, but an unusual energy creature that had the power to alter matter. It had been captured and enslaved by the inhabitants of Deneb IV, and forced to assume the shape of a ground facility that the inhabitants wanted to allow Starfleet to use, in exchange for payment. Once Picard discovered the truth, the creature was released and never seen again.

about that, as the fact that Wesley was without a father was something that I took as my responsibility.

"I will think about it," I said.

✦

"Captain's log, stardate 41263.4. For outstanding performance in the best of Starfleet tradition, Wesley Crusher is made Acting Ensign, with the duties and privileges of that rank."

It was only a few weeks later. The young man had played major roles in a number of missions, and Riker's suggestion stuck in my mind. I had Riker put him on a strict course of study, with the idea he would tender an application to the academy. And since he was now an acting ensign, he was allowed on the bridge. Riker gave him a lot of time at various duty stations, serving in a support capacity. Sometimes he would take ops. I soon forgot my initial resistance to training him, until one morning, when we were on our way to Starbase 74, and La Forge excused himself from his conn position momentarily. A crewman stood by to take his place, when Riker leaned into me.

"Might be a good opportunity for Wesley to get some flying time," he said.

Something about Riker suggesting Wesley take the conn overwhelmed me with fear. What was I afraid of? It only took me a moment to realize… I had to control myself; I could feel Deanna's eyes on me.

"Make it so," I said. There was no reason not to agree.

Wesley took the conn.

Over the years, some who have reviewed my career as captain of the Enterprise have questioned my decision, specifically how I could let a teenager who'd never gone to the academy take the conn of the Federation flagship. My answer is I trusted my first officer, who had trained the young man, and our experiences proved him to be correct: Wesley was an excellent navigator and helmsman. But that wasn't the true reason I did it. The reason that I acceded to it was much more personal.

I enjoyed having Wesley at his father's post.

✦

When we left Earth, I'd been certain, based on Starfleet's reports, that the Ferengi would be the biggest new challenge we would face. It turned out that these concerns were unwarranted; they were not the dangerous adversaries we thought they would be. They were more an annoyance than a threat, a greedy, opportunistic culture whose sole motive appeared to be profit. Our most important encounter with them, however, solved a mystery that had haunted me for a long time.

DaiMon Bok commanded* a Ferengi ship, which had sought us out. He'd made overtures of friendship, wanting to give me a gift: the Stargazer. He'd found it and had it repaired.

I learned quickly that this was a ruse; Ferengi don't give gifts. It is against their religious and cultural beliefs. Bok's true motive was revenge. When he returned my ship to me, we spoke of the "unknown" ship that had attacked the Stargazer, and Bok spat out the answer of who my assailant was.

"That proud ship was Ferengi!" The vessel that had attacked Stargazer was commanded by Bok's son. Bok gave no reason why his son had attacked me, and his revenge plot failed.**

The result was I got my old ship back. We would rendezvous with a Starfleet towing vessel that would take it back to the Fleet Museum in the Sol system. I was surprised at how interested my crew was in it, and during the two days leading up to the rendezvous with the towing vessel, several of them asked permission to tour it.

"What is the crew's preoccupation with my old ship?" I said this to Riker during one of our morning meetings.

"You're kidding, right?"

"I am not kidding," I said.

"Sir, it's Columbus's Santa María, Cook's Endeavour, Armstrong's Eagle, Archer's Enterprise…" Riker said. "Your mission was required reading at the academy. Forgive me if this embarrasses you, but…"

---

*EDITOR'S NOTE: DaiMon" is a Ferengi equivalent of a starship captain, although in their culture a more accurate parallel would be to a chief executive officer of an old Earth corporation.

**EDITOR'S NOTE: Bok had acquired an illegal mind control device, which he used on Picard to get him to pilot his old ship to attack his new one. Bok was unsuccessful, and since there was no "profit" in revenge, his own people removed him from command.

"But what?"

"We all wanted to be you."

It was ironic; those years where I'd felt unknown and forgotten were now the cause of reverence from the crew. It sent me down a different road in terms of my command style. I remembered the choices I'd made as captain of the Stargazer, seeing my role as captain as less a master and more a servant, putting the needs of the crew first. Now I was falling into that god-like detachment. Part of that was the natural outgrowth of the crew's esteem, and part of it was self-protection. I'd lost a lot of friends on the Stargazer, and subconsciously at least I was probably reticent to let myself get too close to anyone.

Still, I wanted to get to know these young people I was working with, and I began to host each one of them for dinner in the observation lounge. When it was Tasha's turn, I had a meal prepared with dishes in the style of French country cooking: roasted chicken with spring onions, tomato tart, mustard-roasted poussin, butternut gratin. She looked at it all in wonder.

"These are the foods of my childhood," I said.

"It smells delicious," she said. I served her a healthy portion, and she began eating. I then offered her a glass of wine.

"I'm sorry, sir," she said. "I don't drink."

"Oh, I'm sorry," I said. "Do you not enjoy it, or is there a medical issue."

"Where I'm from, sir, alcohol and other drugs are abused. People were easier to take advantage of if they were under the influence. I found it was easier to just stay away from them."

"It must have been a very difficult place to grow up. It's an achievement that you were able to escape."

"You never really escape," she said. "You're taught from a young age that you're worthless… that's not something you ever really let go of." I began to understand her bravery; she could risk her life because on some level she didn't think it was worth anything.

"You're worth quite a bit to me, and to this ship." I could see that she was touched by the remark. But it was but a drop of water in a very dark well. I was determined after this conversation to do everything I could to make sure that Tasha felt her life was worthwhile.

I wouldn't get the chance.

"We are here together to honour our friend and comrade, Lieutenant Natasha Yar."

I was with the command crew on the holodeck, in a recreation of a green field, and a burial plot. Tasha had been killed in the line of duty, callously murdered by a malevolent life-form.* It was a profound loss for our crew, and a great failure for me. This was her memorial service, and we watched a holographic recording she'd made; she knew her job put her life at risk, and she felt such a connection to the crew that she'd left this message to be played in the event of her death. She spoke to each of her close friends; I wasn't surprised at the connections she'd formed with them. But I was taken aback at what she recorded for me.

"Captain Jean-Luc Picard," she said. "I wish I could say you've been like a father to me, but I've never had one, so I don't know what it feels like. But if there was someone in this universe I could choose to be like, someone who I would want to make proud of me, it's you."

This touched me deeply. In some sense, I could relate to not having a father, and though I never got over the tragedy of this bright young person's death, I felt some satisfaction that I'd given her something of value while she was alive.

But Tasha's death began a bleak period that would mark the end of my first year as captain of the *Enterprise*. It seemed many chapters of my past suddenly came to a close at that time, and what had been a bright period in my life and career turned into a grim interval. It began with a reunion I'd been avoiding for a long time.

"I waited all day," Jenice said. We were in the observation lounge of my ship. Even so many years later she was still lovely. She was on board with her husband, the well-known physicist Paul Manheim. While I wasn't hiding, I'd avoided being alone with her since she'd come on board. We were finally having the difficult conversation that I had long owed her.

"I went to Starfleet Headquarters to look for you," she said. "But you'd already shipped out." She was composed, but the hurt and anger were coming through

---

*EDITOR'S NOTE: Tasha Yar was murdered by Armus, a strange being who was created when the inhabitants of Vagra II developed a means of ridding themselves of all that was "evil" within themselves. This "evil" formed itself into Armus, a bitter and lonely creature who took amusement in Yar's death.

even after all these years. She tamped it down with an order that sounded a little playful. "So come on, Jean-Luc, let's hear the truth."

"It was fear," I said. "Fear of seeing you, losing my resolve. Fear of staying." She smiled.

"I've thought a lot about this over the years," she said, "and perhaps you're leaving out your greatest fear. The real reason you couldn't stay."

"Which was?"

"That life with me would have somehow made you ordinary." I laughed a little at this, though the brutal truth of it was cutting.

"Am I that transparent?"

"Only to me," she said. Shortly after, we parted amicably, but what she had said stuck with me. Enough time had passed that she'd moved on and was with someone she loved. But I'd given up the chance of a happy life with someone I loved—someone who understood me. And for what? Achievement and recognition? It seemed very shallow.

✦

"You know, I always wanted to own a bar," Riker said.

It was a few days later, and I was sitting outside at the Blue Parrot Café enjoying a drink with Riker and Deanna. The ship was taking shore leave on Sarona VIII, and we were in capital city of Kel. Kel was set on the northern tip of one of the planet's largest continents, at the edge of a vast desert. It had an Earth-like feel; its low buildings and narrow streets resembled ancient French Morocco. As we sipped our elaborate cocktails, we watched the active street life of species from across the quadrant.

"Too bad we can't have one on the ship," I said.

"Where would we put it?" Deanna said.

"Forward station one is just an empty lounge," Riker said. "We could put it there."

"Make it so!" I said. "But we'll need a good bartender."

"I'll start gathering resumes," Riker said.

Just then, Beverly and Wesley came by. I invited them to join us.

"Isn't this great? So many different species." Wesley directed his comments to Commander Riker; he was still a little intimidated by me. "Mom and I just saw the local police break up a fight between a Klingon and a Nausicaan."

"That must have been something else," Riker said. "Hey, Wes, have you seen the amusement center?"

"Not yet," Wesley said. "Mom, can we go?"

"I just got my drink, Wesley," she said.

"Deanna and I will take him," Riker said, with a glance toward me for my approval. I gave him a nod; the atmosphere and the cocktail had me very at ease. The three of them left, leaving me alone with Beverly. We drank and chatted casually, and for the most part superficially. The conversation shifted to our recent encounter with Jenice and her husband.

"She's a lovely woman," Beverly said. "How did you meet her?"

"She cared for my mother," I said. "We were involved briefly." I wasn't comfortable with talking about one old love with another, though I couldn't tell Beverly that.

"Revisiting the past can be difficult," she said.

"Yes, it can," I said. I could see that there was more she wanted to say. The liquor had perhaps made me a little too brave. "Was there something you wanted to tell me?"

"Yes… there's a senior position at Starfleet Medical," she said. "I would like to put in for it."

"You're leaving?" I said. This wasn't at all what I was expecting, and I knew my plaintiveness was too apparent.

"Not yet," she said. "Only if I get it."

"Are you unhappy?"

"Not at all," she said. "The ship, the crew… you… it's been wonderful. It's just that…"

"Jack…"

She nodded.

"Too many memories. I wasn't ready for it."

"It would be a big loss for me," I said. "A loss for the ship, I mean." The Blue Parrot used real alcohol, and it made me a little too honest.

"Thank you," she said.

"Obviously you have my support." I meant that professionally; personally, I was crushed, and as we finished our drinks and waited for the others to return, I fell into a dark silence. I didn't want her to leave.

✦

"Hello, Jean-Luc," Walker Keel said. "It's been a long time."

"Too long, old friend," I said. I'd been asleep in my quarters when the emergency message from him came through. Looking at him on the viewscreen told the story; he was gray, but beyond superficial aging, something was very wrong. Walker had none of the youthful vigor and humor I associated with him. He was very solemn.

"We need to talk, face to face," he said. There was an undercurrent of panic in his voice. "I want you to meet me on Dytallix B."

This would take me off our course and violate my orders, and he knew that. He persisted—I felt I had to agree.

"Something is beginning," he said. "Don't trust anyone."

✦

On Dytallix B, in an abandoned mining facility, I was confronted by three Starfleet captains: Rixx, a Bolian; Tryla Scott, a young woman famous for being the youngest captain in Starfleet history; and Walker. Rixx and Scott held phasers on me as Walker peppered me with strange questions.

"Do you recall the night you introduced Jack Crusher to Beverly?" Walker said. I paused to consider this. A giant lie embedded in the question. Did he think I was an imposter?

"You know full well," I said, "I hadn't even met Beverly then. You introduced them."

"My brother introduced them," he said. This was ridiculous.

"You don't have a brother," I said. "Two sisters, Anne and Melissa. What the hell is all this about?" I was losing patience, but this seemed to be enough for them. Walker nodded to his two companions, who put their weapons away.

"We all came secretly, Picard," Rixx said. "To discuss the threat."

"What threat?"

"Have you noticed anything about Starfleet Command lately?" Scott said. I said I hadn't, though we hadn't had much contact with command.

"Some of us have seen strange patterns emerging," Walker said. "Unusual orders."

They went down a list of strange coincidences, accidental deaths, limited communications. It sounded like a paranoid conspiracy theory. Tryla Scott read the distrust in my face.

"He doesn't believe us," she said.

"You've given me nothing to believe in," I said.

"I think it's spread to my own ship," Walker said. "My first officer hasn't been the same since we stopped off at Earth. Our medical officer says he's perfectly normal, but I don't think I trust him either..."

"Walker!" He was almost raving. I couldn't believe this was the same man. I left the three of them, agreeing to keep in touch, but not at all believing anything they were saying.

I regretted my skepticism. Walker's ship was soon destroyed under mysterious circumstances. I realized they'd been telling the truth: something sinister was going on.

My friend was dead, and I had to do something about it.

✦

"You've done well, Captain Picard," Admiral Satie said. We stood in a communication room in Starfleet Headquarters over the dead body of a Starfleet lieutenant named Remmick. Riker and I had just killed him and the unknown alien that had taken up residence in his body.

Our investigation into the circumstances around the death of Walker Keel led us back to Earth, where we discovered crab-like parasitic aliens had entered the bodies of Starfleet officers, taking over their cognitive brain functions. They were only a few short steps away from conquering the Federation.

"It was some kind of 'mother alien,'" Riker said.

Satie had arrived with several officers shortly after we'd killed the creature. It turned out she was the first to become suspicious of a conspiracy within Starfleet Command, as far back as when she gave me command of the *Enterprise*. She was also the one who sent Walker to me before she herself went into hiding. She had instructed Walker not to tell me she had sent him, in case I myself fell victim to the aliens

I looked down at the remains of Remmick. I'd been taught to cherish life in the universe, I took no pleasure in taking it.

"Once you killed the mother," Satie said, "the others fled the bodies they occupied and died."

"I didn't believe Walker," I said. "If I'd moved more quickly…"

"We all bear the responsibility, Captain," she said. "We must be vigilant."

A few days later, there was a memorial service for Walker on Earth. Beverly and I attended it. It was in the city of Chicago, in an ancient religious church called Rockefeller Chapel. As I listened to the speakers at the service talking about Walker, I felt the loss of my old friend. He'd been such an important part of my life, a person I'd relied on for many years for advice and comradeship. I took for granted he would always be there.

After the service, Beverly, who was very close to Walker's sisters, stayed behind, and I left the chapel alone. As I walked out onto the street, I didn't notice as someone came up behind me.

"Sorry for your loss, Jean-Luc," Guinan said. She was in her usual wide-brimmed hat and long robes, but all in black. I embraced her; I felt such a sense of comfort from her presence.

"It's wonderful to see you," I said. "Where have you been?" She'd long since left the 602 Club, and I'd lost track of her. She seemed to move through the universe with nary a care.

"Here and there," she said. "You ever figure out how to put a bar on your ship?"

"You know," I said, "I just did…" I felt, after the loss of my friend, I had a small reason to be happy.

✦

"Dr. Pulaski of the *Repulse* seems the best option," Riker said. We were going over the resumes of possible replacements for Beverly. She had gotten the position at Starfleet Medical and was leaving that afternoon, as soon as we arrived at Starbase 57. The only person I had in mind for the position was Dr. Ailat, but she'd retired to her homeworld, and I had put off making a firm decision on finding someone else, secretly hoping Beverly would change her mind. But she hadn't. I looked over Pulaski's service record.

"Pulaski is very qualified," I said.

"Is that your decision?" Riker was gently nudging me along. He could tell I was dragging this out unnecessarily, although I'm not sure he knew why.

"Make it so," I said.

"Yes, sir. Now, I think I've got a solution to our problem in engineering." I'd been frustrated with the command structure in that department. The ship was a complicated piece of technology, and the designers had decided on several chief engineers, each with their own area of expertise. But every time we had a problem I was talking to someone different: MacDougal, Argyle, Lynch, Logan. I wanted a more traditional captain-engineer dynamic like the one I'd had with Scully. I needed one person in charge of everybody.

"Let's hear it," I said.

"Geordi," Riker said. "Lot of engineering experience, comes up with creative solutions, and already has a strong working relationship with you."

"He's shown he knows how to take command," I said, "but it could raise some hackles with others who have seniority in that department."

"That's his problem," Riker said, with a smile. "Seriously, he'll figure it out. That just leaves the question of who takes over his spot at conn."

"My preference would be Wesley," I said. "Too bad he's going with his mother."

"You've come a long way," Riker said. I had: I'd come to appreciate the young man, my old friend's son, who'd taken the role of relief conn officer. He would be leaving the ship to accompany his mother to her new posting, after he finished his school term in a few weeks.

"Bridge to Captain Picard," Geordi said, over the intercom. "We're arriving at Starbase 57."

"Very well, assume standard orbit," I said, "and inform Dr. Crusher." I hoped Will hadn't noticed that my voice cracked when I said this. If he had, he gave no indication.

A few minutes before she was scheduled to depart the ship, I excused myself from the bridge, saying I would return momentarily, and went down to sickbay. I don't know that I expected to say anything significant to Beverly; I just wanted one last moment alone with her.

When I got to sickbay, her office was empty.

"Can I help you, sir?" It was Nurse Ogawa, a young ensign who'd just joined the staff.

"I was looking for Dr. Crusher."

"Oh, I'm afraid she left," Ogawa said. This set off a bit of a panic, but I controlled myself, nodded to Ogawa, and left as quickly as I could without looking rushed. I headed to Transporter Room 1. When the corridor was empty, I increased my pace to almost a run, then returned to a walk if someone appeared. I arrived at the transporter room. Chief O'Brien was alone in the room.

"Has Dr. Crusher beamed down yet?"

"No, sir. Not yet." I nodded and left the room. I was short of breath, beginning to sweat. This was no good, and I realized in my tizzy that I'd avoided the most obvious solution to the problem.

"Computer," I said, "locate Dr. Crusher."

"Dr. Crusher," the computer said, "is in the captain's ready room."

I was such a fool. She was of course coming to request permission to leave the ship. I took a deep breath, and leisurely made my way back to the bridge. As I headed for the ready room, Beverly stepped out.

"Oh, I was waiting for you," she said.

"Yes," I said. "My apologies. I was called away." That was a stupid lie; the entire bridge crew was watching us, and they knew I hadn't been called anywhere. I quickly led her back into the room.

"So," I said. "You're ready to depart."

"Yes. Thank you again for letting Wesley stay a few more weeks."

"It is my pleasure. He's a valued member of the crew."

We stared at each other, smiling a bit uneasily.

"I want to thank you," I said. "Your presence here was of enormous help to me."

"I'm sorry I can't stay."

"If you ever want to come back…"

"That might be difficult if you have another chief medical officer."

"I will make it work," I said. She reached out and took my hand, then leaned in to kiss me on the cheek.

"Request permission to depart," she said.

"Granted," I said. She turned and left. Again, I let a moment pass where I could have told her how I really felt about her. I didn't want her to leave, but hadn't the strength to risk stopping her.

Two weeks later, it was time for Wesley to leave, and he came to see me in my ready room.

"Captain Picard, I've thought about this a lot," Wesley said. "I want to remain on the *Enterprise*." I looked at the young man. He was on his way to becoming a Starfleet officer, but he was still young, he needed parenting, and I was afraid of assuming those responsibilities. I gave him an indication that I wasn't sure.

"Captain," he said, "this is where I want to be. This is where I feel I belong." I listened in silence, then dismissed him without giving him an answer. He had started me thinking of my own youth, the feeling of disconnection from my family and home. And here we'd given this young man a place that he felt a connection to. I thought of the father he'd been denied. Nothing could make up for that, but perhaps the *Enterprise* could come close. I decided to let him stay.

It was also a way to guarantee that I would never fully lose contact with Beverly.

✦

"Q set a series of events into motion," Guinan said, "bringing contact with the Borg much sooner than it should have come." We were playing three-dimensional chess in Ten-Forward, the bar that Riker had converted from forward station one. It was a wild success. In a short time, it had become second nature for the crew to gather in this room to relax, socialize, or even work. I was spending time with Guinan after a traumatic encounter with Q, who had introduced us to what would become the Federation's most dangerous adversary. The Borg.

"You're just raw material to them," Guinan said. The Borg are a cybernetic species that assimilated other cultures. They literally scooped cities off of worlds, taking their inhabitants. They would then alter them with cybernetic implants. The minds of the species they assimilate become one with the Borg collective consciousness. This one mind allowed them to work together with deadly efficiency. Guinan spoke from experience: her people, the El-Aurians, were victims of such an assimilation. "Since they are aware of your existence…"

She let her sentence hang unfinished; it was clear what she was implying.

"They will be coming," I said.

"You can bet on it," Guinan said.

"Maybe Q did the right thing for the wrong reason," I said. Q had used his immense power to transport my ship 7000 light-years away in an instant, where we encountered a Borg cube, one of their giant ships. We were no match for them and were only able to escape when I begged Q to save us.

"How so?" Guinan said.

"Well, perhaps what we most needed was a kick in our complacency, to prepare us for what lies ahead." I made my last move on our chessboard, and Guinan saw that I'd beaten her. She smiled, but then it faded as someone else came into the room. I turned to see Mr. Worf, carrying a PADD.

"Here is the list of the missing, sir," Worf said. When the Borg had attacked, they had sliced out a section of the ship. Eighteen people had been in that section and were now missing, presumed dead. I looked at the names on the list, many of which I recognized. Logan, Torres, Whalen, Solis, T'su… young people at the start of their careers. Gone.

A terrible cost for this encounter. I had been too cavalier to refer to this as a "kick" in our complacency.

"Excuse me, Guinan," I said. "I have to go write to their families."

✦

"Dr. Pulaski," I said, "I'm afraid I don't think this is working out." Katherine Pulaski had been chief medical officer for about a year when I decided I'd had enough. She was exceedingly competent in her job,* but she had taken to openly disagreeing with me one too many times, even at certain points insulting me. The news I was giving her didn't seem to be much of a surprise.

"I was going to ask for a transfer," she said. "Because, with all due respect, from the minute I came on board, it was clear to me you didn't want me to succeed in this job."

---

*EDITOR'S NOTE: Indeed, Dr. Pulaski actually replaced Captain Picard's artificial heart in emergency surgery, saving his life.

"I'm not sure that's quite fair," I said, though in a way I knew she was right. "What actions can you point to that support that?"

"I'm afraid I can't point to a single incident," Pulaski said. "It's just a feeling that I had from you that I was unwelcome."

"I'm sorry you felt that way," I said. I couldn't argue with her impressions. I'd kept my distance from Pulaski, and recently had begun silently compiling a list of minor offenses in my mind to justify my dissatisfaction. It was an incident a week before where something happened on the bridge that led me to make up my mind and let her go.

Data sang a song.

I had been sitting on the bridge, flanked by Deanna and Riker. Wesley was at the conn, Data at ops. Worf behind me.

"I spoke to Beverly," Deanna said. I was focused on the keypad on the arm of my chair, pretending to review a duty roster Riker had given me to approve.

"How is she?" Riker said.

"She's well," Deanna said. "Though I think she misses us."

"She definitely does," Wesley said. "I can tell."

"It would appear," Data said, "that she made an incorrect decision accepting that post."

"Sometimes, Data," Deanna said, "you don't know what you've got till it's gone."

"They paved paradise and put up a parking lot," Data said.

"What does that mean?" Worf said.

"It is from an old Earth song," Data said. "I assumed that is what Counselor Troi was referencing, since 'You don't know what you've got till it's gone' is the lyric that precedes it." Everyone laughed.

"I wasn't, Data," Troi said. "It was just a coincidence."

"Sing it for us, Data," Riker said. Data looked to me, and I pretended to be taking note of the situation for the first time, and nodded. As Data began to sing the unusual but sweet song, I fantasized about the future. It led me to contact Beverley directly. I spoke to her via subspace a few hours later.

"What a delightful surprise," she said. We chatted for a while about her job, and how things were on the ship. I then mentioned my troubles with Dr. Pulaski, and that I thought she would be leaving soon.

"So there will be an opening for a new Chief Medical Officer," I said. "I was hoping to get someone with the appropriate experience..." Beverley smiled. She saw right through me.

"I can't keep secrets from Deanna," she said.

"I don't know what you're talking about," I said. "Counselor Troi is not telepathic. In any event, are you aware of any potential candidates?"

"Candidly, Jean-Luc," she said, "I thought being on the *Enterprise* was too difficult, but I'm finding that being away is worse. I miss everyone too much."

"Then come home," I said. "The feeling is mutual." A short while later, Pulaski left, and Beverley returned.

✦

"We've been ordered to Vulcan," I said. "We're going to take Ambassador Sarek to meet the Legarans to negotiate the treaty." I was on the bridge, and had just received the orders. Everyone reacted as I expected. Sarek was a legend, and he had been attempting to negotiate a treaty with the Legarans, an advanced and enigmatic species, for a long time. They'd been discovered by a starship many years ago.* The Legarans were a species that lived in liquid; they looked like large blue lobsters, and had a very advanced technology and culture. They also had no interest in joining the Federation. Sarek had taken them on as a personal project, and spent the last *93 years* attempting to get them to the negotiating table. If this treaty negotiation were successful, it would go down in history as the crowning achievement of his career. And we were going to be a part of it.

I felt that third year on the *Enterprise* was in some ways the true beginning of my captaincy. I was comfortable, I had the crew that I wanted, and we began playing an unprecedented role in galactic affairs. And this, for me, was a personal triumph—a chance to talk with the man I'd been unable to speak to out of nervousness all those years ago, and get his insight into all the history he had made. It would happen, though not how I expected.

---

*EDITOR'S NOTE: It seems that Captain Picard has forgotten that the Legarans were first encountered by James Kirk during his second five-year mission on his starship *Enterprise*. For reference, see *The Autobiography of James T. Kirk*.

✦

"I will not be spoken to in this manner!" It was a few days after Sarek had come aboard, and he was shouting at me. *A Vulcan was shouting at me.*

"Do I hear anger in your voice?" I said. I was baiting him, trying to get him to admit to the truth of the situation. I'd learned of a conspiracy among his aides to hide the fact that Sarek was suffering from a degenerative disease called Bendii syndrome. It made him unable to control his emotions, and through his own telepathic ability he was spreading his emotional outbursts into the minds of people throughout the ship.

"It would be illogical for a Vulcan to show anger! It would be illogical! Illogical! Illogical! Illogical!" He had completely lost control of himself. It was sad to have to force him into this, but I had no choice.

I left him in his quarters to try to regain his composure and went to my ready room. The only option I had was to contact the Legarans and cancel the conference. If the Legarans were to come on the ship with Sarek in this condition, the negotiations would be a disaster. All Sarek's work over the past nine decades would be thrown away. As I faced this unsolvable dilemma, his wife came to see me.

"I must speak with you, Captain," Perrin said. Sarek's wife was human, the second human that he'd married. I found it interesting that a Vulcan, whose entire philosophy was based on controlling his emotions, had chosen for companionship women who culturally were taught to express theirs. She pleaded with me to let the conference continue to save her husband's reputation and legacy.

"The mission can be saved," Perrin said.

"I don't understand," I said.

"If you mind-meld with him," Perrin said, "he will be able to regain control of his emotions."

"I don't see how that would work," I said. "I don't know that I have the mental discipline to control his emotions." Vulcan emotions were known to be even more raw and disturbing than those of a human, another testimony to their culture's success in restraining them.

"You won't need to control them," Perrin said. "You will be a receptacle for his feelings, physically separated from him, allowing him to conduct the negotiations." I looked at Perrin. She had no doubt that I would accede to this request. How did she know? We'd only met a few days ago, and yet somehow she knew that this offer, as dangerous as it was, would be irresistible to me. She smiled knowingly.

My answer: "I can't turn this down."

"Sharing thoughts with one of the greatest men in history? I would think not."

✦

Sarek was in my quarters, facing me. He placed his hands on my face, and I could feel him in my mind… and then his mind *was* my mind. I became vaguely aware that he'd physically left the room, but we were still joined in our minds. Beverly sat close by as the emotions, the memories, flooded in.

"Bedlam!" I said. I could hear myself screaming, but it didn't feel like me. "I am so old! There is nothing left but dry bones and dead friends…" The memories took me over…

"I'm Amanda Grayson," Amanda said to me. She was a teacher, taking human children on a tour of the Vulcan embassy on Earth. I had come out into the hallway, and saw the warm smile and bright eyes, and had let this attraction sweep the logic aside and push me toward her to introduce myself…

My baby son, newly born, crying… I showed outward disapproval for the infant's unrestrained emotion, as inside I felt joy, an overpowering emotional need to protect this innocent, vulnerable creature from a harsh, unforgiving world…

Visions of the aftermath of an explosion. Fire and rubble everywhere while the panicked voice of Amanda implored me to save her…

"I will attend Starfleet Academy…" Spock said to me. He was a teenager, and chose a different path than the one I took. An insult! Was he saying the life I led wasn't good enough for him? I couldn't show him how much it hurt me, I couldn't show him that, even though he was the child, how much I wanted his approval…

"Sarek…" Amanda said, withered, frail, in our bed, her human lifespan so much shorter than mine. I took her hand, and for the first time, showed her emotion. I said the words…

"I love you," I said. But her eyes were closed. She was gone. Had she heard me? Did she know?

"It's an honor to meet you, Ambassador," Perrin said. She was so young, her expression of interest sparkled at me, and I felt that same attraction, but also guilt. Horrible guilt. Amanda had been dead for decades, yet she was the one person I had told that I loved. The feelings I had for Perrin were a betrayal of that love, but yet I pursued those feelings…

Sarek's memories, they consumed me. I fell into Beverly's arms, weeping uncontrollably.

Soon it was over. Sarek had been successful. The Federation had a treaty with the Legarans. Sarek left, and through our connection, I understood the weaknesses of the great men of history, the ambitions, the loves, the loneliness. I could relate to Sarek; I was, in fact, trying to *be* him, to make a difference in the world in which I lived, spreading culture and law in the hopes of being remembered as a force for good. As emotionally wrenching as the experience was, I'd succeeded. It gave me confidence; I was a living instrument of civilization.

As I was often reminded when I described my lofty ambitions, I was also a fool.

✦

"Resistance is futile," I said. I was on the Borg cube, communicating with forty Federation starships. They had gathered in the system Wolf 359 to stop our advance to Earth. The Borg's plan was to assimilate the entire Federation, starting with humanity's homeworld and moving out from there. When I said "resistance is futile," I was speaking as both Locutus and Picard. From Locutus it was a statement of fact: the Borg collective mind did not accept the possibility that any resistance would succeed.

From Picard, "resistance is futile" was a howl of despair. I had been trying so hard to break through, to regain control of myself, but I was pushed aside.

I looked out at the forty ships; the companion beside me spoke.

"They are going to resist," the Queen said.

"Yes," I said. Though she spoke out loud, she also spoke through the collective; all the billions of voices were in my head. The Queen's was the loudest.

We hadn't known the Borg had a queen. She oversaw the organization of the collective, supervised the assimilation of countless species. She was in fact the creator of the Borg; thousands of years old, in her previous life she was a cyberneticist. She created nanoprobes that could enter cells and cure diseases. The nanoprobes also worked in conjunction with cybernetic implants, allowing direct mind-to-mind connection with computers on their world. The nanoprobes evolved, and became a kind of virus that at first infected other members of her species, and then other species they came into contact with. As the collective grew, there was soon a hunger for more species, and they became the Borg.

From the beginning, the Queen seemed interested in me. I knew I was some kind of plaything. Soon after the Borg had taken me, we had disabled the *Enterprise* in battle. But we had stopped short of destroying it. She left them alive to tease me. The collective responded to her control, and she had convinced it that the *Enterprise* wasn't a threat. But there was something else. She had complete control of me, yet she wanted something more. She wanted me to give myself to her. I thought that I had lost myself to the Borg, but the fact that the Queen wanted me in a way she wasn't experiencing meant that some part of Picard had managed to hold himself back. At the time, however, I felt I'd lost. Especially as she took me further apart, forcing me to fight, to defeat my own people.

I saw the ships spreading out around the cube from several different angles. It was a strategy I recognized from both my Starfleet training and my recent briefings. They would attack on multiple fronts, searching for signs of weakness. The lead ship, coordinating the attack, would determine where the weak spots were and move ships to concentrate fire in that area.

"We will counter this strategy," the collective said. I couldn't keep anything from them. They were both reading my mind and they *were* my mind.

I turned to the viewscreen. I was being seen by all the starships who were now closing in. And, in turn, I was looking into the bridges of all those ships as their captains and crews stared at the man they once knew as Jean-Luc Picard.

Admiral Hanson on the bridge of the *Fearless*… He looked determined, hiding his sadness that he was about to try to kill me. The Vulcan captain Storil on the bridge of the *Saratoga*, passionless, ready to do his duty. My old communications officer Chris Black, in command of the *Bonestell*. He looked confused, far from certain that he was doing the right thing.

Robert DeSoto, on the *Hood*, his affability gone.

Marta Batanides in command of the *Kyushu*. Heartbroken.

Corey Zweller, on the *Melbourne*. I hadn't seen him in so long; no longer the young man I had known. Aged, rugged, tired.

Cheva on the *Roosevelt*. Tears in her eyes as she gave the order to fire all weapons.

"Destroy them," the Queen said.

I did. All eleven thousand.

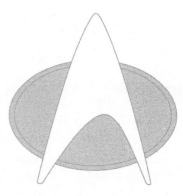

CHAPTER TEN

"HOW MUCH DO YOU REMEMBER?" Riker said.

"Everything," I said. "Including some rather unorthodox strategies from a former first officer of mine."

Riker smiled. I was in Data's lab, naked and infested with Borg implants. Riker had rescued me from the Borg cube. Through me, Data had been able to access the collective, and destroy the cube before it could attack Earth. But I still remembered all the destruction I'd caused, and all of the friends I'd killed. Joking with Riker was an attempt to avoid my pain, which was too much to bear.

I was taken to sickbay, where over the next several hours Beverly removed every trace of Borg technology from my body. Guinan came to see me while I recovered.

"How are you feeling?"

"Almost myself," I said. "Riker says you were of enormous help to him."

"I knew he'd rescue you," Guinan said. "You and I have a date."

"We do? When?"

"I'm not sure," she said with a cryptic smile. "Get some rest." And with that, she left. I didn't know what she meant—Guinan had an air of the unexplained about her, which she enjoyed cultivating.

I was back on duty in a day. I was tired but human again. The *Enterprise* returned to McKinley Station for repairs, which would take six weeks.

Crewmen were free to go to Earth for shore leave. I stayed aboard, however, meeting with Counselor Troi regularly for the first few weeks.

"Did you have another nightmare last night?" she said, as we began one of our sessions.

"Yes."

"Do you remember it?"

"Some of it," I said. The nightmares I'd been having were stark remembrances of recent events, with only a little bit of the usual dream confusion. "The *U.S.S. Roosevelt* was crippled and drifting toward the cube. The collective sent drones to assimilate the survivors."

"Did you know anyone on the *Roosevelt*?"

"Its captain, Cheva..."

"She served with you on the *Stargazer*."

"Yes," I said. "I watched in the dream as the drones took her off the bridge and injected her with nanoprobes."

"Do you remember that really happening?"

"I believe so," I said. "Although in the dream I was physically next to her. She looked at me and asked me to help her. And I put my hand on her shoulder and said something."

"What did you say?"

"'Resistance is futile,'" I said. "I whispered it, it was gentle, like I was trying to tell her not to fight. And then two dead hands pulled her away from me."

"Did you see who the hands belonged to?"

"They were mine," I said. "I was staring at myself as a Borg."

The nightmares were all like this, some obvious imagery tied in with the traumatic events I'd experienced. We talked through these dreams every day, and it helped; the nightmares eventually ended. I felt more rested. Deanna suggested that I consider taking a little shore leave on Earth. I thought I didn't have anywhere I wanted to go.

Then I got a note from my brother's wife, Marie. Robert had married her almost ten years before, and she would periodically write to me. I had given her perfunctory responses, but this had not stopped her from writing. She had told me about Robert, and the son they had. She'd been spurred to write the most recent note when she heard about the *Enterprise* staying in orbit for repairs. She was inviting me to come visit. I decided to accept.

A few days later, I was walking from the village toward the vineyard. It was a beautiful spring day. Along the path, I was met by the vision of my brother at seven; it was my nephew René. He, however, seemed much more pleasant than Robert ever was.

"You know," he said, after we'd walked and chatted for a minute, "you don't seem so arrow... arrow... you know..."

"Arrogant?" I said.

"Yes, arrogant. You don't seem that way to me. What does it mean anyway, arrogant son of a—"

"Let's talk about that later, shall we?"

René led me to his mother, Marie, a beautiful, elegant woman who gave me a heartfelt welcome. She stood in front of the family home, unchanged in all these years.

"Robert can't wait to see you," she said.

"So René tells me," I said. "Where is he?"

I found Robert in the vineyard, tending to his grapes. As his son was the image of him, Robert was the image of his father... our father. Even down to the hat he wore to protect him from the sun. He sensed me approaching.

"So, you arrived all right," he said. "Welcome home, Captain." It was cold and distant. What I expected, and yet, still not what I was hoping for.

I stayed a few days at the vineyard. Though Robert was his critical self, I found myself not wanting to leave; Marie and René were the warm familial embrace that had been missing for me since my mother's death. I was beginning to think that I didn't need to return to the *Enterprise*. Marie made several overtures to me moving back home, and I began to think I could finally have that simple life that had always eluded me. Looking back, it was obvious I was hiding from my feelings. On some level I knew that.

I also, unfortunately, took the opportunity to indulge in the family wine. For the recent years I'd been in Starfleet, most of the cocktails I consumed were made of synthehol, which did not have the deleterious effects of alcohol—you could always stay in control. Not so with the family wine. I had gotten through a bottle one afternoon, when Robert came in. He joined me in a glass.

"What did they do to you?" he asked. I didn't want to tell him about what I'd been through. I got up and went outside.

"Why do you walk away? That isn't your style," he said. He had followed me; he seemed to be looking for a fight. I realized later the truth of it: he *was* looking for a fight, but to help me. I was in a drunken fugue, barely maintaining my control.

I really don't remember exactly what happened. He taunted me, called me the great hero who'd fallen to Earth. I heard his jealousy and resentment towards his responsibility to look after me. But I scoffed at it; to me he'd always been a bully, and now, my years of anger combined with alcohol took over.

I hit him.

We fell through the vines and wrestled in the muddy irrigation ditches. The fight did not last long, not because either of us prevailed, but because we both quickly realized the ridiculousness of two grown men rolling around in the mud. We started laughing at our immaturity. I couldn't ever remember laughing with Robert. The laughter died down.

"You've been terribly hard on yourself, you know," he said. In that moment, I saw Robert understood me, like no one had. The sorrow and guilt poured out of me. The Borg had shown what a fraud I was.

"So, my brother is a human being after all," he said. "This is going to be with you a long time, Jean-Luc. A long time." In that moment, I realized how much I missed Robert. *I missed Robert.*

We got up out of the mud, and he put his arm around me.

"There's something I want to show you," he said. He led me into the house, and went to the hall closet. He took the giant metal key ring that opened the door to the basement, and I followed him down into our family museum.

We walked along the hallway of the famous relatives, until we got to what had been the end. Now there was a portrait of Robert.

And next to it, a portrait of me in my uniform, smiling, arms folded.

"Where did you get this?"

"I had it made," he said. "The first Picard to leave the solar system. I think Father would've approved."

I soon returned to the repaired *Enterprise*, fully repaired myself. Robert had become the brother I'd wanted. Maybe even the father. I realized that I needed Robert; he was the only one left in the world who knew me before I'd become "Captain Jean-Luc Picard," the only person I could show true weakness to.

A few years later, Robert would die. It was a profound tragedy: Robert had maintained the primitiveness of the family home, a primitiveness that made it dangerous, and he and René were killed in a fire in the barn. It is the greatest regret in my life that I took so long to try to fix our relationship. I'd stayed a child too long, angry at how he treated me, and missed out on getting to know him, truly getting to thank him for all the times he was there looking after me. He was the last connection to my childhood, to my family, and he was gone.

✦

A few weeks later, Wesley was finally leaving to attend the academy. Various circumstances had kept him from joining, and in the intervening years I'd given him a full promotion to ensign. But now was the time. On his last day on the ship, there was a goodbye party for him in Ten-Forward.

I noticed Beverly standing alone, watching the proceedings. I went over to her.

"Sad to see him go?"

"It's difficult," she said. "He's so clearly a young man, but for me it's as if my five-year-old Wesley is leaving me."

"He'll be back," I said, although I wasn't sure that was true. I looked over at Wesley standing with Riker, La Forge, and Worf. La Forge was telling some story that they were all enjoying.

"I want to thank you, Jean-Luc," she said.

"Thank me? For what?"

"He didn't have his father," she said. "But thanks to you, he's had a family, filled with love. You helped me raise him." The group with Wesley shared a loud laugh. Beverly gestured toward them. "And he's had the most incredible role models."

"He was born to the best one," I said. "His mother." She looked at me and smiled, tears welling in her eyes. Though it was in public, I gave in to the urge to hug her.

There was something about that moment that changed our relationship; we began to spend more time together. We began a morning ritual of breakfast. It wasn't in any way romantic, but our past had slipped behind us, and we could enjoy the present together.

✦

"Indeed, you've found him, Captain Picard."

I stood in a cave with Data. We were on another undercover mission, disguised as Romulans, on the planet Romulus. In front of me was a man I hadn't seen in 40 years, and though I was at his wedding, we'd never actually spoken.

Spock.

"What are you doing on Romulus?" he said.

"That was to have been my question of you, sir." Spock, now a Federation ambassador, had disappeared four weeks earlier, and then shown up on one of Starfleet Intelligence's long-range scans of Romulus. Command was concerned that he might actually be defecting, and Data and I had been sent on a mission to find him. Our excursion to Denobula all those years before had not been forgotten by the Admiralty.

We were successful in tracking him down, but he initially refused to reveal his reasons for coming to Romulus. Yet, I also had to deliver some profound news to him. News he seemed to anticipate before I could tell him.

"Sarek," he said. "Sarek is dead."

Sarek had died shortly before our arrival on Romulus. At the news of his father's passing, Spock opened up to me: he revealed he was trying to facilitate a reunification of Romulus with its ancient homeworld of Vulcan. It was a mission that had incredible ramifications for the Federation—it would literally redraw the quadrant.

Spock wanted Data and I to leave, but I refused. We could not depart in the midst of such a delicate mission, one that the Federation had in no way approved. On top of which, Ambassador Spock was one of the single most important individuals in the Federation; I had to do my best to protect him. So we stayed to assist him.

As we spent time with him, I learned we had much in common. Despite the philosophy of logic that Spock followed, he was also ambitious—he was now the most famous Vulcan in the Federation, even surpassing his father. But, ironically, he had sought approval from that father who would not, or could not, provide it.

Spock's mission did not succeed while we were there, but he wanted to stay on Romulus and continue his work. As we parted, we talked about his father, and he told me something that I already knew: he and Sarek had never chosen to mind-meld. I offered him a chance to meld with me, and touch what Sarek had shared.

He placed his hand on my face. I felt our minds drawn together…

I saw events from a shared past. It was a strange experience, like two different cameras filming the same scene. A young Vulcan boy, crying after being bullied, his father standing by impassive, and the father's internal struggle to maintain composure, while feeling fear for his son, worry, sadness.

The father's pride as his son helped rescue the Federation president from assassination.

The son, standing at his own wedding, looking out at his father in the audience; the father's secret joy at his son's happiness in that same moment.

Then I saw Spock in the cave, melding with me, closing his eyes in emotion. I was giving this son a profound gift, a gift I'd never had.

✦

"Dad, what's a 'dollar'?" Meribor said. She was my daughter, ten years old.

"It's a unit of currency," I said.

"And what's a 'big yellow taxi'?" Batai said. He was my son, four.

"It's like the carriages that we use to get to other towns," I said. They were referencing song lyrics I'd written out for them. Lyrics I remembered from my previous life. Data had sung it once on the bridge. I had found it quite affecting, so I had looked it up in the ship's database, and had learned the lyrics. In my new life, I had taught myself to play the tune on my flute, and was now teaching the song to my children.

My children.

Years before, I'd found myself on this planet that the natives called Kataan. I had no idea how I got there, and there had been no sign of the *Enterprise*. To make matters more complicated, everyone on this world saw me as someone named Kamin. I thought I'd somehow been transported and looked for any way to return to my ship. For five years, I studied the night sky looking for some clue as to where this planet was. I was living with a woman named Eline, who claimed to be my wife. She loved me despite my insistence that I came from somewhere else. I did my best to hang on to Picard, but the world I was on and the day-to-day experiences of this peaceful, friendly people, who showed me love and respect, pushed Starfleet from my mind. I gave in to Eline's love and forgot my old life.

Except for songs. It was the one thing I'd hung on to, the final link to the life that I had before. I had learned the songs of Kataan but also played songs from distant Earth.

"Mother, we're ready!" Meribor shouted. Eline came from the other room.

"Ready for what?"

"For the concert," Meribor said.

"Not the 'Skye Boat Song' again," Eline said. Eline knew they were left over from something she didn't understand, but she didn't seem to mind. It was only a token, it didn't take me away from her.

"No, we've learned the lyrics to a new one," Meribor said.

"It's my favorite," Batai said. As I played the song and the children sang along, Eline and I caught each other's eyes. The joy of children was something I'd never experienced in my other life—I'd kept my distance from the ones on the *Enterprise*. But now it *was* my life, and their unrestrained enthusiasm and unconditional love delighted me. Watching them grow from tiny helpless creatures, almost immediately developing their own personalities… seeing how they were similar to each of their parents, yet their own people almost from birth.

There were struggles in this life, to be sure. The world I was on was dying, and I couldn't convince anyone to do anything about it. It was frustrating to stand by while I watched this lovely place begin to decline. But it was ultimately a gift, this life that someone had decided to give me, a life in another society, as another man. The simple life that had eluded me as Picard was mine as Kamin. True happiness: children, grandchildren.

And then I woke up from it.

The *Enterprise* had encountered a probe that had linked to my mind; the probe was from Kataan, a world that knew it was dying. They had given me this gift so I would teach the rest of the Galaxy about them.

It was a difficult adjustment to make. On the *Enterprise* I'd been linked to the probe for only twenty-five minutes. But I'd lived a whole life, a whole life where I was happy.

And it was now gone.

I went back to my quarters, lonely, depressed. Riker came to see me. He'd examined the probe, and handed me a small box.

"We found this inside," he said. Riker left me. I opened the box; it was my flute. Or the flute of the real Kamin. I didn't know. I held it to my chest, then realized I knew how to play it. I had never been able to play the flute before. I began to play the "Skye Boat Song." I then played "Big Yellow Taxi" and heard Meribor and Batai singing the lyrics.

"*Don't it always seem to go,*

That you don't know what you've got till it's gone..."

✦

When we arrived in 19th-century San Francisco, we were all almost overcome by the smell.

"Oh my god, it's awful," Deanna said.

"Is that sewage?" Beverly said.

"Yes, and horse manure," I said.

"Maybe a little burning coal," Riker said.

"I think I might throw up," Geordi said.

I, however, had other concerns. We were standing in the middle of a cobbled street, in our Starfleet uniforms. Passersby were looking at us, aghast at our strangeness. Riker noticed it too.

"We need to get some clothes in the local style," he said.

"We'll need money," I said. Geordi took his comm badge off his tunic.

"There's some gold in this," he said. "Should be worth something."

We were able to trade a few of our comm badges (with the circuitry removed) for about ten dollars, which, in this time period, was almost a king's ransom. We used it to purchase some clothing. I didn't know how long we would have to stay, so we would also need food and shelter.

"Look, sir," Geordi said, indicating a sign that read "Rooms for Rent." I knocked on the door. An elderly woman answered.

"Yes?"

"We were hoping to rent a room," I said.

"All of you?"

"Yes," I said. "We don't have a lot of money, so we're going to share."

"You're a strange lot," the woman said. "Who are you?" She seemed put off by us.

"Well, I'm Jean-Luc Picard, and this is… my acting troupe." It was the only lie I could think of that could explain what a group of men and women who bore no resemblance to each other would be doing together.

The woman, Mrs. Carmichael, reluctantly let us a room. And from there we began our search for Data, who'd already preceded us to this time period. He'd followed the Devidians, a strange species from the 24th century, who were using a time portal of their own design to go back to old Earth. They were stealing the life forces from cholera victims, which their people fed on.

I was initially not going to come on this mission, until I received some "encouragement" from a special member of my crew: Guinan pressed me to go. We spent several days tracking the Devidians as well as looking for Data. When we found him, it seemed he'd already done a fair job of tracking the Devidians himself, with some help from people who lived in the period, including the famous author Samuel Clemens, better known by his pen name, Mark Twain. There was, however, one other person there who was also helping him, one I expected to meet. She came to his rented room soon after we were reunited.

"Do I know you?" Guinan said. She was wearing period clothing that somehow still evoked the outfits she wore in our century.

"Not yet," I said. "But you will."

Now everything about my relationship with Guinan was explained; why she seemed to know me when we first met. Her interest in me. I realized that I was also now a part of that unique aspect of time travel that no one has ever been able to properly explain: the temporal causality loop. I was meeting Guinan five hundred years in the past. For her, it was our first meeting, for me, I'd known her for decades. Because of this first meeting, she would recognize me five hundred years in the future. We would form a bond that would lead her to send me into the past to meet her for the first time. Our relationship had no true beginning.

After we defeated the Devidians and returned to the 24th century, I went to see Guinan in Ten-Forward.

"So, what did you think of old San Francisco?" she said.

"The smell was awful," I said. "You're very patient to have kept that from me all these years."

"I didn't want to screw it up," she said.

"It does raise a question in my mind," I said.

"Yes?"

"When I was taken by the Borg," I said, "Will said you were instrumental in getting him to save me…"

"I never told him to save you," she said. "I said he had to let you go."

"But did you know he was going to rescue me?"

"I hoped he would," she said, "or we never would have been friends. Face it, Jean-Luc, we're eternal." I laughed. I felt we were.

✦

"I'm here to relieve you of command of the *Enterprise*," Alynna Nechayev said. She was my new commanding admiral. We'd never met before she came into my ready room to take away my ship.

"I don't understand," I said.

"I need you for a mission," she said. "We believe the Cardassians are developing a metagenic weapon." This was a frightening prospect: a metagenic weapon could destroy an entire ecosystem, releasing a toxin into a planet's atmosphere where it mutates, seeking out and destroying all forms of DNA it encounters. Within a few days, everything is dead.

"Have they solved the delivery problem?"

"We believe they are experimenting with using a theta-band subspace carrier wave," she said. I had experimented with such a device while captain of the *Stargazer*. "There's evidence they're conducting these experiments on Celtris III. I want you to lead a strike team to take out their laboratory."

"Why relieve me of my command? Certainly I could supervise the mission."

"I need the *Enterprise* somewhere else. It looks like the Cardassians are planning an incursion into Federation space. I'm sending the *Enterprise* to engage them in talks."

"I still don't understand," I said. "Shouldn't I be the one…"

"You are an expert on theta-band carrier waves. I want you on the mission."

"I see," I said. It was becoming clear that it wasn't *just* that she wanted me on the mission. "Who will command the *Enterprise*?"

"Edward Jellico," she said. "He brought the Cardassians to the table before, I need him to do it again." I understood it now; there were other officers who could've commanded the mission, and I certainly didn't need to give up command of the *Enterprise*. But Nechayev wanted me to go because she wanted Jellico in my chair on the Federation flagship. He'd gotten a lot of credit for bringing the Cardassian war to a close, perhaps justified, perhaps not. But Nechayev wanted his CV. So I would lead a strike team and lose my ship. She was willing to put my life in danger because she actually had someone else she preferred to be in command of the *Enterprise*.

✦

"What are the Federation's defense plans for Minos Korva?" Gul Madred said.

I was hanging by my wrists, naked in a cold room.

It turned out the mission Nechayev had assigned me was all part of the Cardassians' plans. They weren't preparing to launch a metagenic weapon, they were trying to lure *me* to Celtris III.

I had been captured, held as a prisoner, and tortured by the Cardassians. Nechayev was correct, they were planning to invade Federation space and capture Minos Korva, a system with over two million Federation colonists. The Cardassians were under the misapprehension that I, as previous captain of the *Enterprise*, had been briefed on potential defense plans. They were wrong.

My torturer, Gul Madred, didn't really care. He toyed with me: he was unpredictable and harsh one moment, then kind the next. Making empty promises, then depriving me of food and water. They took me down from my shackles and implanted a device inside me.

"What are the Federation's defense plans for Minos Korva?" he repeated. We'd been through this before, several times over several days. He held up the keypad he'd used to activate the device inside me. I remembered the excruciating pain of it. It felt as if there was no source, no way to stop it, as if all my skin was being pulled off with a white-hot blade. I couldn't bear it. So I begged.

"Not again," I said. "Please…"

"Tell me," he said. I had to say something, but I didn't have an answer to his question. I didn't know. So I lied.

"The Federation will… deploy four starships… led by the *Enterprise*…" I was trying to think of something to make it sound plausible.

"Really? We heard it was seven."

Had they heard? Was he lying? Seven was also plausible.

I didn't know.

"It's seven," I said. "You're right..."

"You're lying. We'd heard three."

"I'm not lying. It's the truth... it's seven..."

"Is it?" He held up the control pad, and turned it on. I screamed.

It went on like this for days.

I woke up one morning to the smell of food. My head lay on his desk. I looked up to see Gul Madred cracking open a large boiled egg. There were two plates of food. Was one for me? I didn't dare ask; I'd learned the decision was not mine. Every decision was his.

"Oh, you're awake. Have something to eat. I insist." He handed me the food, but first only a raw egg with what looked like some kind of pulsating reptilian mass inside that smelled like sulfur. There was also a plate of cooked food, but he wasn't handing me that. I wanted the cooked food, but I couldn't ask for it. The only food he'd given me was the raw egg, so I ate it. This was the learned helplessness of torture. This was different than my experience with the Borg. Madred made the pain he inflicted personal; the lack of predictability forced me to give up. It was a battle of wills in which I could not compete; he controlled my environment, and wanted to control my perceptions as well.

"How many lights do you see there?"

There were four lights over his head, but he told me there were five. He came back to this "game" day after day, dispensing excruciating pain if I did not accept the untruth. I resisted, but Madred had an accomplice: my unconscious mind. It wanted to protect me from the pain. Eventually, I actually thought I saw a fifth light. Madred had altered my reality.

The uselessness of torture as a means of gaining information; I not only would have said anything to end the torment, my mind would convince me it was true.

I was kept in captivity, but it turned out to be pointless. Jellico stopped the Cardassians' invasion plans and successfully demanded my release. It wouldn't end so easily for me.

✦

"We're ready to leave orbit, sir," Riker said over the intercom. We were at Starbase 310, picking up crew and cargo. I was in my ready room. Since returning from my captivity, I had chosen to spend less time on the bridge.

"Very well," I said. I sat in silence.

"We're due at Deep Space 9 tomorrow," Riker said. Deep Space 9 used to be the space station Terok Nor, run by the Cardassians, which I'd visited on the *Stargazer*. The Cardassians had withdrawn, and the Bajoran government had invited the Federation to administer the station. The *Enterprise* would be delivering crewmen picked up from Starbase 310, as well as three runabouts to supply the station.

But I didn't want to go. I did not want to run into Cardassians.

"Sir?"

He needed me to make the decision, the very simple and obvious decision to leave orbit. It was a small decision, inconsequential really. But my captivity had taken away my ability to make decisions. I'd been taught they belonged to Gul Madred. I had to force the words out.

"Make it so," I said.

When we arrived at Deep Space 9, I was on the bridge.

The incomplete gyroscope with dangerous-looking claws reached out for us. When I was last here, the scans showed it was heavily armed. Now, the Cardassians in their exit had stripped it of everything. Still, it took all my self-control to order the conn officer to dock with one of those unpleasant-looking metal arms.

"See," Deanna said, "nothing to worry about." She'd been sitting next to me, monitoring my progress since I'd returned. I smiled. As scared as I was, I did feel I was regaining control.

"Should I begin offloading our cargo?" Riker said. I nodded.

"Has the station commander arrived yet?" I was due to brief him, and then I was to leave.

"No, sir," Data said. "Commander Sisko is scheduled to arrive in two days."

Two days. It sounded like forever.

"I'll be in my ready room," I said, and left.

The two days passed, and eventually, Commander Sisko arrived. He was an imposing man, and I immediately sensed a ferocity about him as he walked into the observation lounge.

"It's been a long time, Captain," he said as we shook hands. There was no warmth in the remark, and I didn't recognize him.

"Have we met before?"

"Yes, sir. We met in battle. I was on the *Saratoga* at Wolf 359."

I felt suddenly nauseous. This was a completely inappropriate thing for him to say, but I should have been ready for it—I'd been so preoccupied with my own recovery, I had somehow missed this on his record. I tried to continue the briefing, tried to find a connection, but this man wouldn't allow it. He had obviously lost people who meant something to him when the Borg… when I… destroyed his ship. We finished, and soon after I left him and his station behind.

As I thought about Sisko, who was still so clearly locked in the tragedy of that attack, it suddenly gave me perspective. I connected my recent imprisonment with the Cardassians to my abduction by the Borg. In both instances I'd been stripped of the most basic human right of self-determination. Linking them in my mind, I was able to step outside of the fear. I was able to let it go. The fear of the Cardassians did not rule me.

I wondered at my fortune over being able to mend my psyche. I certainly had to credit my ship's counselor, Deanna Troi, whose patience, kindness, and professionalism helped me to face the truth of the situations.

But I'm certain I also owed the two mind melds I'd had with Vulcans. I'd transferred to my own mind certain mental disciplines that allowed me to conquer the emotional responses. I suppose the other advantage I'd had was that, over time in my life, I'd become emotionally detached. I hadn't let myself be close to anyone for a very long time. This made the disciplines I'd learned from my contact with the Vulcans that much more natural. It helped me recover, but didn't help in my own pursuit of personal happiness.

✦

"Jean-Luc," Professor Galen said. "I was too harsh." He was lying on a bed in sickbay, his chest burned by a disrupter wound. It was remarkable that he was still alive; he was well over 100 years old, and such a wound would have killed a much younger man. These were his last words.

Three weeks before, he'd come to the ship. It had been over thirty years since I'd seen him, and recently I'd begun to worry about him; for the last several years he'd stopped publishing works in his field. But when I saw him again, he'd lost none of his astuteness or self-assurance. He also still had not acquired any respect for the career I'd chosen. His first evening aboard ship, I took him to Ten-Forward, and asked him why he'd gone so silent.

"I made a discovery so profound in its implications," Galen said, "that silence seemed the wisest course." I asked him to tell me what it was all about, but he shook his head.

"That information comes with a price. Your agreement to join me on the final leg of this expedition."

"For how long?"

"Three months, perhaps a year," he said. It was absurd—I couldn't leave the *Enterprise* for such a length of time. I had to refuse, and when I finally told him, he was furious. His anger at me for my decision all those years ago came flooding out.

"I gave you the opportunity to become the finest archaeologist of your generation. Your achievements could have outstripped even my own, but no, you decided to reject a life of profound discovery. You walked out on me."

He left on his ship. I had hurt him, again. He had been like a father to me; perhaps because I'd been rejected by my own father, I had rejected Galen, but I prefer to think that I just wanted another path.

Soon after, we received a distress signal from him. Yridians boarded his small craft, and they killed him. I never did learn what his discovery was, and knowing the man as I did, I'm sure it would live up to his description as "profound."* But I will always live with a little doubt that if I'd gone with him, I might have saved his life.

It was another overwhelming loss for me, one of thousands of deaths that had occurred since I'd become Captain of the *Enterprise*. Many would wonder how I could keep all the losses from being too much for me, yet it was those deaths that kept me going; only by committing myself to the work of Starfleet and the Federation could I justify in my own mind the sacrifices of others. I had made mistakes, some of which had resulted in casualties, but I did not,

---

*EDITOR'S NOTE: I feel Captain Picard is in fact telling us he *does* know what Galen had discovered. I don't know why he would keep it a secret, unless it might still be classified by Starfleet or the Federation.

would not, let regrets consume me. I had a bargain with the dead; I would keep working, and they would remain quiet. I owed them.

✦

"It was… fun…" James Kirk said. His expression changed. He seemed to see something in his mind's eye that scared him. "Oh my…" he said, and then he was gone.

I'd only just met him, a man history had believed to be dead for 80 years, returning like King Arthur to save us. Unfortunately, our efforts to defeat Dr. Soran* led to Kirk's second death.

I had been inside a temporal Nexus, a strange parallel reality that provided the image of a contented life. My own experience was a Christmas I had never had: family, wife, children, gifts, a tree… It was warm and wonderful, and I knew it wasn't right. I wanted to stay, but the voices of the dead would not let me.

"This isn't real," I said.

"It's as real as you want it to be." It was Guinan, or an echo of Guinan who had been in the Nexus once. The mysteries surrounding her never ceased, and, like so many times in my past, she was there to guide me, like a mythical guardian angel. She led me to Kirk, who was also in the Nexus. Though he wasn't easy to convince, he agreed to leave with me, and help my mission. I would not have succeeded without him.

We were on hard, rocky terrain on the planet Veridian III. It would be impossible to dig him a grave, so I gathered large rocks and placed them around and on top of his body. He and I had worked together to defeat a common enemy, and I felt I was a part of the adventures I'd read about as a child. But it was so brief, it only served to make me want to get to know him

---

*EDITOR'S NOTE: In 2293, on the maiden voyage of the *U.S.S. Enterprise*-B, Kirk had been caught in a temporal nexus, a "ribbon" of energy of unknown origin, which traveled through the Galaxy. People who'd entered it relayed accounts of having their fantasies fulfilled. A man named Dr. Tolian Soran had wanted to enter the nexus, but the only way to do that was by being on a planet that it passed over. He had to change the ribbon's course, and had determined the only way to do that was by destroying the star in the Veridian system. Picard and Kirk defeated his plans.

more. In my short time with him, I didn't find anything unusual about his intellect or personality beyond a kind of boyish energy. Our plan to defeat Soran wasn't clever or complicated. More than anything, the experience showed me that I'd come into my own as a starship captain. Though I had held Kirk up as a hero, I had as much to contribute to the situation as he did. We were equals.

When I'd beamed down to Veridian III, the *Enterprise* had been in orbit and a Klingon warship was nearby. After we had defeated Soran, and I'd buried Kirk, I signaled the *Enterprise*, and they sent a shuttle to pick me up.

I was surprised to see Riker piloting the shuttle.

"Didn't I leave you in command?"

"You did," he said. "I have some bad news. I felt I should bring it to you myself, since I'm responsible."

"The *Enterprise*?"

"It's gone," he said. "The Klingons penetrated our shields. We had a warp core breach. I was able to separate the saucer section, but it crashed on the planet."

"Casualties?"

"A lot of injuries, no deaths."

"We can be thankful for that," I said. I'd just lost another ship, and some of the same insecurities invaded: did I make a mistake? Was there anything else I could've done? This time, the answer came back quickly: no. I then looked over at Riker. I could see he was troubled—I realized I'd gone through this before, but he hadn't. I had a dozen questions as to what exactly happened, but I decided they could wait.

"You can give me a full report later; I'm sure you did everything you could," I said.

"I'm not so sure," he said. I could hear the self-recrimination in his tone.

"Will," I said, "they put us in charge of these vessels, they train us as best they can to be emissaries of peace, to avoid conflict... but there will always be those who look to war and violence for their solution, who operate out of greed and self-interest. We can't blame ourselves for their occasional success. Just be certain the moral arc of history is on our side."

"Very philosophical for a man whose first officer just wrecked his ship," he said.

"It's all right," I said. "I spent the afternoon saving the Galaxy with James T. Kirk. It balances out."

I wish I had a photograph of Will's expression.

✦

"There she is, Captain," Commander Shelby said. Shelby and I stood in the operations center of a dry dock at Utopia Planitia, looking out over a new ship that was almost completed. She'd originally been designated as the *U.S.S. Sentinel*—one of the new *Sovereign* class—but in the wake of my ship's destruction, they renamed her the *Enterprise*.

And they were giving it to me. This time I wasn't court-martialed for losing the ship. By stopping Soran, we'd prevented the deaths of millions, and that seemed to be enough for the Judge Advocate General.

"It's lovely," I said, although I wasn't sure I meant it. The ship was larger and sleeker than my *Enterprise*, but in my personal assessment it was missing some of the charm. I'm sure that was my own sense of nostalgia for something I'd lost, and kept it to myself, as I didn't want to insult Shelby. A few years earlier Shelby had served on the *Enterprise*, and had come back to Starfleet Command to supervise ship design and construction in the wake of the conflict with the Borg. The *Sovereign*-class ship had been one of her projects.

I gave the crew the option of coming with me, since some of the senior staff were certainly eligible for their own command. All but one decided to wait for the *Enterprise*-E to be completed. It was a surprise when Mr. Worf turned down my offer to be chief of security, even with a promotion in rank. I decided to go to see him at his parents' home in Kiev.

"I told him to take the offer," Sergey Rozhenko said. "Why would you leave Starfleet?" We drank hot tea in glass cups, having just finished a meal of beet soup and roasted potatoes.

"Father, please," Worf said. "I didn't say I was leaving Starfleet."

"Then why not go with the captain to his new ship?"

"Sergey," Helena said, "perhaps we should leave them alone to talk." She got up and began to pull Sergey out of the room with her.

"I just asked a question," Sergey said. "Is it so hard to answer a question?" When they left the room, I smiled at Worf.

"They love you very much," I said.

"I am very fortunate," Worf said.

"Whereas I am not," I said. "I would like to hear the answer to your father's question."

"I owe you that," Worf said. He got up and went to the window. "For my whole life, I've looked for a home. Khitomer and my birth parents were taken from me. I've never been fully comfortable in either the human world or the Klingon world. I sought to find my place in the universe. I finally found it… and it was taken from me again."

I didn't realize how profound the loss of the ship would be to someone like Worf. He was in mourning.

"We may be able to rebuild that place on a new ship," I said.

"Forgive me, Captain, but there is a Klingon saying," Worf said. "*Pagh yijach Soch jatqua.*"

I laughed. I had studied enough Klingon to translate it.

"I believe the Klingons have appropriated 'You can't go home again' from the Earth author Thomas Wolfe."

"Impossible," Worf said. "Kahless said it when he returned to Quin'lat after the battle with the Fek'lhri…"

"Point taken, Mr. Worf," I said. "But if you ever want to come back, there will always be a place for you." I soon took my leave and began my walk back to the transporter station in town. I thought about how Worf felt: the *Enterprise*-D had been my home too, and I wondered whether what I said was true, whether I could recreate the same sense of home on a new ship. I remembered going back for my second tour on *Stargazer* and not being able to recapture the feeling of the first. This would be different, I thought.

As I contemplated the nature of home, I fancied I heard a voice. It belonged to a woman, very faint.

"You've only had one home," she said. I searched the area for the source of the voice, but couldn't find it. It spoke again, and I realized the voice was in my head.

"Stop looking for me, I'm not there, Locutus…"

I subconsciously recognized the voice, but I pushed it away: I did not want to remember. It was the voice of the Borg queen. The memories of her had been repressed, the trauma of how she'd used me too difficult for me to face. The Borg were on their way.

A year later, they would return. My crew on my new ship were tested as they never had been before. But we defeated them, and it would lead to my favorite captain's log:

Captain's Log, April 5, 2063. The voyage of the *Phoenix* was a success… again.

This is, as every child knows, First Contact Day, the day Zefram Cochrane flew his own spaceship, the *Phoenix*, past the speed of light, and caught the attention of a passing Vulcan spacecraft. Humans and Vulcans met for the first time, and it would eventually bring humanity to the stars, where they would help found the United Federation of Planets.

And I got to witness it.

And it also almost never happened.

The Borg attacked Earth by going into the past. The *Enterprise* followed them, to stop their plan to assimilate Earth in a more vulnerable period, thus preventing First Contact. They were trying to erase the Federation from history. I began to understand their obsession with us: we were the only people who'd slowed their previously relentless success in assimilating other species.

"Destroy them," the Borg queen said. This time, she wasn't saying it to me; I was strapped to a table in engineering, where she planned on turning me into a drone. She was giving the order to Data, whom she had apparently seduced by grafting human skin on to his body. We were watching the *Phoenix* about to go to warp. Data fired a volley of quantum torpedoes. They headed right for the primitive ship.

"Watch your future's end," the Queen said.

The torpedoes closed in… and missed. Data had fooled her; resistance hadn't been futile. Data smashed a plasma coolant conduit, and the green super-hot gas swamped engineering, killing the Queen and all her drones. We had won, again.

Data and I left engineering, and headed toward the transporter room to reunite with our crew on the surface.

"Captain," Data said. "You had not mentioned the Borg queen in your report on the Borg from your previous assimilation."

"Yes," I said, "I think I repressed my memory of her. But she was on that original cube."

"Which was destroyed," Data said. I knew what he was getting at.

"Yes," I said. "She survived. And she may survive again."

"This time," Data said, "we must remember to include her in our report."

Later, we waited at the Montana missile silo with the rest of the crew and the hero of the day, Zefram Cochrane. He'd just returned in his warp spaceship. His support crew had consisted of Riker and La Forge. He wasn't quite what we expected.

"Now, you're saying this is going to be in the history books," Cochrane said. "How do you spell your names?"

"R-I-K..." Riker said, then, catching a disapproving glance from me, he smiled. "Just joking. If anybody asks you don't remember our names."

"What are your plans now that you've completed this trip?" I said.

"You said the aliens were coming, do you think they'll pay me a lot of money for my ship?"

"I do not," I said. "The Vulcans aren't interested in money."

"Oh," said Cochrane. "That puts a little crimp in my plans. What do the history books say I do next?"

"It's a little vague," Riker said. "Best play it by ear."

"I don't think these aliens are going to show," Cochrane said. "I'm going to bed."

"Just hold on," Riker said. He indicated the sky as the familiar design of a Vulcan scout ship broke through the clouds.

"Holy shit,"—this from Cochrane.

✦

"So Shinzon, the Praetor of the Romulan Empire," Admiral Janeway said, "was your *clone*?" She sat in my ready room, having come aboard the *Enterprise* to receive my report after we'd returned to Earth from Romulus. It was an interesting experience reporting to her; several decades ago I'd had to report to her father. She was much more affable.

"Yes," I said. "It would appear someone in the empire got hold of my DNA and embarked on a project to replace me." I understood her disbelief.

I myself had confronted this younger copy of myself, and I still had trouble accepting it.

"Wouldn't it take some 50-odd years to grow a clone that could be mistaken for you?"

"They were able to accelerate his age," I said. "But there was a change in government, and the project was discarded. They exiled him to the dilithium mines on Remus."

"And yet from there he was able to rise to power and overthrow the Romulan government."

I nodded.

"I suppose he had the advantage of good genes," Janeway said. I smiled, but the encounter had disgusted me. I had seen some of myself in Shinzon's ambition, but his upbringing had led him to be sadistic and Machiavellian. He had successfully conspired to kill the entire Romulan Senate, and start a war with the Federation. In our conflict, he'd killed a good portion of my crew, including one of my closest friends. Janeway read my expression, and regretted her remark.

"Sorry, Jean-Luc. You are not responsible for his actions."

"I appreciate that."

"You've suffered terrible losses," she said. "It must be especially difficult given the death of Commander Data." Difficult did not cover it; it had been traumatic. Data had rescued me from Shinzon, and in doing so sacrificed his life. I had always taken comfort in the fact that Data would outlive us all, and become a living witness to the history we all shared. He had been my companion for a very long time, and I wouldn't let him go so easily.

"He left us a remembrance," I said. I tapped my communicator. "Picard to Bridge, please send in B-4."

A moment later, B-4 entered. B-4 was a prototype of Data that we'd discovered on the mission. Before Data had died, he had downloaded all his memories into this avatar.

"Hello," B-4 said.

Janeway stood up and shook B-4's hand. "It is nice to meet you."

"Why?" B-4 said.

"His positronic brain is not as advanced as Data's," I said. "He may never be at the level Data was…"

"Oh my goodness, this is pathetic."

I turned; it wasn't Janeway. In her place was Q.

"Q, what the hell are you doing? Where's Admiral Janeway?"

"I sent her to a Kazon prison camp in the Delta Quadrant. I'm kidding, take a joke. She's fine."

"What are you doing here?"

"I'm here to express my condolences," Q said. B-4 held out his hand to him.

"Hello," B-4 said. Q looked him over with disgust, then turned to me.

"Are you really willing to put up with this?"

"Q..." I stepped forward, raised my hand. "Don't."

"Don't what?" He stared at me and smiled that Q smile. I knew what he intended, and it seemed wrong. I had to try to stop him.

"I respect Data's sacrifice," are the words that came from me but I didn't mean them. Q had the power, and I was tempted. Very tempted.

"You know, normally I would force you to ask me to use my power," Q said. "But I'm not doing this for you... I'm doing this for me. I miss him."

"Why?"

"Shhhhh..." Q snapped his fingers. He was gone in a flash, and Janeway returned.

"Jean-Luc," Janeway said. "What happened?" But I wasn't looking at her. I was focused on B-4. The android's childlike expression was gone, in its place a much more familiar, confident bearing.

"Data, is it you?"

"I believe it is, sir," said Data.

Data was back, and very much himself. There was something about this event that put my entire life in perspective. Q knew this was what I wanted, and I had not protested forcefully enough to stop him. Usually, my moral compass was clear on issues like this, but I'd lost some of my bearing. I couldn't see what was wrong with this, because I didn't want to have to accept the loss of Data as I had had to accept the loss of so many loved ones before.

The ship continued on, but it wasn't the same. Worf had been right, I had to relearn the lesson that I couldn't go home again. Riker and Deanna had married soon after he'd been offered his own command, and they left. Geordi and Data had stayed behind I think out of loyalty to me, and I felt I was holding them both back; they both could have had their own ships.

I had been in space too long. It was time to step down, it was time to move on.

One morning I was telling all this to Beverly over our regular breakfast, as we sat together on the couch in my quarters.

"What are you going to do?"

"I don't know," I said.

"Well, this makes what I have to tell you a little easier. I'm leaving the *Enterprise* as well. I've been offered command of the medical ship *Pasteur*." This shouldn't have been a surprise; Beverly had in the last few years shown an interest and ability in command. But I was surprised nonetheless, and a little panicked.

"That's wonderful," I said. "I'm very happy for you."

"You don't really sound happy for me."

"I'm sorry. Somehow, when I decided to leave the *Enterprise*, I didn't think I'd be leaving you. I'll miss you."

"I'll miss you, too."

What happened next surprised the both of us. I kissed her, and we were caught in a passionate embrace. We broke, and I looked at her, the woman who'd been in my life for so long, but always at arm's length. The moment I had decided to be free from my ship, I realized I didn't have to deprive myself of her any longer.

"Beverly," I said, "will you marry me?"

CHAPTER ELEVEN

"WELCOME TO VULCAN, AMBASSADOR PICARD," T'Pring said. She was one of the members of the High Council, striking and statuesque and 154 years old. She greeted me at T'Plana-Hath spaceport in the city of ShiKahr. With her was a small entourage of Vulcan diplomats, who welcomed me to their world. ShiKahr was a beautiful ancient city, surrounded by desert and the characteristic Vulcan red rock mountains. It was home to the Federation embassy.

I was led to a waiting hover transport, and our driver took me and the other diplomats to the embassy. We sat in silence for the entire trip—there was no small talk on Vulcan. Most humans would find this awkward, but my preparations for this assignment convinced me not to give in to the impulse to "chat." It was important that I have the respect of the Vulcans I would be dealing with, and showing human insecurities would not help. I felt ready for this new chapter.

When I informed Starfleet Command that I wanted to resign my commission, there was a flurry of protestations from every admiral that I knew. Many of them wanted me to stay, guaranteeing me a promotion, but I turned them down. I was marrying Beverly—that was my priority.

After leaving the *Enterprise*, Beverly and I had moved into temporary accommodations at Starfleet Headquarters, and from there we had to move quickly on our wedding plans, as she would be assuming command of her ship in a matter of weeks. We put our invitation list together. There was one name

I put on the list that worried Beverly, but she finally agreed. We planned the ceremony for a few days before Beverly was to ship out.

The wedding was at my family home. Marie no longer lived there, having left after the tragedy she faced when my brother and nephew died. I didn't expect she would return for the wedding, but she sent us a lovely note. We arrived there a few days before the wedding took place.

"It's beautiful," Beverly said. "Is it sad for you to be here?"

" 'Things without all remedy should be without regard,' " I said. " 'What's done is done.' "

"Those are Shakespeare's words," she said. "What would you say?"

"I'd say let's have a grand wedding."

It was a very large affair, and I was touched at the number of crewmates and friends who made the effort to return to Earth to be a part of it. Guinan officiated; at some point in her long past, she had been a clergy, although I wasn't sure where or for what religion. Wesley was my best man, the image of his father, which made it a little strange for both me and Beverly, but we didn't discuss it, we just had a wonderful time, dancing and drinking. It was a truly magical day for me. I don't know that I ever felt joy as complete and unrestrained as that day. I looked at Beverly, so happy and beautiful. I could hardly believe we would finally be together. I was 79 years old, and felt that my life was just beginning.

At the end of the reception, an elderly man I didn't recognize walked over to me.

"It was a beautiful affair, Jean-Luc," he said.

"I'm sorry," I said. "Have we met?" He smiled. For a brief flash, his face changed, and I was staring at Q. Another flash, and the old man returned.

"Thanks for inviting me," he said.

"I wasn't sure how to get you an invitation," I said. "But I figured you always seem to be looking over my shoulder, so putting it on the list was enough. Why the disguise?"

"Guinan hates me," Q said. "As do a few of your other friends. I didn't want to cause a stir."

"Thank you for coming," I said. "And for what you did for Data."

He smiled, and with a flash, was gone. Some might ask why I would've invited someone who'd been such a nuisance to me over the years. I would respond with an old aphorism: you can choose your friends, but you can't choose your family. And Q was, unfortunately, family. In some sense, I owed him. He had tested and tempted me; in our encounters, I was pushed to my limits, I had to be the best person I could be. It would always verify my ethics and morality, but I also had to confront some of my very serious flaws.

There were several dignitaries there, and we were honored to have the Federation president as a guest. Andrea Brand had retired from Starfleet several years before and had been elected to the Federation Council. She had the year before been elected president.

"Congratulations, Jean-Luc," she said to me. "I was wondering if I could have a word with you in private before I leave?"

"It is my wedding, Madam President."

"It won't take long," she said. We took a short walk away from the festivities. "What are your plans?"

"I haven't made any," I said, which was the truth. I had decided to throw myself into building a life with Beverly, and for the first time in my life was not really thinking about the future.

"I would like to appoint you Federation Ambassador to Vulcan," she said. "There is concern that the Vulcans and the Romulans have begun secret talks regarding reunification. Your knowledge of the Vulcans would make you invaluable." I had never considered a career in politics, but President Brand's argument was compelling. I told her I would think it over.

The next day, I raised the subject with Beverly over breakfast.

"You're a wonderful diplomat," she said. "I can think of no one better for the job."

"The problem is… we just got married."

"I think I can arrange to be in the vicinity of Vulcan now and again," she said. "After all, I'm the captain."

"Already planning on abusing your authority?"

"We can't all be as selfless as Captain Jean-Luc Picard."

"Thank god," I said.

I called President Brand and accepted her offer. I received a briefing and certification, and Brand arranged for Beverly to take me to Vulcan on the *Pasteur*.

When it was time for us to leave, I insisted on piloting the shuttle myself, just so Beverly and I could have a few more minutes alone. We landed in the

Pasteur's shuttlebay. As the rear door of the shuttle opened, I saw a large number of the crew waiting.

"Commanding officer *Pasteur* arriving," I said, and the crew stood to attention. Beverly looked at me and smiled; she leaned in and gave me a kiss, then moved to the lectern to read her orders.

"To Captain Beverly Picard, stardate 60768.1, you are hereby requested and required to take command of *U.S.S. Pasteur* as of this date. Signed Rear Admiral Kathryn Janeway, Starfleet Command."

I smiled in awe and pride.

The few days it took to get to Vulcan were an interesting experience for me. The crew seemed to want to cater to my every need, and I couldn't figure out whether it was because I was an ambassador or because I was married to the captain.

We made it to Vulcan, and she took me to the shuttle bay. Seeing her in command of her own ship was revelatory. She had always been a forceful presence in sickbay, but the ease with which she transferred that to the bridge was impressive. She was a remarkable woman, and I was consumed with love for her.

"Goodbye, dear," she said. "I'll be back soon."

"I'll hold you to that," I said.

✦

T'Pring and her diplomats took me to the Federation embassy. There was a large gathering of staff waiting to welcome me. I wasn't used to this level of pomp and circumstance, but did my best with the introductions. T'Pring said whatever I might need, I shouldn't hesitate to ask, that all of Vulcan welcomed me. She then left with her entourage. I let out a silent sigh of relief; I don't think T'Pring knew that I'd mind-melded with Spock, the man she'd left at the altar.

I quickly got myself into the day-to-day routines of being an ambassador. It was complicated, bureaucratic work. I was representing the president of the Federation on this world, and Vulcan's unique role in that Federation was more delicate than I thought. I was fortunately spared the usual ceremonies and parties that ambassadors typically had to attend—Vulcans found them "illogical." But there were a number of other situations that would require a great deal of tact. I often found myself stuck between Federation members who wanted Vulcan help in a specific area of study or technology, and the Vulcans, who were not the most collaborative of species. There was also the Romulan–Vulcan situation, and trying to get information out of the High Council was proving to be a challenge.

I spent the most time dealing with individuals from other planets of the Federation wanting to visit Vulcan and helping them navigate Vulcan's strict visitation and immigration laws. After a few months on the planet, I came to understand the reason for these laws: it was the most peaceful society I'd ever seen. There seemed to be no fear, no anger, no sadness. Just calm. Outsiders often proved problematic.

"I was taking my morning walk," I said to Beverly, during one of our evening talks via subspace, "and I saw a Tellarite talking to a Vulcan woman."

"Oh, they're such pigs," Beverly said.

"This may not be a secure channel, Captain. We need to be diplomatic."

"Yes, Ambassador."

"So the Tellarite is yelling, 'Hey, I just want to buy you a drink.' The Vulcan woman says she's not thirsty. The Tellarite then says, 'Come on, you know what I mean,' to which the Vulcan responds, 'If you're inferring you wanted to use a drink to initiate a mating ritual, Vulcans mate only once every seven years.'"

"Did he buy it?" Beverly said.

"No, he said she was lying, to which she gave the usual, 'Vulcans never lie.'"

"Which in and of itself is a lie. Was the Vulcan pretty?"

"Not as pretty as you."

"I was just curious." I laughed, and we ended our conversation with a promise to see each other soon. We didn't. I didn't blame her; she was a starship captain, and her duties kept her from any personal priorities she might have. Over the next three years, Beverly and I were together for no more than four weeks. It was an irony that we'd spent all those years together on the *Enterprise*, and now that we were married we barely saw each other. I didn't have an expectation she would sacrifice her career for our marriage, but it hurt nevertheless.

My job as an ambassador settled into routine, and I found the emotional distance of the society I was in familiar; I decided I would have made a pretty good Vulcan. But I also started to get restless. Even at my advancing age I wanted a little more action in my life.

I was about to get it.

I was in my office trying to expedite passport applications for some children of an Andorian on the Federation Council, when I received a subspace call from an old friend.

"Captain Data," I said. "To what do I owe the pleasure?" He was in my old ready room on the *Enterprise*-E.

"Sorry to disturb you, Ambassador," Data said. "I'm sending you some information attached to this transmission. Please look it over."

On my screen, a long-range scan of a star system appeared along with a familiar-looking device emitting high levels of subspace interference.

"What system is that?"

"The Hobus system," Data said. "It is in Romulan territory."

"It has the characteristics of the subspace engine the Denobulans built."

"That was my supposition as well."

"Do the Romulans have something to do with it?"

"Negative. They are in fact sending a strike force to the Hobus system."

"The people of the Hobus system have been periodically subjugated by the Romulans," I said.

"Perhaps they heard about the Denobulans and were looking for a means of escape."

"But the Romulans probably assume it's a weapon…"

"Starfleet has tried to warn them," Data said. "The Romulans will not respond. Their strike force will be there in a matter of hours."

"There is one person I can call," I said. "Meanwhile, please come to Vulcan, we may need you."

"Yes, Ambassador," Data said. "That was my thought as well. We are already on our way."

I left the Federation embassy. Over the years, I had been forced to develop a small intelligence network on Vulcan to gather whatever snippets of information I could on the reunification talks. I also kept tabs on the movement of the diplomat who was spearheading the discussions with Romulus, and, if my information was accurate, he was currently at the headquarters of the Vulcan High Council.

I entered the building and went right up to the receptionist.

"I want to see Ambassador Spock," I said. The receptionist just stared at me.

"I am unaware of an Ambassador Spock…"

"Vulcans do not lie," I said. "He's upstairs negotiating Romulan–Vulcan reunification." The receptionist stared at me for a while longer, then went to get help. A few minutes later, I was led into a conference room.

"Ambassador Picard," Spock said. He stood with T'Pring. Neither one of them looked pleased to see me, but then again, that's always hard to tell with Vulcans.

I apologized for the intrusion, then explained the situation.

"The Romulan government is still quite paranoid," Spock said. "I sincerely doubt I can talk them out of their attack. But I will try."

I wanted to go with him, to add my voice to his, but he didn't invite me. I think he was probably right not to, as frustrating as it was. I went back to my office, where the passport applications were still on my desk.

When the *Enterprise* arrived in orbit, things picked up again. Data brought me aboard and took me to the stellar cartography room. Spock was already there, along with the ship's first officer, Geordi.

"I was unable to convince the Romulans," Spock said. "We will now have to pursue other options, as the situation has deteriorated."

They showed me a map of Romulan territory. On it, a spreading mass of light was expanding from the Hobus system.

"Is that a supernova? That's impossible, the Hobus star wasn't nearly that old."

"You are correct, sir," Data said. "The Romulans attempted to destroy the subspace engine, but appear to only have damaged it. It was accidentally set off."

"The damaged subspace engine caused the Hobus star to go supernova," Geordi said. "A supernova that exists in both normal space and subspace."

"Because it exists in subspace as well, the supernova will spread far beyond the Hobus system," Spock said. "It will consume Romulus in a matter of days."

"And then move on to Vulcan and the rest of the Alpha Quadrant," Geordi said.

"We must stop it." I turned to Spock, "I remember from our meld you had an invention called 'red matter' which you could use…"

"Ambassador," Data said, "we have already taken steps to carry out that plan."

"You can't take a Federation ship into Romulan territory," I said. "Perhaps Geordi…"

"Already have my engineers on it," Geordi said.

Data and Geordi had things well in hand; they had just included me out of courtesy. Data helped Spock build his red matter device, which he would use to consume the supernova. Geordi's unmarked vessel would allow Spock to enter Romulan space without causing an interstellar incident.

On the day Spock left, I went to see him off.

"Good luck, Ambassador," I said.

"You are aware, Picard," Spock said, "that I do not believe in luck."

"You are also aware," I said, "that I know that's not true."

I never saw him again.

✦

"I'm afraid, Jean-Luc," President Brand said, "I'm recalling you."

Spock did stop the subspace supernova, but he had failed to do so before it reached Romulus. The Romulan homeworld was destroyed, and Spock was now missing, presumed dead. The Vulcan High Council blamed me; I had ignored protocol.

"I understand," I said.

"I could've made a case for you ignoring protocol if Romulus had been saved," Brand said. "But as it is, you're to leave immediately."

Data was still in orbit and offered to take me back to Earth. On the way, I communicated with Beverly.

"I'm so sorry," she said. "What do you think happened to Ambassador Spock?"

"I don't know," I said. "But I think he's alive somewhere."

"How do you know?"

"You always retain a bit of a person you've mind-melded with, and you feel it when they die. I felt it when Sarek died. But the piece of Spock is still alive in my mind."

"I guess you weren't cut out to be an ambassador," she said.

"I guess not."

"I'll get back to Earth as soon as I can," she said.

"You take your time. You have a ship, and a job to do."

"But what about us?"

"There's time for us," I said. I wasn't sure there was, but I would wait for her.

✦

I stood on the plank on top of the tanks, punching down the crusts of the fermenting grapes. It was getting more difficult for me to do this work myself, but I had no choice; there weren't many people on Earth interested in producing wine. The year before, a Klingon had answered my advertisement that I was looking for help, but I turned her down. I didn't think a Klingon and I would work well together.

But I was excited. This would be my third vintage since coming back to the vineyard. For the first vintage I'd harvested the grapes two years ago. They would be bottled soon. I had high hopes for the Picard vintage of 2393. As difficult as the work was, I'd learned to enjoy it, finally.

I finished mixing the tanks, and got down. The sun was setting, and I decided to go in and fix myself some dinner. I might try Beverly on subspace tonight, although it was sometimes difficult to reach her. She had promised to be home for my birthday, and I was very much looking forward to that; it would be my ninetieth. I imagined she might arrange for some of our other friends to be there as well. It would be lovely to see some of the old crew again, and hear about their new adventures. And then they would leave, and that would be fine as well.

After dinner, I settled down with a cup of Earl Grey tea, and took one last look at this volume I've written. It reminds me that I've really lived my life alone, for better or worse. But that's who I am, and I feel lucky to have the life I've had. I've seen more of the Galaxy than one man is owed, and met more than my share of the great men and women of our time. I feel proud of whatever small role in our civilization that I've played. But now, it's up to others to make the history.

For me, I'm happy making my father's wine.

EDITOR GOODMAN'S ACKNOWLEDGMENTS

Thanks to everybody at Titan Books, especially Laura Price and my editors Andy Jones and Simon Ward, for all your patience and hard work, and, again, patience; Dana Youlin for whipping the manuscript into shape; Russell Walks, a wonderful artist, for your collaboration and for lending your talents to creating all the amazing photos; Dave Rossi, again, for making me an author; John Van Citters, for listening to Dave Rossi the first time, and then continuing to let me do this.

André Bormanis, for all those questions you answer promptly, completely, and with good humor; Mike and Denise Okuda, for all your work that makes this book possible; Mike Sussman, who suggested why Picard put Wesley at the helm; Admiral James Stavridis, for his memoir *Destroyer Captain: Lessons of a First Command*; Steve Kane, who recommended I read *Destroyer Captain: Lessons of a First Command* by Admiral James Stavridis; Bryan Wolf and Brian Lazarus, great lawyers; Brannon Braga and Rick Berman, who made me a *Star Trek* writer.

Patrick Stewart, for obvious reasons; Seth MacFarlane, without whom I wouldn't get to do any number of amazing things, including working with Patrick Stewart; my friends Mark Altman, Adam-Troy Castro, Howie Kaplan, Anne Lounsbery, Scott Mantz, Glen Mazzara, Dan Milano and Austin Tichenor, because you read the last book; my family: Fred, Phyllis, Bill, Jason, Rafael, Crystal, Anthony, Steven, Julia, Emma and Steve; my sisters Ann and Naomi, carrying on our mom's legacy with me; and Talia, Jacob and especially Wendy, for your love, attention, humor and care, despite my annoying work habits.

ABOUT THE EDITOR

David A. Goodman began his writing career in 1988 as a staff writer on *The Golden Girls*. After getting fired from that job, he worked on over 20 other television series, among the more relevant: *Star Trek: Enterprise, American Dad*, and *Futurama*, where he penned the *Star Trek* homage "Where No Fan Has Gone Before." He is best known for his work on *Family Guy*, where he served as executive producer and head writer for over 100 episodes. As of this writing, he is working with Seth MacFarlane on the new show *The Orville*. He lives in Pacific Palisades, California with his family.

OS 11-16-17
AG 1-18-18
PK 3-22-18
FI 5-24-18
WH 7-23-18
OM 9-??-18
TG 11-??-18
ST 1-28-??

DISCARD

ST 1-28-19 KP